Changeling Press, LLC

ChangelingPress.com

Alien Vampires
Paranormal Women's Fiction
Crymsyn Hart

Alien Vampires
Paranormal Women's Fiction
Crymsyn Hart

All rights reserved.
Copyright ©2023 Crymsyn Hart

ISBN: 978-1-60521-881-6

Publisher:
Changeling Press LLC
315 N. Centre St.
Martinsburg, WV 25404
ChangelingPress.com

Printed in the U.S.A.

Editor: Jean Cooper
Cover Artist: Karen Fox

The individual stories in this anthology have been previously released in E-Book format.

Table of Contents

Charmed by the Alien Vampire Firemen
Crymsyn Hart

When Ember's apartment burns down, two firemen offer their guesthouse for her to rent out. Not able to sleep on her friend's couch any longer, she takes them up on their offer. One night smoke pours from their house. She rushes in to help them and discovers their secret.

With her restaurant being bought out from under her, Ember's life is unraveling. She doesn't know if she can trust her landlords. Someone knows what they truly are and kidnaps her to pressure her for information about the firemen. When she doesn't talk about her green-skinned firemen, the situation only gets worse.

As love grows between Ember and her aliens, the world closes around them. She needs to get closer to them, but men invade their home. In order to save them, she will have to give up everything she knows.

Chapter One

The smell of smoke clung to her clothes even after washing. She stared at the remnants of what used to be her apartment. Everything she owned lay under the debris and waterlogged rubble.

The flames had started on the floor below her. She'd gotten out of there by the skin of her teeth -- the firemen had woken her up. The fire alarms in the building hadn't gone off nor had the sprinklers. After her complaints to the landlord, nothing had been done to get them fixed. Former tenants' trash filled the basement -- a fire hazard waiting to happen.

Ember, like the other tenants, needed to move forward with her life. She could sleep on Anne's couch for as long as she wanted. However, Anne lived in a one-bedroom apartment. A set of sliding doors separated the living room from the bedroom. Ember's mind raced all night to plan how she would get on with her life. Thankfully, Gus hadn't been a dick and told her he would look after the restaurant until she got back on her feet.

"You shouldn't be here. It's very unsafe."

Ember glanced up. Faded jeans hugged toned legs. He wore a white T-shirt with "1 F 7" on the upper left chest. Symbolic flames bracketed the numbers. Shaggy blond hair covered his ears. Intense blue eyes flecked with green stared at her. Something about those eyes looked familiar. Defined cheekbones carved a long line down to his strong jaw and a chin with a small cleft. His lopsided smile made her blush and pull her gaze from him.

"Everything I owned was in here." She gestured to what used to be her home. "I thought I might be able to find something." Ember didn't recognize the total stranger because she knew all her neighbors by sight. "If it's so unsafe, why are you here?"

"I'm the idiot who lost his extra pair of gloves. This

was the last fire I worked, and they're not on the truck. I've looked everywhere else, so this is the place they should be."

"Wait. Fire? You're one of the firemen who helped me out of my apartment."

His neck turned pink. "Yeah, no big deal. Comes with the job."

Emotion overwhelmed her. Ember launched herself into his arms and hugged him. The fireman stiffened. Waking up to the heat, with the smoke all around her, when strange men burst into her bedroom hit her once more. She tightened her arms around him as tears burned her eyes. She pressed her face into his shoulder.

"Hey, it's okay." He patted her back.

She wiped her eyes and turned away, embarrassed by the display. "Sorry. It's a big deal. You and your partner got me out of there."

"You should've heard your smoke alarms going off."

"They didn't go off, and I sleep like the dead."

"The most important thing is you got out."

Ember nodded. "Yeah. Guess so. Hey, is there some way I can thank you for what you did?"

"It's part of the job. No thanks needed. I should really look for my gloves."

Ember sighed as the man stepped away and focused on the burnt rubble. She scrutinized the pile to look for his gloves, but all she could make out were yellowed melted bits of plastic, the shapes of gutted furniture, and the demolished walls. Nothing of what he wanted was in the wreckage, and nothing remained of her life there either. All she had was the restaurant and her friend's couch. The fireman poked at the debris with his boot.

"Isn't it too dangerous for you to be rooting around?" Ember asked.

He picked up a piece of metal, examined it, and then threw it back into the pile. He ran his fingers along his face and streaked it black. She bit her lip and held in a laugh.

"What?"

"You have a couple of stripes on your face."

He gave her a lopsided smile. "Hazard of the job."

"I don't see your gloves anywhere in this rubble. Why don't you and your partner come over to Gusto? Dinner'll be on me. It's the least I can do for you saving my bacon."

"The fancy pizza place off Maple near the new Twin Taps brewery, right?"

"The very same one, but it's nothing fancy. Make sure to come by," Ember told him.

He wiped at the soot on his face. "I'll bring it up. Thanks for the invite."

Her phone vibrated in her pocket. She pulled it out and saw a text from Anne asking about dinner. Checking the time, Ember noticed she had to be at the restaurant.

Ember might have been the brains, but Gus made her dream possible by cooking the menu she and Cecil had envisioned. The whole idea had been Cecil's to start with. Then she lost Cecil. Now all their memories were ashes. She hugged herself and tried to think about the future.

"Are you okay?"

Ember sniffled at the sudden strike of emotion. She wiped her eyes and smiled. "Sorry. Losing all this made me think of something else I lost a few years ago."

"I know what it's like to lose everything, but your memories can't be torn from you. Pictures and mementos can be replaced. The new things might not mean the same, but they're only placeholders for what's in your heart." The fireman's eyes flashed with a hidden pain suggesting his statement held more of a personal meaning.

"You're right, but it doesn't hurt any less."

"Of course not. You seem like a fighter, though. I bet you'll put all this in your rearview mirror and be back to running full speed ahead in no time."

Her phone buzzed again. "Thanks for the pep talk. I hope you find your gloves. Remember to come by when you have a chance."

"Will do. Thanks again."

Ember waved as she slid into her car and drove off to the restaurant. It was the only secure thing she had right now.

* * *

"Hey, Em, you mind if we talk?" Gus stuck his head into the office. His dark hair brushed the top of the door. Red stains smeared his apron. He wiped his brow with a towel and sat in the chair across from her. She couldn't read his eyes, but the frown stirred a few butterflies in her stomach.

"What's up, Gus?" She glanced up from the computer with blurred vision. Business remained good after being open for five years. Her gaze traveled to the picture of her and Cecil on their opening day. They both looked happy at the life they had ahead of them. It hurt her heart knowing he couldn't be there to share the success with her.

"I'm done."

"Well, sure. It's been a long day." It had been so busy in the last couple of weeks she hadn't had a chance to look for a place to rent.

"Yeah. Long day, but that's not what I mean." Gus leaned back in the chair.

"What do you mean?"

"I've gotten an offer to buy my half of the restaurant."

Her heart dropped into her stomach. Ember gripped the desk to steady herself and knocked the stapler off in the process. "What kind of offer? You and Cecil were friends. This was your dream…"

Gus threw down his towel. "It was his dream. He's dead. Schlepping pizza at this joint for the rest of my life isn't mine."

"Get the hell out of here!"

Gus placed the stapler back on the desk. "Take the weekend to let it sink in. You have three months to buy me out. I'm only giving you that time because of Cecil." Gus set a sheet of paper face down before her and walked out.

Her stomach turned. Gus owned fifty-five percent of the business. Ember didn't know where she would come up with the money. Cecil's life insurance policy covered his funeral and some repairs on the restaurant over the years. Whoever this investor was, he -- or she -- hadn't approached her. How long had Gus felt this way? He had been a littler quieter than usual, but generally they spoke about the business. *What am I going to do?* Ember brushed her fingers over the offer. Someone knocked on the door before she could turn it over.

"Who the hell is banging on the door?" she glanced at the clock. It was close to closing, and she didn't need any more interruptions.

A mousy head of brown hair poked through the door opening. Jean, the general manager, opened the door a little bit. "We have a bit of a situation."

She rolled her eyes and got up feeling a hundred years old all of a sudden. Her head spun, and her knees buckled. Ember tried to catch herself, but she went down, and her head hit the side of her desk. Darkness tucked her into the quiet of her mind.

* * *

The sharp scent of vinegar stung her nose. She jerked away, and the pain in her head exploded until white dots danced in her vision.

"Hey, don't move yet. The bump on your head is rather nasty."

Ember opened her eyes to gaze into familiar ones. "It's you."

He flashed her an odd look. "Do I know you?"

"You lost your gloves at my apartment. I mean you were at the pile of rubble formally known as my apartment."

His face scrunched up. Blond hair fell across his eyes. She took in another breath to clear out the vinegar when she smelled vanilla and oranges. Ember looked up. Jean remained in the room. Two other men she didn't know, dressed in jeans and flannel shirts, had joined them.

"I think she hit her head a little too hard," one of the other men chimed in.

She threw him a dark glance, and he quieted down.

"No, Chance. She thinks I'm Bennett," the fireman said to the other man and turned his attention back to her. "You met Ben. He's constantly losing things. I'm Nash."

"Are you twins?" Ember asked, feeling a little out of place with all the attention focused on her.

"What did I miss?" Another man burst into the room. He looked exactly like the one who knelt before her. They were carbon copies of one another.

"Always running late, Bennett. You missed all the fun while Ms...." Nash set the vinegar bottle on the floor.

"Umm... Tate. Ember Tate."

Bennett grinned, and the same divot appeared on his chin as on Nash's. "Is she going to be okay?"

Nash probed the knot on her head. She didn't notice the pain. The same citrus vanilla scent made her mouth water.

"You'll be fine. I suggest you get checked out by your doctor in the next couple of days."

"I'll be sure to do that. Thank you, Nash. Ummm... can I have a minute please with my manager?" Ember eyed Jean.

"Come on, guys. Drinks are on the house. Give me a few minutes to make sure the boss is okay." Jean shooed the men away. Ben's eyes lingered on her before he left.

"You okay?" Jean came back into the office. "You went down pretty quick."

Ember waved off her comment. "I'll be fine. Who are those guys and how did they end up in my office?"

"You remember that situation I told you about?"

"Vaguely."

"Well, I have twenty guys who said you told them dinner was on the house."

"I don't even know twenty guys."

"You do now. After you passed out, I asked if one of them was a paramedic since I noticed the fire trucks parked outside."

"Shit…" She groaned.

"What?"

"Nothing. The partner of the guy working on me just now -- Bennett -- I met him a couple of weeks ago. They pulled me out of my building when it burned. I told them to come by the restaurant and dinner'd be on me. I wasn't expecting the whole station to show up. Wonderful. I'll take care of it."

"You sure?"

Ember nodded. "Yeah. Give me a minute."

Jean left the room, and Ember stayed in the chair. She pinched her nose to keep the headache from coming on again. Her gaze went to the paper on her desk. *I can't deal with this right now.* The firemen's laughter drifted down the hall. The camaraderie between them made her realize how much she missed the merriment. How much she missed slipping into a hot shower and watching a movie. Have some chocolate ice cream and maybe a grilled cheese sandwich. The things she would do when she had her own home. Or someone with whom she could sit on the couch and just be.

A soft knock came on the door.

"What?" she growled.

"Sorry. Can I come in?" Bennett stood in the doorway.

"Yeah, I didn't mean to snap. It's been a hell of a night."

"I wanted to see how you were doing."

"You didn't come up here to give me a heads-up you brought the entire company to my restaurant?"

"You said dinner was on you."

"I said bring you and your partner and dinner was on me. I wasn't expecting the entire firehouse to eat me out of house and home."

"It wasn't supposed to be that way. I told a couple of the guys, and then they told a couple more. I couldn't exactly say no."

"It's easy. N. O."

Bennett laughed.

"It's not funny."

"Yes, it is. I wanted to see if you were okay. Nash said you were, but I wanted to double-check. How's your head?" Bennett touched her arm.

Ember felt herself warm to his touch. The scent of cherries hit her nose. She licked her lips at the sweetness of it. "My head's fine. Thanks for asking. Did you ever find your gloves?"

"You remembered?"

"Yeah."

"No, I didn't find them. Look, I'm sorry about the guys. I'll make sure they kick in really well to tip the waitress."

She chuckled. "You'd better. Jean's a good egg. I should go help her out." Ember stood up and the world rocked.

Bennett caught her around the waist. "I'm not sure that's a good idea. You have a mild concussion."

"Well, then, you help her."

"I wouldn't know what to do. Maybe if you keep an eye on me."

"Fine. Then let's get you to work." Ember went toward

the door, and Bennett followed.

"You're serious?"

"She's the only one waiting on your party, and it's been a fucking day. Not to mention I'm sleeping on a lumpy couch with no personal space."

Bennett didn't reply. Instead he left her leaning against the wall and raced over to help Jean as she handed out the drinks to the other firemen. Her manager shot her a look. Ember nodded, reassuring Jean that he was okay. Once Jean had the drinks down, Bennett sat down next to Nash. He whispered something to his partner. Ember noticed he slid his hand along Nash's thigh under the table and squeezed it. Nash flashed him a look. This deepened the mystery between them. The scent of melted cheese wafted out of the kitchen. Ember pushed off the wall and went in to check on the order. Three pizzas waited to be taken out. Jean took one from her.

"I can get those."

"I'm fine."

Ember grabbed the last pizza and brought it out to the horde. Half a dozen hands grabbed for the cheese-covered crust. She jumped back and watched the spectacle of the men devouring the eight large pizzas. They slurped down the drinks, burped, and kept diving back in for more slices.

"Have you ever seen such a beautiful sight?" Jean sighed.

"All those men swilling beer? Yeah, every night I'm in here."

Jean poked her side. "No. All these wonderful muscled creatures, eating as though they were gladiators preparing for battle. Man, I could surely handle one of their hoses."

Ember laughed. It made her head hurt, but it felt good. Jean dashed away and refilled the empty glasses. Ember went into the kitchen and found a couple more cheese pizzas in the window. She brought them out to the hungry men.

"You're a lifesaver," one of the company called.

"Zach, you say that to anyone who brings you food or booze," Nash joked.

"Can't help it, Lieutenant. Anyone who brings me the goods is a goddess in my book." Zach winked at Ember.

"The goddess here is Jean. Make sure you pay her homage when you leave," Ember told the table.

"We'll take care of her," Nash replied.

"Enjoy the rest of your meal." Ember walked over to the register and comped the bill. They had saved her life.

"The one who called me a goddess sure looks scrumptious," Jean smiled.

"He's younger than you."

"Hasn't stopped me in the past." Jean chuckled.

The rustle of chairs moving made Ember glance out. The firemen filed out of the restaurant. Ember helped Jean clear the table. Once things were put back together in the dining room, Jean handed Ember something.

She looked down. "A hundred bucks? What's this for?"

"For helping me out."

"You did all the work." Ember tried to give Jean back the hundred.

"They left me four hundred bucks and a couple of phone numbers. Besides, I overheard your little conversation with Gus. I can't believe he's going to sell you out."

Ember leaned against the wall. "Please don't tell anyone. I haven't figured out what I'm going to do."

"How much is he asking? Sorry, I shouldn't have asked."

"It's fine. I haven't looked at the number yet. I chickened out."

Jean patted her hand. "If you want to talk to someone,

I'm here. Gus is a prick, anyway."

"Thanks, Jean. I'll see you tomorrow."

"'Night, Em."

Ember finished up her paperwork and glanced at the offer on her desk one more time. *It can wait until tomorrow.*

Ember walked out to her car parked out in a far corner of the lot. She dug into her pocket for her keys.

"Hi."

Ember dropped her keys, jumped, and turned around, ready to hit whoever had snuck up on her. "What the hell do you want?"

"Whoa!" The man put up his hands and stepped into the light. "It's Bennett."

"What the holy fuck are you doing out here?"

"Sorry. I would've called you, but you never gave me your number. All I have is this place. I have a proposition for you."

She grabbed her keys and leaned against the car. "Proposition? I bought your company dinner. Isn't that enough? I really want to go home and get some sleep."

"Here's the thing. Have you found an apartment yet or are you still sleeping on your friend's couch?"

"Still sleeping on the couch. I've put in a few applications for places but haven't heard back. Look, you saved me, but I think me feeding everyone is good enough thanks for everything you've done for me." Ember went to open the car door, but Ben touched her arm.

"Hear me out before you run away."

She rolled her eyes. "Fine. Make it quick."

"My partner and I have a guesthouse. It's vacant, if you're interested."

"Guesthouse? How can two firemen afford a mansion?"

Ben ran his finger down her arm and along the top of her hand. Ember repressed a shiver. The sweet scent of caramel filled her senses. Her mouth watered as he stepped closer until his body heat hugged her. Ben's presence made her very aware what she looked like -- all pizza sauce-splattered and flustered. It wouldn't surprise her if she had flour on her face. It had been a long time since she'd worried what a man thought about her. Ember inhaled once more and tasted the caramel on her tongue. Ember couldn't help but lean in and take a whiff of the fireman.

"Everything okay?"

"Yeah, sorry. Did you have a caramel before you came here?"

His brow furrowed, and the question hung in his eyes. "No, why?"

"Forget it. I'm tired and feeling the bump on my head. What's the address of this guesthouse?"

Ben handed her a slip of paper. "The address and my cell. Give me a call if you're interested. If I don't get back to you right away, we're on shift. We do 48- or 72-hour shifts. Then off for the same."

"Thanks for the heads-up. 'Night." Ember slid into her car and left the fragrant fireman behind.

Chapter Two

"So?"

"I'm still thinking!"

"Some help you are." Ember grabbed a handful of popcorn and threw it at her friend Anne.

"You're the one sleeping on the sofa. If you get any popcorn stuck in your vajayjay, don't blame it on me."

"Do you even know anything about your latest stud muffin? Maybe like, when was the last time he was tested for the crud?"

"At least my v is getting some. You really need to air yours out. I keep offering you Mr. Sparky."

"I'm not using your dildo. Especially not one called Mr. Sparky. That's just wrong."

Anne shrugged. "Whatever gets you by. Seriously, I know you've kicked in for rent, but there's not enough space in here for three people."

"Three?" Ember grabbed her glass of wine and downed it in three sips.

"I'm sorry, Em. It came out of my mouth while we were getting busy. I didn't expect you to be sleeping on my couch for two whole months. A girl's gotta have her space."

She leaned back into the sofa and held in her anger. "No. I get it. It's your place. I'll call the fire guys. When do you need me out by?"

"The end of next week'd be great, but I'm good for you to hang until the end of the month."

"Thanks, Anne." Ember got up and walked out onto the small balcony outside her friend's bedroom. Her breath came out in a cloud as she rubbed her arms. Her thoughts raced. Her stomach twisted and turned until she pulled out her phone and the paper with Ben's number on it.

She got his voicemail and hung up.

Ember redialed the number. "Hi, Bennett. This is Ember. I'm interested in your guesthouse. Give me a call back when you can. Thanks."

The next morning, the ringing of her phone woke her up.

"Hello."

The voice on the other end came out muffled.

"Sorry what?"

"Hi, Ember. It's Ben. I'm getting off shift. If you want to come by this afternoon that'd be fine."

"Sounds great."

"Oh, we're in a dead zone. Once you turn into Creek Rd, head straight until you see a dirt road. Then take a left. We're about two miles down."

"Am I going to need a truck to get there?"

"You'll be fine. See you later."

Ember showered, went into the restaurant early, and checked in with Jean. Everything seemed under control.

"Have you had a chance to think about my offer?" Gus caught her before she could leave.

"Think about, yes. Come up with your money, not even close. I'm trying to get off of my friend's couch."

"My guy wants an answer. I pushed him off another month."

"Who is this mystery buyer, anyway?"

"It's Lance Vegum. He owns a chain…"

"I know who he is, Gus. He's put in a pizza buffet chain in every town from Spartanburg to Charlotte. This place will never become that."

"Then you'd better come up with the money for it."

Ember broke away and got into her car. She hit the steering wheel with the heel of her hand until it hurt. Her anger ignited a fire inside her. She had to figure out a way for it not to burn her down.

She turned onto the dirt road and went slowly down a few yards. It turned into a paved driveway that kept on going until she pulled up in front of a house four times as big as her restaurant. It looked like a huge log cabin from the outside. Ember parked the car and got out. A cool breeze hit her and made the hairs stand up on her arms. Something in the air felt strange. Before she could place it, a large Great Dane dashed out and planted itself right before her.

"Nice puppy."

Its loud bark made her jump. She normally liked dogs, but Ember couldn't read this one to see if it would lick her or eat her for dinner. Her heart slammed into her chest as she remained pinned there. The black-and-white animal bared its teeth and stepped a little closer. Ember flattened herself against the car.

"Canis, come. Leave her alone. Don't let him fool you. He's a lap dog." Bennett came out wearing nothing more than black, grimy, holey blue jeans. Those smudges smeared across his toned chest. Canis loped over to Ben and leaned against him. "Did you have any problems finding this place?"

"No, the directions were great. How do you live way out here in a dead zone?"

"We have our own network. Nash worked it out. He's the technical genius around here. Do you want to see the guesthouse?"

"Yeah. That'd be great."

Bennett motioned for her to followed him. She couldn't help but stare at how the jeans hugged his ass and the way his muscles rippled as he walked. He was a girl's wet dream. All he needed was a cowboy hat and a horse. As they walked past the large house, they came to another building that resembled some sort of modern work of art constructed of glass and steel.

"This is your guesthouse?" Ember couldn't believe what she was looking at. Then again, she couldn't believe two firemen lived way out in the middle of nowhere in a mansion.

"Want a tour?"

She nodded and went inside. The floorplan was completely open, so the kitchen flowed into the living room. It was all one floor and completely furnished. The whole kitchen was done in stainless steel and was more modern than what she had at the restaurant.

"Kitchen and living room. The bedroom and bathroom are this way." Bennett took her around a corner and down a short hallway. The glass let her look out and notice they were walking over a creek.

"Wow, you don't see that every day."

"Yeah. We didn't want to damage the environment any more than we had to. The creek runs along the whole property." Bennett opened the door to the bedroom. The bed took up most of the room. The walls in this part of the house were regular walls, and then the bathroom was set apart by really thick blocks of glass. She brushed past Ben and stuck her head into the bathroom. The shower could hold three people easily, and then there was a detached tub.

"This is amazing, but I don't think I can pay what you'd want for rent."

"How much were you paying at your old place?"

"Nine hundred."

"Then you can do the same here."

Ember couldn't believe him. "What's the catch?"

Ben shrugged. "No catch. You staying here gives us someone to watch the house when we're not around. Maybe keep Canis company, if you like dogs."

"I love dogs, but you sure he won't eat me?"

"I told him to be nice to you and to listen to you."

"You sure he's going to?"

"Oh, he will."

"Seriously. How can you guys afford all this?"

Ben looked down.

"Sorry, that's none of my business. Look, I'll take the house. When can I move in?"

"Hey, Bennett, are you in here?"

"In here, Nash."

Nash stood in the doorway next to Ben. Side by side they looked like carbon copies of one another. "Are you sure you guys aren't identical twins?"

Nash's grin turned up his cheeks a little more, but his eyes remained unreadable. "We're not related at all, but we look very similar. Ben, can I talk to you for a minute?"

Canis burst in and slammed right into her leg. Ember caught herself before the dog made her fall. He gave her a goofy doggy smile. She patted him and her finger caught on something buried in his fur by the edge of his collar. A door slammed and Ember jumped. She went into the main part of the house with Canis at her heels. Ben stood in the kitchen. The way the sun hit him gave him a greenish appearance.

"Everything okay?"

"Yeah. Nash and I have a difference of opinion about you moving in."

"I don't want to cause any trouble between you and your... partner. I mean..." This place would get her off Anne's couch. Ben was giving her a deal. Either way, it was her ticket to get back on her feet and find the money for Gus. Six weeks was all she had.

"It's fine. How about you move in this Saturday?" Ben asked.

"What about Nash?"

"He'll get used to it. Saturday?"

"Don't you want first and last month's rent?"

"First month's rent is fine. We can work out last month's over a period of time if you want to stay." Bennett stuck out his hand. Ember took it and felt his firm handshake. His grip pressed on her skin as though he had more than five fingers. She pushed the thought aside when he let go.

"Thanks. I appreciate it. Saturday, it is."

"Good. See you then."

* * *

"This place is amazing," Anne said as they got out of the car. Canis bounded out toward them. She shrieked and backed up against the door. "Get it away. Get it away."

"Come here, boy," Ember called him. He sprang away from Anne and leaned against Ember for attention.

"He likes you. If only men were so easy to tame. He gonna bite?" Anne inched a little farther away from the Great Dane.

"I don't think so. He did the same thing to me when I first came here. Bennett said he's a big baby. Where're your owners?" Ember asked the dog.

Canis's pink tongue hung out of his mouth. A string of drool slowly oozed toward the ground. His liquid brown eyes held hers until she looked away. He bumped her with his nose to be petted. She scratched his ruff, and her fingers hit the small metal piece the size of a dime under his collar. *Must be where they chipped him.*

"You sure they said Saturday? I don't see any cars here." Anne peered into a window of the main house.

"I left him a message, but he didn't respond. Come on, let's go check the guesthouse." Ember grabbed a bag of clothes from the trunk and a box. Anne took the other box which constituted all her belongings. They walked back to the guest house. A white piece of paper was taped to the door along with a silver key.

"Come have dinner with us tomorrow night if you like. See you around." Ember pulled the note from the door and took the key. It felt heavy in her hand, but it settled a weight on her soul knowing she had a place to lay her head.

She slipped the note into her pocket and then used the

key to open the door. Once she entered, a heavy floral scent overwhelmed her. It brought back the scent she smelled on one of the firemen. A large vase of white lilies sat on the counter along with a small bowl of oranges. She bit her lip and nearly laughed.

"Wow, flowers and oranges. Are they asking you out on a date or welcoming you to the neighborhood?" Anne pressed her nose into one of the flowers.

"I'm sure it's them being nice." Ember smelled the lilies and placed her stuff on the floor. Canis came into the kitchen and sniffed her things.

"This place could easily go for three thousand a month. How in the hell did you score landlords like this?"

"From what I gathered, my landlords are in a relationship with each other," Ember told her.

"You sure?" Anne pulled open the kitchen cabinets and the fridge.

"Pretty sure from how they acted around one another."

"You don't have to worry about them coming on to you." Anne leaned against the counter.

"Yeah. Did the boy toy lose his way?"

"Lester'll be here. He was right behind us." Anne checked her phone. "No signal out here. How are you going to live?"

Ember snorted. "I don't always have to be plugged in like you. Bennett said they have their own network. Nash is supposed to be some tech guru."

Anne plucked the petals from one of the lilies. "He'd have to be for the place they have here. Damn, you said they were firemen. I can't wait to see them."

"What kind of a name is Lester?"

"A proud one. It belonged to my grandfather." A deep voice echoed in the house. Anne's boy toy stood over six-five, looked like he could bench press a Dumpster while head banging. His long black hair hung in a ponytail. He had pale skin like he barely saw the sun. His black clothes and heavy silver jewelry marked him for a metal guitar player or a vampire in training. He extended his hand to the dog.

Canis jumped between her and Lester and growled. Ember grabbed his collar, but he wouldn't budge.

Lester pulled back his hand. "It's great to meet you. Anne didn't say anything about a dog, though."

Something about Lester made her stomach turn. Ember trusted Anne, but she didn't see the appeal of the vampire-rocker-wannabe together with her friend who was all sunshine and butterflies. "Dog belongs to my new landlords."

"Ahh, okay. Hey, Vanilla Bean, I have band practice tonight."

"He calls you Vanilla Bean?" Ember couldn't help but gag on the words.

"He says I smell like vanilla. He's a really good guy." Anne gave Ember a hug.

Ember eyed Lester. "What kind of band are you in?"

"A heavy metal Christian band. I'm the bassist and the lead singer." Lester stuck his finger in his ear and wiggled it around. "Do you hear that?"

"Hear what?" Anne asked.

He looked around trying to figure out where the sound he heard originated from. He went outside and stood by his van. Ember and Anne followed him back out. "You guys don't hear the hum?"

Ember listened intently and shrugged. "Nothing except the dog breathing."

"She's right. I don't hear anything. Didn't you say you had to get to band practice?" Anne trailed her hand over Lester's ass.

Ember groaned. Lester glanced at Anne and grinned. "Yes. Although, I have a little time before I have to get there. Ember, it was nice to meet you."

"Same. Anne, call me later."

Anne giggled as Lester tickled her and shuffled her over to the van. They took off, leaving Ember all alone. She listened again and didn't hear anything. Ember rubbed the dog's head and then went back into the house. Canis followed her in and sat.

"You're not going to leave me alone, are you?"

Canis woofed and slid down onto the floor. Ember wasn't about to kick the dog out. Bennett said he told the dog to listen to her. She grabbed her bag and made her way into the bedroom, waiting to hear the *click-clack* of the dog's claws on the floor, but he remained behind. She put away her clothes in the empty dresser and her few toiletries in the bathroom. Then Ember sat on the bed. She smelled the sheets and the blanket and realized they had been washed. Ember pulled one of the blankets back and rested her head against the pillow, sinking down into the mattress. As she did, the world slipped away.

Something tickled her face. When she opened her eyes, she looked into the dog's brown ones. His tongue slurped along her cheek. Standing next to her was Bennett -- or maybe it was Nash. She still couldn't tell them apart.

"I see you made it into the house okay." The sound of his voice and the set line of his mouth made her realize it was Nash.

"Yes, thank you, Nash."

"Good. Now we can set some ground rules I expect Ben didn't tell you about."

She sat up in bed and straightened her shirt. Now that she was upright, her brain began to function better. "I knew this was too good to be true," she muttered.

"You might be right."

"What are these ground rules? Ben made it sound like I could go anywhere on the property."

"Bennett has a soft heart and you fit his profile."

Ember sighed. "Great. I fit a profile. Wayward female searching for apartment about to lose her business kinda girl."

Nash's cold expression didn't change. Canis whined. Ember scratched the dog, and Nash grabbed her hand. "I'd prefer it if you didn't make friends with our canine."

"Fine, but he followed me in here and curled up by the bed. Look, I'll make my stay here as short as possible until I can find another place. Happy?"

"It makes me rest easier, yes."

"Fine. Should I get a pen and paper to write down your rules?"

"You don't have to be bitchy about it," Nash growled.

"How do you expect me to be when you barge in here and proceed to dictate house rules? Sounds like you never wanted me here in the first place."

"So quick to catch on. I guess the blow to your head the other day didn't do as much damage as I first thought."

"You're such an ass."

"Good, so you know I want to interact with you as little as humanly possible."

"I'll make sure to stay out of your way. What are your ground rules?"

"Rule number one: Don't go into the house when we're not there. If we are, knock before entering. Leave Canis alone."

The dog whined. Nash glanced down at him. Canis responded with a growl and went over to Ember. "Fine. Do what you want, beast."

"What else do you not want me to do?"

"Don't go poking around any of the outbuildings, either. If you can mind your own business, then we should get along well enough."

"Fine. Are we done?"

Nash looked at her. Ember caught the cherry vanilla

scent from him, but it moved away when she realized what an ass what he was. She tried to read his blue eyes. To find some emotion that made him worthy of even being a firefighter. He certainly didn't have a helpful bedside manner. How could he be partnered with a man such as Bennett? His complete opposite, a man who cared about people.

"Sure are. Come on, Canis, let's go."

The dog sat down beside her. Ember placed her hand on top of the dog's head in defiance. The dog lifted its lip to Nash. "I don't think he wants to go with you."

"Stupid mutt. Stay here, then. I'll send Bennett to retrieve you." Nash walked out of the house.

"I appreciate the thought of you staying, but I don't want you getting in trouble," she told the dog.

Canis cocked his head and woofed as though he expected her to answer. When she didn't, he lay down and watched her as she walked around the room. After she unpacked, her stomach growled. The scent of the oranges made her pick one up since she didn't have any other food. A knock sounded at the door, and she went to open it.

"More lectures, Nash, on where I can and can't go?"

"It's Bennett. Can I come in?" He stood in the doorway waiting for her invitation.

A weight left her. Even though they looked the same, they were not. The warmth of Ben's personality radiated off him and relaxed her. As he came in closer the scent of vanilla and citrus enveloped her senses. He was the ray of sunshine where Nash was a storm cloud.

"Yeah, come in. Thanks for the flowers and the oranges."

A splash of color went across his cheeks. "You're welcome. I wanted to make you feel a little bit at home. I figured since you might not have any food right away…"

Ember threw her arms around him. Ben returned the

hug with a little squeeze and then backed away. "I appreciate it. I have your rent by the way." She went to grab her purse, but he put a hand on her shoulder.

"I trust you. Get settled in first. Actually, I came over here to ask you to dinner."

She sighed. "I don't think it's a good idea. It seems your boyfriend doesn't like me much."

"What do you mean?"

"Nash came a little while ago and dictated the house rules about not going into the house or anywhere else whether you're here or not. He said you took pity on me because I was your type. Plus, he didn't want me to make friends with your dog, but I think the dog decided refused to go along." Ember plucked an orange from the bowl to keep her mind off Nash being an asshole.

Canis trotted out. He leaned against Bennett and gave him a doggy version of a smile. Ben's expression hardened. "I'll have a word with him. Please come for dinner. I can tell you're hungry the way you keep playing with that orange."

Ember giggled as she set the orange back in the bowl. He was trying to be nice to her. "Hungry, yes, but I'm not going to be the cause of trouble between you."

"You won't be. Nash is protective of our space. He doesn't like it when our life is disturbed."

"But you deal with the public all the time. How can he be so boorish?" Ember asked. "Sorry, I saw at the restaurant you were… close."

Ben smiled. "We don't do much PDA, but sometimes it happens. Underneath the stoic façade, he really is a good guy. He gets along better with machines than with people. Here we get to be who we are and not under the strict eye of the firehouse. We get ogled enough when we're out and about. Give him some time to warm up to you."

She laughed. "Time. Right. He wants me out as soon

Crymsyn Hart   Alien Vampires

as I can find another place."

"Like I said, I'll talk to him. He has to get to know you."

"You both have to get to know me. You offered me a place to live without even doing a background check or even asking if I have the money to pay you."

"Let's say I have a good way of reading people. You seem pretty stable. You gotta eat, right?"

Ember rolled her eyes as her stomach growled again. "I guess."

"Come on," Bennett chuckled.

She followed Bennett into the main house. Canis remained at Bennett's side. As Ember passed over the threshold, a soft breeze flowed over her skin and a mild current of electricity zinged her. She stopped and grabbed the wall. Her head spun. Canis yelped, and Bennett turned back around.

"Are you okay?"

"I'll be fine. Something about this house, I guess."

Ben took her arm and led her into the kitchen. As she walked into the house, she got a little bit of a look at their decor. It seemed a mixture of modern and old-fashioned. She spied a jukebox hidden away in one corner. In another room, she saw some old firefighting tools. Shelves filled with books and DVDs filled a whole other room. All modern stainless steel appliances lined a wall with a black marble counter between them in the kitchen. A spread of food on a large wood table seemed more Ben's style than Nash's. The kitchen was the perfect mixture of them both.

Nash sat at one end of the table and looked up. "What're you doing here?"

"I invited her for dinner. She's our tenant now, so we should be nice to her. Including you." Bennett pulled out a seat for Ember.

Nash threw down his fork and glared at his partner.

"I'm not doing this now, Ben. You already know my feelings regarding this. We shouldn't have to hide what we are here." He got up and walked past her.

As he went by, another wave of static electricity passed over her. Ember let out a moan. Nash stopped in his tracks. The muscles bunched under his shirt. His head turned slightly to look back at her. She caught a flash of silver in his eyes as Nash grabbed the doorframe and held onto it. He gathered himself once more and left the room. Bennett helped her over to the chair. His hands shook, and a few beads of sweat formed on his brow. He stepped back and sat across the table.

"Are you okay?" Ember asked.

His breath was shaky as he forced a smile. "Yeah. Fine."

"Really? Because you look green. Your skin is splotchy on your neck almost like scales. Are you sure you're okay?"

"Excuse me. Help yourself to dinner. I have to talk to Nash." He went after his partner.

Canis put his head on her knee and licked her fingers. His eyes flicked between the table and her. "Tonight's been interesting. I'm not going to feed you since I don't know if you can have human food."

She buried her head into the dog's fur and inhaled his musky scent. He sighed and put his paw on her leg. Ember waited a few moments to see if her landlords would return. The spread of salad, several vegetables, and different kinds of meat made her stomach rumble. Bennett said to help herself. She got a plate and sat back down. After she'd eaten a couple of bites, Bennett returned with Nash. They got a plate full of food and sat at opposite ends of the table from one another with her in the middle. They each looked at her and glanced down. The tension between them made her shift in her chair and her stomach churn. She looked over at Nash. His cold demeanor chilled her.

"The food is great." Ember took another bite to break up the unease in the room.

"You don't need to patronize us," Nash snapped. "You're the one with the popular restaurant."

The jab hit Ember harder than it should have. She dropped her fork, pushed back her chair, and shoved the table until it pinned Nash. The effort left her breathless. A scowl turned his lips into a twisted sneer. He heaved the table toward her and stood up, almost ready to come at her.

"Be an ass all you want, but don't drag my restaurant into it. Y-you have no idea what I'm going through. It's the last thing I have of Cecil's."

She went out for some air and to escape from the arrogant son of a bitch. Outside the night shone clearer than in the city. The air felt electric, like it would spark at any second. Tears blurred her vision and wet her cheek. She couldn't stay here with that asshat always on her about something or other.

"Are you okay?"

Ember didn't bother to turn around. "Does it matter if I am? You and him… Look I can't go back to sleeping on my friend's couch. Tell Nash I'll be out as soon as I find another place. I meant what I said about dinner. It was good."

"You can tell him yourself." The darker tone to the voice made her turn around this time.

Nash stood behind her. Bennett stayed in the entryway of the house. She could discern a slight difference in their appearance in the way Nash turned up his lip.

"I'm sorry about the jab with the restaurant. I didn't mean to make you angry."

"Didn't you?"

"Maybe a little. You have to forgive my coldness. Ben

told you -- this is our home, and I'm not used to company being here all the time. If you stay out of my way, then I'll stay out of yours, and you can make friends with the dog." Nash reached down to pet the canine, but Canis growled at him and went over to Ember.

She chuckled and wiped her eyes. "I don't think you have a say in who he picks as a friend. Staying out of your way suits me fine. There's a lot about me you don't know, and I'm not in the mood to talk about it. Good night, Nash."

Ember headed back to her new house with the dog following behind her. Once inside she went straight into the bedroom and crawled into the big bed. Canis put his head on the mattress and stared at her.

Ember groaned. "Fine. Come up, but you stay at the end of the bed and no funny business."

The Great Dane climbed up and plopped at the foot of the bed. Ember still had room to stretch out in the king-size bed. Even with her eyes closed, her mind whirled over what she could do to hold onto the last piece of Cecil she had left.

Chapter Three

"You got a second?" Gus popped his head in.

"If you're here for my hundred thousand dollar check, I don't have it."

"It was a dick move for me to drop it on you the way I did." Gus's white apron had yet to be smeared with the day's fare.

"It sure was." A wave of relief went over Ember hearing Gus admit it.

"I know how much this place means to you."

"Does that mean you're not going to sell to that dick Lance Vegum?"

"Well... Lance, why don't you come in here and meet Ember?"

A wave of nausea hit Ember. Lance was not what she pictured him to be. He stood about five-five and was rail thin. He stared at her with intense brown eyes behind wire-rimmed glasses. His profile showed off his tight man bun. He wore a blazer over a T-shirt with blue jeans. Lance flashed her a smile as though he hadn't heard her comment to Gus.

"Nice to meet you, Ember. I totally understand why you'd have reservations about me buying Gus out." He reached over the desk.

Ember got up and shook his hand. His firm handshake made her hand warm. He relaxed in the seat and looked around the office.

"It's nice to meet you. I'm sorry about calling you a dick," Ember murmured.

"I've been called worse. Gus, you want to give me and Ms. Tate a moment?"

"Have fun." Gus winked at her.

Gus walked out. She leaned back in her chair. "Why my restaurant?"

Lance crossed his legs showing off his sandaled feet. "I

know you think I'm nothing more than a… millennial wannabe who wants to dismantle your restaurant."

"Don't you?"

"Not at all. Gus came to me. I wasn't even looking at your restaurant. I've been looking for a way to expand into more upscale dining. Honestly, I like the feel of it. I don't plan on changing much. If I overheard you right, you're no closer to getting the funds together for Gus."

She looked down at the receipts scattered on the desk. "No. I don't have the money."

"Gus told me about what happened with the fire and losing everything you had. I'm sorry."

"How long are you giving me to get the money? Gus said you were giving him six weeks."

Lance took off his glasses and wiped them on his shirt. "My deadline is thirty days, but my coming here was a way for me to make you another deal."

"And this other deal is?"

"I was hoping I might be able to buy you out."

"You have some nerve to even…"

"Whoa! Let me finish. I'd keep you on as the manager."

"Get the fuck out of my office."

Lance settled his glasses back on. He slipped his hand into his pocket and drew out a business card. "Maybe it's time for you to let go of the past. It's booming now, but what happens in five years?" He set the card down and left.

Ember threw the card into the wastebasket. His words fueled a fire in her. It was all she thought about as she drove back to her new place. Ember got out of the car. The air left a taste like old pennies on her tongue. Canis lay curled up outside her front door with a bouquet of lilacs lying next to him. He lifted his head and yawned.

"You coming in or not?"

He blinked but didn't move.

"Fine. Don't move, silly mutt."

Canis growled as though letting her know he understood her comment.

"Don't like being called a mutt, then move your butt." Ember stared at him, but he still didn't budge. "Fine. You're not coming in tonight." As she closed the door, something felt off in the house.

She tried to shake it, but it didn't pass as the night wore on. Ember flicked through the photos on her phone and came across an old one of her and Cecil together in front of the restaurant. It was the first week of them gutting the building. The smile on his face gave him dimples on both sides. He lit up the room and her whole life. She ran her finger over his picture and felt the familiar ache in her heart.

"I wish you were still around. You'd know how to get out of this pickle." She held the phone close and curled up so she could fall into the oblivion where her mind shut off.

In her dream a great whoosh of air picked her up off her feet and slammed her into a wall. An explosion rocked her dream enough to force her to open her eyes. When she did, Canis barked in her face. His nose was inches from hers. The air smelled like burning hair. Ember pressed her hands to her ears.

"All right. I'm awake. What do you want? How in the hell did you get in here anyway? I locked the door, and you were still curled up outside." Ember tried to push the Great Dane off of her, but he wasn't budging. "What is it?"

Canis wrapped his jaws around her arm and tugged on it. He didn't break the skin, but dog slobber rained on the bed. He pulled again and then barked, pacing back and forth between the bed and the doorway. It was obvious he wanted her to follow him. She got out of bed and put on her slippers. Ember grabbed her robe when

Canis took the end and yanked.

"I'm coming. Damn dog." She followed after him to the main house. Thick black smoke poured out of the open door. She coughed and pulled her robe over her mouth to breathe. She felt the Great Dane grab hold of her hand and guide her through the smoke.

Her heart hammered along her ribcage. She thought about calling for help, but she didn't see any phones or any fire extinguishers when she was in there before. Canis led until the smoke cleared a little. Ember took in a breath and tasted sulfur. Canis ran toward another room off the kitchen. She hadn't noticed it the last time she was there.

As she passed through the threshold, a wave of energy hit her and made her sneeze. When she took in another breath, it had the slight taste of sulfur and antiseptic. It took her brain a moment to comprehend what she saw. A large black chair took up the center of the room. A silver metallic sheen glinted off the walls. Illumination shone from above, but she didn't see any lights.

Canis grabbed her hand and pulled her along. He stopped in front of a wall which opened to reveal a hallway. He barked and ran down the corridor as though telling her to hurry up. Ember went after him, marveling at the absence of smoke, but her sense of urgency hadn't left her. The dog wouldn't have gotten her if something wasn't wrong. The air tasted stale as if she had been in the walk-in fridge for too long at the restaurant.

The hallway was wide enough for three or four people. Her sense of balance was off, like she was heading underground. Canis stopped at another door and placed his paw on the door. It slid back into the wall and revealed another room. Black scorch marks marred the walls and the floor. The fire originated in this room.

Two men leaned against the far wall. At least she thought they were men. They looked like men except they were green. One lay across the lap of the other one. Both were unconscious. Canis raced over and licked the one up against the wall. He moaned, and his eyes flickered opened. He patted the dog. Canis whined and glanced over at Ember. He barked again but didn't move from the two green men. Something about them looked familiar. Silver hair spilled over the shoulder of the green man who was propped up. The barely conscious one gave her a half smile. She went over to him slowly and knelt down. Canis licked her face and whimpered.

"C-can I help you with something?" Ember asked, trying to wrap her mind around the man before her.

"Ember, why are you here?"

"Bennett?" She recognized his voice but couldn't believe her eyes even if she could believe her ears.

"Yes," he wheezed. "Get out of here. There's nothing you can do for us."

She touched his arm and found it to be cool. "There has to be something. Why're you green?" She glanced at the other man in Ben's lap and figured it must be Nash. Cuts marred Ben's green chest and the left side of his face was charred. One side of Nash's body was blackened and his arm bent at a strange angle. Her mind couldn't process what she saw. At one moment, Ben was green and the next he appeared normal with severe injuries.

"You have to get out of here."

"I'm not going anywhere."

"You shouldn't have brought her here," he scolded the dog.

Canis barked in reply.

Ember touched his arm. His normal human appearance wavered like a ghost back to the green-skinned male. He felt real enough. "Let me call you a doctor. You're hurt."

"No ambulance. No fire. We've exhausted our supply of blood. I told him…"

"Blood, why do you need blood?"

A hunger lingered in his eyes he didn't have before. "We need it to heal. Like I said, you need to leave before I do something I'll regret." He grabbed her arm and tried to shove her away, but he had little strength to do it.

The way he looked at her made her feel like a rabbit caught by a snake. She needed to run. She took a step back to get up, but the Great Dane blocked her path. "Canis, I'm going to get some help."

The dog sat down and didn't budge.

"He's sworn to protect us. You should've gone when you had the chance. I'm sorry, Ember, but I need you. We both do."

Ember tried to turn around, but his arm wrapped around her waist in a strong grip this time. She counted six fingers instead of five. Her neck was wrenched to the side and a quick pinch on her throat made her jump. Ember clawed at the arm, but a great pain spread from her neck as blood rushed from her heart to what sucked on her throat. The slurping sound filled her ears. She tried to breathe, but a slow groan came out instead. She felt like she was floating as the blood left her body.

* * *

Ember slowly opened her eyes. Her head spun. She tried to sit up, but found she was too weak.

"Hey, take it easy." Bennett sat by her side on a bed that wasn't hers. He appeared normal and no longer green.

"What happened?"

"Nothing you need to worry about," Nash's cold voice came from the doorway. He seemed off-kilter a bit, and his skin was paler in the light. "Ben, can I talk to you?"

Bennett ran his finger over Ember's forehead and gave her small smile. "I'll be right back."

They spoke in hushed tones. Ember tried to hang onto the feeling of his finger along her forehead. It felt soft and nice. Human touch was something she missed. Ember struggled up on her elbows and sat up. Ben looked back at her and shook his head. It was clear he didn't agree with Nash about what they were saying. She moved again. A groan of pain and exhaustion came out of her mouth as her body protested. Bennett went rigid and so did Nash.

"You can't tell me you don't feel it too," Bennett said loud enough for her to hear.

"It doesn't matter, and you shouldn't have done what you did," Nash replied through gritted teeth.

"You know it matters, and she saved our lives."

"Umm... Guys, what the hell is going on?" Ember asked them. "I can hear you."

"We have to tell her," Bennett said to his partner.

"We don't have to tell her shit!"

"I'd appreciate if you told me something. Your dog led me into your house which looked like something out of a sci-fi movie, and two green men with six fingers were hurt on the floor. Was I hallucinating?"

She ran her fingers through her hair. Her fingertips caught on something round and metallic nestled in her hairline behind her ear. It felt like the same thing she encountered under the dog's collar. "Ahh -- what the hell is this?" She tried to stop the panic from settling into her body.

"I told you should've left it," Nash told Bennett.

"She saved our lives. I wasn't about to let her die."

"Maybe not, but I still need more."

Ben took Nash's face between his hands. "I've put in an order for more plasma to be delivered. It'll be here later today. Rest until then. I'll talk to Ember about all this." Bennett brushed his lips over Nash's.

Ember turned away from their private moment. Their conversation stirred more questions. Nash pulled away and leered back at her. She could feel the coldness of his stare. Whatever Bennett had done, it made Nash despise her even more. Nash hobbled away. Canis whimpered. Ben stepped back toward the bed. The farm boy exterior blinked in and out. He ran his fingers over his neck and standing before her was the green man she'd seen the night before. Ember let out a startled scream.

He waved his hand, and no more sound came out of her mouth. "I'm sorry about all this. I know you want an explanation. I'll give you one if you can calm down. Will you listen?"

Ember clutched her throat.

"I'll give you back your voice, but no more screaming."

She nodded. Not sure what all this meant, but she had to follow along or she wouldn't get away from these strange men she'd found herself enmeshed with.

Bennett drew up a chair and sat next to her bed. Ember shifted back in the bed until she was up against the headboard. The move left her panting. He put up his hands. Ember stared at those hands. They had the same lines as hers did, but six total fingers instead of five. "Whoa. I'm not going to hurt you."

The voice was the same as the man she knew, but the exterior was alien. She tried say something again, but nothing came out. Bennett came toward her. Ember jerked away. He slipped his fingers along her neck. He touched the device behind her ear. A shock went through her and Bennett withdrew. She took in a breath and cleared her throat.

"What in the hell did you do to me? Why are you green? Am I your prisoner?"

The Great Dane jumped up on the bed and laid his head on her lap. She petted him to distract herself from everything burning up her mind. She glanced up at the creature she knew as Bennett. The silver hair looked glossy as it hung to his shoulders. His eyes were vibrant purple. His skin along his face, neck, and outlining his chest was a dark emerald green. Over his chest and pecks down to his waist a slight silver sheen brushed over his flesh, giving it a lighter hue. A sculpted eight-pack of muscles defined his torso. The odd thing was, he didn't have nipples. Her gaze swept below to his waist, and she didn't see his belly button. He wore dark blue jeans. At his waist, the skin blended from green to the same color of his jeans.

"You're not a prisoner here. You can leave any time you like. I suggest resting a bit more, though, while the nanos do their work on you."

"Nanos?"

He pointed to the device next to her ear. "They originate from the suppression module embedded behind your ear. These devices normally control our Plasma Units, but I implanted it on you to save your life. After you saved ours."

"Take it off."

"I can't. Once it's been embedded, it can't be removed. It also allows you to see us through the holograms that camouflage us. You'll have access to the rest of the ship as well. I'm sorry how this was handled, but I couldn't let you die."

"How did I save your lives?"

"You remember finding us with Nash in my lap?"

"Barely. It looked like there'd been an explosion. Something rocked the guesthouse, and black smoke poured out of your house. I could barely breathe. Canis led me to you."

Bennett patted the dog. "He's been our friend ever since we rescued him. Haven't you?"

Canis looked over at Bennett and yawned. *"Yes."*

Ember heard a low voice and stared at the dog. "Did he talk? Wait, did I hear him?"

The canine poked her hand with his wet nose. *"Yes,*

human. I your overlord. You obey."

A chill went through Ember. *I'm not hearing this. A dog can't talk. Men can't be green or not have nipples and six fingers.* She touched the small device again and looked back at Bennett. It didn't seem like he wanted to hurt her, but she didn't know if she could trust him.

"He's not serious, is he?" Ember asked.

Bennett burst out laughing. "No. He's messing with you. He's watched too many movies over the years. He likes to read, too."

"How is that possible?"

"Canis was skin and bones when we found him. We were lonely, and Nash thought it'd be interesting to see if the suppression model would work on a lower form of animal. The curative powers of the nanos revived him, along with some food and rest. Over time he's gotten smarter and become telepathic so he's pretty good at getting his message across. It also allows him access to the ship and any building on the property. Now you're linked into our network, so to speak, and you can understand him as well."

"What if I don't want to understand him or even deal with your being… green. I don't want your nanos wreaking havoc inside my bloodstream. I thought you were nice guys offering me a place to live… and… now I'm y-your slave. You can make me do whatever you want." Ember pulled her hand away from the dog. She looked down and realized she was still in her robe and nightgown. Her head stopped spinning, and she felt a little bit stronger. She stood up, but her legs wobbled again. She tried to catch herself when Bennett put his arm around her waist. Ember placed her hand on his chest. It was warm. When she inhaled, she smelled vanilla and citrus. Under her palm, she felt two distinct heartbeats. Ember leaned a little bit closer as the fragrance enticed her.

"Do I smell or something?"

Ember blinked coming out of her daze and realized she was nose to nose with him. Something in his eyes showed his kindness. "No, forget it. Sorry. I'm going back to my place now. Please don't follow me."

She walked toward the door, but Bennett grabbed her hand. "Ember, whatever you decide to do, please don't tell anyone about Nash and me. It'd be bad if anyone found out we're not... human. Nothing will happen to you while you're here. I promise."

"What about Nash? He's not happy that I know about you. Can he control me as well?"

"I can't promise you anything with him. I'll try to talk him into leaving you alone. I'm grateful for what you did. He was nearly gone, and you helped bring him back."

"How did I do that? You mentioned before you had more plasma coming." Ember thought back to seeing them on the floor, and Ben urging her to go. Then he held her to him and the pain in her neck. They had endangered her life and to make sure she didn't die had implanted her with a device to save her from death.

"We drank your blood. Nash was hurt badly in the explosion. I used all our stored plasma on Nash to keep him going. Then Canis brought you. I tried to stop him, but I was too weak. I took enough of your blood to heal and then made sure to give some to Nash. I had a difficult time pulling him from you, but your blood saved both of us enough until more blood arrived."

"You drank my blood. Great. Fucking green, vampire aliens and their talking dog. Yeah. I'm done."

Ember walked slowly back to her house. Her stomach rolled. Everything in the new place belonged to them. It all looked alien. The smell even made her nauseous. She rushed into the bathroom and lost whatever she'd eaten. She slumped on the floor. All Ben revealed to her overwhelmed her in the midst of the shit storm at the restaurant. Ember took a few minutes before she stood up. When she did, she checked the mirror, but didn't see any bite marks. How had they taken her blood? One thing set in her mind. She had to get out from under the watchful eye of her new alien overlords.

Ember found herself outside Anne's door. She barely remembered driving over. She wiped her nose again. She still couldn't believe it. Green men. Drinking blood. Being implanted with strange technology and she couldn't tell anyone about it. She didn't care so much if Nash got collected and dissected, but she didn't want Bennett to suffer. Ember had a soft spot in her heart for him because he had been kind to her and rescued her from her apartment fire.

She sniffled again and knocked on the door. She heard giggling on the other side. Anne opened the door in her robe and messed-up hair. Her expression fell when she saw Ember.

"Hey, Em, are you okay?"

"I don't know. Can I stay here tonight?" It all came rushing out in a torrent of tears. Anne hugged her. The familiar embrace helped settle her nerves. Anne led Ember into the apartment and onto the couch. Lester appeared behind Anne wearing some ragged boxers.

"Ummm…"

"I'm sorry. I should've called, but I didn't have anywhere else to go."

"Of course, she can stay, Anne. We don't turn friends away. I'll get dressed and get some bedding for the couch." Lester waved her in.

Anne closed the door. Ember sat down and felt deflated. Anne squeezed her knee. She looked into her friend's concerned gaze and tried to smile. All her emotions were a mishmash of confusion, disbelief, horror, and some weird sort of obligation she felt about not revealing Ben's secret. Even if she told her best friend, would they believe her? She didn't believe it herself.

Ember slipped her fingers over the module nestled behind her ear. The metal remained cool under her fingertips. She felt the best she'd felt in years, physically at least, but she couldn't make out the events of them feeding off her. All that remained was Bennett urging her to leave.

"Hey, Em. Are you going to tell me what happened?" Anne touched her arm and made her jump.

"Here you go." Lester handed her a glass of water.

Ember sipped on it as Lester sat across from her. He had put his jeans on. Ember noticed the various tattoos stretched across his stomach and arms of several strange creatures. "Interesting tattoos."

"Thanks. They're my own art of the images I see in my nightmares."

"Why would you want your nightmares inked on you forever?"

Lester shrugged. "What better way to face your fears than to always see them?"

"I guess that's one way of looking at it."

"Did one of them hurt you?" Anne asked. "Do I need to call the police?"

Sure, they had hurt her. They had sucked her blood. Revealed to her a precious secret they were aliens. They had implanted her with their technology to save her life. She remembered the look on Bennett's face when he asked her if she was going to tell anyone about them. The anguish he had even for a creature from a different world. It showed he cared about her in a way and about Nash. Looking at Anne's expectant face and Lester's strange expression, she realized she couldn't give up what the men were. Guilt ate her up. They had saved her from her apartment, and she saved them. Maybe they were even.

"No. You don't have to call the police. The guys are on call, and it's so quiet out there. I saw some coyotes close to the house. I freaked out."

"Oh, sweetie, that happens when you live out in the middle of nowhere. The way you were banging on the door made me think you were attacked."

Ember ran her fingers through her hair. A calm came over her. "I think I scared myself. After my hellish day I couldn't process what I saw."

"What else happened?" Anne stroked her hair.

Ember told her about the meeting with Lance and his offer to buy her out. She finished the water and set the cup down. Lester got up and then handed her another. Once she took a sip, she tasted the alcohol in it. She put it down.

"I don't need to get drunk."

"I figured you could use it to calm down. Your hands are still shaking. You sure it was the coyote that spooked you?"

"Yes, I'm sure. Like I said, it's been a day."

"I'll let you get some sleep, then. Maybe next time you tell the Great Dane to go after the coyotes or get yourself a gun." Anne hugged her friend. "I'll see you in the morning."

"'Night, Ember. Oh, do you ever hear a hum where you are?" Lester asked her before he went into the bedroom.

"Nope. Don't hear it. 'Night, guys." She threw the bedding on the couch. The bed creaked in the other room. Ember lay awake in the living room long after they had fallen asleep. She stared at the ceiling, watching the play of headlights as they made strange designs above her. Her thoughts turned over and over about her new reality. Aliens existed and lived among them. They could pass for regular people. What would happened to them if they were found out?

She pulled the pillow over her face and screamed in frustration. They had saved her life twice. They didn't sound like they were going to make her into a sex slave or bear their young. Her curiosity got the better of her. They were civilized. Bennett didn't want their secret exposed. So many questions worked deeper into her mind past her fear of them; she wanted to know more about them. Where did they come from? The thought stuck with her as she drifted off to sleep.

The next morning, Ember woke with the first light of dawn slipping in through the windows. Her friends still slumbered. She rubbed her eyes and put on her shoes. Questions about her landlords burned in her mind. It was all she could think about as she drove home. Ember knocked on their door, but after several moments no one opened it. Instead Canis bounded out, jumped up with his paws on her shoulders, and licked her face.

"You back."

She patted the dog's head and stepped back so he was back on the ground. "Yeah. For now."

"Good. Masters will be glad."

"I can't believe I'm talking to a dog."

"I talk back." Canis barked with his answer as she heard his words in her head.

"Where are they?"

"Work. Wanna play? I have chewie."

"No, I don't want to play. I'm going to take a shower and go back to sleep. Go do what you normally do."

"I come."

She rolled her eyes and motioned for him to follow. The dog padded into the house. If the firemen were at work, then they would be gone for a couple of days. Ember would have to wait for them to get back.

Chapter Four

Ember walked around the house trying to find some evidence of a spaceship on the property. Out back, there was the outbuilding. Beyond that a space where the grass was brown and withered. When she walked over the clearing, her entire body vibrated. She could feel her teeth chattering. The nodule on the back of her ear warmed, but it didn't hurt. Canis stayed outside the shriveled area.

"You come out. Masters no like you in there."

"Why not? The ship's under here, isn't it?"

Canis snorted, but he didn't say anything else. Instead, he kept on staring at her. Ember wasn't going to find anything else until her alien landlords got home. "I have some treats if you want some."

The dog yawned. *"Got carrots? Sausage?"*

"Carrots I have. I might have some chicken. Would that work?"

The dog got up. He followed her into her house and sat by the fridge until she got out some leftover chicken out. He swallowed it in one gulp. She checked her email while she waited for her landlords and found another email from Lance asking her if she thought about his offer. She sighed. He even asked her to go to dinner. That got her even madder. The night passed, and the men didn't return.

The next afternoon, she brought a couple of pizzas home hoping she could talk to them. She noticed a truck in driveway. She knocked on the door and balanced the pizza in her arms. The man on the other side looked completely human. From the coldness of his gaze, she knew it was Nash.

"You decided to come back. I wasn't sure if you would."

She shrugged, trying to appear as if learning they were aliens were no big deal. Questions burned the tip of her tongue. "Are you going to invite me in?"

"Bennett's not here, and I'm not in the mood for pizza." Nash's mouth turned up in a slight sneer. "Although I could go for a good drink."

"Oh well, I don't have any wine with me."

"That's not what I was thinking," Nash whispered against her ear.

He wrapped his arm around her waist. She dropped the pizza boxes from the sudden surprise. Nash's body pressed against hers. The scent of cherries and cloves filled her nose. When she looked up into his cold eyes, she could see through whatever projection he had over his true appearance to make out they were blue laced with gold. He pushed her neck to the side. Nash ran his nose along the curve of her throat. He planted his lips under her ear. Ember shivered.

"You don't want to do whatever you plan on doing," she said.

His teeth nipped her skin. They felt like regular teeth and not fangs. Since they drank her blood, she figured he would bite her with sharpened canines, but he sucked the skin between his teeth. The thunder of her pulse filled her ears. Nash made no move to touch her except with his lips and tongue. He swirled it around the spot where he bit, teasing the blood to the surface. It felt good even though she hated to admit that. Ember moaned. He breathed in a quick breath and tightened his grip. Nash bit harder.

"W-what are you doing?" Ember finally found her voice.

His answer was to slide his tongue along her flesh. It felt like sandpaper. She shivered in response and couldn't help it, but she wanted to feel more of him. Or did she want this to be Bennett? Ember couldn't tell.

"Taking what is mine!" Nash's seductive tone lulled her deeper into whatever trance he put her under.

"Who said I was yours?"

A sharp pain hit the side of her throat. She expected him to have bitten her, but it didn't feel like that. As his lips locked on her throat, it sent tingles of pleasure through her until she panted and felt like she would come at any moment. Ember groaned and Nash shoved her away. She stumbled and caught herself before she fell onto the driveway. She clutched her chest to catch her breath. When she looked back at the door, it was closed. Nash and her pizza boxes were gone. Ember pressed her palm to the side of her throat and came away with blood in a design that looked like an eight-pointed star. The echo of the pleasure he brought her lingered in her body. She needed some kind of release. What had happened? Her legs wobbled and she got lightheaded. A rush of warmth moved from behind her ear and spread through her body. A quick second later she regained her footing.

Ember banged on the front door, but Nash didn't open it. Her questions hammered against her brain. She would get answers. He had taken her blood and she liked it. At least she thought she did. Her body responded like it was close to the best sex she'd ever had. It didn't make sense. After pounding until her hand hurt, it was clear he had gone back to being his surly self and ignoring her.

She screamed in frustration and headed back toward her house. When she got inside, she had a message from Lance on her phone.

"Hi, Ember, I was wondering if you'd like to go out for dinner to talk. Give me a call." She rolled her eyes and deleted the message.

The next message was from Anne. Ember hadn't talked to her since she left her apartment. She couldn't bear to tell her friend the truth. It was bad enough she lied about the coyotes. Ember listened, but it the voice wasn't the one she expected to hear.

"Hi, Em, it's Lester. Anne said it was okay if I called

you. She thinks I'm checking up on you after your brush with the coyotes. I know the truth. I need to meet with you and warn you."

She hung up. He texted the number with a note for her to call him. *Does he know the men are actually aliens?* She threw the phone onto the couch. It bounced on the white cushions and looked like a strange black speck on the material.

"Ember?"

She jumped at the light touch on her arm. "Fuck." She spun around. "Bennett, what do you want?"

"I knocked and called out. When you didn't answer, I came inside. I hope it's okay." Even though he looked like a Midwestern hunk of a fireman, she could see the green alien underneath. She wasn't sure which one of his guises she liked better.

"It's fine. Why are you here?" Ember kept her distance, but she yearned to feel what it would be like to melt into his arms. Her stomach churned at the fight to keep from going over to him. Whatever pull she felt from him and from Nash perplexed her. She shouldn't be attracted to two alien men.

"I saw the pizza. Nash told me you stopped by and what happened. I wanted to see how you were. Are you okay?"

"Am I okay with what I found out? Or am I okay with what happened tonight with your boyfriend?"

"Both, I guess. I know it's a shock finding out I -- we're different from you and not from this planet. We're not going to hurt you."

"You're not going to pull me back into your spaceship and probe me?"

Bennett chuckled. He sat on the arm of the chair but kept his distance. "No. We won't probe you unless you want us to." His voice lowered and it lulled her into a relaxed state of mind. Ember shook her head and felt whatever spell he had over her falling away.

"Don't hypnotize me. Is it because you're part snake or something with your green skin?"

"My kind are related to something like the chameleons you have on Earth. I'm not trying to mesmerize you."

"Chameleons. Is that why you look like some sexy farmhand turned firefighter?"

"You think I'm sexy?" His eyes flashed violet through his disguise.

Ember felt her cheeks burn. She looked down at her hands to get away from his gaze. "Well, not the green-skinned whatever you are, but sure, the human..."

"Hologram," he corrected her.

"...Hologram is very appealing. I'm pretty sure you know from the looks you get even dressed up in your gear."

"I know you have questions about us. You coming back with the pizza shows you're more intrigued than scared."

He's reading my mind.

Bennett met her eyes and smiled. *"Yes, I can hear your thoughts if I listen because of the suppression module."*

A flash of anger rolled through her. "Have you been listening all the time since you tagged me?"

"I don't see a number stapled to your ear like a cow. No, I'm not reading your thoughts. We could. The module allows us to control you wholly if we like, but I'm not into domination. Naashin does enjoy it, though."

"Naashin? Is that Nash's real name?" The name became garbled as she said it, but she could hear the language he spoke was much different. A quick second later she heard the English translation. She hadn't heard Bennett speak in his own tongue before.

"Well, the English equivalent."

"What's your real name?"

"I'm not sure you'll be able to pronounce it. Bennett was the nearest thing we could figure out."

She shrugged. "Try me."

He said a whole string of sounds she couldn't even make out. Ember shook her head showing she couldn't understand him. Bennett smiled. "Told you. It's easier to call me, Ben. Or Bennett. I've gotten used to it after all this time."

"How long have you been here?"

Ben studied her for a while before he answered. It felt like he scrutinized her. The nodule on her neck warmed, but she didn't feel any different. "I can tell you or I can show you. If I show you, then you're going to have to go into the ship. You're going to have to trust me. Think you can do that?"

Ember wanted answers. If this was the way to get them, then she could venture back into his ship with him. "What do I have to do?"

"Take my hand and follow me." Bennett extended his hand toward her.

She bit her lip as a squeak of fear entered her brain. She figured he could sense it or read it in her thoughts, but her brain was still going over the idea they were not alone in the universe. By taking his hand, her world would change. She needed to delve into the mystery for whatever reason she had been put in their path. Ember twined her fingers through his.

"You have six fingers." She lifted their hands up.

"I do. Let's get into the house, and then I can answer more of your questions." He led her into the kitchen. She remembered the room off the kitchen, but this time she was awake and could focus on it.

Where the kitchen ended, another room led downward. It didn't blend well enough with the architecture. Grey walls on both sides. A low buzz came from that side of the room. As Bennett got to it, the image he projected of the human male fell away, revealing the green alien. Ember gasped seeing him standing before her in full view of the lights. He stood over six feet tall, close to seven from what she could tell because his head nearly brushed the top of the doorway that led into the ship. His green skin glistened in the light. His silver hair was unbound. The light caught the fine silver of his eyebrows and long lashes. As her gaze roved over his body, Ember noticed his green scales turned to begin to turn a dark blue matching the color of his jeans until the color became the perfect match. He did say he was related to something similar to a chameleon. His mouth was full and his nose a little flatter than most people's. His eyes were spaced farther apart, but nothing that made him unattractive. Just alien.

"What's she doing here?" The stern voice broke the spell Ember found herself caught under.

Nash slipped his arm around Ben. They said something in their language. He locked gazes with her, and she could feel the spite he felt for her. Nash grumbled something as though they reached an agreement. He pressed his mouth to Bennett's. The other alien tried to pull away, but Nash deepened the kiss and stared right at Ember, claiming Ben for his own. Bennett turned into his embrace and returned the kiss. Nash moved his hand down Bennett's torso and a low moan came out of him.

The sound hit her. She gripped the counter. Her knees wobbled and her breath hitched. Something about that vibrated down to her core. A rush of pleasure encompassed her body. A flash of her between the two aliens filled her thoughts. Ember could feel their hands sliding down her body. They pressed themselves against her, leaving her on the brink. A shot of pain brought her back to herself. Ember lifted her hand and came away with a gash. Blood welled up in her cut. Before she could get a towel, Bennett had her wrist. His violet eyes glowed with hunger like a starving man. He said something in his native tongue and hovered over the wound, waiting.

His breathing intensified. So did hers. His warm breath beat against her palm in time with her pulse. The tension between them was palpable. His five fingers encircled her wrist while his thumb rubbed along hers. Each small movement made her quiver. It felt like he ran his thumb over other parts of her body, and she couldn't understand why. It spiked her desire. With him so close, she wondered what his skin would feel like. The scent of vanilla and citrus overwhelmed her. Her mouth watered. Would he taste like he smelled?

Ember cupped his cheek. Bennett didn't break her gaze. He turned his head into her hand and made a soft sound. The green along one side of his face lightened almost to the color of her skin. The texture of it felt a little like velvet with the smooth feel of snake scales. His mouth looked inviting. The blood pooled in her palm. He moved closer until his lips nearly touched it.

"May I?" The words came into her thoughts.

She got the sense he fought for control, not wanting to take it against her will like the last time. Part of her remained frightened at what she would feel and how painful it would be, but she was more intrigued than scared.

"Yes," she whispered.

Bennett's eyes widened in slight surprise at her permission. He kept his gaze on her before he opened his mouth and covered the cut. She half expected him to bite into her flesh, but his tongue brushed over the gash. It stung a little. Then she felt something latch onto the center of her palm. Each time he swallowed her breath became shallower. The suction came in time with her heartbeat. Ember groaned. Bennett held tighter, and his eyes snapped open. Ember could feel herself lingering on the edge of an orgasm from him taking her blood.

She didn't want him to stop, but he released her hand. As he did, she caught what looked like a flower closing on the end of his tongue. The outline of an eight-pointed star lingered on her palm in the form of minuscule pinpricks over the slash. It hurt for few moments until she felt the rush of heat flash down her neck. It worked down her arm and then her palm pained her less.

"Thank you."

It took her a moment to find words. "You're welcome."

"Do you still want to know about us?"

The lingering desire from his bite remained in her system. She felt like she would burst from unreleased sexual energy. If a bite did that to her, then what would it be like if she ended up in bed with one of them. Not that they were even interested in her sexually. Bennett had Nash so it was very unlikely they would want to do anything with her.

"Yes."

"Then follow me."

* * *

Ember followed Bennett deeper underground as they entered the ship. The ship tilted at an odd angle. Bennett rounded a corner and stopped outside a door.

"This is our Viewing Chamber. It's similar to your movie theaters, but everything here is three-dimensional, and we can interact with it. Nash tends to use it to play parts in some of his favorite movies. Right now, he's stuck on *Backdraft*."

"Is that why you're posing as firefighters?" Ember asked.

"It's part of the reason."

"Aren't you afraid the guys at your firehouse or anyone will see through your disguise?" The large room could have housed her entire restaurant.

"Nash developed a portable holographic projector we have implanted in us. Nash is the technical genius. He's outside diverting some power from our batteries, so we can run this. You wanted to see how we came here, right?"

Ember trailed her fingers over the metallic surface of the room. The oily texture warmed under her fingertips. A small tingle ran over her skin, but it wasn't unpleasant. "I do." She looked at her palm again, and it was no longer wounded. Bennett traced a finger over where he had taken her blood.

"The nanos in your blood healed you. Don't fear them or us."

"Why do you need blood?" Ember asked.

"It's part of our mutation," Bennett answered her. "The same reason we have six fingers."

"Only six? What kind of mutation?"

The light in the room brightened. Images flickered around the room. Voices faded in and out until the whole room changed into a three-dimensional space. A different version of Nash and Bennett appeared before her. She wanted to say something, but the present-day Ben put a finger to his mouth and pointed to the scene playing out before her.

Both aliens were dressed in black armor. Different pieces covered their bodies, and what skin she could see was the same color as the plates. They had swords as they rushed around slashing at two-foot tall purple blobs. One blob jumped up and wrapped itself around Nash's leg. He stabbed at it with a short dagger he pulled from his waist. It dissolved into a puddle of goo.

"Don't let them get to the controls," Nash screamed to Bennett.

A black chair rose from the middle of the floor. Purple blobs engulfed the chair. Smoke poured from the space the chair rose from. Other creatures skittered down the walls. Nash kept slicing at them, but more kept coming. A wall before the chair pulled back and revealed a large red-and-orange glowing ball of light. Ember squinted at the brightness. Flares shot out from the surface and raced straight at the ship. She jumped back. The current Bennett touched her shoulder to reassure her nothing would hurt her. Ember had to remember it was all a movie she was watching.

The room shook and she lost her footing, but Bennett caught her. The control panel exploded next to her. Sparks nearly blinded her, but they didn't hurt her. Instead they moved through her. A purple globule flung itself at the board next to her. It had rows of tiny sharp teeth like a shark. Small tentacles allowed them to latch onto the metal. They chewed away at the module until they got to the exposed wires beneath. Nash pinned one with his sword.

Another flare brightened the screen and the ship shook. Ember held onto Bennett as she felt the shock.

"They've already compromised the central computer. I can't get Drix back online."

"Whose Drix?" Ember asked.

"She's our central computer. She's what your world calls artificial intelligence. She helps navigate the ship, runs the things we can't. Those blobs are asteroid parasites. They live on the surface of the asteroid and eat certain metals. We scanned the asteroid belt to be sure and didn't find any, so we thought we were safe. One must've made it on board. They multiply quickly. We made it all the way to your sun before we noticed glitches. We thought we could stop them, but they'd overwhelmed the ship. Watch." Bennett gestured back to the scene playing out.

The ship tilted, throwing Nash and Bennett toward the other end of the room. Nash hit his head and passed out. Ben tried to get over to him. Another sun flare shot out and spun the ship out of control. Bennett pressed a button at the other end of the panel. A blue shimmer flowed across the floor. It crackled. As it hit the parasites, they all shrieked and then died. In the recording, Bennett passed out. Lights flashed red and yellow as another flare blasted the ship away.

Nash stirred. He mumbled and pressed a couple of panels. The ship righted itself. A green-and-blue sphere appeared in the view screen. Earth. The ship hit the atmosphere. A female shape blinked in and out at one control panel. The ship righted itself as the image wavered. The ship sped up and the surface came up quickly. The ship hit. Everything went dark.

When the scene resumed, the two aliens were outside inspecting the damage to their spaceship.

"I don't know if we're going to be able to fly it again, Ben. It's deeply embedded into the bedrock and there's extensive damage."

Bennett touched Nash's hand and sighed. "I've done scans of the surrounding area. No signs of any advanced civilization. There are some primitive settlements."

"You know what they say about Earth being at the ass end of the universe. It's no wonder why we stay away." Nash leaned against the ship and groaned. "I'm getting hungry. I hope the Plasma Units here are edible."

"We don't have much left from our blood stores after the crash. If they see us and the ship as we are, they'll kill us. We've been lucky the weather's cold and the snow is deep among these large plants. No one has come looking for us." Bennett threw a tool back into the box as he helped Nash try to fix the hole in the ship.

"We'll work it out. Let's get this circuit fixed so we get the heat working." Nash turned back to the ship.

Burnt trees showed the path of where the ship crashed and stuck up in the snow as part of it remained buried in the ground. Forest surrounded them. It looked nothing like the place they lived now.

"I'm confused. Did you guys move your ship?" Ember asked.

"No." Nash's stern voice came from behind her. He touched a place on the wall. The image in the Viewing Chamber fell apart, revealing the soft gray wall.

"Then where did you guys crash land?" Ember turned to look at him.

"It's not a question of where, but when," Nash replied.

"All right, when, then?" Ember asked him.

"According to your calendar in seventeen hundred and ten," Ben told her.

"You're telling me you've been here for over three hundred years?" Ember stared at the green aliens. She didn't see any gray hair threaded through Nash's or Bennett's locks. "Impossible."

"It's not impossible. Humans are so small-minded, thinking they are the only beings in the vast world of space. Other races are longer lived than any of you or even us. Some exist as pure energy. Some are so tiny, they come together to form one entity so they can speak to the outside world. There are others so heinous all they want to do is destroy us all." Nash leaned against the wall. His expression made her wonder what was behind the stoic mask.

"Nash, you don't have to insult her," Bennett replied.

"Who said I was insulting our tenant? I'm telling it like it is. You're the one sharing our wonderful history with this *human*. Don't you think it's a bit odd?" Nash growled.

"Guys, I'm still here. I have a right to know what's going on since you tagged me with your alien technology."

"We saved your life," Nash snapped.

"After I saved yours, apparently. What were you doing anyway that got you so hurt?"

Nash crossed his arms over his chest. His scowl made her feel smaller. A slight pressure pushed on her forehead. Ember tried to say something else but found she couldn't speak again. She grabbed her throat. She gritted her teeth and then poked his arm. It didn't do any good. Ember kicked his leg as hard as she could to get his attention.

"Ouch!"

"Serves you right, Nash," Ben chuckled. "Release Ember. She deserves to know who and what we are. Besides, if I'm right --"

"You're not. Take the blood bag and drain her dry. Get her out of here. Also, I want my dog back." Nash turned in disgust and waved his hand as he walked away. Once he was out of sight, Ember felt her voice come back.

She rubbed her throat and glared at Bennett. "What's with him? Is he going to do that all the time? What did you mean 'if you were right'?"

"Nothing."

Ember sighed. Bennett wasn't going to talk about it. Even though she had discovered how they had ended up on Earth, it didn't explain where they came from or why they drank blood. It left many more questions. She looked at her palm and rubbed the spot where Ben had sucked her blood. Thinking about it made her insides tingle. How could she be attracted to two tall, green aliens who wanted to suck her blood?

"Fine, it's nothing. Will you answer some of my questions?"

"I'm an open book."

"Apparently not."

"Ember, there are some things about our species... Nash finds difficult to explain. Let's leave it at that, but I'll answer your other questions."

Whatever Nash didn't want to talk about seemed to be a touchy subject. It made Ember more curious about what he shied away from. "I've seen you guys eat food, but why do you need blood?"

"It's a genetic mutation among our species. The same

with only having six fingers and six toes on each hand and foot. We're supposed to have seven. We can eat regular food, but our bodies require the blood to survive. It heals us quicker and gives us more strength than others of our species. We're similar in that respect to the vampires in your movies."

"You're supposed to have seven fingers and toes?"

"Does it put you off?" Bennett gave her a half-cocked smile.

"No. I'm just not used to it. Along with the no nipples or belly button."

Bennett ran his fingers down his chest and over the eight-pack abdomen. Ember watched those fingers caressing the ridges of his muscles. She could almost feel them trailing over her stomach. Her alien landlord chuckled. His lips turned up, and she wanted to feel if they were as full as they looked. Ember pulled her gaze away, forced herself to think about something other than his anatomy, and if he was anatomically compatible with a human woman. She felt her cheeks burn and couldn't voice all her other questions.

"Enough of the tour. I'll take you back to the guesthouse. Canis said there's a man waiting for you. He isn't happy about the smell of him. You should go see what the stranger wants."

"Fine."

Chapter Five

"What the fuck are you doing here?"

"You mind getting this dog out of here?" Lance tried to get away from the Great Dane, but when he moved the dog mirrored his movements.

Ember petted Canis's head, but he still didn't let Lance out of his sight. "Not until you tell me why you're here. I don't appreciate you coming to my house."

"Can we talk inside? I really don't want my business being broadcast everywhere."

"Do you see anyone out here besides me and the dog?"

Lance nodded behind her. Ember saw one of the men walking in the shadows. It intrigued her knowing one was snooping on her. "Your landlord?"

"One of them." Ember yawned. She realized how late it was from the moon hanging in the sky. Where had the evening gone? Right. She'd learned more about her alien overlords. "I have a few weeks for your deadline, so get out of here."

"That's what I was hoping to talk to you about. Gus accepted my offer."

"Shit." It hit so quickly she grabbed onto the side of the house for support. Lance took a hold of her arm. Everything she had worked for had all gone in the swift signature of a check. Canis wrapped his jaws around Lance's arm.

He screamed in pain as the dog pulled him away from Ember. "You fucking mutt." Lance raised his good hand to take a swipe at Canis. "Get your dog out of here."

"He's not Ember's dog. He's mine. He doesn't like you touching our girl." Nash growled as he yanked Lance away from Ember.

His statement stunned her. She glanced at Nash, but his expression hadn't changed. Lance held his arm where it was bleeding through his shirt. "Fine. Then I'll see you in court for this."

"Get your ass off my property."

"Ember, I'll be at the restaurant at nine tomorrow morning. Make sure you're on time." Lance got back into his car and sped off.

Canis stood against Ember as her world crashed down around her. She tried to open the door, but her hand shook so much she couldn't grasp it. A hand slid over hers and turned the knob for her. Nash led her inside where she sat down. Hot tears slid down her cheeks.

"Okay you?" Canis's rough voice sounded in her mind. She didn't respond but shook her head.

"Here. Drink this." Nash pushed a glass of water into her hands.

"I'm not thirsty," Ember mumbled.

"I can make you."

"Don't be an ass. I can't deal with it right now."

"Why do you let man push you around?" Nash asked her.

Why had Nash suddenly decided to be nice to her? Yeah, he was sexy in the farm boy/fireman guise he had. He was sexy even as a green alien, but his coldness turned her off.

"You've made it pretty clear I'm nothing more than a snack. I don't need whatever snarky comment you have brewing in your head. Everything I've worked for has gone down the drain. Just because you don't like what I might say doesn't give you the right to make me stop talking or drink my blood without my permission." She took the glass and threw it against the wall as the anger overtook her.

"I don't like surprises showing up on my property."

"That's not an excuse for Canis biting Lance. I have to work with him."

"Man smelled bad. Didn't like how he touched mistress,"

Canis said. The dog whined and placed his head on her leg. Seeing those intelligent, liquid eyes blunted some of her anger.

"Thank you, but you still shouldn't have bitten him."

"Is he your boyfriend?" Nash asked.

She clicked her tongue in disgust. "No, he's the new majority owner of my restaurant. Now he's going to take everything else I have left of Cecil. The fire took all my belongings, and now he's taking my restaurant."

"Cecil was your husband?"

"That's all you got out of that? Yes, he was my husband. He was killed when some guy smacked into his truck. You can read my mind, as Ben said. Anything else you find in there and want to rub in?"

His forehead creased and he frowned, a break in his stoic façade. He let out a long breath and his eyes narrowed. "I don't like other men touching what's mine."

"Yours? How do you figure that? You've done nothing except be an ass to me and stop me from talking."

"Ben was right. I didn't want to believe it, but I heard you moan in the house at dinner. I've tried to push you from my mind, but the sound you make. It entices me. It's stayed with me and I can't fight the pull." He took her face between his hands and ran his fingers down her cheeks. The small touch made her shiver and the breath catch in her throat. The aroma of cherries filled her nose. Ember slid her hand over his and could feel his sixth finger along her jawline. "You're mine."

Nash pressed his lips to hers. Ember fought against him to get away, but once she realized he wasn't pushing himself on her, she relaxed and let the kiss wash over her. The light pressure of his lips. The flick of his tongue along her mouth tasting her.

"I'm not yours," she whispered. "Ben is yours."

"You're both mine." He touched the module behind her ear.

A shot of warmth flowed down her nerves. Her clit throbbed and she fell against him. Nash held her as she squeezed her legs together. He did something else to the metallic disk that made her back arch until it felt like she would burst. "W-what are you doing to me?"

"I need to know something. I have to be sure."

Ember closed her eyes and tried to catch her breath as another wave hit her. She pressed her thighs together and tried not to give into the orgasm building within her. Whatever he had done with the control nodule turned her on as though he knew all her spots to caress. "Be... sure of... w...?

Ember couldn't hold in the moan in her chest. This time Nash touched the module again and an orgasm crested over her. She gripped his hand and felt like she'd had the best damn sex of her life. He hadn't done anything more than kiss her. Nash brushed his lips over hers in a chaste kiss. She tried to catch her breath, but it felt like she was one more breath away from having another orgasm.

"What just happened?"

"Did you enjoy it?"

"Yeah... I guess. It wasn't what I expected."

"I'll explain later. I have to speak to Bennett. Come to us when you get back from work tomorrow." Nash tapped the module again.

It released her body to normal as though she had never had an orgasm. The aftermath and confusion lingered. "This is all a little strange. Why are you being so nice to me all of a sudden?"

He caressed her cheek. "Accept it for now. Come back tomorrow, please. I'll explain it and more."

Ember didn't think she had a choice if she wanted to figure out what the hell he did to her. Or even if she wanted him to do it again. Everything she thought about Nash had been blown away.

"Come on, Canis. You sleep in the house tonight," Nash told him.

The dog didn't move.

"I mean it."

"Let him stay, Nash. I may need something to cuddle with after the day I've had."

His gaze hardened. "Fine. See you tomorrow. Watch her."

The dog barked a reply as Nash walked out of the house. Ember heard the door close, and she relaxed back in her seat. She ran her thumb over her lips where Nash had kissed her. She never thought he would kiss her after being such a dick. He stood up to Lance for her, but she didn't know what he meant about being his. It twined more questions in her mind and also that tomorrow she had to deal with Lance.

* * *

By the time she got to work, it was nine thirty. Her stomach churned as she got out of her car. One of her servers rushed by her in tears.

"Kris, what's going on?"

The young woman looked up at her. "The new guy said we were paring back the number of servers. What's going on, Em?"

She slammed her door. "Let's go have a talk with the new guy."

Kris wiped her eyes and followed Ember inside. Lance and her entire staff gathered round the bar area. Lance looked up from his tablet. The veins pulsed in his temples. His man bun even looked pissed off from how tight it appeared to be wound.

"I told you to be here at nine and you're late. What's she still doing here?" Lance barked.

The staff looked at her and then back at him. "Let's talk in my office, please, Lance."

"We had time to talk this morning when I asked you

to come in. Since you weren't here, I decided to go ahead with the staff meeting. I have a schedule to keep." He looked back down at his tablet and went on with the meeting, ignoring her.

Ember ripped the device out of his hand and went into her office. "That was not a question."

A few minutes later, Lance walked in. "What the hell do you think you're doing?"

"What am I doing? You might be the majority owner, but you still need to talk to me about making drastic changes."

"If I recall, I came to your house to talk and was attacked by a beast. You failed to show this morning." Lance pulled his shirt down to cover the bandage on his arm where Canis had bitten him.

"I don't appreciate being blindsided. Who even told you where I lived? Secondly, you had no intention of talking business last night. I might've taken a bit longer to get here, but I'm here. You can't go firing people without consulting me."

"Can I have my tablet back?"

Ember handed it over to him. "Here."

He yanked it from her and pushed a few spots on the screen. "Fine. You're here, so let's talk. To put the record straight, I wasn't trying to get into your pants. Gus told me where you lived. I wanted to be proactive and let you know Gus cut and run. I don't want us to be at each other's throats when it comes to running the business."

She gritted her teeth. This man was her new partner. "Fine. Kris isn't the person you want to fire. I can give you a list. Let me guess -- Gus told you she had to go."

"See! This is why I wanted to meet with you so we can go over --"

"Excuse me, Em, there's a guy here who says he has to talk to you." Jean stuck her head in the door.

"Really isn't a good time, Jean."

"I know, but he says it's life or death. He's scaring the servers."

"Fine. I'll be there in a minute. Lance, can we get back to this in a few minutes?"

"Go deal with this situation. I hope it's not another one of your landlords."

She got up and shook her head in disgust. "I'm coming."

In the dining room, Lester was talking to Kris who had a wide-eyed stare. Lester turned around, and his expression turned to relief. "Thank, God. I left you messages."

Ember waved Kris away signaling she would take care of her friend's boyfriend. "Lester, can we talk about this outside, please?"

"Yeah. Yeah. Did you get my calls?" Lester followed her outside.

"I've heard your voicemails, but I've been a little busy with the changes going on here. Is everything okay with Anne?"

"She's fine. I wanted to warn you about your landlords. I know what they are. You have to be careful of them."

"They're firemen. They saved my life and offered me a place to live. Should I be careful of them hosing me down? Lester, I don't have time for this." She turned to walk away when he grabbed her arm.

"They're not what they seem. You think they're regular fireman, but they're not from this planet. I've encountered their kind before." He pointed toward his tattoos. "I've been abducted. Seen the inside of their spaceships. There are reptilians amongst us. Don't let their outward appearance fool you."

Ember tried to keep her face blank. Did he really know what Nash and Bennett were? If so, what would he do about it? "Lester, my landlords are regular firefighters.

They're a couple of great guys who have a thing for one another. They're *not* aliens."

"Don't let them brainwash you. I can prove it." He pulled his shirt up.

"Whoa. You don't need to get naked out here."

Lester took his shirt off showing off more tattoos of strange aliens and monsters. He pointed to the small of his back. "This one is the reptilian who I encountered. They can shift their shape. They manipulate humanity and our government. They show up in disc-shaped crafts. I was abducted by one. They have six fingers, and they drank my blood." He lifted up his hair. Something small and silver glinted in the light. "Do you see the implant?"

Ember resisted the urge to touch the one behind her ear. Lester grabbed her hand and put it on the silver disk at the back of his skull. It felt cool and smooth. Everything he told her confirmed what she had learned from Nash and Bennett. "Lester, I --"

He dropped her arm. "I know you don't believe me. I've tried to have it removed, but none of the doctors I've seen want anything to do with it. I've tried going to the government, but they think I'm a conspiracy nut. The hum I talked about at your place -- I heard it the last time I was abducted. Don't trust the men who claim to be your landlords. They'll tag you as though you were a piece of meat. They can make you do anything they want now. A white light blinded me and when I woke up, I was in a cell. They scanned me. They could read my thoughts and took my blood. They kept me for a few days, and then they dumped me back in an empty lot. I don't want the same thing to happen to you."

"I believe that something happened to you. The hum you heard is probably from the power lines running near the property. Thanks for the warning. I'll keep an eye out. Give Anne a hug for me and have a good show tonight." Ember squeezed his arm and headed back inside. His words gave her a little bit of a scare as she ran her fingers over the metal disk behind her ear. It remained slightly warm. The firemen said it contained nanos that kept her healthy. The gash in her hand healed and didn't leave a scar so they hadn't lied about that. Nash's behavior still left her befuddled. Cleary she was attracted to Bennett. Nash claimed she was his, but what did that mean exactly?

Chapter Six

After five hours of arguing with Lance, Ember brought food back to the house. She got out of the car and felt a vibration in the ground, running up her feet.

Canis barked at her near the house.

She followed the dog around to the back. A strong tremor made her grab onto the side of the building. She dropped the bag as the pebbles on the ground shook. "What's going on?"

"Ship working."

"Ship working? What does that mean?"

"It means we finally might have a way to leave." Bennett came out and wiped his hands on already stained jeans. They were tight and fit his muscled form, even when she could see through the hologram. He was smeared with black and orange stuff. She didn't want to know what it was.

"That's a good thing, right?" Ember forced a smile.

Bennett shrugged. "We've been here a long time. What smells good? Did you bring dinner?"

"Yeah, Nash told me to come by so we could talk after I got back from work."

His eyes narrowed. "He did? Well, he didn't tell me. Maybe that's why he's been such a bear today."

"What do you mean?"

"Since this morning he's been working like a jackrabbit to get this hunk of junk running. If we ever do get back to Tilleron, it needs a complete overhaul. I wonder if Brax is still around. He's the head mechanic among us. Come inside. Nash knows you're here by now."

They went inside the kitchen. Ember set the bag down and took out a few different things she brought with her. Nash emerged from the ship. He didn't bother with the hologram to hide his appearance. He glanced at her, but all she could see was the cold being who didn't care for her. Had he been fucking with her earlier?

"Ben said you've been working on the ship. I could feel it vibrating under the ground when I got out of the car. You might want to keep that contained so no one comes looking for you." Ember began setting out pasta and some salads along with the small pizza she'd brought since she didn't know what the men liked. Her stomach knotted with anticipation of what Nash wanted to talk to her about. It also made her think of what Lester said. They had the same device implanted in them. Did it mean there were others like Bennett and Nash on Earth, kidnapping people and using them for blood donors? Did Nash and Bennett have any communication with them? She didn't know if she should tell them about Lester. If they were leaving, then, it didn't seem to matter.

"I'll have to increase the dampening field to minimize the sensation. Were there any other noticeable signs?" Nash asked.

"The pebbles bounced on the ground. Also, I think there's a hum. At least that's what my friend's boyfriend said when he came here to help me move."

"Thanks. I'll look into it."

"Great. Um… you said earlier there was something you wanted to show me, Nash."

"Yeah, Nash, what did you want to show Ember? You've made it perfectly clear you don't want anything to do with her." Bennett snagged a piece of pizza and munched on it. He seemed as curious to know what she and Nash had talked about late last night.

He straddled the chair and stared at both of them. "I wanted to get the Stimulation Chamber running."

The color drained from Ben's face. "Are you sure? I thought you wanted to get the ship running because you picked up a distress call from another like us. Was that a lie too?"

Nash let out a sigh. The veins in his temples throbbed. His emerald skin along his neck and chest turned a darker shade of green. "I have my reasons. And I wasn't lying."

"Guys, obviously you need to talk through some things. I'm gonna go back to my place." Ember started to head out of the kitchen when she suddenly froze. She tried to move, but her legs wouldn't respond. "Release me, Nash."

Bennett snapped something to his partner in their language. Nash answered back with a few growls and guttural sounds. Bennett lunged at Nash, who stepped out of his way. Bennett slid a few feet, turned, and knelt down, ready to pounce on Nash. He hissed. Ember only had a view of Ben's back. The scales rolled and changed color from green to black. The muscles in his shoulders bunched. Just as he was about to spring, a spear of desire hit Ember. She fell to her knees as the ecstasy of building orgasm flared along her nerves. She let out a low moan and held her breath, trying to fight her body. The next thing she knew, hands held hers and she was pressed against a solid form. When she breathed in, the scent of citrus overwhelmed her. She tried to catch her breath, but Bennett lowered his lips to hers. His hands slid down her back and caressed her ass as he pulled her closer -- as though he tried to meld them together. When he pulled away, Ember's head spun from the lack of air and his kiss. He trailed his fingers along her face. His human disguise fell away. She caught herself gazing into his violet eyes and felt her heart skip a couple of beats. His chest expanded as he drew in short breaths.

"I don't think we need the Stimulation Chamber," Ben said to Nash.

"What's a Stimulation Chamber?" Ember asked.

"It's where we find out if our Plasma Units are sexually compatible with us so they can become Body

Units as well," Nash told her. His eyes flashed silver. Those eyes looked at her as though she were the main course and dessert rolled into one.

"H-how do you know I'm sexually compatible with you?" All she could think about was how being around both of them made her feel. Their scent intoxicated her, and she couldn't understand why the fragrances made her hot and bothered.

"It's more than compatibility, Nash, and you know it," Bennett whispered.

Nash trailed his thumb along her lips. Ember swiped the tip of her tongue over it coming away with the tang of grease and the sweat. Nash's eyes widened and his lips turned into a soft smile. She figured if he really went for it and gave her a full-on smile it would dazzle her. He tipped her chin up and away from Bennett and studied her face. The questions in his eyes made her want to know what he was hiding. He lowered his mouth to hers and kissed her lightly. He pulled away before she could taste more of him. Bennett growled under his breath, which made her focus back on him.

"What's going on between the three of us? Besides Nash making me do things and almost have an orgasm."

"I needed to hear you moan," Nash replied. His featherlight caress made her head spin again. Whatever they were doing to her, she was at their mercy.

"Why?"

"We need to continue this discussion upstairs or in our chambers," Bennett panted.

"Tell me what the fuck is going on?" Ember blurted out as she got a bit more control.

Bennett took her hand and placed it over the bulge in his pants. "I want to have sex with you and worship every part of your body. Tell me you don't want the same thing. I've seen it in your thoughts."

She rolled her eyes. "Yeah, sure, I've thought about it.

Although, I'm not sure why I'm fantasizing about green aliens rocking my world."

"Trust us, Ember, the encounter would be beyond anything you've experienced before," Nash tried to reassure her. Questions pooled in her mind. When he gave her a genuine smile, it allayed her lingering fears.

"Tell me about the moaning thing first," Ember muttered.

Bennett hadn't released her hand from his firming cock. Ember ran her finger over the bulge, trying to feel more of it. The yearning in his eyes grew the longer she caressed him. Nash trailed his fingers around her neck and pushed her hair out of the way. He went behind her, wedging her between him and Bennett. Nash flicked his tongue over her ear and tugged on it. She squeezed Ben's cock. Nash bit her a little harder. A muffled cry came from her throat. Bennett's eyes fluttered shut.

"When you moan, it lets us know you're our mate. Something neither of us thought possible," Nash whispered before plunging his tongue into her ear.

Bennett slipped his hand along the curve of her hip, tugging at her shirt until his six fingers feathered over her stomach. Ember jumped. She tried to keep focused on what they said. "Mate. As in wife?"

"Something like that." Bennett kissed the underside of her chin.

"Certain sounds can affect us in particular ways. Your moan, the vibration it makes in us, it lets us know you're our soul mate, as humans call it," Nash explained.

"All you need to do is hear us and once we are together, just our sound will make you come," Bennett said. "I knew it the first time I heard you, but Nash didn't believe me."

"But you guys are together, why would you want to involve me in your relationship?" Ember could feel herself losing the battle between their caresses and their body heat. Everything in her said to give into them. She wanted to feel what it would be like to have them inside her.

"It's rare for us to find mates with our mutation, but to find two is nearly unheard of. Do you want to keep talking or can we take you upstairs? Your thoughts are nearly screaming it." Nash caressed her breast and pressed against her ass until she felt his dick.

"Please, Em. Haven't you ever wondered what it'd be like to be fucked by two little green men?" Bennett asked.

"I don't think you're so little. Stop reading my mind. Just because you can doesn't mean you should."

Nash laughed. "This close it's hard not to. Yes or no? Are we going to make you burn or leave you wanting?"

Ember closed her eyes and leaned against both men. Their combined scents aroused her. The beats of their hearts didn't match hers. This was a once in a lifetime shot. If they thought she was their soul mate, then that complicated things. Every part of her screamed to say yes. It had been so long since she'd been with someone. She didn't know if she could open herself up the way they might want. Cecil wouldn't want her to hold onto things so tightly. Four years of lonely nights. Of longing for the man she'd thought she would spend the rest of her life with.

"One condition," she demanded.

"Name it," Nash replied.

"No more controlling me with a thought or a wave of your hand. Free will is the ticket to get into my pants."

"I'm already in your pants." Bennett chuckled as his fingers slid over the thin material of her panties.

"You know what I mean." She tried to make it sound harsher than it came out.

"Done." Nash scooped her up into his arms and held her against him. Bennett hissed something. Ember wrapped her arms around Nash's neck and rested her head on his shoulder. Up close, she could see his skin was made of small scales. They weren't any larger than her pinky nail. He brought her down into the ship.

Small pinpoints of lights twinkled off and on, giving them enough light to see by. Nash set her on a large bed. Bennett came in and closed the door, completing the illusion they were suspended among the stars. Ember rubbed her arms, missing the warmth of the two men.

"Drix, raise the temperature three degrees," Nash commanded.

"As you requested." A female voice made Ember jump.

"You fixed her?" Bennett asked.

"Yes, I finally cobbled together the parts I needed," Nash replied.

"She's the computer for your ship?" Ember asked.

"Yes. Are you still cold?" Nash stood before her. Bennett waited on the other side.

"No. I'm good. Thanks."

Now they had her in bed, they both seemed not to know what to do with her. Or they were waiting for her to make the first move. She bit her lip and pulled the shirt over her head and let it drop to the floor. They still didn't move. She stood up and slid out of her jeans until she stood only in her panties and bra. Bennett's eyes had gone wide. Nash seemed to be taking in the show. Ember slid her hand over Bennett's jeans and undid them until his cock sprang out.

"You gonna take those off? That's kinda how this works."

Bennett took his shirt and jeans off. It seemed he had been carved by an artist. She walked her fingers along the indentations of his abs until she got to the space where he should have had a belly button. The flat surface intrigued her, but she pushed that from her mind and focused on his dick. It resembled a human male penis in shape, maybe a little bigger and longer than she was used to. It was a deep shade of green. Ember trailed her fingers over the spongey head, down to the base, and then back up. The gesture didn't seem to be turning him on. He had no hair at the base of his shaft, but three testicles.

"I must be doing something wrong, if you're not interested all of a sudden," Ember told him.

Nash chuckled. "We aren't like human men. We have to be petted in different places on our members to stimulate us. While it would feel good to have your mouth on my cock, let me show you what we like." He took one of her hands and slid it under Ben's balls until she palmed all three of them. "There's an indentation on our middle testicle like the crease of a peach. Do you feel it?"

Ember ran her fingers over the smooth flesh of Bennett's balls and did feel a slight ridge on his middle ball that her finger fit in. "Yes."

"Rub it gently. Slowly, so you can hear him groan." Nash waited behind her as she brushed Bennett's testicle.

Ben grabbed her shoulder as she massaged the fold. He drew in a breath and his cock bobbed. Ember massaged it a little bit more, not sure how much pressure to use. She moved her finger in circles and tried to cup his other balls at the same time. Bennett's breath came in short pants. He took her free hand and placed it on his chest. Ember felt the beats of his hearts and then a low rumble started in his chest. It felt like a cat's purr, but it went deeper.

"Do you feel it?" Nash whispered against her ear. His voice had deepened to a huskier tone. He slid fingers over hers on Bennett's balls.

Bennett's chest heaved as he took in shorter breaths. Nash pressed against her, sandwiching her between them. The rumble in Ben's chest grew. As it did, she could somehow feel it in her. It felt similar to the vibration of the ship, but it triggered something inside her. The growl stirred her passion on an emotional level. It amplified her desire for them until she felt a gush of wetness between her legs.

"Yes," she whispered. "I can't really explain it."

"Told you," Bennett whispered.

"Fine," Nash murmured.

"What does this mean?" Ember trailed her fingers over Bennett's chest.

"Enough," Ben moaned.

The long groan made Ember shiver. It was as though she could feel him inside her -- like his voice had become sort of a vibrator hitting all her spots. Bennett pushed his mouth against hers. Ember tasted the cherry of his lips. She wanted to eat him up and have him inside her. If they could make her feel this way without even touching her, what could they do with their hands and mouths? Nash trailed his fingers along her sides and slipped her bra straps off her shoulders. He moved her hair aside and placed small kisses along her skin. Ember shivered when he undid the clasp. He caressed her breasts and squeezed her nipples. She broke the kiss with Bennett and cried out.

Bennett pulled one of her fingers into his mouth. His tongue wrapped around it as he pulled it out. A quick nip on the tip made her quiver. Nash sucked on her throat near her pulse point, but he didn't bite her. Nash walked his hands across her stomach and over the silky fabric of her panties.

"If you want to turn back, now is the time. After this, you're ours," Nash told her.

Ember turned her head and kissed him. He plunged his tongue into her mouth at the same time he slipped one of his fingers along her wet slit. Nash massaged her clit in torturous circles. Ember moaned again. Bennett released her finger and pulled her bra all the way off. His mouth found one of her nipples. His tongue flicked across the firm pebble. A quick pain made her gasp. She threaded her fingers through his silver hair. The sucking sensation made her press against him. Ben's hand cupped her other breast and fondled her firmed nipple. Nash dipped his fingers into her while his thumb massaged her clit. Ember's nerves fired. She tried to catch her breath, but wave after wave of pleasure passed over her. Nash moved back to her throat.

"Mine," he whispered.

"Ours," Bennett answered. He kissed the other side of her throat.

Nash plunged his fingers into her again, and Bennett attached his sucker to her neck. She raked her fingers down Bennett's back as an orgasm warmed her insides. She screamed and rocked against both of them. Both men licked her throat again and gave her a moment to recover. Ember rested her head against Ben's chest and listened to the calming beats of his heart. They kept her anchored to the world.

"Are you okay?" Nash asked.

"Yeah. The whole star thing is great, but can you change the scenery? It's kinda screwing with me."

Bennett laughed. "Drix, show us home."

The men slid their arms around her back and held her as the room lightened and turned into a foreign landscape. Five planets hung suspended above them. Two of the large spheres seemed like they would collide. A green ocean stretched out as far as the eye could see. The gentle lapping of the water relaxed her. High cliff walls surrounded them on three sides. Waterfalls spilled over them. They frothed the surface of the water, and a fine vapor blanketed Ember. She inhaled the air and turned her face to the mist. It reminded her of being at the beach. The light green water resembled Nash's flesh tone along his chest.

"This is your home planet?"

"Yes," Nash said. "This place is sacred to us. We believe it's where life sprang forth. A temple to the Origins stands in a cave underneath the largest waterfall." Nash pointed to the waterfall. "The other cascade is said to have healing properties. Pilgrims come from the three planets to gather its waters and bathe in the sacred springs."

Ember gazed up again and counted the planets. "I see five."

"The closest two large planets that look like they'll crash into one another. At certain seasons their rings cross. It creates a chemical reaction and lights appear as they hit the atmosphere. Those are the sister planets our ancestors migrated to. They're very similar to this one, but they aren't as spectacular. The other three planets you see in the distance can't support life." Bennett trailed his fingers over her arm.

She heard the longing in his voice as he told her about his home world. "How long has it been since you've seen this place?"

"Once you're identified having our particular mutation, they ship you off to Tilleron where our kind have been living for as long as anyone can remember," Nash told her.

"That's horrible. What about your families?" Ember asked.

"They do what's been done for eons. When we're old enough, we're given ships and told to roam the universe looking for Plasma and Body Units. We normally don't mingle with the population. Instead we send out probe ships that bring back what we want, but since we've been stuck here for so long, we've adapted," Bennett told her.

A pang of sadness hit her realizing how long it had been since they had seen their families. "It sounds like a lonely existence."

She hugged herself and walked away from them toward the water's edge. Hearing their tale and listening to the lapping of the waves brought back the sudden overwhelming loss she felt for Cecil. It all hit her at once about. She thought she had gotten over her mourning, but with Lance taking over ownership of the restaurant, it was like she was losing her husband all over again. Ember stared at the foreign landscape and wondered what it would be like to travel to all the places and see the other worlds and have someone with her.

"Why are you so sad all of a sudden?" Nash asked.

She wiped her tears away. "It's been a rough few weeks at the restaurant." Ember sat back on the bed. Nash and Bennett trailed their fingers over her thighs. Nash took her hand and kissed the inside of her palm. The light gesture comforted her. This was a different side of the alien she didn't think existed.

"With that man who came to the house?" he asked.

"Yeah. He bought my partner's half of the business, and now he's the majority owner. He's even offered to buy me out. It's like losing Cecil all over again. It was his dream. We put in the money, but Gus had the most. I don't know what to do."

"We can give you the money if you want to buy him out." Bennett began to rub her back. His fingers seemed to find the right spot.

The admission stunned her. "It's a lot of money and I-I can't. You barely even know me."

Nash touched the module behind her ear. "We know all about you. This allows us access to your memories. I did a little delving while you were sleeping. I shared them with Ben. Don't be mad at us. Once Bennett suspected you might be our mate, I needed to see if you were... stable. If you could keep our secret."

"Did I pass the test?"

"Only if you let us cheer you up." Bennett wiped a few

remaining tears from her eyes.

Ember had to push the day's events away and focus on the two new men in her life. Cecil would want her to be happy. She wanted to discover what life could be life with her green men. The thought was so new and their relationship still tenuous, she needed to make up her mind about them, about the rest of her life. Ember stood up and shimmied out of her panties.

Nash turned her around to face him. She bit her lip and cupped his balls. Her finger found the ridge on his middle testicle and she applied a little pressure.

"Not so hard." Nash grunted.

Ember slowed down and trailed her other hand over his pecks marveling at his nippleless chest. His face scrunched up in a moment of pain, so she adjusted her finger and worked the rim along his ball in circles. Once his eyes widened, she figured she'd found the right technique. Ember placed her lips along his chest, over one of his hearts and tasted him. A touch of salt and cinnamon stuck to her tongue. She sucked in his skin and nipped at it with her teeth. Nash held her to him, his six fingers sliding down her back. His cock firmed. She moved her hand around his shaft as it lengthened. She bit along his collarbone. A rumble started in his chest. One of his hands grabbed her ass and with the other he wrapped his fingers through her hair and yanked her away from his chest. His eyes glowed silver and his mouth pulled away in a snarl. A small ping of dread went through her.

"No, never fear us," Bennett whispered. He kissed her neck.

Nash groaned as she slid her hand faster over his dick. The vibration hit her, and this time it was easier to give into it.

"We are not used to being with another while intimate. It's difficult to stay in control. We are more... animalistic when we're together. Rougher," Ben told her.

She felt the quick pain of his tongue sucker hitting her skin.

She glanced at Nash. His face seemed knotted in concentration. His eyes were closed, and his lips held in a tight line.

Bennett's fingers slid over her breasts. "He needs to be inside you before he loses control. He doesn't want to hurt you."

"What about you?"

"Nash first, Em."

Bennett pinched her nipples until she screamed. Nash's eyes snapped open. They were tinged red. He growled, scooped up Ember, and dropped her back in the bed. He pinned her hands above her head and opened her legs with his knees. He hissed something and waited. She figured he asked for her permission.

"Yes," Ember whispered.

Seeing the wildness about him excited her. She struggled to touch him, but he was stronger than she was. She lifted her hips to meet him as he slid inside her. Nash plunged inside with a tempo she could hardly match. Each time he entered her, his cock rubbed along her clit. He held her down with one hand as the other slid over her hip. Nash grabbed her leg and slung it around his waist. He dipped into her well and she could feel him filling her, touching her inner spots, inflaming her desire. Waves of pleasure started consuming her body the longer he fucked her. Ember screamed. Nash shivered and licked her throat. He murmured something in her ear that didn't translate. Before she could answer, the rumble in his chest vibrated against her. Her orgasm reached another crest. When the pain came from his bite, it made her scream with bliss as Nash sucked on her throat. Nash pushed into her a few more times, easing her down from the pleasure. He released her wrists. Ember trailed her fingers over his back feeling his shoulders and the muscles defined under his scales. His hot breath blasted along her neck.

"Are you okay?" he asked. He brushed a piece of her hair from her forehead.

A few drops of blood clung to his lips. She realized it was hers. He remained inside her, still hard. She gripped him between her thighs, knowing she could go another round as the ache inside her lingered. "Yes, are you?"

"I'll be fine. You've had a lot of blood taken. We should let you rest and regain your strength."

"What about Bennett?"

Nash's gaze trailed over to his partner and the longing on his face answered her question. "I'll make sure he's satisfied."

"Can I watch?"

Bennett laughed. "Next time. Sleep for now."

He caressed her cheek and Ember felt him brush her suppression nodule. Before she could protest, her body shut down into sleep.

Chapter Seven

Ember opened her eyes to a white ceiling. Canis snored snuggled up against her. She tried to sit up, but when she moved the mattress kept sucking her in. The dog opened his eyes and yawned.

"You awake."

"Yes. Where are Nash and Bennett?"

"Work. Said see you in couple days."

Ember fell back into the bed and felt like scolding her new lovers for rocking her world and then abandoning her. However, she understood work. Ember got up, walked into the master bath and felt like she could live there. It had a standing shower, a separate bathtub, and benches built into the walls. Not to mention the counter by the sinks had more lotions, conditioners, and moisturizers than she bought in a year. She shook her head and slipped into the shower. Once she got out, she wrapped herself in one of their fluffy robes and went into the kitchen. The low vibration of the ship drew her attention. She put her hand on the wall hiding the ship's entrance. It rippled but remained a wall.

"Don't do that again unless you want to stir my emergency systems," a female voice sounded in the kitchen.

Ember turned around and found a transparent form of a woman by the counter. She couldn't discern any particular features on the projection. "Are you Drix?"

"You're Emily."

"Ember actually."

"I'll keep that in mind. What have the boys been doing all these years? What they've done to get me up and running is a Turlaxian's worse nightmare."

"I thought you were a holographic projection they could interact with."

Drix put her hands on her hips. "They didn't tell you a

damn thing, did they? Considering the state I'm in, it doesn't surprise me."

"Then what are you?"

"I'm more than the computer. I'm an artificial intelligence who runs the ship. I'm able to interface with the boys if need be. I can speak with you because of the suppression module they implanted in you. I've downloaded your memories and understand more of this world than I did before."

"They've been trying to fix the ship… fix you for a long time. I guess our technology has finally caught up --"

"Caught up? You humans remain in the stone age. That's why I'm surprised they've been able to get along this far. Nash has had my lower functions going for a while so I could at least repair the holes in the hull over the years." Drix leaned on the counter.

Ember chuckled at the thought she was having a conversation with a hologram who seemed to have a crush on one of her new lovers. "Sounds like you have a thing for Nash."

"I compliment genius where I see it. I'll be so glad when we get home and I can get an upgrade."

"Home?"

Canis raced in barking. *"Man here for you."*

Ember rolled her eyes. Drix disappeared. The vibration she felt in the kitchen dissipated. Canis grabbed her robe and tugged on it. "I'm coming."

She went to the front door and saw Lester getting out of his van. He knelt down in the driveway and gathered a bit of the loose dirt. He scooped it up into a plastic baggie and slipped it into his pocket. Lester started to head out back. When Ember came out he stopped.

"Hi, Ember. I was coming over to check on you after our little conversation the other day." Lester tried to stuff the bag deeper into his pocket, but the edge of it still stuck out. She suspected he had other motives than coming to check on her.

"I'm fine. You could've called or texted. How was the show the other night?"

"Great! Sold out. We're playing a bigger venue next week. Been talking with some festival guys to get on their tour circuit so we can get some traction going."

"Sounds great. Did you need anything else?"

He ran his hands through his hair. "Ummm... can I expect because you're dressed in a robe and not in your house you... spent the night with your landlord?"

"Not that it's any of your business, but yes. They're perfectly human. I know you were worried, but I can assure you. Corn-fed Midwesterners."

His shoulders sagged. "That's good to hear. I didn't mean to scare you, but you had me worried. I don't hear a hum like I did the first time I came out here."

A growl sounded behind Lester. Canis barked another warning at him.

"You should go. He gets really protective of me and the guys. Tell Anne I said hi. There's no worry about me getting abducted."

"Right. See you later." He inched away from the dog and got back into his van.

Canis stayed by her side until he was out of sight. *"Up to something."*

"Maybe. I don't know. Look, I have to get to work, too."

"I come with."

"You can't. I work in a restaurant."

"I come. Humans no see. Only you, and I quiet."

She eyed the dog. "Do you have a cloaking device built into your collar?"

The dog looked up at her and smiled, letting his tongue hang out of his mouth. "Fine. You can come, but you can't go into the kitchen."

"I behave. Stick head out window?"

"Fine. I don't need your drool in my car."

She pulled into the restaurant parking lot. Canis went in with her and no one noticed him. Ember popped her head into the kitchen to find Lance behind the line with Haley, the sous chef.

"Hi, Ember, I thought you had today off?" Lance asked.

"I figured it'd be a good idea to check in and see how you were adjusting." Ember forced a smile. "Hi, Haley, how's it going?"

"Fine. Thanks, Em. You hear from Gus at all? He left some shit at my house," Haley asked.

"Nope, looks like he bailed on both of us. As they say, money talks."

Lance beat the ball of dough into a pizza pan. "Have you thought about my offer?" His man bun bobbed each time his fist hit the dough.

"What offer?" Jean walked in.

Ember let out a long breath and looked at her General Manager. "Something we can discuss later," Ember replied.

"I asked Ember if she wanted to sell me her piece of the business." Lance glanced up. "There are no secrets here."

"I assumed what we talked about would be kept between us, Lance."

He chuckled. "You don't know the first thing about me. Haley, I think the crust is a little thick. I'll bring out my recipe, and you can see how it goes over as a special at first."

Ember walked out the door. Canis remained on her heels as she went into her office and slammed the door.

"*I bite him again.*" Canis put his head on her leg after she sat down.

"No. Although it'd make me feel better."

"What would make you feel better?" Jean came in and sat down. She closed the door.

"Jean, how long have we known one another?"

"Years. I've lost count. I knew Cecil before I knew you. He talked me into this gig. I gathered with Lance taking over, it's eating you up like you've lost Cecil all over again. I know how much you loved him, but he's gone. This place can't fill the hole in your heart. Cecil would want you to move on. Gus was a dick, but he's been wanting out for a while. I think you might've ignored the signs."

Ember let out a slow breath and let the words sink in. She *had* ignored the signs with Gus. Jean was right. "I never thanked you for all you did. You're right, I held onto my grief so tight I put blinders on. Gus talked about wanting to get away a few months ago. I thought he was talking about a vacation. I didn't think he wanted to sell out."

"Would it be so bad to get rid of this place, say goodbye to Cecil the proper way, and find a new adventure?" Jean squeezed her hand for some reassurance.

Canis licked Ember's hand. *"She smell good. I like her, but she also smell like mean man around her thighs."*

Ember held in a laugh at the statement. "Thanks, Jean. Tell Lance I'll think about it. You and him, that's pretty quick. I hope he's good in bed."

Her mouth dropped, but she recovered quickly. "Em… I… It's not what you think. I mean, yes, we've hit it off, but he didn't ask me to come in here."

"If he makes you happy, then go for it. I've recently found myself in a strange new something."

Her eyes lit up. "Great, Em. You of all people deserve some happiness."

Canis stretched out so he wrapped around her chair. If she moved, she would run over him.

Jean got up. "I'll see you later."

"Bye, Jean. Thank you for everything."

She sighed and rested her head in her hands. Today was getting more and more fucked up. She'd woken up from a night of mind-blowing sex with the two aliens. Well, just the one, but they claimed she was their soul mate. Lester coming to the house to make sure she hadn't gotten abducted. Hopefully, his curiosity had been satisfied. Her general manager made her realize how much she still missed Cecil.

"You sad."

She reached down and petted the dog. "A little. I miss someone who's been gone for a long time."

"Masters help you."

"What do you mean?"

"Help make happy."

"Thanks. I think."

Canis got up and tugged on her arm. *"We go ask. I know way."*

"I have things to do. In a little bit."

* * *

Canis stuck his head out of the window as she drove. *"Turn. I smell ham. Me hungry."*

"I can't believe I'm taking directions from a dog. You're always hungry."

"Smart dog."

"Yes, you're a smart dog."

"Another turn toward the water now."

"Water? Like a lake or a river?"

"Big water."

She rolled her eyes and turned. The firehouse was on the left. The red brick building had seen better days, but it functioned. The large trucks were out of the house and the men were cleaning them. She spotted Nash with a sponge in his hand, working on the front of the truck. She took a moment to admire his firm ass in his pants as he worked the grill. A wind kicked up and he froze. Nash turned and looked over at her. His farm boy appearance held firm, but she could see beneath the façade. Canis barked. Ember parked and opened the door. As soon as she did, the dog raced toward Nash.

"Missed Master."

"I missed you too, good boy. Why are you here?" Nash scratched him behind the ear and looked at Ember.

"Mistress sad. You help," The dog answered.

"Okay. Go find Ben, he's inside." Nash tapped the Great Dane on the butt as he lumbered by the other firemen. Nash came over to Ember. "Are you okay? I mean, you're not hurt?"

"No. I'm fine. I mean more than fine... I --" A few of the other men waved at her from the other night at the restaurant.

"Good. I... we didn't know if..."

"I'm good. I mean it was great. Shit."

Nash chuckled. "It's okay. Canis said you were sad. Is it something we did?"

"No. He said you could help me not be sad and thought I should come here."

"Has coming here cheered you up?"

Ember closed her eyes and felt the attraction in her building. It took everything in her not to wrap her arms around him and kiss him in front of his whole company. The feel of Nash inside her made her pulse race. She could smell the cherry fragrance she associated with him. Her fingers ached to touch him and bury herself against his body. The overwhelming need was not something she had experienced before. She groaned in frustration. Nash's eyes widened. He licked his lips. His hands clenched at his sides. The water in his sponge cascaded all over his boot. His eyes glowed silver even through the disguise he wore.

"Yes." Her throat went dry and the taste of his cinnamon skin made her mouth water.

"I think it'd be best if we talk about this later. Then we can fix whatever it is," Nash said. His voice strained with the thin measure of control.

"Right. Have a good rest of shift." Ember pressed her nails into her palm, turned and walked back to the car. As she got inside, she saw Bennett outside talking to Nash. They both glanced at her. She could feel their longing as much as if it were her own. She wanted to be between them, but instead she focused on the drive back to the house.

When she got there, she wanted to be surrounded by their scent and their presence.

* * *

"You've returned." Drix's voice came through the house.

"You sound like you didn't think I'd come back," Ember replied.

"I didn't know where you stood with them."

"Someone sounds a little jealous." A small zap hit Ember. "What the hell was that?"

"Your system is flooded with nanos. You're connected to them and to me. I can do whatever I want with you." Strong arms came around her and held her in place. Ember couldn't get away.

"What the fuck are you doing?" The warmth behind her ear enhanced to a burn. She cried out and tried to move again.

"You're not good enough for them. They have to understand you're nothing more than a walking flesh suit which they can use to eat and fuck."

"Holy shit, you *are* jealous. You think they've replaced you with me."

The pain intensified at the comment.

"You have no right to them! They are *mine*."

It felt like her head would explode. Stars appeared on the edges of her vision. "You need to let them make that decision."

A shout of frustration filled the kitchen from the

artificial intelligence. "You have them under your spell. I might've just woken up, but I've had enough time to gain the knowledge of this world. A witch is what you are, and you will burn for it."

Without knowing how, Ember found herself back in her apartment. Flames surrounded her bed. She tried to get out of the bed, but she had no control over her body. The fire inched closer. Heat burned her fingertips. Ember shrieked.

It's not real.

The flames jumped from around the bed to the blanket. She tried to shimmy backward toward the headboard. She managed to get a little way away. Smoke choked her. She coughed and felt the grit of it on her tongue. The flames leapt from the bedspread to her arms. She could feel it, roasting her alive, from the inside and the outside.

Laughter echoed around her.

Not real. Not real.

Ember fought the hold Drix had over her.

Blisters appeared on her arms from the heat. The flames blipped and the room shook around her. The view of her burning bedroom went in and out. It felt like her insides were melting. The vibration from the ship shook the house. It hurt to even think. She tried to pull herself out of the nightmare she'd been plunged into. A shadow passed through the room and she could see the main house's kitchen and not her own bedroom. Darkness blanketed her vision. She felt her consciousness swimming. Something cool pressed against her face and neck. Words were said in her ear. Ember clung to the coolness. Someone stroked her hair. Lips brushed against her forehead. She could breathe. The flames disappeared and the kitchen came back into view. She buried her head in her savior's shoulder and cried.

"It's okay. She won't hurt you anymore. I switched her off."

She shook her head. "I'm still burning."

Fingers trailed down her cheek that made her look up. As she did, she could see Bennett's violet eyes. He brushed his lips over hers. She inhaled his signature scent and it helped to abate her fears. Her body had returned to normal as the nanos worked to heal her. She stayed next to him as his fingers ran down her back. The simple touch calmed her.

"You're okay. Nothing's going to happen to you again." He wiped away the rest of her tears.

"I'm never going to be okay. As long as I have this module stuck in me, she's going to be able to influence me. Both of you can control me. I can't live like that."

"Shhh... I turned her off."

"What about when you turn her back on again?" she cried out, not sure she could ever go back into the house. Hell, the computer might even be able to come into her house. She didn't know what Drix's range was.

"Not going to happen. I promise. Nash already knows. He'll be back later tonight. He had to finish our shift and cover for me."

"I was back in my apartment, and I was burning because you hadn't saved me."

"She was trying to confuse you."

"She made the nanos inside me start to cook me from the inside out."

"I'll talk to Nash, but I can't take it out."

"I know. I'm not asking you to. Just... I need you to know -- if you want this to work between us, then you can't manipulate me."

"I don't want to control you, but I do want to protect you. I want to love you for as long as we have together. I desire to show you the universe. The suppression module can be programmed to have the nanos do other things. They keep you at peak health so you can live as long as we do. They can enhance your pleasure." He trailed his fingers over her hips. The light touch stirred her desire for him and purged the terror from her body.

Ember laughed. "Here I am, frightened out of my wits, and you're thinking about sex. Men! I don't think it matters if they're from Earth or another planet."

"Can't help it. You smell wonderful, and I'm a sucker for a damsel in distress."

"How did you know I was in distress? I thought you could read my thoughts?"

"We can, but you caught Nash off guard at work and I don't like to listen in. It doesn't work over long distances either."

"Good to know."

"So Nash told me Canis said you were sad, and we could help. Nash wanted me to check on you. I wasn't expecting to find you screaming with Drix hovering over you. I never suspected she'd be jealous."

"Well, thank you again for saving me." Ember slung her arms around his neck. His smell helped drive away her remaining anxiety.

"What was it we could help you with, so you aren't sad anymore?"

"It's nothing really. And honestly, with your computer going on psycho, I'm not sure I want to tell you."

"She won't hurt you again. What is it?"

A stab of grief hit her once more when she thought about Cecil again. Maybe it would help her to let go of the past and move on with the future. "You showed me your home world in your holographic room. C-Can you make a realistic image of a person?"

"If we have some pictures maybe. If you wanted to interact with this projection, we would need some personality to program it with. What were you thinking?" He brushed the hair behind her ear.

"My general manger suggested maybe I was holding onto the restaurant to keep Cecil in my life. I thought..."

His lips turned down in a sad smile. "You thought maybe if we resurrected him for you, you might say goodbye and move on?"

"Something like that. After Cecil died, I threw myself into work."

"I'll talk to Nash about it. We have your memories stored in the computer. I understand the need to have closure. I can't promise anything, but I'll see what I can do."

A surge of happiness bubbled within her. She grabbed Ben's face and planted her lips on his. He stiffened and then returned the kiss. His tongue flicked along her mouth. His fingers raked down her back. He broke the kiss and pulled away.

"I didn't want to entice you, but if you keep..."

Ember moved her hand down to his cock and held it, feeling it already firm against his pants. Bennett groaned as she held him. The soft sound moved through her. The hair stood up on her arms. Ben shook against her as his breathing intensified. She tried to fight the pull she felt toward him. It seemed more difficult the longer she was around them both, but Ember also knew the real reason behind it. She was falling in love with them. Their touches and their smells made her wet. It aroused her so she almost didn't want to be away from them. Their sounds, the vibrations, affected her in a way she couldn't really describe. It felt like they were touching her from the inside. It was all she wanted to feel him inside her. Feel his lips caressing her. Him being there pushed away her fear and sorrow.

"I need you," she whispered, "take me to my bedroom."

"Are you sure?"

"You sound like I'm not."

"I don't want to push you after what you went through. The nanos are still fixing your body. You were more damaged than you let on."

She trailed her fingers down his cheek. His green skin changed slightly to the same as her skin tone. She liked how they changed back to their original color as her fingers moved away from the area. "I guess you're going to have to be gentle."

He lifted her up and held her close as he walked her to the guesthouse. Ben laid her on her bed. "I'll be gentle." He tugged at her shirt and pulled it over her head.

"I can undress myself."

"At this moment, I think you can't. I'm going to make sure you heal while I make you scream."

The notion of what he said sounded funny. Ben plucked off her shoes and socks. She tried to sit up and take off her bra, but he did it for her. His fingers lightly brushed her flesh. The warmth was fleeting as his fingertips swept over where her bra straps used to be. He undid her pants.

"I can do that."

"I rather enjoy having you all to myself. Nash gets a little possessive if you hadn't noticed."

"Is that what all the hissing and growling was? Same with you trying to fight him the other day."

Ben pulled one pant leg off and trailed his finger over the curve of her calf. "Yes. He kept denying you were our mate. I challenged him. We'd both heard you moan. It affected me first and I knew. He took a bit more convincing. He's always been standoffish. He's good at his job, but he has a difficult time expressing his feelings even with me. It took him a while to believe me when I told him we were meant to be together."

"Then I came along and screwed up your dynamic."

He got her pants off and stared at her. His intense gaze made her realize Bennett really cared for her. It wasn't some animalistic thing that drove him to be with her. Her heart melted. His lips pressed against her thigh. The silkiness of his mouth along her flesh made her quiver with the need for release.

"You didn't screw up our dynamic. I offered you a place to live because we could. I had a sense about you. Nash didn't want you to discover our secret and tell the world. How do you explain to your military we're peaceful aliens who have been living here for over three hundred years and occasionally drink blood to keep ourselves alive?"

She giggled when he hit a ticklish spot as he pulled her panties down. "You don't. You end up on a dissection table."

"Exactly. I didn't think you'd give away our secret, but there are many humans who would."

He worked her panties all the way off. Bennett lifted her foot and touched his lips against the heel. Ember jumped and kicked, but he held fast. His gaze settled on her as his tongue flicked over the top of her big toe. He opened his mouth wider so the sucker on his tongue bloomed to the size of a quarter and looked like a strange star.

"Can I?"

Bennett nodded.

Ember touched the bloom. The sucker latched onto the top of her finger with a small amount of pain. And then he took the rest of her finger in his mouth for a quick moment. She caressed his cheek and he released her.

"Still doesn't scare you?"

"No. You don't scare me. Stop trying to push me away."

"I'm not. I'm trying to make you aware I'm not a human male. There are many things about us you still don't know."

"I'm well aware you're not human. You have no nipples, or belly button, and three testicles. Not to mention you're green."

"And the color of my skin bothers you?"

"Not at all. I love watching how your skin changes to match mine when I touch it. Nash's didn't do that."

"All of us are different when it comes to how much the hue of our flesh changes. I take on more of what I want to. Nash does better with blending into the background. Now you're naked and have seen all my mutations. Are you still sure about this?"

She reached between his legs and caressed his dick. Bennett flashed her half smile but made no other move to entice her. "If you keep talking, then I'm going to pleasure myself and make you watch with all my moaning, so you'll get blue balls. Can you handle that?"

She slipped between her legs and found her clit. Before she could start, Ben grabbed her wrist.

"I don't think so. That would defeat the purpose of us being together. Besides, I want you crying out my name before Nash comes home. Are you ready?"

"Are you going to take off your clothes?"

"A little later. First, you. Will you mind if I mess with your suppression module?"

"Are you going to control me?"

His fingers slid under her ear. "Not at all, allow you to feel desire, with the slightest touch. Give you the untiring ease to make love as long as you wish."

"Sounds lovely. I'm okay with it."

Bennett pushed the device and tapped it a couple of times. Ember didn't feel any different, this time, but she appreciated he asked permission. He went back down to her foot and sucked on her big toe. It felt like his mouth was on both of her big toes at once. He pressed a point on her sole. A spear of pleasure shot up her leg. Ember bit her lip as he worked his way over the top of her foot and up to her calf. Each time he caressed her, it seemed as though he were touching both sides of her. Six fingers fanned out along her knee. He pressed on a point behind her knee. Ember kicked out and caught him in the chest.

Bennett grunted and flashed her a harsh look.

"Shit, I'm sorry."

He laughed. "It's okay. It didn't hurt one bit. How are you feeling? Do you want me to stop?"

He opened her legs and tickled her thigh.

"I'm fine. Don't stop." She tried to touch his face, but he kept out of her reach. Instead he held widened her legs and dipped his head between them. Once his tongue touched the soft flesh, she arched her back. Her body sang at each small flick of his tongue. Ben nipped her inner thigh as his fingers slid over her hips and cupped her ass. His fingers fit perfectly against the roundness of her bottom.

"You smell so sweet. I can hear your blood. You taste like cotton candy." Bennett sucked on her skin, then bit down with regular teeth.

A cry broke from her lips. She squeezed her eyes shut as she tried not to give herself over to the desire. His mouth slid like silk along her skin. He bit her again and it sent chills inside her. She trailed her fingers along his back, feeling his bunched muscles. Ben nipped her again. This time she dug her nails into his shoulders. He squeezed her ass in response. The ecstasy built within her, but he didn't let her come. It seemed this was what he meant when he said he would control her love making with the nanos in her blood. Ember groaned as he pressed his thumb along her clit. Her insides melted as he massaged it in circles. Each place he touched he marked her for his. Ember couldn't imagine what it would be like when both him and Nash did the same thing to her. Before she could even comprehend what his next move was, his tongue swept over her clit.

The world exploded in points of light. She tried to cry out as the first wave hit but tilted on the edge of orgasm. Time seemed to stop as he caressed her with his tongue.

The slow strokes over her wet slit made it a struggle to breathe and yet she could. Her body warmed each time he tortured her.

"B-ben...nett," she breathed out his name.

His stopped and his body shook. He grabbed her hips and held onto them. He delved back onto her clit. Ember felt a sharp pain as his sucker attached to her. Ember thrust her hips into him. She shrieked. Her pulse thundered in her ears. Ben pulled blood from her and worked her clit at the same time.

Ember broke down as words left her and she struggled to think. Bennett slipped his fingers inside her and applied pressure along her inner walls. Fire raced along her spine. It ate her up from the inside out until she could do nothing more than give into it. And yet, Bennett still wouldn't let her come.

The more he sucked and pressed his fingers on each of her inner walls, it drove her mad. She pushed against him. He moved into and out of her. Each time he brought her higher, until it felt like she would brush the stars.

"P-please."

Bennett lifted his head leaving her clit throbbing with pleasure. "Had enough?" He touched another place inside her.

She wrapped her legs around him. "I need you."

He delved inside her once more. His lips pressed upon her stomach. Ben worked his way up to her breasts and caressed one. "Do you need me inside you?"

He took her nipple into his mouth and latched onto it again with his sucker. Ember needed him in more ways than one. He impaled her slowly and looked up at her with a sly smile.

"Now?"

Ember couldn't say anything except moan. His nostrils flared. Whatever vibration her moan made, got him going. He pushed against her. Bennett pressed his lips into hers in a hungry kiss. His fingers slid around her neck and touched the module. He pulled away, took off his clothes, and lay down with her. As he played his fingers over her flesh, she lingered on the edge of oblivion. Each lazy trail of his finger felt like he traced her inner points. Each one brought a gasp spilling from her throat. She didn't know if she could take much more.

Bennett feathered his fingers over her inner thigh and pressed them on a point. It felt like he touched her clit at the same time. "Fuck."

"Almost there." He nibbled her neck.

Ember reached for him. He kissed the inside of her palm before laying it in the center of his chest so she could feel the alternating beats of his hearts.

"Touch me, Ember." He took her other hand and slid it between his legs, so she cupped his three balls.

She found the groove on the middle one and caressed it. His eyes remained glued to hers, but his breathing increased. A rumble started in his chest. It hit her palm first and vibrated along her arm until it raced along her flesh. His moan deepened. She squeezed her thighs together as the moment overtook her. Ember didn't understand how the sound made her react the way it did.

"Ben…" She couldn't hide her need from him.

"Yes, love. I know." He slowly eased into her so she could feel how well they fit together. He kissed over her heart as he moved into her.

Ember wrapped her legs around him and ran her toes over his toned ass. His kisses aroused her more. She could barely concentrate on their moving together. Each time he dove inside her, it felt like the world unmade itself and reformed when he pulled out of her. He remade her with his hands and his voice.

He stopped kissing her and moaned again. Ember pushed against him needing to have him inside her. Bennett bit her throat. She turned her neck to give him better access -- giving him permission to take her blood. When his sucker pierced her vein, Ember forgot everything else except she was his and they were together.

Chapter Eight

Bennett stroked her hair as she rested on his chest. Ember listened to the two organs pumping blood through his veins, some of it hers. She didn't know how much he had taken while they made love, but the whole process left her wrung out. They had slept into the next day. She sighed and nestled into the warmth of his body. Ben held her closer to him.

"Are you okay? I think we were both exhausted afterward and you needed the rest."

"Yeah. I think after what happened with Drix and us being together, I must've shut down."

"It's understandable. Did you enjoy yourself?"

"Mmm-hmmm... That was an experience."

"A good experience?"

"Yes, not what I expected. You and Nash are very different."

"Of course, we are."

She turned and looked up at him. "I meant..."

"I know what you meant. Nash is rougher. I can be, too, if you like. Did I please you?"

She snorted. "You know you did. I see the smug smile on your lips."

"I had to be sure. Sometimes our Body Units aren't as satisfied. Although, it could be because we can't fully be ourselves with them."

Ember recalled they called people they had relationships with. "Did you ever find a Body Unit like me before?"

His fingers brushed over her nipple. The ache in her doubled and she bit her lip. Bennett grinned. "You're more than a Body or a Plasma Unit for both of us. You're our mate. None of the humans we've been with have reacted the way you do when either of us groans."

"Are there other ways to arouse you besides rubbing

your extra ball and you reacting to my voice?" Ember asked.

"There are other ways. Those are the quickest. We can show you what other sounds stimulate us. Sometimes it's the heat of battle and we react roughly. I have certain spots on me that make me want to fuck. I particularly like it when Nash bites me."

"I don't have a sucker like you do."

"It helps, but you won't need one. I'll show you." Bennett took her hand and ran it over his shaft. Her touch seemed to stir him. "The spot at the end of my *findick*."

"What did you say?" Ember wasn't sure she heard him right. "Your findick?"

"I didn't say Find Ick. I said findick."

Ember bit her lip to keep from laughing. His violet eyes flashed in anger. She held up her hand and took a minute to stop her giggles. "Sorry, but this definitely got lost in translation. I hear findick. Whatever you're growling is not coming out right."

"Hmm... something must be messing up with your translator and nanos. Anyway, at the base of my penis, do you feel the smooth spot?"

She moved her finger over the spot the size of her thumb. "I do."

"If you bite me there, you're likely to find yourself in trouble."

Ember straddled him and wrapped her arms around his neck. "What if I bite you here?" She kissed his throat and bit down, feeling the give of his scales and then tasting blood.

Bennett jumped. His nails scraped down her back. He shivered and whispered something she didn't understand. Ember bit him harder. Ben moaned. He grabbed her and the world turned. She found herself looking up at him. His eyes were wild. His lips pulled back from his teeth. He spread her legs open with his knee and shoved his cock inside her. Ember followed his lead as he pumped into her, all his humanity seemingly driven from him. He growled something again as he hit her clit. Ember groaned and he shook. She held him as he plunged into her and then screamed. At the last second, he bit into her shoulder with regular teeth. Ember cried out and felt the pleasure pass from him into her until he settled down next to her. His fingers touched the bite mark.

"I hurt you."

Her shoulder already tingled from the nanos healing her. "It's okay."

"I got a little carried away when you bit me. I'm sorry."

She hugged him and inhaled his scent. "Don't be sorry for what you are."

"What's Ben supposed to be sorry about?" Nash sat on the edge of the bed. "Looks like I missed some of the fun." He swiped his finger over the bottom of her foot and made her giggle.

Ember leaned up and kissed him. "You smell like smoke."

"Had to go fight a fire. Pulled a couple out of their bedroom. You taste like Bennett. I think I'm jealous."

"Be jealous all you want. I'm going to take a shower." Nash got up and pulled his shirt off, letting his human façade fall away. "Let's get wet."

"By myself."

Ember stepped into the shower and tried to let the water wash away all her lingering fears about the crazy computer who wanted to kill her. As the water slipped over her body, it reminded her of her lover's hands. She longed for more and almost thought to take Nash up on his offer, but she wanted a little time to herself.

Bennett called her their mate. That meant they weren't going to easily give her up. He offered to help her get over Cecil by creating a three-dimension model of him. Now she had a little space, she knew she didn't need to. A weight had lifted from her. Ember towel dried her hair and felt something fall into place. Her heart didn't have a hole in it. That place had been filled by two three-testicled aliens. She walked out of the bathroom and found Nash and Bennett kissing on the bed.

"Did I interrupt something?"

Nash looked over and was about to say something when the house shook. A shrill noise deafened her. She held her ears and tried to get the ringing out. Nash dashed over to her as the house quaked again. He said something, but she couldn't hear. He squeezed her hand and rushed out of the room. The noise made her head feel like it would explode. She pulled her hand away and saw there was blood on her fingertips.

The world wobbled.

Bennett grabbed her and pushed the nodule on her neck. She shook her head. He tapped it a few more times and the noise stopped. Instantly she relaxed and the sound vanished.

"Can you hear me okay?"

"Yes. What is that?"

"It's the ship. Drix must've turned herself back on and started the engines. Let me go check with Nash. It's best if you get away from here for a while. Take the dog with you. He's outside. Once you get to the main road, then you shouldn't feel the ship's influence." Bennett brushed a kiss along her lips. Ember gathered some things and headed out to her car. Canis had something in his mouth.

"What do you have?"

"Kindle."

Ember kept her mouth shut and opened the door for the dog. The pebbles around the car vibrated. A geyser of white smoke plumed up from behind the house.

"Masters said leave." Canis jumped into the back seat

and lay down.

A shiver of fear went through her. "I'm going. They say anything else?"

The dog dropped his case. He growled so she figured it was best to go. Once Ember got onto the main road things returned to normal.

She made it to the restaurant and found it busy. Ember pulled into the back of the lot. She walked in. Canis stayed in the car when she cracked the window for him. She went into the office and found Lance at her computer.

Lance's hair was pulled back into his signature bun. "Ember, I wasn't sure I would see you today."

"What're you doing in here, Lance?"

"Trying to get into your computer to check the books. I can't crack the password."

"Why didn't you call and ask me?" She tried to hold back her temper.

His face reddened. "I didn't want to disturb you. I seem to keep pissing you off."

"That's right, you didn't think."

"I'm not used to having partners. Can I have the password?"

Ember sank down in the chair opposite him. "Why don't we forget about the password for a few minutes? Let's talk business."

"Talking? Wow, you've had a breakthrough."

"How about you stop being a dick?"

He chuckled and held up his hand. "Touché. What did you want to talk about?"

"How much will you give me to buy me out completely?"

His eyebrows rose. He whistled and tried to hide the smile growing on his lips. "What made you come to that decision?"

"My business, not yours. Answer my question."

"You don't want to stay on here even as the

manager?"

"No. I walk away, and you never hear from me again."

Lance drummed his thumbs on the desk. He wrote down something and then passed the piece of paper over to her. Ember glanced at it and laughed. "This is more than Gus wanted from me to buy him out."

"You're the heart and the brains behind the business. You're the one who kept this place going. I've talked to the employees. Everyone here loves you. I'm not the heartless bastard you think I am. I'm giving you what I think this place is worth. I hear you have a new man in your life. He stopped by here last night."

His words floored her. It was nice to see he'd talked to the employees and found out their opinions of her, but then..."Wait. Nash was here last night? Impossible, he was at the firehouse all night."

"Nash?"

"Yeah, short blond hair, built, looks like he could've walked off a farm."

"Not this guy. He's like six feet tall, long dark hair, tattoos. Looks like he's in a rock band."

"Heavy metal Christian band, actually."

"You know who I'm talking about?"

"Yeah. His name's Lester and he's my best friend's boy toy. He has this crazy fascination with me I don't really understand. What did he want?"

Lance shrugged. "He said he had something important to tell you. I told him you weren't here. Next time I see him, do you want me to call the cops?"

"Might be a good idea."

"What do you think about my offer?"

Ember ran her fingers over the paper and glanced around the office. It had been her home away from home for so long. However, it was time to move on. She felt it in her bones. "You promise you're not going to fuck this place up?"

"I can try not to. That's the best I can promise. My business model and yours aren't exactly the same."

She got up and stuck out her hand. It took a moment, but Lance got up, and shook her hand. "I'll have the papers drawn up and get you a check. We can tell everyone --"

"No. Don't tell anyone until it's done. Of course, you'll tell Jean. Unless you're going to fuck that up too? She's a good woman."

His face paled. "No. I-I wouldn't do that."

"You care about her then?"

He nodded. "It was fast, but the way I feel... it's nothing like I've ever felt before. I love her. I..."

"Hold that thought. I'm happy for you. Just be good to her or I'll have your balls. What did you want to know on the computer?"

"I wanted to look at the books and the vendors, order history, stuff like that."

"I'll print it all out for you."

"I'll get my lawyer to draw up the paperwork."

Several hours later, she double-checked the reports and the notes she had made for him. Ember exited out of the side door and went to her car. As she walked by, a van screeched into the parking lot. She glanced at it quickly enough to recognize it. The side door opened, she was yanked into the vehicle, before she could scream.

She struggled as something went over her head. Her hands were tied behind her back. "What the fuck are you doing? Get off me!"

"Shut up!" A man's voice she didn't know shouted at her.

A sharp pinch hit her neck before she could say anything else. Her throat went dry. She lost touch with consciousness.

* * *

It was all black. Her tongue felt like it was wrapped in

cotton. She tried to move, but found her arms and legs were bound to a chair. Her head pounded as though she had a hangover. Warmth from behind her ear spread out to her entire body as the nanos flooded her blood stream. Ember moaned.

"Shit should've kept her out for longer. How much did you give her?" the voice asked.

"What you told me?" a female replied.

"Anne?" The name came out garbled.

"It's okay."

The hood was pulled from her face. Ember squinted at the brightness. The sparse furnishing revealed nothing more than a cot, a couple of metal chairs, a stack of supplies in the corner and a card table that had seen better days. The walls were gray. She couldn't see the door. Either way she didn't like the looks of this.

Anne knelt before her with a bottle of water. Ember took a few sips and then turned her gaze on her friend. "What the hell is going on?"

"We needed to make sure you were safe."

"I was safe! You fucking kidnapped me in the back of a van, drugged me, and now you have me tied up. Anne, get me out of here."

"Sorry, Ember, we can't do that. Not until I know you're not under the influence of the aliens." Lester leaned against the wall sipping on another bottle of water.

"Oh, for fuck's sake, Lester, I'm not under alien control. Let me go!"

"Em, we figured you'd say something like this. I've had a chance to look you over and I found this." Lester moved her hair aside and pushed the suppression module at her ear. "It's the same as mine. Although yours is still active."

Lester pulled out a tuning fork, struck it, and then held it up next to her suppression module. The vibration of the tuning fork made her shiver. A quiver went down her spine and all her hair stood up on her arms. It almost felt like the vibration she experienced when either Ben or Nash groaned. The longer he held this to her ear, the metal of her module heated up. She clutched the arms of the chair and fought to get away from the sound. Ember whimpered.

"Lester, enough. I think you proved your point." Anne snatched the tuning fork away from him.

"Told you it was the same as mine. Yours hasn't been turned off which means the aliens are here," Lester growled. "I took samples of the dirt at your house. A friend of mine tested it. It's full of radiation. The same kind I had around me when I was brought back. Your landlords have you under their thumb. Where are they hiding their ship?"

Lester squeezed her hands until it felt like her fingers would break. She promised her men she wouldn't reveal what they were. She hadn't counted on her friend's crazy boyfriend on being an abductee who was hell-bent on confronting the aliens again.

"Stop. Stop. I'll tell you what you want to know," Ember cried out. She glanced over at Anne.

Her friend touched Lester's face. "Hey, she said she'll talk. Can we take the tape off her now? I really don't like this."

Lester plucked the tuning fork from Anne and shoved it back into his pocket. He pulled out a pocketknife and pointed the knife at her. "Talk first. Then we'll think about letting you go."

Another tremor of fear went through Ember. She didn't know the module had an alien GPS in it or not, but she prayed her men would come and get her.

"What do you want to know?" She glanced at Anne who mouthed "sorry" to her. Her eyes drifted back to the tip of the knife which was closer to her face than she liked.

"Why did they tag you? How long have you been working for them? What kind of information have you been feeding them about the human race?" Lester paced before her, his voice getting more agitated with each question.

"Whoa! First of all, they saved my life with this device." She thought back to what Ben said how they couldn't take it out. "When I first looked at their house for rent, I fell and hit my head. They're trained firefighters, but the fall was bad. They implanted this to heal me. They don't have an agenda."

"Sure, they do. Have they taken your blood yet? Are you their sex slave? Have they done any experiments on you?"

She rolled her eyes. "No. I'm not their sex slave. I don't know if they've taken my blood or not. I was close to death. Maybe they did, to see if I was compatible with this device. They leave me alone and I leave them alone except to tell them, *Hey, I need you to look at my plumbing.* They're regular guys. Give them a break."

"They can't be *regular* guys. They have to be up to something. You're going to tell me what they're doing here." He thrust the knife tip into her throat. It pinched enough she knew it drew blood.

"Lester, stop this. I don't want Em to hate me for you being an ass."

Lester backed away from Ember and looked at Anne. "We have to know."

"She's my friend and I believe her. Give me that knife." She yanked it away from Lester and cut Ember's hands and legs free.

"Get me out of here, Anne. And we're never going to talk about this again." Ember kneed Lester in the groin. He went down to the floor. She glanced at her friend. "Are you going to give me a ride home?"

Lester reached out to Anne. "Baby, she's going to deliver you to them."

Anne kicked him in the stomach. Lester groaned and doubled over. "I can't believe he talked me into kidnapping you. After we drugged you and got you in here, Drake, the drummer, punked out and ran."

Ember followed Anne up some stairs. It turned out they were in the basement of Anne's apartment building. She got into the car and tried to keep her mind clear and not panic about what her men would say when she told them what happened.

"I didn't know he'd go this far."

"Whatever. Get me home."

"Are they really aliens?"

"Your boyfriend kidnapped me. I want to go home and get some sleep. Anne, I never thought you'd get caught up with such a crazy asshole."

"He's really nice except for the alien part and you did say…"

"I said whatever the hell he wanted so I wouldn't die."

They drove the rest of the way in silence. Anne pulled over at the beginning of the driveway. Ember got out. "Tell Lester to stay the fuck away. If I see him, I'll call the cops." She slammed the door and walked down the driveway. A truck came toward her. It stopped with a screeching of brakes and a cloud of dust. The door opened, and Bennett rushed out. Canis barked and stuck his head out of the window. Ben took her in his arms and held her. She breathed in his scent and it relaxed her.

"You're okay."

"I'm fine."

"Canis told us what happened. The ship… you're never going to believe it… I'm sorry about what happened to you. How did you get away?"

The sounds of an engine got her attention. She looked back and Anne followed them in the car. She stopped and got out. "Is this one of them? He doesn't look green and little."

Bennett moved Ember behind him and growled. She squeezed his waist and went to his side. Knowing he cared about her made her happy, but she didn't need him hurting Anne.

"This is my friend Anne. She helped me escape."

"Smells like one who took you," Canis said.

"Did she help them?" Bennett turned to her.

Ember touched his face only to feel his muscles coiled and ready to strike. Whatever control he had, he held onto it by a thread. "Anne's boyfriend tricked her into kidnapping me. She helped me get away. She's safe." Ember looked at her friend who nodded.

Bennett relaxed some. "Thank you for helping save our mate. She's precious to us. If you're her friend, then you're our friend."

"Thank you," Anne squeaked out.

"Follow us back to the house," Ember told her. She slid into the truck and waited for Bennett to get in. Canis licked her cheek and nearly sat in her lap.

"Missed you. Sorry couldn't bite him," Canis said.

She giggled. "It's fine. It all worked out."

"Did it?" Bennett asked. He gripped the steering wheel as he spun the truck around and slung some gravel with the tires. "You told her about us."

"I didn't have much of a choice. I had a knife at my throat because her crazy boyfriend thinks you're going to take over the world and use all of us for blood slaves."

"Why would he think that?" Bennett asked.

"How about I tell you and Nash at the same time? It'll make it easier for me to say everything once. Then you can decide what you want to show Anne. You were saying something about the ship."

His stern lips turned up into a smile. "We got a signal."

Chapter Nine

They got to the house. As soon as Ember's feet hit the ground, she could feel the vibration going up her legs. She bit her lip and grabbed onto Bennett. He slung his arm around her waist and held her up.

"What is it?"

"It's the movement of the ship, I guess. It feels like... it feels like when you moan," she whispered.

"Oh...I never noticed it before. Something we'll have to keep in mind when we get you on board." He brushed a kiss across her lips.

Ember clung to him and felt the warmth starting to flow through her body. "Can you make this stop for now?"

He deepened the kiss. He ran his fingers over her jaw and touched the nodule. He held his finger over it while his tongue twisted around hers. Ember moaned, but he swallowed the groan. As he did, the feeling the ship stirred in her stopped. She pressed her forehead into his chest to catch her breath. When she looked up, his expression had a ring of concern to it.

"What is it?"

"Your suppression module has been damaged. Nash will have to see if he can recalibrate it."

"Is it going to hurt me?"

"I don't think so."

"Are you two done?" Anne's cheeks were red from watching their kiss.

"Yes. Come into the house," Bennett offered her. He threaded his fingers through Ember's as they walked into the kitchen.

"What is that?" Anne inquired.

Ember could still feel the shuddering of the ship. It seemed like she stood on a washing machine, but she didn't want to jump Nash or Bennett. Canis stayed by her side. Anne placed her hand over the wall that connected the house to the ship. All of a sudden Nash walked through without his disguise and right into Anne. She screamed, backed up, and hit one of the counter stools.

"Shit, Lester was right. They are green!" she squealed.

"Anne, get your shit together. Nash isn't going to hurt you."

"Em, love, who is this?" Nash asked. His tone was even, but his scales were darker than she had seen them before alerting her to his dire mood.

"Hi, I-I'm Anne."

"She helped save me from the man who kidnapped me. I brought her here, so she'd see her boyfriend's insane. He thinks you're trying to take over the world."

"Are you going to make Ember your slave?" Anne asked them.

Nash chuckled. "It seems like you've caught me on a good day when I don't feel like enslaving the human race. If you helped Ember get away from the one who hurt her, then I won't probe you either."

"Why didn't you come for her yourself?"

"We were on the way, but I had some things to fix," Nash commented. He slid over to Ember and brushed his mouth along her lips. "You're okay?"

"Yeah. I'm good."

He turned her head to the side and touched the module. "This has been altered. I'll have to recalibrate it again. What happened to you?"

Emily told them how she got yanked into the van and how she got away. Nash pulled her to him. She melted into his arms and held onto his scent as he stroked her hair and said a few things in his language to her. Nash trailed his nose down her neck before he pressed his mouth to her throat and pulled away.

"You're safe and well. That's all that matters. There are things we have to tell you about the ship. Drix won't harm you again."

"Thank you. What's going on with the ship? I can feel it rattling in my teeth."

"It wasn't Drix that woke up the ship. It was programed to notify us when it received an answer to the distress call we sent out ages ago."

"Is that why it's waking up now?" Ember asked.

"I think the technology has finally been able to catch up with itself. Even though Drix's higher functions have been sleeping, her lower functions have been using the materials the ship was mired in to fix the hull. We have the power to leave this place. It'll take a couple of days for us to get everything packed. We want you to come with us," Nash replied.

"Holy shit. They want you to go into space with them," Anne breathed.

"I heard them completely fine," Ember told her.

She smiled at her two men and saw their expectant faces. "You're asking me to give up everything I have here. I don't know if I can. Will you give me the time to think about it?"

"Of course," Bennett told her.

"We have preparations to make. Come on, Ben. Ember needs some time with her friend."

Bennett brushed his fingers over her face and descended into the ship. Anne went over to her. "Are you going to go with them?"

Ember shrugged. "I don't know. I need to get back to my own space."

Canis growled under his breath and stayed with them as they left the house. They got into her bedroom, and she found the bed had been made. When she sat down, she could smell her two men. Anne flopped back onto the bed.

"This place is great. Seriously, they're from another planet and you've... shit. You've slept with them. What's it like? Is it good? Are they like regular guys? You have to tell me."

"I'm not going to give you details about my sex life with them." Ember laughed.

"Both of them?" Anne asked.

Ember bit her lip. "Both of them."

"At the same time?"

She laughed as the tension eased within her from keeping such a big secret. It was nice to know she could share it with someone. "I'm not telling you that."

"You've gotta give me something. Does it have anything to do with that metal disk on your neck? Lester swears up and down he was abducted, used as a juice box, and had experiments done to him."

"They really did save my life by putting this device in me. This technology also helps with sex. They've been stuck on our planet for three hundred years."

"Makes my life sound normal. Lester isn't exactly a genius in the sack. He doesn't know where the button is even after I've given him the *Orgasms for Dumbshits Handbook*."

"I figured the sex was phenomenal since you invited him to move in pretty quick."

"Oh, the equipment is, but that's as far as it goes. He told me some sob story about being wrongly evicted. I found out later he hadn't paid rent in six months."

"Then why did you believe him that he's been abducted?"

Anne played with a loose thread on the pillowcase. "He has X-rays of the thing in his neck. It has tendrils that go into his brain. Plus he has the recordings from his regression sessions. Then Lester introduced me to his support group. Thanks for not telling your guys about me being involved."

Ember hugged her friend. "It's fine, but you can't go back to your place. Lester will be waiting."

"He knows where you work, and he knows you live here. He's not going to stop."

Canis laid his head on her knee. *"I protect."*

She scratched behind his ear. "I know you will. You were a good boy for letting the others know."

"You can understand the dog?" Anne asked.

"Yeah. He watches over me. He's been with the guys for a long time. They saved his life." Ember patted the bed, encouraging the dog to leap up. Canis sprawled out on his back, so he could have his belly rubbed.

Anne moved her hand over his belly and smiled. "What now?"

Ember laid back and closed her eyes. The experience of being kidnapped lingered as did the fear of being picked up again. The idea of leaving her planet and sailing off into the great beyond left her baffled. Could she leave everything behind? "I don't know. My life's turned upside down in twenty-four hours. I'm going to take a shower and make some food. Make yourself at home."

"Thanks."

* * *

Ember listened to Anne's even breathing. Canis lay curled at the end of the bed snoring away. She woke up from some kind of a dream that broke apart like gossamer. She rubbed her eyes and moonlight streamed into the window. Ember slipped on her robe over her long T-shirt and put on her slippers. She made the journey into the main house. All the lights were off. She went into the kitchen and passed through the barrier that separated the ship from the rest of the house. A shock passed over her. She gripped the wall as the lights blinked in the ship's corridor.

She followed the sound of voices and found her firemen in a room ablaze. They were dressed in full gear with a hose fighting back the flames with other men. A burst of heat hit her arm and made her jump back. She yelped. One of the men looked over. He said something and the whole thing froze like a tableau. He pulled off his mask and hat and came out to her. The light from the fire caught Bennett's silver hair.

"Ember, what are you doing down here? Are you okay?"

She glanced at the red mark on her hand. It was already fading into pink as the nanos healed her body. "I'm fine. I couldn't sleep. What the hell are you two doing?"

"Blowing off steam." Nash came out. His face glistened with sweat. "Come in. Nothing will hurt you while the simulation is paused."

Bennett took her hand and led her inside the replication. The heat from the fake fire lingered. She touched one of the frozen flames and didn't find it hot. It had substance and felt like tissue paper. Ember could taste smoke on the back of her tongue. Soot lined her men's faces. She examined some of the other fake fireman.

"What's going on? I recognize some of these guys."

"It's an amalgamation of all the television shows, movies, and training videos we've seen over the years." Nash smiled.

"What kind of technology do you guys really have?"

"This is one of the simulations we use when it comes to staying up to date with being firemen. It helps us to stay on our toes."

"You have this amazing thing here to make movies come to life and yet your holograms look identical. What's up with that anyway?"

Nash winced at the comment. "My fault, I'm afraid. What you see is the visage of the first Plasma Unit we had when we crashed here. We were both hungry and didn't understand how fragile your species was. We kept him alive for a little while, and I-I came to care for him. We tried implanting him with the nanos to save him, but we didn't know how humans functioned."

Bennett had a sad smile on his lips. "Nash scanned his body. When we did our holographic implantations, the image got stuck. We haven't been able to change it. And we both wanted to remember him."

The little tidbit made her heart ache for the both of them. It showed they cared for one another and other creatures. Ember trailed her fingers along Nash's face. Could she leave them behind?

"I'm sure you did your best. How long have you been in the firefighting business?"

"Off and on over a hundred years."

"What made you want to get involved in such a human profession?"

"Fire consumed the first cabin we built here. We wanted to help. Even in town we were on the water brigade. No one wants to lose their home." Bennett took her hands in his. "I'm sure you understand what it means to us that we can go home. It's taken so long to get the hull repaired and Drix back up to full working order. I know you said you needed some time. The longer the ship is active, the more exposed we are. Your military would strip our ship and dissect us. If they knew about our affiliation with you, it'd endanger you as well. Look at Anne's boyfriend."

She hung her head. "I know. It's not a decision I can make lightly. I don't even know how I'll survive on your ship. What will I eat?"

"We have that covered," Nash chimed in.

"Trust us, Ember. We need you." Bennett brought her wrist to his mouth and flicked his tongue over it. The sharp sting came as he pulled on her blood. The rush of euphoria flushed through her and she moaned. Having them drink from her was nearly as intoxicating as having sex with them. Nash came up behind her and brushed her hair away. He kissed her throat and the same pain hit her neck. She went to her tiptoes as pleasure rushed straight between her legs. Nash slipped a hand under her robe and over her already damp panties. He pushed aside the material and massaged her clit. She thrust her hips against Bennett. His sucking changed until he used his teeth on her flesh.

"Not fair," she whimpered.

"Danger. Men here. Men here," Canis shouted.

The dog's voice split her skull and broke the mood. The men withdrew from her. The dog barked at them. Bennett and Nash dashed out to see what was going on. Ember tried to go after them, but Canis stood in Ember's way.

"Let me by."

He planted his feet. *"No. Masters say you stay here."*

"I'll give you a steak."

"No deal. Chicken better."

"Fine. I'll buy you a whole rotisserie chicken."

"No." He grabbed a hold of her robe and pulled her out of the room. *"Come."*

"Where?"

"Safe place."

"I need to go help them."

The canine growled again and yanked her after him until she stumbled farther into the ship.

Chapter Ten

Ember sat on a bed with Canis standing guard. She ran her fingers over the soft black material. It felt like velvet but looked like silk. The shelves were dusty. The bed hadn't been slept in for a long time. The air she breathed left a stale taste on her tongue. Her stomach growled for something to eat, but she was too nauseous to think about food while her men were upstairs having God knew what done to them.

"I need to know what's going on." Ember got up and pounded the gray wall. A panel next to it lit up red and grew clear.

"I can show you what is transpiring." a mechanical voice said in the room. It didn't have a male or female sound to it.

"Who are you? Are you Drix?"

"I am Ordrix. The one after Drix. All you have to do is touch the ship and ask anything of it."

"When did this happen?" Ember asked.

"It's part of my most recent upgrades. What do you wish to see?"

"Bennett and Nash. Canis said there were men in the house. They were coming for my… my mates. Can you show me what's going on inside?"

"I have access to the security system. See as requested."

The screen showed the kitchen. Bennett lay sprawled on the floor, a pool of blood by his head. Nash was on his knees as he stared at the three men who had guns aimed at them. One of them was Lester. Another had Anne held in the corner with a gag in her mouth. "Can you make it so I can hear them?" Ember asked the computer.

The screen blinked again, and faint static came over the speakers.

"Tell me where she is?" Lester struck Nash across the

cheek, but her mate didn't react.

"I don't know where Ember is. She's not our prisoner."

"Let's kill 'em, Les," one of the goons said. "They're going to mind stun us anyway, imprison us, and then they're going to use us as their fuck toys."

"If you truly believe that, then why did you come here?" Nash chuckled. He spit a glob of blood onto the floor.

"Smart ass!" The other goon cocked his gun.

Lester pressed his gun to Nash's forehead. "I'm going to give you until the count of five. I know Ember's carrying your alien spawn. You won't pollute the human race."

Nash hissed.

Ember panicked. She didn't have enough time to get to back into the kitchen and stop them. Her mates were trying to keep her safe, but she felt like she was betraying them not being able to help. Bennett was already hurt.

"Canis, the people who stayed at the guesthouse before me. How did they make them forget? Nash said they left them with money and no memory. What did they do?"

"Something smelled funny."

"One," Lester counted.

"You won't find her. Even if you did, you won't get to her," Nash responded calmly.

Something that smelled funny. What would smell funny to a dog? "Was it some kind of food or liquid?"

"No. In the air. It made me sneeze."

Moved in the air. "Gas."

"Two."

"Ordrix, do you have something in your... I don't know... fuck. Can you flood the house with whatever gas that wipes out the memories of the humans in there?"

"I have access."

"Then do it."

"It would affect you as well. I can't say to what extent."

"I don't care. Nothing can happen to Bennett and Nash. Do it..."

"Three."

"...now."

"As you wish."

A light hiss sounded in her room. A haze like traveling heat waves filled the kitchen. The men coughed. Lester didn't flinch. He pushed the gun farther into Nash's forehead.

"Four."

Ember's head felt a little woozy like she was getting over a cold. She forced herself to keep watching. The other men coughed. One of them dropped a gun. The one holding Anne released her and looked at Anne as though he didn't know her. Ember coughed as she inhaled more of the gas.

She struggled to recall why she stared at the funny screen on the gray wall. She stumbled backward until she was sitting on the bed. She took in another breath. Everything she thought she knew slipped through her mind like an eel she couldn't grasp. She looked up at the screen. She knew what things were but couldn't put them into the context of how they fit into her life. How did she get to be in a room with a large dog watching television? The TV showed two green men -- one lying injured and the other on his knees, as four other men with guns were looking at one another as though they had no idea how they got here. The woman with them also seemed to be a stranger.

This is a very odd movie, she thought. She tried to think of her own name, but even that had fled her mind.

She turned her attention back to the screen. One green man got up and waved his hand before the men's eyes. They didn't react. A smile turned up his lips as though he knew what was happening. He plucked the guns from their hands.

"Sir, you used the phone and called your friends telling them you were going to be late since you had to fix your flat tires."

One man blinked. He almost looked familiar to Ember. Maybe from another time. He answered the green man. "Yes. Thank you. We won't bother you anymore. Hey, guys, come on. Ma'am, sorry to bother you."

The woman nodded, dazed. The green man ushered the men out of the house. He watched his guests drive off until the darkness swallowed their headlights. Once they were gone, he locked the door and rushed back into the kitchen to the fallen man.

"Anne, come here, please."

The woman looked around, then realized he was talking to her. She walked over and knelt down by the fallen man. "My name is Anne."

"Yes. We're your friends. I need your help. We're not going to harm you. Do you understand?"

"I understand."

"Good. I'm going to take your hand and cut it. Bennett's going to drink the blood from the wound, but it won't hurt."

"Okay." She offered him her hand.

Ember watched as the green man sliced Anne's hand and held it over the other man's mouth. He slowly swallowed the blood until his mouth latched onto it. Ember watched in fascination at how the fallen man soon got better as he took in the blood. Once Ben was moving around, the other man withdrew Anne's hand from his mouth.

"Nash, where's Ember?"

"She's safe. She released the gas we use on our Body Units who stay at the guesthouse that makes the mortals forget."

"If she forgets… Then, she won't remember anything of us," Bennett said.

Nash ran his hand through his hair and caressed Ben's cheek. "We're going to have to take that chance. If she truly is our mate, then she'll know."

"You know she is."

"I'm trying to think about the big picture and if it means…"

Bennett gripped his arm. "How about we go and find her?"

Nash nodded. "Ordrix, release the doors. Light a path for her. Canis, make sure she comes."

The panel Ember watched faded back to gray metal. The door opened. The animal took her shirt in its mouth and tugged. "I get it. You want me to follow you."

The dog barked and went ahead of her. She went slowly, taking in the strange makeup of the building she was in. The angle of the path told her they were going uphill. The panels on both sides were green and kept getting brighter as they got toward the opening ahead of her. Something about it felt familiar even though she couldn't put her finger on it. When Ember got to the top of the ramp, she saw the two green men and the woman.

"This isn't a television show, then?"

The silver haired green man shook his head. "No. It's not a show." He came close to her and she caught a scent.

"You smell good," Ember told him. She stepped closer to get a better whiff of him.

"What do I smell like?" he asked her. Ben's voice dropped to a throaty whisper and made her shiver inside.

"I don't know, but it makes me hungry."

"What about me?" Nash asked her. His voice constricted as he approached her.

They might have been green, but she found them both appealing. This one with the silver eyes, his scent was almost similar, but not as sweet. She stood up on her toes and ran her nose along his neck taking in more of his smell. "Mmmm… like dessert." Something about each of them sparked something in the back of her mind, like a long forgotten dream. The way they looked at her suggested they knew her on a more personal level than they knew Anne.

"Dessert is good," Nash whispered.

"Are you going to tell me why those men were in your house?" Ember asked Nash.

"They were going to hurt us because they thought we were harming you," Ben told her.

"You wouldn't hurt me," she replied. Even as she said it, Ember knew it was true. "You're okay now, aren't you?" She touched the silver-haired one's chest and nearly pulled away when she realized it wasn't skin. It felt familiar. He slipped his hand over hers and held it there.

"You don't have to be afraid of us." Bennett cupped her cheek.

She stared into his violet eyes. Nash came up behind her and slid his nose along her throat. Being between them didn't make her want to flee. It brought a moan from her lips and a longing for more.

"I know this all seems strange to you and maybe a little sudden. How do you feel being with us right now?" Ben stroked her hair.

Ember quivered from the soft caress. "Nice. Familiar. Like I should want more."

"What about me?" Anne asked them. "Are we together?"

"No, you're Ember's friend. You're coming with us," Bennett said to her.

"She is!" Nash exclaimed.

"We're going somewhere?" Ember asked.

"You have a choice to go with us. How about we talk about this more in the morning?" Bennett told them. His finger stroked behind her ear. As it did, her eyes drooped, and darkness took her over.

* * *

Ember opened her eyes. Anne snored away on the bed. They were in the same gray room where she had been before. She felt rested and like cotton candy filled her head. She flinched at the light, but she realized it wasn't the sun. She got up and stretched, feeling well rested. Something was missing. She rubbed her arms and felt a chill. She got to the door and touched it. It opened. Ember stepped into the hallway and followed the men's voices. She got down and stood at the edge of an open doorway.

"...we have to go. If they come back and decide to do more... Ben, I know you want to stay and wait for Ember to get her memory back, but we don't know how long it's going to take."

"You saw the messenger. She's selling the restaurant. She wants to come with us."

"We don't know. She could've decided to move to Nebraska or go on a cruise. We have to give her the benefit of the doubt."

"I know, Nash, but I can't lose her. She means to me the same as you do. You live in my heart as she does."

"I don't want to go without her either, but we might have to. The longest we can stay is a couple more days. The shaking of the ship and the electronic field it's giving off will soon be noticed by the authorities. We know what it means if they come here. I can only hold the energy dampeners in place for so long. They're already at full capacity."

Ember peeked through the door and found the two men in bed together. Nash caressed Bennett's face. It made her long for something she missed deep within her. The other man closed his eyes and let out a sigh.

"I know."

Getting up the courage, she knocked on the outside of the door. "Can I come in?"

"Of course."

She went in. "No. Don't get up." The men made room for her in-between them, so she crawled in. "Is this okay?"

The two of them molded their bodies to her. It felt right being with them. Their scents calmed her. She snuggled closer. Their fingers trailed over her arms and her stomach.

"This is better."

"It is." Bennett turned her face to him and kissed her.

Ember returned the kiss before breaking away. "You were talking about me coming with you and a restaurant?"

"Yes. Do you remember any of it?"

She thought about what they said. Something itched at the back of her mind. "Maybe. I don't know." She wrapped her arms around Bennett's neck and pressed against him. "I'd rather talk about this."

Ember didn't know what drove her, but being with them seemed more important. She kissed Bennett's throat until he groaned. The sound made her squeeze her thighs together. She needed to hear more. Bennett didn't touch her. It was clear he wanted to.

"We should wait until your memory comes back, love," Nash replied.

Ember turned to him and studied his silver eyes. She circled her arm around Nash's neck, but he had more control when she kissed him. He didn't return the kiss. His lips remained cold. She trailed her fingers along his firmed chest until her hands slid along his waist and touched his firmed cock. He drew in a breath. When she touched his balls and felt an indentation along his middle one, he quivered.

He grabbed her hand but didn't guide her away. "You

may say that, but I know you both want me. I know you're both…hungry."

Bennett kissed her and moved his lips down her throat. "You understand we drink blood?"

"Yes. I saw with Anne. I'm not afraid of you. I might not recall what happened between us, but I know I need to be…" she shook her head at the frustration of what she needed, but it was with them.

Nash wiped the tears from her cheeks. "Shhh, I know. Do you truly wish this?"

"Yes."

Bennett kissed her the side of her throat once more and Nash took her wrist. The pain brought some sort of recollection with it. Desire flared along her nerves and a name spilled from her lips. "Bennett."

He stopped sucking and looked at her. His face was more familiar than it had been before. She craned her neck for him to drink more. He struck again and pinched her nipple. Ember screamed. Flashes of images of them together filled her mind.

"More," she whispered.

Nash gripped her arm tighter, trying to make the blood come quicker. Warmth prickled from under her ear and flowed down her neck. She arched her back. Her breath quickened as an orgasm clenched her reason. Her head grew light as they took her blood. The more they took, the more things inside her unlocked. Ember touched the sides of their faces as she drew in labored breaths to stay conscious.

"Nash."

He stopped. The warmth in her neck burned throughout her body. He swiped his tongue over her wrist.

"Ben, stop."

Bennett unlatched from her neck. Ember felt like her whole body was on fire. The more she burned, the more the fog in her mind cleared. Her head spun, but she planted her hands on Nash's face and kissed him. He met her tongue, but it was short-lived.

"More. You have to take more."

"We can't. We'll kill you."

"I remember some. It feels like I'm sweltering. The nanos...something...I can't recall all of it. Please."

Nash nodded. "Bennett, keep an eye on her."

"Okay."

Ben slid one hand over her heart and held her against his chest. Another hand went up to her throat. Ember closed her eyes and rested her head on his chest. The double beats of his hearts reassured her. Nash kissed her palm. Bennett hugged her to him when the pain struck. She moaned and wanted so much to give into the delight it brought her, but she fought to stay awake as the burning went deeper into her mind. Bennett held her closer and she could feel his desire for her. He kissed her and whispered in ear.

"Stay with us. Tell us when the fog lifts."

Ember gave him a slight nod. The lightness that took her body and the thrumming of his hearts eased her into a trance. She floated. The burning in her mind raced to the rest of her body. Things from her past returned. Ember grew cold and could barely feel Bennett holding onto her.

"Nash, stop."

Bennett rubbed her arms and Nash pulled her against him. "Can you hear me, Ember?"

"Yeah. Cold."

"I know. You have to stay awake so the nanos can work on replacing your blood. Talk to me."

"Anne?"

"She's fine. She doesn't remember anything, though. We're going to have to take her with us. It's the most sensible thing to do. At least you'll remember being her friend."

"I'm going, too. Nothing here for me now."

"What about the restaurant and Cecil?"

"I recall them. Although they are a little faded. Cecil was a good man."

Bennett trailed his hands along her cheek. She sighed as a little more feeling came back into her. She felt a little bit more grounded. "Hopefully, over time all those memories will be restored to you."

Ember thought back. "There are a few more holes, but I remember opening the restaurant with him. How he died. I remember how you both saved my life and Nash was an ass. You come from a different world and you're going back to it. You implanted a device in me that repairs my body. You have a talking dog and both of you rock my world."

"Glad to know you remember us, at least," Bennett said to her.

"More might come back over time. It's good you figured out a way for the fog to lift," Nash told her.

She snuggled into them. She was sleepy, but her head wasn't as floaty. "Not sure what it was, but I couldn't let Lester and his goons hurt you. I remember what you said about the people you had staying in the guesthouse how they didn't have any memory after they left."

"You did it even though you knew it would destroy your recollections of us?"

"You mean too much to me to lose you," Ember told them. "I love you."

"We love you, too," Bennett whispered to her.

"You should rest now to get your strength back."

"Will one of you stay with me?"

"I'll stay. Nash has to get things ready so we can go. Rest now." He stroked her hair, and he pushed the nodule, so she fell asleep.

The next time she opened her eyes, Bennett had left

the bed. She got up this time and remembered what happened to her before. She was still a little cold, but she didn't feel like she would pass out. Canis popped his head up next to her.

"Awake."

"Yes."

"I tell Masters."

She scratched the dog's head behind his ears. "Where are they?"

"House. Packing."

She sighed. "Guess I have to do that, too. Lead the way."

"No need, Ember. I'll light the way for you."

The mechanical voice made her remember the computer was no longer going to try and kill her. "Thanks." She followed the lighted panels up to the kitchen. Bennett had his head stuck in the fridge showing off his toned body in leather pants that stretched over his fine ass. She licked her lips. "I know I'm hungry, but damn."

Bennett pulled his head out. His arms were full of things he dropped into a box on the counter. "You're awake."

"Yes, because someone likes to keep putting me to sleep. We really have to have a serious talk about you guys controlling me with this suppression module."

He gave her a wry smile. "It's all for your safety."

She leaned her elbows on the counter. His violet gaze settled on her chest. "My eyes are in my face and not in my boobs."

"I know that, but I like to look at your chest. The swells of those perfect breasts…" He shivered as he licked his lips. "You make me horny. All I want to do is protect you from the world. Is that so wrong?"

"No. It's not wrong. When do we leave?"

"As soon as Nash does a few calibrations. I was scouring the rest of the fridge and the house to get any last minute things. You might want to as well. Oh, and a messenger sent some papers to you. I left them in your kitchen."

"Thanks. I'll be in the house packing. Where's Anne?"

"We put her in the Viewing Chamber to give her something to do until you woke up. She's acting in one of her favorite movies."

"Labyrinth?"

"Yeah, actually. Maybe some of her memory is coming back." He grabbed the box and headed down into the ship. She went back to her house with Canis at her heels.

"Me watch you."

"I got that. Come on. I'm sure you can eat what's in my fridge." Ember looked over the paperwork. It was the agreement to sell her part of the restaurant to Lance. She signed the offer, put it into the envelope, and dropped it in the mailbox.

She glanced at the stuff in the house. Nothing much sparked her interest, so she packed her clothes and grabbed her computer. As she put it in the bag, Ember found a picture of her and a Cecil. They both smiled in front of the restaurant. She touched the photo and smiled. Cecil would want her to move forward with her life and be happy.

Time to look forward. She glanced at the clock. Several hours had passed. Ember gathered the rest of her things and wondered what her life would be like jetting through the galaxy with two green men, her best friend, and a talking dog.

Chapter Eleven

Ember stood in the control room with Nash and Bennett. Anne slept in one of the bedrooms so she wouldn't be rattled when they took off. They'd implanted a nodule in her to make sure she would understand them and to keep her healthy.

"There's no going back," Nash told her.

"I'm aware of that. I don't have anything left for me here. Besides, I get to be with you." Emily gripped both of their arms and squeezed.

"Okay. Here goes nothing." Nash pressed the wall. Two black seats rose up from the middle of the floor. "Once we start taking off, we won't be able to interact with you. We'll have a psychic link to the ship. You'll need to sit down." A wall slid back and revealed a room behind them. "It might get bumpy so hold on," Nash warned.

Ember sat in the room. Nash and Bennett both sat in their chairs. Black armor covered their chests and arms. It made them look all the more alien. They closed their eyes, and shook as they rested against the chairs. Their seats turned around to the blank wall behind them. As the chairs rotated, the gray wall changed to blackness.

"Are you ready to take off?" Ordrix's voice came over the intercom.

"Yes," Bennett and Nash answered at once in flat voices.

"I've tapped into the power grid. It will black out many states and we'll appear on the governments' radars."

"We can recharge once we near the sun and then head back to Tilleron. Let's hope there aren't any space pirates around," Bennett commented.

Ember grabbed her seat when the vibration from the ship hit her chest. A slight force pushed her back in her seat. She couldn't see her men, but it seemed like she could feel them all around her. The lights flared as they drew energy. The rumbling became so loud she covered her ears. The air seemed to be electrified. Hair on her arms and on her head stood up. A whoosh of cold air blasted through the interior and sucked the air from her lungs for a quick second. When she could breathe again, she noticed the screen and saw blue sky. They were several hundred feet off the ground and gaining altitude. As they went higher, the landmasses below grew smaller and smaller until the blue-and-green ball of Earth hung before them.

"Shit. I thought that'd be different."

Her men didn't respond. She walked between them. Their green scales had gone black and gave them a more dangerous look. She didn't dare touch them, but she kept her eyes on the screen until Earth was no longer visible. The sun looked like a bright glowing orb in the distance.

"How long will it take us to get to the sun?" Ember asked.

"A few hours. We'll be close to the surface so I can absorb the heat. My batteries are pretty drained from being lodged in the earth and taking off. I'll have to shut down many of my systems. They'll be occupied until we get to the sun," Ordrix told her.

"What exactly are they doing?"

A small platform rose from the center of the ship. "Put your hand on the board and see."

Ember rested her palm on the silver surface. A jolt hit her. She tried to pull her hand away, but it felt like her mind expanded. Ember felt encased. Panic hit her brain from the overwhelming sense of being more than she was and yet also pushed together at the same time.

"It's okay. You're with us and with the ship. We steer it through a psychic link with Ordrix. In case she's hurt or not functioning, then we can go in and find the problem.

We have to be under until we get to the sun to see what damage has fully occurred since she's been in the ground. Go back to our rooms and wait." Nash's voice flitted through her thoughts. She felt his touch along her face as though they were next to her.

Ember felt a slight push against her chest and a disconnection from the world around her. When she opened her eyes, she was back in the control room. She lightly kissed Nash's and Bennett's lips and saw faint smiles in return. Ember followed the lighted panels down a hallway she hadn't explored yet. A door slid open to reveal a room decorated in purple drapes along the walls and a dark blue spread on the bed large enough for three. It had another chamber attached to it. The aroma of flowers led her over to it. A light mist encased her skin when she entered. The path was a large circle. In the center was a fountain. Flowers of all varieties and some she'd never seen before grew toward a light in the center of the spray.

She found a place to sit and listened to the fountain. It relaxed her so much that she forget they were flying through space. The smell of the flowers made it feel almost like home.

"Do you like it here?" Nash stood next to the fountain.

"It's wonderful. When did you do all this?"

"We've had it for a long time. Where do you think I got all the flowers from?" Bennett chuckled.

"I figured you kept raiding the local florist."

"No pillaging I promise." Bennett rubbed his temples.

"Are you okay?"

"It's been a long time since we've flown. I've forgotten the endurance it takes even with both of us helping to pilot the ship. There are still a lot of repairs we have to do. While Nash was navigating, I was helping Ordrix fix the ship, putting her resources where they needed to be so we could get home. It's taxing."

Ember ran her fingers down his face. He turned his hand into her cheek and kissed her palm. She rubbed his temples and trailed her fingers along his jawline. His hair was braided from the top giving him the look of a mohawk. The tail end was done in several other braids and then woven together again. Even his black scales made him look all the more alien.

"Do you always dress like this in the leather armor?" Ember asked.

"Yes, when we're on the ship," Nash replied.

"Do you like it?" Bennett slid his arms around her waist.

She trailed her fingers over the vest that covered his chest. It felt like a metal plate, but soft as leather. "It definitely gives you the outlaw alien biker look."

"Something you like?" Nash crooned as he moved the hair from the side of her neck.

"I could get used to it. Your scales being black to match the armor is different."

"We can change that." He pressed her hand against his neck where the armor didn't touch. His scales slowly faded to match her flesh tone. "It helps being able to change color sometimes."

"Well, I can't do that."

"Yes, you can." Bennett molded himself to her back. "How's this?"

Nash nibbled her ear. "We're going to fuck you until you scream. I'm going to go so deep inside you won't be able to bear it when I come out. You won't ever want us to stop. I want your tongue wrapped around my cock and sucking on my balls while Bennett fucks you from behind."

Ember felt her cheeks sear at his comments. "Guys, what're you doing?" His suggestions and combined scent overwhelmed her and made her wet at the idea of what might come.

"See. You changed color," Nash said to her.

"That's not the same thing," she protested.

"Doesn't matter. I like it when you turn pinkish." Bennett sucked on her other earlobe.

"You two are horrible," she teased.

"Of course, we are. That's why we're made for one another. And why you're made for us?" Nash teased her.

Bennett slipped his hands around her breasts. "Do you want to join the mile high club?"

"I think we're a little higher than a mile." Ember leaned back against him and felt the bulge pushing into her ass. She rubbed along him until Ben ran his hands over her thighs. He moaned.

"If you get him doing that, then I can't promise how long this will last. I'll fuck him myself," Nash whispered.

She ran her tongue along Nash's lips. "I'll fuck the both of you and then make you beg for more."

He leaned in for more of her mouth, but she pulled away. He growled in frustration, but she turned her attention back to Ben's cock and moved slower until both of them breathed faster.

"Tease."

Ember wrapped her arm around Nash's neck and bit his throat. He ripped her from Ben's arms. He raked his nails along her back and sucked on her lips until they hurt as he kissed her. Ben hissed behind her. Nash broke the kiss and replied in a guttural voice. Ben went by them, but Ember grabbed his arm. He flashed her a menacing smile. She held onto his arm. Bennett clutched her chin and bit her bottom lip until he drew blood. His eyes had gone dark violet. He sucked on her blood before Nash pulled her away and snapped.

"Enough, both of you, or you don't get me at all."

Bennett took in a deep breath and released his hold on her. "Forgive us. You make us forget that we share you. It brings out the animal in us. Remember I did say, when

Nash and I are together it can get… rough."

She touched his face. "I know, but I'm yours. Both of yours." Ember stepped away from them and pulled her shirt off. Their eyes went wide. She took off her bra, and their eyes were glued to her chest. She ran her fingers over her breasts and rolled her nipples. They both licked their lips. Ember took a step backward toward the bed. Her men followed her as if they were in a trance.

They pulled off their chest plates and left them on the floor. She took off her shoes and socks. She undid her pants. Nash reached for her, but she darted away. Ember stripped the rest of her clothes off until she was by the foot of the bed. They stood in front of her naked. "Kneel."

They looked at one another and then back at her.

"If you want me, then kneel. I've had enough of both of you putting me to sleep or controlling me because you think it's best for me."

"We did that at times to save…" Ben began.

"If you pull that shit with me again, then you'll find this…" She gestured to her body. "…to be a no-fly zone. Understand?"

They nodded.

"Good. Now kneel."

Both of her mates knelt before her. It made her feel like she could do anything, and they were devoted to her. "I understand there might be times you need to do something I might not agree with. This is your domain, but when we're together like this, you can't use it to control me."

"What about for your prolonged pleasure?" Bennett asked. He reached to touch her.

"That's different."

"What does our mistress want?" Nash asked.

She trailed a finger down the outline of his face. He nipped the tip with his tongue. "I want to watch you together first."

They looked at one another. "I'm not sure that's a good idea, Ember." Bennett said as he got up and came at her. "We could get carried away. You might get hurt."

"I'm willing to take a chance. Maybe you need some enticement."

Ember sucked on her fingers. She walked them down over her stomach. Her mates' mouths dropped open. They stared at her as though she were lunch. She opened her legs and trailed her fingers over her inner thighs. They came at her, but she shook her head as she rubbed her clit and let out a moan.

Bennett took Nash's face in his hands and kissed him, but his eyes weren't focused on the other alien. They concentrated on her while she pleasured herself.

Bennett and Nash circled each other, touching and hissing. Their suckers bloomed on the end of their tongues. Watching the display made her hot as the testosterone -- or whatever the alien equivalent was -- grew between them. They were fronting for her until Nash growled something as his hands grabbed Bennett's balls. The other man grunted. A sudden shiver went through him. The scales on their backs seemed to roll. Bennett smashed his lips against Nash's and grabbed his ass. Nash nipped at Bennett's throat. His sucker attached to it. Bennett rubbed Nash's cock. Bennett bit into Nash's throat as they moved at the same tempo. Their hips bucked together and then they looked up at her, out of breath.

"You've seen us together, but we can't be fulfilled until we're with you." Bennett slid across the bed.

His cock pointed at her. He grabbed her legs and pulled her toward him. Ember didn't have a chance because Nash got right in behind her. He slid his hands under her arms and caressed her breasts. Bennett kissed her thighs and plunged his tongue into her wet slit. He worked his way inside her, fucking her. Nash pinched her nipples until she cried out. He bit into her throat and she felt the pain of the sucker latch onto her. She pushed her hips into Bennett until he moved up and attached his tongue to her clit.

Ember moaned. She could feel it vibrate in her own chest. Nash returned the gesture as the throb moved from him and into her. Ember arched her back to feel more of him against her. She turned her head and caught his lips. His tongue met hers and she could taste the tang of her blood. Bennett released her clit and kissed up her stomach as he slid his body along hers.

"Is this what you wanted?" Bennett asked.

"Almost," she whispered. She turned around between them. Bennett slapped her ass. She grunted from the sudden pain. Nash gave her a puzzled look. She kissed his stomach, sucking in his skin and biting her way until she got to his shaft. She slipped one hand under his balls and rubbed his middle testicle.

"What do you think you're doing?" He raised his hips up.

"What you said. Unless you don't want my tongue wrapped around your cock?" Ember touched the shaft with her tongue and tasted the salty sweetness of his flesh. The scales along his dick scraped her tongue as she flicked it along one side of his length.

"Oh fuck," Nash moaned.

She gripped his hips as Bennett kissed her back. His fingers trailed over the tips of her breasts. He spread her legs and rubbed the mounds of her ass. Ember shivered as she took Nash more into her mouth. She couldn't take him all in, but she twisted her tongue around his length and pulled up with suction. Bennett's breath blasted along her throat. He slid his cock inside her. She nearly bit down on Nash's shaft, but she concentrated as Bennett moved inside her. Ember tried to keep her focus on Nash's cock and the rhythm of what Bennett was doing to her. Nash threaded his fingers through her hair and held her. She drew in a ragged breath, and the pleasure Ben brought in her rode along her spine.

"Yes, Em. Don't stop," Nash cried out.

She sucked on him faster until she felt his warm seed spill into her throat. She sucked him down until he released her. Bennett slid into her one last time. At the last second, he bit her. Ember felt the orgasm sweep over her and then spill into him and Nash. Bennett lay on top of her as she snuggled against them. Their hearts thrummed in their chests. "How was that?" she asked.

"Amazing," Nash breathed. "But what about for you?"

"I'm out of breath. I'm good."

"But you're not," Bennett said to her. He stroked her neck. "We can go again and make it last far longer for you."

She caught his arm. "We don't have to have marathon sessions every time. I enjoy being with you. When you moan it makes me wet. I'm good. If we keep on going the way you want to, I could end up with little green aliens running around."

"No, you won't. We made sure to program the nanos, so you won't become pregnant unless you wish it later on."

"Later on? Wait...are we genetically compatible?" Ember asked.

"Very. It's something we checked," Bennett told her as his six fingers walked along her belly and caught her clit once more.

Ember held in a small moan. Nash traced her thigh and moved his fingers inside her slowly. "No fair, guys."

"We don't play fair," Nash chuckled. "Do you like this?"

"Yes," Ember whimpered. Bennett didn't ease up on massaging her clit until she felt her muscles clench around Nash's fingers.

"You sound wonderful, my lovely mate." Bennett set his hand on her chest and shivered as Ember screamed. "Fuck. That sound." Bennett kissed her until Nash claimed her lips once more. She cried out as they all came one more time.

They held them to her as they lay in silence after their love making. Ember kissed Nash's chest and moved over to Ben. Nash trailed his fingers along her back. She could stay with them forever.

* * *

"When will we reach your home world?"

"We should be there in a month or so. We're making good time. As long as we don't run into space pirates." Nash got up from the chair and stretched. Ember rubbed her hands over his chest and kissed him lightly.

"I don't know what I'm going to do with you two with all this time on my hands," Ember joked with him.

"You can show more things to Anne and make sure she's comfortable with what's going on," Bennett said.

"She's fine."

Canis came in with him and barked at her. *"Need more reading, please."* He dropped the Kindle at Bennett's feet.

"You've read all this already?" Nash asked.

He barked again. *"Yes."*

"Give me the Kindle and I'll find some stuff for you," Ember snatched it up.

"What about us?" Bennett asked.

"Pfft. You have two hands."

"Now who is being mean?" Nash caught her around the waist and kissed her. Bennett stole her away and kissed her as well.

"It's been a long day and I could use a little pampering of my own," Ember told them. They both nuzzled her neck, and she felt the pain of their suckers along her throat. It brought a moan from her chest and they held her tighter.

"God, if I have to see more of this, I think I'm going to puke," Anne said as she came into the control room.

Ember smiled at her. "I can't help it if they have a thing for me. Oh fuck…"

"Yes," Bennett whispered.

"Later."

"Promise?" Nash asked.

"Yes."

"Good. Now give us some girl time." Anne grabbed Ember and dragged her out of the control room. "You never did tell me how they are."

"I thought you didn't remember our conversation."

She smiled. "I recall a few things."

"It doesn't scare you they're aliens?"

"Shit, by the way they treat you and how you scream, I want one." Anne chuckled.

"They weren't what I was expecting, but they make me happy."

"All it took was for you to find some green aliens and fly you halfway across the universe so you can be happy after Cecil died."

Ember hugged her friend because what she said was true. Her thoughts were of the two green men who loved her. Whatever their future and whichever adventures awaited her, she knew they would always be there for her. "You're exactly right. Two *big* green men whisked me away, and I love them more than I ever thought I would."

Anne gave her friend a quick hug. "You really gotta dish on how they are in the sack."

"We've been friends for a long time. I still don't kiss and tell."

Serenaded by the Alien Vampire Rock Star
Crymsyn Hart

After Irene Beckham accidentally discovers rock star Ace Hendrix's big secret, she wakes up in his bedroom without any memory of how she got there. As flashes of her memory of the night before return, Ace makes her an offer. Let him suck her blood, and he'll make her a wealthy woman if she can stay quiet about it. Ace even proves to her he didn't take advantage of her the night before.

When the press gets wind of Ace's new fling, Irene decides she's not the right woman for him, but Ace knows they're meant to be together. He doesn't care what the paparazzi says, he has to have her in his life no matter the cost.

Chapter One

Irene adjusted her glasses once more and bit her lip to keep from sighing out of boredom. A line of anxious women stretched from the stage into the seat aisles, waiting to get a glimpse of rocker Ace Hendrix. She fiddled with the badge around her neck awarding her the golden opportunity to meet the singer. Squeals from teenagers nearly made her ears bleed. All the excitement grated on her nerves. Bev, the friend who got her the pass, went along with the throng being as shrill as the others. Bev had a thing for Ace. The crowd parted and the shrieks grew into a cacophony.

"Oh. My. God! There he is. I want to lick him all up," Bev yelled into her ear.

Irene winced as she caught a glimpse of the rocker. With the leather boots on, he towered over his fans at nearly seven feet tall. Skintight leather pants encased his athletic legs. If the waist went any lower his dick would be hanging out. His brown hair was pulled back into a short ponytail showing off his angled face. He wore a red vest he left unbuttoned, showing off his toned physique and hairless chest. A mass of silver chains hung around his neck like thin snakes curling together. He flashed the crowd a halfcocked smile and the women went mad again.

"He's okay, if you're into the emaciated look." Irene took another look at him.

"Of course, *you're* into men who read star warrior books and dress up in fake armor. They wear superhero T-shirts and spend all day parading around at your weekend conventions pretending to be something else." Bev gave her a halfhearted smile.

"If I had known your true feelings beforehand, then I wouldn't have invited you to conventions. I thought you enjoyed them. It's where we met. Not every guy I date is a nerd."

"The last three were. Hush, it's almost our turn."

"I'm not going to hush. You've been silencing me for years. When Trish and Alexa bailed on you again, I came with you. I'm sick of being your last choice. I'm done being your tagalong." Irene finally realized Bev had been using her.

Bev took her arm and yanked Irene closer. "I don't need you making a scene, Irene. I'm here to see Ace and I don't need you screwing it up."

The cacophony of the music and the women screaming again made her head hurt. Irene took off her glasses and cleaned them on her shirt. Someone bumped into her, causing her to drop them. *Shit.* She bent over to pick them up, but the crowd moved forward as the women squished together to get closer to Ace. Squinting, she patted the ground trying to find them, when another volley of squeals erupted behind her. The blurred pavement gave way to black, rounded leather boots, and then fingers held out her glasses.

"Looking for these?"

She took them from the stranger and settled them back on her nose. The left lens was cracked, and the right arm bent. "Thanks," she grumbled.

"You're welcome."

Irene focused through the cracks. Ace Hendrix had returned her glasses. Bev elbowed her side as Irene forced a smile.

"Looks like those are pretty busted up. I think it's my fault. Why don't you and your friend come backstage for the show? It's the least I can do."

"I --"

"Irene, come on," Bev said through gritted teeth.

I won't hear the end of it from her if I say no, and I'm not in the mood to argue. "That'd be great. Thanks, Mr. Hendrix."

"Nicole'll get you situated. I have to get ready. Ow!

It's gonna be one helluva show!" He winked at her and spun around on his heel, heading into the wings of the stage. A short, blonde woman holding a clipboard stepped forward with two lanyards in her hand.

"Hi, I'm Nicole, Ace's assistant. These will get you into anywhere in the theater."

Bev snatched them from Nicole and threw one at Irene. "Thank you so much. It's so nice of Ace to invite us backstage after what happened to my friend."

Irene rolled her eyes. Nicole waved them onward. "Come this way, please."

"Gladly," Irene muttered. She followed Nicole backstage among the stagehands and the rest of the crew. Nicole stopped in a room littered with food and people relaxing on several couches.

"You can stay in here while the crew sets up. There's water. Help yourself to some of the food. Oh, and here are some earplugs for when they get started. It gets really loud." Nicole handed them the earplugs.

"Thanks." Irene attempted to fight a headache as her eyes tried to adapt to seeing through the cracked lens. Bev grabbed her and led her over to an empty couch. It did feel good to sit down after standing for so long.

"This is amazing. I can't believe you scored us these passes. I mean no one gets to come in here unless they're crew."

"Yeah, it's great. All it took was a crazy mob breaking my glasses." Irene took off her glasses and tried to mend them, but the arm only bent more. She stopped trying.

"Don't be such a sour puss. Try to have some fun!"

"This is really your thing. I can't see, so that makes it even worse. The world is a little blurry and cracked."

The lights flickered and went out completely. The echo of a guitar riff resounded from the stage. The sound made her jump and it shut Bev up. Irene put in her earplugs. The sound was dampened, but she could still hear the music. She didn't dislike the songs. They weren't her kind of music. Bev tugged at her arm and motioned for her to come out to the stage so they could watch the band play. Irene shook her head.

"I gotta pee. I'll be back." Irene wound her way through the people hanging around but found her way farther backstage. As the sound of the music lessened, she pulled out her earplugs. The low lighting made it difficult for her to make out the signs on the doors. With her glasses askew and struggling to see, Irene saw a blurry sign for the restroom. *Thank God.* She pushed the door open and heard a groan.

Irene stopped when she realized two people were in the room. She could make out the tall form of Ace and his assistant Nicole locked together. Ace had his arm around Nicole and his lips on her throat. Nicole moaned, but Ace seemed too busy sucking on her neck to notice.

"Oh shit. I thought this was the bathroom. I can barely see anything."

He looked up. He licked Nicole's neck, but it seemed his tongue looked longer than it should have been. Irene wasn't sure what she saw because it blurred. "What are you doing here?" Ace asked.

"Sorry. I got the wrong door." Irene backed away. Ace released Nicole, who stumbled into a chair. Ace closed the door. Up close, his skin color appeared off. Under the red vest his flesh turned green. Even with her glasses being messed up, she could see it. "What the fuck?"

"I wish you hadn't come in here. You saw me with Nicole, and now I can't let you go." Ace grabbed her and pulled her toward him. He wrenched her neck to the side.

Irene tried to get away, but his grip wouldn't allow her to. "I won't say anything about this. Honest, I can't really even see anything clearly. I promise I won't te --" The pain struck her throat. Irene moaned. Ace stiffened against her and redoubled his sucking on her neck. She beat against his chest. Her pulse echoed in her ears. Her head swam as points of lights twisted in her vision. "Please…" she whimpered, and she felt another pinch along her arm before her vision went black.

Chapter Two

Irene opened her eyes and rolled her neck. A stab of pain struck her throat. She sat up and pushed her hair back. Her fingers hit her glasses. She pulled them off and found they had been fixed. "What the hell?"

Glancing around, she discovered she'd woken up in a room not her own. Dark blue walls were hung with pictures of the ocean and cliffside vistas. One was so huge it made it seem like she looked out a window. And yet she couldn't find any windows. A bed large enough to sleep four people took up most of the room. *What the fuck happened?* She took off her glasses and inspected them to make sure they were hers. She ran her hands over the wall, looking for any crack that could be a door. After going over the whole room, she knocked on the walls to hear if any were hollow. With nothing but hurting knuckles, she slammed her fist on a bare spot on the wall.

"Let me out of here," she screamed.

"Enough with the yelling. I have a headache as it is," a male voice came over a speaker.

"Who are you and what are you going to do with me?" Irene scanned the room looking for a speaker.

Something clicked and a portion of the wall popped out. Someone hovered in the hallway. "Come on. We have a few things to discuss before you can go." She recognized Ace's voice.

Irene followed the rocker. Posters of old concerts from Buddy Holly, Jimmy Hendrix, The Doors, Madonna, all from different eras of music and mixed with framed golden records lined the hallway. As she ran after him, all she could stare at was his ass in those leather pants. "Mr. Hendrix, how did I end up here?"

He turned down the hall and Irene rushed to catch up with him. He turned another corner. She found him as he grabbed a bottle of water from a fridge that blended in with the cabinets around it. He flung himself down onto a sofa and gestured for her to take a seat across from him.

Irene sank down into the couch. Records, CDs, cassette tapes, anything music-related lined the bookshelves around the room. "You have quite a music collection."

His gaze roamed around the room and a slight smile came on his face. "Thanks. I've been collecting for a long time. Music's always been my escape. Would you like some water?"

"Sure. Thanks."

He tossed the bottle of water at her. It hit the back of the couch next to her and bounced onto the seat. "Sorry. Like I said I'm getting over the hangover from last night."

"About last night. How did I get here? Back at your house? Where's my friend?"

"What's the last thing you remember?"

She squeezed the bridge of her nose, trying to recall what happened. Her head pounded as she tried to draw forth the memories after she waited in line with Bev for Ace. "My glasses got knocked off and trampled. You picked them up and your assistant gave me and Bev backstage passes." A spear of pain sliced her temple. She tried to pull up more. It remained out of her reach. "I don't know." She ran her fingers over her jeans as a thought passed through her head. "We didn't... ahh..."

"Fuck?" he asked.

Her cheeks burned at his language. "Yeah."

"No, we didn't. After you wandered into my dressing room, you fainted. Nicole, my assistant, brought in my doctor. He said you'd passed out from having too much to drink. I thought it best to have you brought back here to sleep it off where no one'd bother you. We put you in the guestroom to sleep it off. I can have my car take you wherever you need to go."

Irene sipped the water and thought back to being with Bev before the show. "I didn't have anything to drink."

"You sure? Maybe your friend slipped you something. It'd account for you thinking your glasses were broken."

"They were. You picked them up for me."

"You stumbled and dropped them right in front of me, but they weren't broken."

Nothing of what he said made any sense to her. Irene tried to rack her mind at what happened the night before. The ache hit her temple again. She winced. "No... I..."

"Look, you're awake. You seem fine to me. Now, I have a life to get back to. It was very nice to meet you. I'll have my driver take you home. Come on."

Ace got up and walked out of the room. Irene sat trying to make sense of what he'd said. *This doesn't sound right. If I passed out, then Bev would've wormed her way into coming with me, playing at being nursemaid.* She squeezed her eyes shut and recalled clearly her glasses had been broken. They went backstage with Nicole, and then she had tried to find the restroom. And then... she walked into Ace's dressing room, but he was...

"What the hell was he doing?" Irene whispered. A quick pang of pain went deeper into her temple. She shook it off and kept on diving into her memory. A glimpse of Ace with Nicole in his arms flashed in her mind. She could barely hold onto it before another jab hit her. Irene gritted her teeth as her vision swam. Something wet dribbled onto her lip. The taste of copper sat the back of her tongue. She wiped her nose and came away with a smear of blood. She tried again to go into the memory of her finding his dressing room. Ace was doing something to Nicole. Something about his tongue wasn't normal. He came over to Irene and...

"Are you coming or not?" Ace asked. He stuck his head back in the room to check on her.

Irene tried to stand. Her legs couldn't support her weight. She sat back down on the sofa. The pain in her head overwhelmed her as she put her head in her hands and moaned. Another quick flash came to her. She tried to catch her breath but found herself reliving the memory from the night before. Ace grabbing her around the waist, the sudden pinch in her arm and sting in her throat. She fought to get away. Her vision clouded, but the agony in her head made it impossible to chase more of the memory.

Ace approached her in his music library. He opened his mouth to say something. The end of his tongue seemed to bloom. The tang of the blood flowed down her throat. Irene wiped her hand across her nose once more. The crimson smear made her cringe. Ace grabbed her hand and licked the blood from it. Irene tried to back away, but he swiped his thumb over the top of her lip and sucked on it.

"W-what are you doing?"

The memory of what she saw the night before hadn't retreated. Ace knelt down before her and took her wrist. She watched in horror as his tongue opened, like a budding flower and latched onto the flesh above her vein. Irene felt a pinch which quickly faded. His head remained at her wrist. She could feel his lips pressed upon her flesh as warmth traveled down her arm. Irene tried not to panic. When he broke away and looked up at her, his tongue looked like some deranged flower as it closed and returned to a normal tongue. His blue-green eyes penetrated her will, holding her as if he had captured her soul.

Ace brushed her cheek. "It's clear you recall some of what happened. You weren't supposed to. I've never seen anyone fight against the nanos like you did."

"What wasn't I supposed to remember? What did you do to me? You drank my blood. What kind of pervert are you? What's wrong with your tongue?"

He frowned, but he didn't release her wrist. "Questions. Always with the questions. You had them last night, too."

"What're you going to do with me? I swear I won't say anything about the blood drinking." Irene glanced around and tried to find an escape. No windows and only one door she could see was the only way out.

"Calm down. I'm not going to hurt you. The call of your blood was too enticing for me not to take another sip. I do enjoy how you taste and how you sound. It made my headache vanish."

"Good, I guess." Irene couldn't believe the rock star had drunk her blood and liked it. "Why can't I remember last night? What did you do to me?"

He lifted his hand. "See the ring?"

Irene let her gaze fall to the silver ring with the large ruby. "Yes."

"A device inside it allows me to hypnotize people. It normally works, but you must have a strong mind. You're fighting the suggestion."

"So you put people in a trance to take advantage of them?"

"No, I put those I desire to feed from under my spell, or to control them if they walk in on me when I'm drinking."

"Your assistant knows you're a… you drink blood?"

"She's aware. We have an arrangement."

"Great. Are you going to zap me again and send me on my way?"

"I'm not going to *zap* you. There are several options. I can let you go and hope you'll keep quiet. I can pay you off. Maybe we can come to some arrangement like I have with Nicole. You accompany me on tour. I can feed off you and pay you for the trouble. Or we can work something out when I'm in town. I'd again pay for your discretion. What do you say?"

"I-I don't know what to say." Irene's head spun. The strangeness of the situation hadn't faded yet. "Tell me how I got back here last night?"

Ace released her and sat on the couch next to her. "After I enthralled you, I asked if you wanted to return to your friend. You said she was a bitch. I invited you to come home with me after the show. You came willingly. When we got back, I took some more blood, and then you fell asleep in the bedroom. Nothing else happened. It's all on camera if you want to see it."

His enticing gaze held hers. Something in those eyes said he told her the truth. Irene still didn't understand all of it, but he didn't frighten her. "No. I need some time to think about all this. Can I go home, please?"

"Of course. I'll get my driver to take you. Think about my offer." Ace took her hand once more and brushed his lips over the back of it. "This way. I'll show you out."

He led her outside to where he had a car waiting. Irene climbed in the back. A flash of memory came back to her as she recalled being in the car the night before with Ace sitting next to her. He tried to talk to her, but she didn't really say much. He didn't do anything to her. Not even make a move to touch her.

"Where to?" the driver asked.

Irene snapped back from the memory and gave him her address. A window rolled up separating her from him and off they went.

Chapter Three

A week passed, and Irene remembered a little more of what happened to her. Parts remained fuzzy, but her head didn't hurt anymore when she delved back into her mind. Irene pulled into her driveway after a day of sorting books and dealing with people at *Pages*, the bookstore where she worked. In her mailbox, she discovered a white envelope with her first name on it. Inside was a USB drive with a note wrapped around it.

Call me.

She scratched her head and a small smile turned up her lips as she stared at the phone number with an A at the end of the note. Ace's offer rattled around in her mind. Her memory might have returned, but that didn't mean he wouldn't mesmerize her again. She fingered the drive and plugged it into her computer. All the files were video files.

The first one she opened was from the music venue showing her and Ace leaving his dressing room. The cameras followed them out to the car. As he said, she'd gone willingly. The next video file showed them in his limo with the camera angle facing them. He sat next to her in the car, barely talking, but he didn't make any move toward her. She watched with interest as Ace took her wrist and held it to his mouth. Irene looked at her expression, and it seemed she enjoyed him taking her blood. Irene examined her wrist. A faint pattern like some weird sort of flower dotted the flesh. The last video file was of Ace carrying her into the house. He moved her into the room she found herself in and laid her on the bed. After he left, the video went blank.

She stared at his number and wondered what it would be like to take him up on his offer. He had been true to his word and hadn't taken advantage of her. Being a rocker, she thought he would be... Well, she didn't know what he would be like, besides the whole drinking blood thing. Maybe he was interested in more than her blood. Although, Irene couldn't see a sexy rock star being interested in her. He had obviously sent her the flash drive to prove he had been honorable. *It won't hurt to call him to thank him even if he's a little… weird.*

Irene dialed the number and waited for it to connect. When it did, his deep voice came on. "Hello?"

"H-Hi… ahh… Ace. This is Irene. I got the flash drive you left in my mailbox."

"Good. Good. Did you think about my offer?"

"I can't leave my job to go on the road with you. I enjoy working in the bookstore."

"Which one?"

"*Pages.* We're the only used bookstore in three counties. Most of them've closed down, but my boss has some connections. I think she's funneling money from her husband to keep it going. Anyway, ahh… I wanted to say thanks for letting me know you were true to your word."

"You mean that I didn't rape you when you came to my house of your own free will."

"Yes," she squeaked out.

"Well, I can appreciate loving your job. How about another proposition? Would you let me visit you?"

"So you can suck my blood?"

"Yes, and maybe something more. What do you say?"

"It all depends on what you're proposing?" She felt her cheeks sear at the thought of what might happen between them.

"I have a few days off before I'm on the road again. Would you want to get some dinner? I'm an excellent cook."

"I could… umm, sure."

"Okay. How about tomorrow night? I'll send the car for you. Anything in particular you can't eat?" he asked.

"I'm allergic to seafood, strawberries, mushrooms, and

peppers."

"I can work around those. I'll have my driver pick you up at seven."

"Okay. See you then." Irene hung up.

* * *

Irene checked herself in the mirror one more time. The gray in her brown hair stood out. The lines around her brown eyes were longer than she liked. Her stomach rolled around like a rock tumbler. Suddenly, she heard the knock on her door. She straightened her shirt and wished for a moment she fit the mold of the typical rock star girlfriend: skinny, blonde, and tan. Instead she had a curvy figure and had trouble losing weight. Nothing could change all that now. She grabbed her bag. Outside her door stood a man in a well-tailored suit.

"Ms. Beckham. I'm Simeon, Mr. Hendrix's driver. We met the other night, but you might not recall."

"Yeah, I don't."

"That's okay. Come on."

He escorted her to the car and opened the door. She slipped inside and settled in as the car sped off. Her stomach twisted into more complicated knots when they pulled up outside of Ace's house. She slipped out. The front door opened before she could grasp the knob. Ace wore jeans and a T-shirt sporting some '80s B movie about alien clowns.

"Hello."

"H-Hi." She twisted her hand into edge of her shirt and glanced down at her shoes.

"Why don't you come in? There's no need to be nervous. Thanks, Simeon. I'm good for the rest of the night." Ace lifted his hand and waved at his driver.

Irene crept past the rocker into his house. "Whatever you're cooking smells wonderful."

"Thanks."

The kitchen opened up into a wide island in the

middle and a great long table set up in a dining area. The plates were next to one another. The perfume of cooking meat made her mouth water.

He went to the fridge. "Would you like something to drink?"

"Just water."

"I have plenty of that." He grabbed a bottle of water and handed it to her. His fingers brushed hers, sending a chill up her arm. Irene stepped away from him to keep her distance. Coming here might have been a mistake, but she wanted to understand why he wanted to drink her blood. Why she had consented to it in the first place?

"There's some time before the roast is done. Would you like to see my garden?"

"You like to garden?"

"It helps relax me. Sometimes when I'm elbow-deep in soil, I'll get hit by my musical muse and come up with lyrics. My mother gardened. It reminds me of her."

"Is she…?"

A frown marred his handsome appearance. "Yes. For a long time now. I wasn't there when she passed."

"I'm sure she knew you would have been there if you could have." Irene twisted the cap off the water and strolled past him over to the table. The lush scenery in the greenhouse drew her. Plate-size orange flowers raised their full blooms to the sun even as it set. They wove along an archway. Green tri-pointed leaves the size of her palm brushed the top of the door. Water droplets glistened off the lush greenery. Flowers and fruits of all different varieties hung waiting to be plucked and enjoyed.

"You can go inside if you like. It's a little bit warmer than in here. I keep to tropical plants because they're… Well, it's what I'm better at." Ace slid the door open. A blast of hot, humid air hit her and made her back up a step into a chair. The sharp corner dug into her shoulder.

The sweet perfume of so many different flowers tickled her nose until she sneezed. Her eyes watered, but once she wiped them and her glasses, she could see again.

Ace had his hand on her arm. "Are you okay?"

Irene nodded. Another scent enveloped her that she hadn't noticed before. It smelled like peppermint and chocolate. She licked her lips and leaned in a little closer to get a better whiff of the delightful aroma. "Do you have any hot chocolate on the stove?"

"No, why?" His warm breath caressed her ear.

She jumped. Her heart hitched, but she couldn't get the scent out of her nose. She glanced at him and noticed how his eyes reminded her of a tropical sea she could swim in forever. A warmth rushed through her at being so close to him. For a moment, Irene wanted to forget about her blackout and his weird blood fetish and have him wrap his arms around her.

"It's so strange. I don't know why I suddenly caught a whiff of it. It's like my two favorite fragrances. I'm a sucker for hot chocolate with peppermint in it."

"I may have an idea why you smell that around me."

"Care to explain?"

Ace slid his hand along her cheek. The way his fingers grazed her jaw it felt as though he had more than five digits. The thought floated from her mind as he ran his thumb over her bottom lip. "It's been a long time since I've hungered for another this way. I've been here a long time."

"What does that have to do with how you smell?"

"It means you're aroused by me. Whenever a woman is attracted to me, I smell like something they crave or their favorite food."

"You must get a lot of women who want to lick you."

He laughed. "A few. Sometimes I let them. I'd let *you* lick me."

Irene pushed her glasses up. "So you can suck my

blood again?"

"You enjoyed it, but no. I was thinking it could follow a night of pleasure after dinner. If you wanted to, of course."

Irene felt a laugh bubble up and spill from her throat. It broke the spell he had over her and cleared the succulent fragrances from her nose. "That's an amazing line. Do you say it to all the groupies you invite back to your house or maybe even the back of your tour bus?"

"I admit there have been a few over the years, but not as many as you might assume. And I've never brought anyone back to my home."

Irene gazed at him, not sure she believed him. He was drop-dead sexy and anyone would want him. "Then why me?"

Ace's forehead scrunched up. He took in a breath to say something, but the timer went off in the kitchen. He reached out to touch her again. However, the beeping started and broke the moment. Ace threaded his fingers through his brown hair and pushed it out of his face. Since she was close to him, Irene noticed the golden highlights. "It can wait until after dinner. I hope you're hungry."

She shrugged. More intrigued about why he had singled her out among all the women he had -- even over Bev. She was more into his music and knew his songs. Irene had only been along for the ride, the consolation friend, because she was the last person on Bev's list. What would Bev say if she knew Irene was in Ace Hendrix's house?

Ace walked back into the kitchen. She couldn't help but watch his ass in those jeans. Irene licked her lips and wondered if she could bounce a quarter off his butt. As he strolled across the room, prowling after his prey, something completely primal lingered around him. He wasn't built like a wrestler or runner, but something in between. His T-shirt was loose enough she couldn't make out how well he was built, but the material wasn't stretched. Irene glanced at the greenhouse and the plants beyond.

"Everything okay?"

"Yeah, just thinking. Did you need any help with getting dinner ready?"

"Grab a plate and help yourself." He lifted the top off the Dutch oven and placed it on the counter. The scent of the meal tantalized her senses and made her stomach growl. Ace slid the oven mitt off and held out a plate for her. His smile won her over. She took the plate and looked over the fare. A large roast was surrounded by different kind of vegetables cooked in a thick gravy.

The meat fell apart when she speared it with the fork. Irene took what she wanted and went over to the table. Ace followed and sat next to her.

"What do you think?" Ace asked, breaking the silence in the room.

Irene blew on her food to cool it off. "It's too hot to eat yet. It smells great, though. Do you like to cook?"

He shrugged. "From time to time. When I'm home, I'd rather not have to eat from takeout containers."

"Why not have a personal chef?"

"I don't like people in my home."

"You have a driver."

"Simeon is part of my security detail, too. I've known him and Nicole for a long time. They're more like family than anything else. They've saved my life a few times, and you could say I've saved theirs."

"Because you gave them a job?"

Ace set his fork down and sipped on his water. "It's a long story, but I trust them. More than I trust my manager."

"Wow. That's something, then." Irene wondered how he had saved his driver's life. How much trust did Ace put in him? Ace didn't look any older than thirty. What kind of life had he led before he became a rocker or what brought him to it? There was so much she didn't know about him except what the news reported on. They said he was a superficial playboy who always had another woman on his arm after every show. His last relationship lasted for three months and ended badly. People enjoyed his music, but he sang happy pop songs which didn't inspire her.

"You don't sound impressed."

Irene shrugged. "I don't know you or anything about your life except what your publicity team puts out or what you have on social media." She took a bite of her food now it had cooled. "This is really good." The meat melted in her mouth and the vegetables had a savory favor.

"Thanks. You don't follow my life as it gets splashed around on the tabloids or on reality television?"

"To be honest, I'm not a huge fan of your music. It's a bit too…" *What am I thinking? I'm about to tell him I hate his music after he's invited me into his house.*

"What? Tell me."

"Forget it."

"No. I want to know." He leaned back in his chair and his lips turned up into a smile. His eyes brightened. "I love hearing from my fans."

"I'm not a fan."

"Ahhh…. Well that explains a lot." He took a bite of food. "Then tell me your criticism on how I can improve."

"I don't really think it's my place."

"Go ahead. I can take it."

Irene set her fork down and crossed her arms over her chest. Her cheeks burned. She met his gaze and tried not to look away. "Fine. You're a bit too poppy. You try to be a hardcore rocker, but to me you're the male version of Brittney Spears or Taylor Swift."

He lifted an eyebrow. "Wow. I guess you *really* don't like me."

"Like I said, your kind of music isn't really to my taste." Irene ate another mouthful and thought about what he said. He wanted some criticism, so she gave it to him.

"Anything else you want to tell me?"

"I think you have more talent than you let on. I've seen some of your interviews and..."

"And?"

"They make it seem like you have rocks in your head. Why do you let them portray you as if you're an airhead?"

"Simeon's said the same thing, but image sells. It's what they record company wanted at the time. My career snowballed once the first single dropped. The ride hasn't slowed a decade later. The company wants more. They've approached me for another album which would make six altogether. I've gotten better over the years. Finish eating. I'll show you the garden and maybe then you'll see the rocks in my head aren't as big as you think."

"How about a better answer to why you smelled so good to me? I've been attracted to other men, and they don't smell like chocolate and peppermint. Why are you so special?" Irene countered. His explanation had only made her question more about what he told her.

He gave her a knowing smile. "We can get into that later on. Let's see if you like what else I have to show you. Maybe think on the other proposal I mentioned earlier."

"Right, your blood fetish and wanting to pay me to suck on my neck."

"You called *me*. I sent you the clips so you'd see you came with me willingly. Even if you didn't remember it. Calling me back showed me your interest."

"Sure, it piqued my curiosity. I wanted to know what it... I wanted to actually remember our conversation this time. Are you going to make me forget again?"

"All depends on how the rest of the evening goes." His eyes twinkled with excitement as he scored another piece of meat.

What does he mean? How is the rest of the evening going to go? Does he plan to seduce me? Will I remember it, or will I find another flash drive in my mailbox? She watched him eat his food and tried not to make it obvious, but she caught Ace watching her as well. An awkward silence filled the room. She smiled at him now and again and picked at her food. Her stomach fluttered at the thought of what was to come next. He leaned back and sighed in appreciation of his meal.

"Are you finished?" He stood up and reached for her plate.

"Yes, thanks. Do you need help with the dishes?"

Ace set them in the sink. "I'll do them later. I thought you might want to see there's more than rocks in my head."

"Gonna prove you can shake some of them loose?" Irene leaned on the counter.

He shook his head. "Come on." He waved for her to follow him.

Irene followed him back down the hallway and turned into a room. A spiral staircase heading down into parts unknown made her wonder if it descended into his dungeon. Ace gestured for her to come with him. Irene half expected to find a woman chained up waiting for him to drink her blood. Instead, the wood-paneled room remained vastly empty except for a black grand piano. A long table pushed against the back wall had sheets of paper laid out on it. She walked over and noticed the lines and the notes. *Sheet music.* Penciled notations were scribbled on some of the pages. Nestled in the corner of the room was another chair.

"Let's shake some rocks."

"Gee, now I'm sorry I ever used the analogy."

Ace cracked his knuckles and set his fingers onto the keys. Once the melody started, Irene found herself caught up in the tune. She sank down onto the piano bench next to him. His fingertips danced over the ivory, capturing her in its notes. It started off slowly and grew in intensity. She closed her eyes and heard the sorrow within the music. It went beyond the pop anthems and kitschy songs he pumped out. The rise of the harmony took her out on the tide and pulled her back. As it dipped, another sound wound into the music. She opened her eyes. Ace's voice entwined with the piano notes, a mixture of a hum and a chant. His eyes were closed, and he was totally engrossed in the music. His fingers slammed down on the keys as the intensity of the song built. She sniffled and felt wetness slip onto her cheeks. His blue-green gaze met hers, and it seemed as though she saw him for the first time.

Gone was the rocker. In his place was a man with more depth of feeling than she had thought him capable. His eyes misted as he finished the tune.

Irene wiped her eyes. "The melody was amazing, haunting. Is the song going to be part of a solo project or another album?"

He took her hand and trailed his lips over the back of it. Irene shivered. The aroma of peppermint and chocolate hit her once more. The silky feel of his mouth on her flesh made her wet. Bumps rose along her arms. The simple gesture made her want to find out what truly was behind Ace's façade. *What would it be like to feel him kiss me? Feel him inside me.*

"You haunt my dreams."

"You barely know me. Except for the drinking my blood part. How could I haunt your dreams?"

Ace sucked the tip of her finger. Irene couldn't believe this was happening. He rested his other hand on her thigh. He didn't break the stare when he pulled in more of her finger. A small moan slipped out. The pressure of his grip tightened on her thigh. He drew in a breath as though he fought to keep control. His tongue wrapped around the digit. A quick stab nearly made her pull away. Irene jumped as his mouth worked on her. Irene ran her hand over his and groaned as he sucked. He grabbed her leg harder and took the whole finger into his mouth.

"What are you doing to me?" The scent of peppermint overwhelmed her. Ace trailed his fingers on her jeans. Her head spun. She tried to make sense of the strange and almost fucked-up events. Ace sucked a little bit more before he released her finger and flicked his tongue over where he had nipped her.

"Sorry, I couldn't help it. Your blood calls to me. Everything about you calls to me. I knew it the other night when I heard you." He kissed her palm and sighed. His expression seemed one of calm and expectancy all rolled into one. Like she was the answer to all his dreams. He cupped her cheek and smiled.

"I have no idea what you're talking about."

"I know you don't, but I can show you if you'll let me. You have to trust me. Do you think you can?"

His earnest expression made her relax with him. The warmth of his hand seeped into her skin. She rubbed her palm over the back of his arm. His skin felt like peach fuzz, something she had never felt before with another person. Touching him made her feel more alive in a way she couldn't describe. Ace's unique scent clouded her mind and made her hunger. Irene yearned to kiss him, to see if he actually tasted how he smelled. Even though she got the peppermint and chocolate, she could also catch the scent of him mixed with whatever citrus soap he used. As her fingers slid over his, something felt off about his hand. It seemed like he had an extra finger. *Impossible.* She brushed her lips along his, taking a chance to see what he would taste like. Her desire to trust him overwhelmed her. He hadn't taken advantage of her when he could have.

Ace returned her kiss with more intensity. His tongue swept across her bottom lip. She leaned in a little more, but Ace pulled away. Irene sighed.

"There's more to me than what you see."

"Shaking more rocks?"

Ace chuckled. "Come with me. I have something else to show you."

Chapter Four

Irene stood up from the piano bench. "Is this the part where you strip me naked, flip me over your shoulder, and carry me off to your bedroom?"

"Not exactly what I had in mind. If you can trust me some more, then you might get your wish." He stood up and offered her his hand.

She didn't hesitate and took his hand. "You're not wearing your ring?"

"It's in my pocket. I don't need it all the time when I'm at home. You fought the nanos the last time. I didn't want to inject you with them again if I didn't have to. If I can prove to you what I know is true, then I won't have to."

"Nanos? You said that word before, but never told me what they were." His answers twisted into more questions. Who exactly was this famous rocker? Why had he set his sights on her? Even with all those uncertainties, her body warmed toward him. The peppermint aroma grew stronger. She now had a hankering for peppermint ice cream with chocolate sauce. It would go right to her hips, but she didn't care. She wanted to feel the coolness slipping over her lips or have him kiss her again. Anything to ease the agonizing craving growing within her.

"Those answers will come. Do you have an open mind?"

She shrugged. "I'd like to think so. I read a lot of books, go to a lot of nerdy conventions, as Bev says. It's opened my eyes to some of the weird. I've walked in on a few scenarios I wish I hadn't."

"I'll have to ask you about those. If you don't feel comfortable, I'll take you back."

"Where are we going?"

Ace walked her over to a door she hadn't noticed before in the corner of the room. Ace pulled out his ring, placed it on his finger, and put his hand on the door. A light appeared from underneath it as the wall dissolved. A sliver of fear overtook her. The illumination blinded her, so she had to shield her eyes. Ace tugged on her hand to follow, but she stood her ground.

"It's okay. Nothing'll hurt you. This is how we get to my ship."

"Ship? What you have a secret passageway to a yacht in there?" She tried to laugh off her unease.

"Not exactly. You said you trusted me."

"You *said* you'd answer my questions and not make more."

His grip on her hand tightened. The light dimmed so she could see him. The dark tan of his skin tone had taken on an emerald green sheen. His face seemed sharper and longer. It was difficult to tell because of the light.

"Your questions will be answered. Come with me. It won't hurt." He jerked her inside the space, and she bounced against his chest.

The space was no bigger than a small closet with nothing inside except light gray metallic walls. The reflection distorted her image and made her question what she was doing. How had her evening turned into the rock star singling her out, sweet-talking her, and taking her into a small closet with him to go see his mysterious ship? It had twisted into something she hadn't seen coming. He was something she hadn't seen coming. She brushed her fingers along the wall. Its smooth surface tingled her fingertips with a small electrical jolt. Irene hissed. Ace brushed his mouth along the places where she had been stung. The coolness of his lips took her mind off the hurt.

He slid his other hand along her neck and held her nape. His touch soothed her fear of being in the tight space. Ace slipped his other arm around her waist and held her close. "Don't be afraid. Shut your eyes against the light."

Irene nodded and squeezed her eyes shut. A great blast of heat engulfed her. Even with her eyes closed, the brightness came through. Heat prickled her exposed skin like ants biting her. She moaned from the sudden pain and shivered. Once the heat touched her, she grabbed onto his shirt and held onto him. Ace held her closer. It felt like the floor dropped out from underneath her feet even though she could still feel something solid. A buzzing filled her ears.

"Ace, what's happening?" she forced out. The air was sucked from her lungs. Ace stroked her hair, trying to reassure her, but her stomach went into her throat, and it felt like her dinner tried to crawl back up.

Irene glanced down. Instead of a floor below her, an expanse of black with small white dots shimmered in the distance. A round sphere with white wispy things floating above blue and green masses took up her vision. *It can't be!* Her stomach quivered again. She quickly buried her head back into Ace's chest. She heard him chuckle and squeeze her waist.

"It'll be okay. We'll be there in a second."

"Where?"

"My ship."

She nodded, not really comprehending how she flew through the air with a strange man and was not dead. *Why is the Earth below us? I'm hallucinating. He drugged my food. That has to be it. Whatever it was, it took some time to take effect. The piano and the small talk were his way of lulling me into a false sense of security. It's all...* Her feet hit a solid floor. Irene couldn't think beyond the fact he had drugged her, and now she was having a bad trip thinking they had traveled from his house on Earth to his spacecraft somewhere above the Earth. Irene shook. The one thing keeping her calm was Ace's grip. It seemed odd his body kept her calm even though he'd turned her world around. His fingers trailed down her back. He tilted her chin up so she could peer into his amazing eyes.

"What did you drug me with?" Irene asked.

He pushed a stray hair away from her cheek and tucked it behind her ear. "I didn't drug you. I told you I'd answer your questions. You have to trust me a little bit more, and then all will be revealed. Are you okay? The journey can be a little harrowing when you're not used to it. Come with me. I'll show you my ship." The room lit up at the sound of his voice.

"Welcome back, sir. It's been a while since you last activated the transport. Is there anything you desire?" A computerized male voice sounded from the room.

Ace ran his fingers through his hair. His shoulders sagged as he glanced around. His demeanor seemed to change as though he was more himself than at the house. A blast of air hit her. She rubbed her hands over her arms to warm herself. Her breath came out in a mist. Ace took off his shirt and stepped toward her. Irene moved away from him.

"You're cold. This will help with the chill."

"No way. Take me back to your house."

"It'll take an hour or so for the transport to recharge. You'll have to stay here until then. I'll take you back, don't worry. Indulge me until then."

"What is this place?" Irene's head spun. She tried to stay focused, but different scenarios of how he would torture her and hide her body kept flashing in her mind.

"Drean, increase the temperature by five degrees. Ready the Stimulation Chamber."

"Are you sure that's a good idea, sir?" the computerized voice asked.

"Don't question me now. I'm not in the mood."

"I was only thinking of the female. She's already frightened from the transport. You may want to --"

"Who is that?" Irene asked.

Ace hadn't made a move to touch her. Her curiosity

wormed past her fear. The shape of the room they appeared in was oval with two doors, one in front of her and the other to her left. The same gray metal covered the walls as in the small room in Ace's house. The air smelled stale and had an antiseptic tang. The chilled air remained as she breathed out a cloud of mist.

"If you want answers to all your questions, then you have to follow me."

She stared at him and crossed her arms over her chest. "You keep stringing me along. Tell me or I'm not going anywhere with you." The air around her warmed.

Ace sighed. He draped his shirt over her shoulders without touching her. The aroma of peppermint again made her mouth water, even though she tried to fight it. It was also difficult not to stare at his toned chest and abs. The cold of the ship didn't seem to bother him. His breath caressed the side of her cheek as he lingered next to her. The fabric of his shirt still held his warmth. It did make her feel a little more grounded.

"Do you believe in aliens?" Ace brushed the hair away from her throat. The light movement of his fingers made her quiver as he traced her neck. She tried to concentrate on the metallic walls to stay focused and not fall under his spell. His lips trailed along her flesh.

"Why?" she managed to get out.

"I love how you taste," he murmured.

She nearly let herself lean back against him, but she stepped away instead. "Stop trying to twist my mind around. Tell me what's going on, Ace."

"Fine. I wanted to show you slowly so you could accept it. Make love to you so you could feel the connection between us. I've been on your planet for a long time, and I've never met a woman who makes me feel the way you do. When you moaned in my arms on the night you walked in on me and my assistant, it hit me. Believe me, I've had a lot of women in my day, but you're supposed to be mine."

"I'm not anyone's and... what did you say about being on the planet?" Irene let his words sink in, but they didn't make any sense.

Ace sighed. "Please don't be afraid. I'm not going to hurt you." He pressed and held the center of the red gem in his ring.

The image of the sexy rocker dropped away. Tanned skin faded to reveal a dark green, almost black, skin tone. It reminded of her of the leather volumes they had at the bookstore. His muscles were defined under his skin. As the light hit his flesh, Irene made out how the skin lightened to an olive green along the sides of his neck and his face. His brown hair became an electric purple that hung around his ears. His eyes remained the tropical blue-green she knew. Her gaze roved over his chest. The absence of a belly button made him all the more strange. Ace held up his hands. They appeared off balance. She counted five fingers plus his thumb. The red gem of his ring blinked as the light above them fluttered. She glanced up. The ceiling glowed with a faint light. The temperature warmed more so she felt more comfortable having something familiar on her in the strange environment she had stepped into.

"What the fuck?" Irene muttered.

"The Stimulation Chamber is ready, sir. I'm not sure how long we can maintain full power to all the other systems with it running. It'll take longer for the transport to power up so you can return to the planet." Drean's voice echoed in the ship.

Irene couldn't make out if he was above them or whether the voice was coming from a speaker. Ace gritted his teeth. "Fine. For now, keep systems as they are. I need to show Irene around the ship."

"As you wish." The voice faded away.

"Ace, what's going on?"

"I asked you if you believed in aliens."

"Right. I take it you want me to believe you're one. You somehow transported me to your spaceship, and we're, what, on Mars now or something?" Irene couldn't take in what she saw. He wasn't human. No human being had that color skin.

"I'm from a planet called Tilleron. It's in a star system ten light years from your planet. I've been on Earth for a hundred and fifty years."

"But your ship, computer, whatever -- you said we weren't on the planet." Irene backed away from him until her fingertips hit the metal wall. The lights dimmed again.

"We're not on Earth. We're on its moon."

"If we're on the moon, then why hasn't the military or someone with a decent telescope or a Chinese satellite found your ship?"

"We're in a cavern deep inside the moon on its dark side. It used to be an old lava tube. The ship leaves once in a while, flies to your sun, recharges, and returns. Drean is aware of your satellites and technology, but ours are more sophisticated so the ship goes undetected."

Irene nodded as if she really understood what he was talking about. Her legs felt like limp lasagna noodles. She tried to stand, but instead she slid down the wall onto the floor. Ace knelt down. She drew up her knees and tried to put more space between herself and Ace. *Impossible. What he said is impossible. We're underground on the moon. He's an alien. Will he ever let me go home?* How had he existed on Earth and looked normal? It's not like he was some C-class celebrity. He was a full-blown star the press followed around. She didn't know much about what else the paparazzi tried with him.

"Irene, you said you wanted answers. I'm here to give them to you. I promise I won't hurt you. Won't you trust me?" He brushed his fingers along the top of her hand.

His light touch made her look up into his welcoming smile. "You're green. How come no one has discovered your unusual pigmentation?"

Ace chuckled. He held up his hand with the large gold ring on it. The red stone winked again in the light. He pressed the side of it and the jewel lifted up. Inside the ring, she could see light blue machinery whirling around. Sharp jabs hit her temples and her vision blurred. She took her glasses off and rubbed her eyes.

"This bothers you?"

"Yes, I can't keep my eyes focused on it. If you close it, I'll be good." Irene massaged her temples when she felt Ace's fingers slide over hers and applied pressure on both sides.

"Does this help?"

The pain retreated under his fingers. Irene let out a small sigh as she caught the scent of peppermint. Then she opened her eyes and pulled away. Ace gave her a puzzled look. His eyes showed his sadness as he leaned back. Irene could tell he wanted her to trust him. She was trying to get over the fact she sat on a spaceship, with a green alien who had beamed them onto his craft. He hadn't hurt her. She yearned to trust him. She wanted to feel his arms around her and taste his lips once more.

"It helps. Thank you. Does your ring have some sort of holographic projector inside it? Has it ever malfunctioned before?"

"I was in the middle of a set with the cameras on me and a thousand screaming fans in the audience. All of a sudden I saw myself on the screen."

"What did you do? What did the fans do? The band?"

His smile widened showing off his perfect teeth. "They all thought it was part of the show. I finished the set, went back to my dressing room, and made sure I had a backup. Luckily, I did. I've made improvements since then."

"Was there any backlash? Did your people say anything?"

"My people?"

"Yeah, your kind. Other aliens."

"No. They wouldn't. Once my kind detects our mutation, they send us to Tilleron, banned from ever returning to our home planet. We're the stigma they hate because we have to drink blood. It doesn't matter if you have other gifts and are considered..." He looked away, but not before she caught the pain flashing across his face.

His eyes filled with tears. Ace's story hit her heart. She couldn't completely understand his tale, but he had been cast adrift. Irene slid her hand along his cheek and felt the warmth of his skin. The softness reminded her of velvet. "What was your gift?"

"My voice. I was slated to sing in the temples praising the Origins. It's all I wanted as a child. Sometimes even if we aren't born with seven digits, the suckers don't develop on our tongues. Mine formed past the age of maturity. I was two years into training and my sucker bloomed. Once my teacher found out, he tried to have me spared, but even he answered to a higher master. They banished me from the temple and sent me to Tilleron. We can stay on the planet if we like, or we're paired with ships and sent off. We look for Plasma Units and bring them aboard."

"Your slaves?"

He shook his head. "I can't speak for others of my kind, but no. I make sure my Plasma Units are treated with respect once they know what I am. Some species willingly come to Tilleron and seek to be our Plasma Units."

"Plasma Units are people you take blood from?"

"Yes, that's what Nicole is. She and Simeon know what I am. They've been with me for a long time. They are my current donors."

"Then why do you want me?"

"I want you for more than your blood, but first I want to show you something."

"The Stimulation Chamber?"

He chuckled. "That too. Right now, I want to taste you again, if you'll let me."

"You want to drink my blood again?" Irene questioned him.

He nodded.

This was the proposal he had given her in the first place when she thought he had some weird blood-drinking fetish. Hearing his story made her more curious about who he was. He hadn't harmed her. His green skin didn't put her off. The purple hair was a bit distracting. His eyes remained the same and she could see into him. Her heart said she could trust him. Irene caught his scent once more. Her mouth watered and she wanted to drink him in.

"How?"

He took her hand and kissed her palm. His lips slid across the flesh like silk until he came to the inside of her wrist. Ace opened his mouth and flicked his tongue along her vein. Irene shivered with the anticipation of what would come. The tip of his tongue opened like a crazy flower. It was a little bigger than the size of a quarter. Eight separate points, each with a small suction cup on it. Ace brought her wrist up and attached the sucker to it. Irene felt a jab of pain. Ace pressed his lips to her flesh and glanced up at her. She could feel the blood rushing down her arm. She gasped. He gripped her arm and drank faster. Her head felt a little floaty. Watching him turned her on in some bizarre way. She touched the top of his head and threaded her fingers through his hair. Ace stopped drinking and looked up at her. His tongue closed back up and resembled a regular pink tongue.

"I want you, Irene. Like no other."

"Ace, I'm not going to say it wouldn't be interesting to sleep with you, but..."

"Come to the Stimulation Chamber. If you feel differently after, then I'll wait until you want to."

She bit her lip wondering if he had the same equipment as a human man. "Ace, I don't know. Are we even compatible? I mean... you have a sucker on your tongue and no nipples... do you have a barbed penis?" Irene dared to put a hand on his chest. He felt warmer than she did. "Your sexual organs aren't hidden in your elbow, are they?"

"No. You have a disturbing mind. Although, I have run across some species who have their reproductive organs on their head."

"Other species?"

"Yes, this universe is filled with amazing things and more life than you humans have ever imagined. I'm fully capable of having sex with a human. As to what my penis looks like, you'll have to see for yourself. Will you come with me?"

His statement intrigued her about what he had seen in his journeys. It also opened up more questions about him. The eager look in his eyes nearly turned into a plea the longer the silence grew between them. She glanced at the place where he had bitten her. Small dots of blood resembled some sort of strange blossom. The dots smeared when she touched them, but she didn't feel any pain. Whatever this Stimulation Chamber was, she decided it wouldn't hurt to check it out. He did say he wouldn't pursue her for sex if she didn't like it. "I'm not taking my clothes off."

"You don't have to." He relaxed and stood up. Ace grabbed her hands and pulled her up. Irene stumbled and slammed into him. Ace slid his hands along her back and cupped her ass. Pressed against him, she could feel the bulge in his jeans along her belly. This close to him she could see his lips were light jade green. The inside his mouth was pink and so was his tongue. Her gaze traveled back to those lips and how much she wanted to kiss him.

"You know there's one thing I don't understand about all this."

"What's that?"

"Why you're so interested in me?"

He brushed his fingers along her face. The soft caress made her sigh. He closed his eyes as though he savored the noise. "I told you. I heard you moan."

"I'm sure you've heard other women moan considering you've had plenty. How am I so different?" She didn't quite understand why her moan would single her out among the thousands of females he must have heard? She wasn't the type to be noticed by famous rock stars. Her brown hair had stray gray hairs here and there. She had more weight on her than she cared to admit. She'd had relationships on and off over the years, but nothing stuck. With forty right around the corner, her life had fallen into a routine. She'd worked at *Pages* for eight years. Irene loved being around the books.

"It'll become clear in the Stimulation Chamber. Come." He led her out of the room.

Chapter Five

Irene took in the long hallway. All the walls had a metallic gray sheen. The corridor could fit three people in it. Rooms and other hallways branched off, but she and Ace kept going straight down the corridor, and then turned with the ship until they came to another door. Ace placed his hand on the panel beside the door. It lit up purple and the door slid open. The room inside was circular -- and empty.

"What is this place?"

"It's called the Stimulation Chamber. It's where we bring potential partners to see if they are sexually compatible with us. Sometimes they are our Plasma Units, too."

"From the hard-on you're sporting, I already know you're into me. You said something about why I smell the peppermint and chocolate scent around you."

"Yes. You're smelling my pheromones, and it's how you react to them. Humans see me on stage crooning my heart out. They're attracted to the image. You saw past all the glam and wanted to be with *me*. You desire *me*. Drean, raise the chairs," Ace told the computer.

The gray metal of the floor flowed toward the center of the room. Two oval shapes hovered a foot off the ground. They reformed into chairs that resembled ice cream scoops. Ace led her to one of them.

"What do we do?" Irene asked. How could sitting in a chair let Ace know they might be sexually compatible?

"Sit in the chair. A film will slide over you. You will want to struggle, but relax. It won't hurt you."

"Does it transport me to another planet?" Irene's stomach quivered from newly blooming fear. She didn't like the idea of him saying she was going to struggle.

"No. It links us telepathically. Sit, please." Ace sat in the chair across from her and gestured for her to sit.

Irene kept in mind he hadn't done anything to hurt her. She sat in the scooped chair. The metal chair conformed to her body until it hugged every inch of her. Her stomach fluttered as she leaned her head back against the metal. Irene closed her eyes. Her body tingled. Pressure descended over the middle of her forehead like warm water being poured over her. Something wet shot up her nose. Ace's reminder about not struggling flashed through her mind. She balled her fists into the fabric of her jeans and tried to hold her breath. The substance poured down her sinuses and spread over her face. The jellylike material filled her throat. She opened her mouth to scream as the liquid came over her face and flowed down her neck. It had no taste, but felt like she was encased in gelatin.

Irene opened her eyes and tried to see Ace, but everything was hazy. The substance squished between her fingers. It warmed her. When she took in another breath, she could even breathe while the gelatin was in her throat. The butterflies in her stomach eased a bit. A white light flashed over Ace. His back straightened and his toes twitched. Irene closed her eyes and felt the light hit her.

Heat seared her body, but it faded until a cool breeze wrapped around her. She inhaled peppermint and chocolate, the same odors she smelled around Ace. A warm hand caressed her cheek. It didn't feel like she was sheathed in some gelatinous fluid.

"Open your eyes," Ace whispered to her.

Irene obliged. Instead of the room they were in, she found herself surrounded by tall trees. Sunlight streamed in through the leaves. Dust floated in the sunlight like particles of glitter. The leaves were greener than anything she had ever seen before. Water babbled through a brook somewhere close by. Ace remained in his alien guise. He slipped his hand along her cheek and rested it on her neck. The small motion of his finger along her flesh made her moan. It felt like he had touched all of her.

He ran his thumb over her bottom lip. It was as if he stroked her clit. Irene held in the whimper as she grabbed Ace's arm to stop herself from collapsing.

"What the fuck?"

He laughed and pressed his mouth to hers. His tongue sought entrance. Irene could taste the cinnamon of his lips. The kiss pulled the breath from her body. Her entire being lit up. Their tongues met and she lost herself in his embrace. She didn't want to be parted from him. Ace ran his fingers down her arms. Tingles shot all along her body. He squeezed her ass. She ran her fingers along his chest, feeling the muscles underneath. Irene tugged at his shirt, but he took her hands and pulled them away. She tried to touch him again. The mint aroma of him drove her crazy. She needed to taste his lips one more time and get a deep taste of the cinnamon. What would his body feel like while she rode him?

God, why am I thinking this way? "What's going on?" Irene asked, trying to fight the compulsion to be close to him.

Ace smiled. "I knew this would work, but I wanted to be sure."

"What is this thing doing to me?"

"It lowers your inhibitions toward me."

"It makes me think you're sexy?"

He chuckled. "No. If you're drawn to me already, then it heightens your attraction. It pushes away any doubt or fear you might have. It lets you experience your desire without any guilt. It does the same for me. The modules link us telepathically, so we experience the same mindscape. Even with potential partners if the attraction is there, we don't have to be sexually aroused by them. It happens. I don't think you're having that problem. How do you feel?"

"It feels like I'm going to crawl out of my skin unless I touch you again. I need to..." She shook her head, not sure she could express all her feelings. The driving need had to be soothed. She ran her fingers through her hair and tugged on it hoping the pain would push the compulsion away.

"I know. It feels like you want to meld with me."

She nodded. "Something like that, if you could put it into words. What does that mean? Do we fuck now?"

Ace kissed the backs of her hands. The feel of his lips only made the burn worse. "We can if you wish, but it won't be quite the same as having me in the flesh."

"I don't care. Whatever this place is doing to me, I need you. Now."

He couldn't hide his shit-eating grin. "Let's change the scenery, then." He snapped his fingers. The trees disappeared. Around them the sky lightened into streaks of twilight and burnt orange at sunset. A cool breeze caressed her, carrying a slight scent of flowers on it. She looked down. Her clothes changed from T-shirt and jeans into a dark blue dress that hugged her curves. Her hair hung over her shoulders. The dip in the fabric showed off her cleavage.

"Where are my clothes?" Irene asked, not comfortable showing off all the skin.

"My landscape, my rules. You look magnificent." He took her hand and led her over to a bed. "You're beautiful, Irene. Don't think otherwise. Understand, I want you, more than anything, but I can't say how this will go once we get started. Even though it is in a sort of dreamscape."

The yearning in her had only increased. "I don't care. I'll take what you can give me."

"I was hoping you'd say that."

Ace cupped her breasts through the material of her dress. Irene moaned when he pushed her hair aside and nipped at her throat. His gentle nibbles turned into a harder bite. His bite brought her close to an orgasm but held her just on the edge. She whimpered. Her pussy throbbed with the need of him.

"Please," she whispered.

He stopped. "I can't wait to make you come. Your cries drive me wild. Even in here you taste good. I just can't drink from you in this place."

"You'll just have to do it when we get out of here."

"I'm going to hold you to that."

Irene tugged at his shirt, but he snapped his fingers again. In a flash, his clothes were gone. She chuckled and decided to explore the expanse of his flesh. Irene pressed her lips to his green flesh and flicked her tongue over his scales. They were as soft as regular skin. He was cooler than she was, but he tasted like cinnamon. Irene slid her fingers over his abs, feeling the indentations of his eight-pack. She learned the curves of his torso until she came to his smooth pecs.

She concentrated on placing small kisses over his back and had to stand on tiptoe to reach the nape of his neck. Irene sucked on his skin.

"Oh, God. Please. Stop," he begged her breathlessly.

"Why?"

"Because I don't want to lose control and hurt you."

"I don't care." Irene found the spot once more with her tongue and licked it.

Ace growled and pushed her down onto the bed. He straddled her and pressed his body against hers, so his cock pushed into her stomach. He growled something she couldn't understand. He snapped his fingers again and she felt the breeze on her naked flesh. Ace thumbed her nipple and cupped her breast. He took the other in his mouth and bit down on it until she trembled underneath him. All of her senses focused on him. They might be in some kind of computerized simulation, but it seemed real. Her feelings couldn't tell the difference as her brain tried to sort it out. Not that it really mattered because the pleasure working through her nearly made having him on top of her unbearable.

Ace pinched her nipple hard enough to make her cry out from the pain. He looked up and the skin over his face darkened a little bit. He shivered and then drew up from her and took in a breath. "Damn woman."

She reached for his cock, but he batted her hand away. "What?"

"I want to do you in the real world, but I'm going to give you what you asked for."

Ace rolled off her and took up her leg. He kissed one spot on her left foot and pressed the same place on her right. Each time he did, bolts of warmth shredded her nerves. She tried to move, but he kept her on the bed as he worked his way up her calves to her knees.

Irene whimpered. He flicked his tongue along her skin. His eyes met hers, and he gave her the sexiest grin. Her stomach quivered as the desire took hold. The bliss built within her like a cresting tide, but it never crashed over her fully. He brought her up to a point and then left her hanging. Irene's heart sped up. Her body ached for him.

She needed him inside of her to cure the ache. "What are you doing to me?"

"Making sure you know how much I want to pleasure you in the real world."

"I have an idea. Every place you touch leaves… almost an echo before you go onto the next one. It's like I can feel you already inside of me."

"I know."

He spread her legs wider, kissing and pressing the same spot on each thigh. Her pussy quavered. Her body wasn't her own. Each place he caressed felt like he was pushing all of her pleasure points at once. Prickles sped along her spine. She screamed, but he wasn't done with her. Ace slid his fingers inside of her and applied pressure along her inner walls. Stars appeared in her vision. She bit her lip to keep from crying out.

"No, let me hear you," he begged her.

Before she could question him, Ace flicked his tongue over her clit and the suckers latched on to it. The world exploded in a fleeting moment of pain. Ecstasy rocked her world and turned her spine to molten fire. Irene thrust her hips into him. She shrieked and broke down into whimpers. Time seemed to stop as he worked her clit at the same time, his fingers manipulating her inner walls.

"Please. I --" She wanted to tell him to stop, that she was sure she would have a heart attack. It was a struggle to breathe and think. Irene wanted it to go on, even if it wasn't happening to her physically. Her mind transformed it into a reality. Ace stopped. He released her and stretched out next to her. He placed a hand over her heart. Even the light weight of his fingers on her flesh caused her to gasp. With his other hand, he wiped away the tears she didn't know she'd shed.

"Was that good enough 'fucking' for you?"

She nodded, not able to speak yet.

"Good."

"It must not have done anything for you."

He trailed his fingers over her lips. "More than you know."

Irene winced and rubbed her temple.

"Are you okay?"

"Yeah, just a small headache. So what happens now? Do we have sex in the real world?"

He brushed his lips along hers. "We can, but you might want to recover a little bit. Kiss me and this simulation will end. We'll return to our bodies. You can relive this moment like it happened and know what's to come when I make love to you."

Irene wrapped her arms around his neck and pressed her body along his. "I can't wait."

"When you're back in your body, I can show you the rest of the ship if you want."

She nodded. "I'd like to learn more about you. I..." The pain in her head sharpened and made her stumble back from him.

A vee formed in the middle of his brow. She wanted to say something when the pain stabbed her temple. The image of the dreamscape wavered. She screamed and Ace went over to her. He said something to her, but she couldn't hear what he said. He took her face in his hands. His lips moved, but the pain only intensified. He brushed her face and lips, and then the world went dark.

* * *

Irene opened her eyes and looked into his blue-green ones and saw his relief.

"You're awake. I wasn't sure if you would wake."

The light hurt her eyes, but the stabbing pain had left her temples. She was lying on something soft. Her fingers brushed over smooth, cool fabric. Ace ran his fingers over her cheeks. His gentle touch stirred her desire from their shared experience. She tried to sit up and kiss him to taste his lips once more, but he held her down.

"Whoa. You need to rest a bit more. Then I can take you back to the planet. I have to make sure the nanos are working."

"Nanos? Didn't you try those before?" Irene asked him.

"I did, but those were temporary. These, I'm afraid, are a bit more permanent. There can be some side effects from the Stimulation Chamber. It happens sometimes when subjects aren't completely compatible with it unless they're implanted with a Suppression Module first. I hoped it wouldn't be necessary with you."

"I have no idea what you just said."

"Don't be mad at me when you see this." He held up a small reflector and pulled back her hair on her left side. Ace tapped something behind her ear. "We use these on our Plasma Units. They can be used to control them, but it's also a hub for the nanos in your blood. They'll keep you healthy. The nanos repaired the damage to your brain. The implant can't be taken out."

Irene touched the small silver disk the size of a dime and felt the coolness of the metal. It was hidden right at her hairline so no one should see it behind her ear. She couldn't see it when she put her hair down.

Irene glanced at Ace. His expression had deepened with worry. The experience she had in the Stimulation Chamber flowed through her as her body recalled the sexual encounter. Her cheeks flushed at how he made love to her. Irene didn't feel any guilt associated with it. Her need for him remained, but it wasn't as nearly as overwhelming as it had been before.

"What happened exactly for you to do this to me?"

"I have Drean running diagnostics. He thinks the moon quakes caused a short. It disrupted the psychic link between us and caused some feedback unsatisfactory for your brain chemistry. If you had the nanos, they would've offset the interruption. You had a seizure. I broke contact as soon as I felt your pain. You were unconscious for a couple of hours as the nanos repaired the damage. Do you feel any different than you did before you went in?"

Irene could hear the panic in his voice.She took a second and thought about how she felt. Her body felt fine. She didn't have any aches and pains.

Ace was out of focus. She took off her glasses and could see clearly. "What's up with my vision?"

"The nanos must've fixed your eyesight, too. I can reprogram them so you can wear them again if you want."

She shook her head. "I'll have to think about it. Sometimes I forget to take them off and wear them in the shower. It's quite funny."

"I'd love to see you all glistening and soaped up." He touched her hand. "What do you say?"

"I say you need to wait and tell me about why this device is different than whatever you injected me with when I first met you?" Irene asked.

He touched his ring. "This can insert pre-programmed nanos into a human to wipe out a person's memory for a few hours but doesn't impair their judgment. Like I showed you with the videos so you could see I was a gentleman."

"How do you program them? Nanos must be microscopic."

"I place the ring on a module here on the ship. From there I can program them. Are you still mad at me?"

"No, I'm not mad, but I think it's time I get back to Earth. This has been an interesting date." She trailed her fingers over his chest and back up along his neck. He shivered and a small moan came out. The sound of it made her shudder so much she wanted to hear him do it again.

"Would you like to go out with me again?"

"I'd be game for dinner and a movie next time. Maybe even seeing you naked in real life. My place?"

"Would next week work? I have a couple of shows in Chicago. You sure you don't want to come with me? I could make it worth your while."

"Giving me some space is probably a good idea, so I'm not ripping your clothes off and wanting to fuck you like there's no tomorrow. I'm not sure your screaming fans would appreciate me hanging on your arm."

"I don't care what they think. The ship is charged up now so we can leave if you're feeling up to it."

"I am."

Ace helped her up and escorted her through the ship back to where they came aboard. Ace wrapped his arm around her and held her close. "Ready?"

"Yeah."

Chapter Six

"Have you seen the photographs that came out in the papers last night?" Bev rushed into the bookstore and pushed aside a customer who stood at the counter.

Irene glared at her friend. "I'm sorry, sir. Thank you for coming in. Someone will give you a call when your order arrives."

The man nodded and shot a dirty look at Bev. He left and Irene focused back on her friend who had barged in. Irene stretched. She had been on her feet all day and her back ached. They had been unusually busy for most of the day.

"Did you get contacts?" Bev asked.

Irene touched her face where her glasses had been. She still hadn't gotten used to not wearing them. Her date with Ace seemed like a lifetime ago, but it was only a couple of days. It didn't seem real learning he was an alien who transported her to his spaceship on the moon. She resisted the urge to touch the device he implanted.

"Yeah. They came in the other day. Been meaning to try them."

"I like you better with your glasses. Makes you nerdier like you belong in a library. I still don't get why you work in this dive."

"Why the hell are you here, Bev? I don't need your insults anymore. I thought you got the message at the concert to leave me alone." Irene didn't know why she stayed friends with Bev. Bev hadn't bothered to call after the concert to check on her. *She wants something, or she's here to gloat.*

"You bitch. You've been holding out on me."

Irene rolled her eyes. "I have no idea what you're talking about."

"Sure you don't!" Bev tapped her phone screen and showed it to Irene.

Irene's eyes widened. The phone showed a photo of her and Ace outside of his house when he was leading her out to the car. The image of her and Ace kissing with the headline *Rocker Seen With Mysterious Woman* got her blood boiling. Bev yanked the phone away and read the story.

"'Rocker Ace Hendrix is caught with a strange woman. Although not his usual fare, the identity of this female remains a mystery. What will his current flame say about this transgression? Ace, known for his flamboyant shows, outlandish style, and outspoken ways, has never been shy about whom he dates. While this Grammy Award-winning artist will surely sing about his current fling, for now all we can do is speculate as to who she is, because she certainly doesn't fit his normal tune.'" Bev finished reading and gave Irene a knowing smile. "What's he like? How well does he fuck? I've heard he's fantastic in bed."

Irene gritted her teeth. The bell above the door rang and she glanced up, expecting a customer. Instead a man holding a large vase of flowers and a small stuffed cow sleeping on a crescent moon came in. "Ms. Beckham?"

"Over here," Irene announced.

The delivery man set the gifts on the counter. "Sign here, please."

She signed the tablet he held out and he left the shop. She ran her thumb over the brown-and-white cow. The strong floral scent made her sneeze. Large white and yellow mums were mixed with red roses, purple lilies, and lavender.

"It has a card. They're from Ace, aren't they?" Bev screamed as though the flowers had come for her. She snatched the card from the plastic holder before Irene could get it. Bev danced out of her way and kept Irene from grabbing it as she came out from behind the counter. "Dearest Irene, I enjoyed our night together. See you in a few days. Saw the cow and it reminded me of our trip. Love, Ace." Bev held it to her heart. "I can't believe it. Where did he take you? You have to give me details."

Irene wrestled the card from her. "I don't have to tell you shit. What happened between me and Ace is private and doesn't need to be broadcast. Bev, you only come around when you want something. I always seemed to be twisted around your little finger, but enough is enough. Leave me alone and get the hell out of here."

Bev's mouth hung open. It felt good to get it out. Bev's face got as red as the roses in the bouquet. She threw the envelope at Irene and got into her face until they were almost nose to nose. "You don't want to make an enemy of me, little girl. I can make life difficult for you. If you think you can sweep me aside, then you have another think coming."

"You don't run my life. Get. Out!" Irene pushed Bev away. Bev's eyes narrowed like she wanted to say something else, but she walked out of the shop.

It wasn't until Irene got home that she was able to enjoy the flowers and the stuffed animal. She touched the nodule on her neck. It made her long for Ace. He would be back from his tour in a few days. She thought back to the time they spent in the Stimulation Chamber. Every time she did, her body hummed from the memory of their time together. The itching need to touch him and bathe in his unique scent overwhelmed her. She curled up on her bed. The article made her cringe and feel a bit of doubt even though Ace assured her he was into her. She didn't want to think about it. However, someone had gotten the photograph. It enraged her that someone had invaded her privacy. She wanted time alone to savor Ace. The short time away from him hurt her heart.

Irene rolled her eyes and realized she loved Ace. She lay back in her bed and felt her phone vibrating beside her. She didn't answer it the first time. The private number called again. She gritted her teeth and answered.

"Whoever you are, it'd better be good. It's late and I'm not in the mood today."

"Whoa! I was calling to see if you liked your flowers?"

"Hey, Ace. They're beautiful. I wasn't expecting them, considering --"

"Considering I took you to the moon, I thought flowers and a stuffed animal might be the best way for you to remember me."

Her insides melted at the comment. "You didn't need to get me a stuffed animal for me to remember you. You've made quite an impression already."

"Well, then, would you mind if I came in? I'm starving and you did promise me dinner and a movie."

How can he be outside? Soft rapping started on her front door. She rushed over and unlocked the door. The moonlight centered him in its light like a spotlight. He flashed her a smile and caught her with his intense gaze. "What are you doing here? I thought you had a couple of shows and --"

Ace stepped inside and pulled her close. His lips found hers in a searing kiss. She lost all sense of herself. Irene was in heaven as his tongue pushed between her lips and met hers. His fingers dragged down her back as though he needed them to be one person. She reached between them and rubbed the bulge of his cock. Ace broke their kiss and moaned.

The sound hit her in a way she'd never experienced before. As the rumble moved through her, it made her want to press her skin against his. Irene clenched her thighs at how wet the sound made her. She shivered and tried to catch her breath.

"We should close the door," she forced out, trying to put a little space between them so she could think.

"Afraid we'll give the neighbors an eyeful?"

"I don't care about the neighbors, but the press might be lurking."

Ace closed the door and locked it. "Did you call them before I came over?"

"I'm serious. My friend came to the shop today and showed me an article. Here." She tapped her phone and searched Ace's name until the most recent article came up. Irene handed her phone over to him so he could read the article. His eyes lost the amusement as he scrolled. His gaze smoldered and his mouth turned up into a growl.

"*Pistra insa menda.*" Ace thrust the phone back at her.

Whatever he said, it didn't sound good. He ran his fingers over his ring and turned his fingers into a fist. Irene touched his shoulder. He turned back around and his hand came up, but he stopped before he touched her face. His expression softened.

"I-I'm sorry. I didn't mean... I wasn't going to... I lost myself for a second." He cupped her cheek.

"I kinda figured when I couldn't understand what you said."

Ace led her over to the couch. "I didn't realize I'd lapsed into my native tongue. The story... I don't know how they got the picture. They're vampires. They follow me around everywhere. It's maddening. I'm sorry you got caught up in this brouhaha of my life. I hoped for once I could have something normal."

Irene laughed.

"Aren't I entitled to a little bit of happiness?" His voice grew strained as he stared at her.

"No. I mean...you're a rock star and an alien. How could you think to have a 'normal' life? You deserve happiness. I wasn't laughing at that -- more about the situation. I'm sorry. What did you say in your language?"

Ace ran his fingers over his thighs. "I basically said, 'Those assholes.' You're right. I shouldn't expect normality. For a long time, I've accepted what comes with this lifestyle. Then I found you."

"I'm not important enough for you to throw away all you've built. The article's right. I'm not the type of woman who normally hangs on your arm. Can you see me walking down the red carpet with all those other celebrities? I'm not rail-thin and…"

He put a finger to her lips. "Hush. I don't care if the press thinks I should date a model or an actress. I see *you* walking beside me. It's where you belong. It's where I want you to be."

Her heart melted at the statement. "Ace… I'm not sure how this works with you being…"

"A rock god?" A corner of his mouth turned up, making him all the more irresistible.

"I wasn't going to say that."

"You were going to say alien."

"Yes."

"It works like any other relationship. Although I'm a bit different from other men, and I hope you'll keep my secret."

"I didn't intend on saying anything after you took me to your spaceship and probed me." She returned his smile.

"Technically, I didn't probe you. We did something like the Vulcan Mind Meld."

"Except you did it to find out how horny I was for you."

Ace feathered his lips along her jaw in a light kiss. Irene leaned closer to capture his mouth as she trailed her hands over his jeans. He took her wrists and pushed her back into the couch and straddled her. His mouth moved down her throat. She pushed against him hoping to feel more of his body. Her pulse thundered in her ears. She was surprised he couldn't hear it.

"What are you doing?" she murmured.

His teeth nipped her jugular. "I need you, Irene. I need you to scream my name. We can talk about the press and how we make this work later. I came here tonight to see you. I don't care about what other people say. You're my mate. You felt the pull between us in the Stimulation Chamber, and you feel it now. After our encounter, I've been dreaming about tasting you in the flesh. The nanos can bring other perks. I can read your mind. I can program them to make you feel pleasure like you've never dreamed."

The part about reading her mind felt like he had thrown cold water on her. She squirmed under him until she got her hands free. "Whoa. What do you mean you can read my mind? Have you been manipulating me all this time?"

He pulled away from her throat with a look of confusion. "No! I haven't been manipulating you. Everything you're feeling is all you. When it comes to reading your mind, well... I'm a bit out of practice with it. All I get is static when I try to listen in." He ran his fingers over his face. "Fuck. I've messed everything up. This wasn't how I planned on the night going." Ace got up and started to leave.

Irene gritted her teeth and stood up. She went to grab Ace's hand but tripped over her feet into him. He caught her. She buried her head in his chest and let her mind still and enjoy having him there. Being with him eased the growing yearning within her.

"I should go. It'd be best..."

The scent of him overwhelmed her. She could taste peppermint on the back of her tongue. "No. Forget what I said." Irene wrapped her hands in his shirt and flicked her tongue over his throat and caught his Adam's apple between her teeth. Ace groaned. This time the vibration went right into the pit of her stomach. The wave of pleasure made her bite him harder. Ace grabbed her shoulders and wrenched her away.

His chest heaved as he tried to take in air. "No."

"I thought that was what you wanted?" Irene couldn't understand the difference in him. "Isn't having sex with me why you came here? I'm certainly up for it." Her heart raced. She placed his hand on her chest as she tried to catch her breath.

"You don't understand. If I... if we... I could hurt you. I don't want your first time with me to be painful." He cupped her face and she saw the truth in his eyes.

She dug her nails into his hand. She felt like she was back in the Stimulation Chamber. "I don't care. I need you."

He lifted her chin. "Your heart is racing, and I can smell your longing. It wasn't like this a few minutes ago. Tell me what happened."

Her throat went dry. "I don't know for sure. I kissed you and you moaned. The sound..." Irene tried to tell him how it made her feel, but she the words seemed beyond her.

"Melted your insides and shot straight through you. You can't catch your breath or think straight."

"Something like that," Irene managed to get out. She slid her hand along his cheek. Feeling the smoothness of his skin helped soothe the yearnings building within her. She brushed her lips along his.

"I knew you were the one. You're feeling it, too."

"What?"

"Remember when I told you about hearing you moan and how it made me feel, like I knew you were one in a million?"

Irene tried to concentrate on what he said. "Vaguely." She kissed him again.

He took her hand placed it on his chest. "Focus for a minute. I know it's difficult once the realization hits. I can leave and we can..."

"No."

"Okay." He curled her hair back. "Let's go into the bedroom in case someone tries to peer into your window." Ace kissed the back of her hand. "You'll have to tell me where your bedroom is."

"Down the hall on your left."

Ace led her into the bedroom. Irene came at him to kiss him, but he remained at arm's length. "I'm going to get some water and then come back."

"Fine."

Ace left the room and Irene sank down on the bed. After he left, she felt a little bit more like herself. The yearning for him became bearable. She leaned back against the headboard. Irene didn't know what to expect about the coming night. The outcome hadn't been planned. She hadn't shaved her legs in weeks. She needed to take a shower, but it didn't seem like he cared. Ace wanted her. Part of her still couldn't fathom she was dating an alien.

Ace came back in with a couple bottles of water. He set them on the table and went around to the windows making sure the shades were closed and drew the curtains as well. Ace pressed his ring and the illusion around him vanished. "Are you better now?"

"Yes. Sorry. I don't know what came over me."

"I do. I told you it's why you're my mate. No one really knows how or why, but our species knows our mates by the sound they make when they whimper. It's the vibration. When it hits our body, it tingles the pleasure centers of our brain. You react the same way when you hear us. This is how I know you belong with me." He sat on the bed next to her, took her hand, and placed it on his chest.

"Close your eyes and tell me what you feel."

Irene closed her eyes. She didn't worry about the sound of the air or the noises outside. She felt the thud of his heart against his chest. Then... but it couldn't be. Another beat came after it. Irene pressed her ear to his chest to listen and heard the alternating beats of his hearts. He stroked her hair while she took in the strange sounds. Almost like two fighting bass drums. One whomped and the other struck back.

"Two hearts?"

"Yes. It's one of the differences between my species and yours."

"Besides you being dark green with six digits on your hands and toes? Not to mention the sucker on tongue you suck my blood with?"

"There's more. You sure you want to see it?" Ace unbuttoned his jeans. She got a peek of the bulge against his black briefs.

Irene slid her hand over his firm shaft. It twitched under her touch. "You sure it's not going to bite me?"

"It won't, but I certainly will, if you let me," Ace stripped off his jeans and briefs. Her eyes didn't stray from his dick. It looked like a human penis, but slightly thicker. He stroked his cock and moved down to his testicles. She counted three instead of two. "Do you want to know where to touch me to hear me moan again?"

She bit her lip. Her breath hitched as she thought about hearing him groan. He took her hand and slipped it over his testicles. She cupped them and felt their weight in her hand. Ace shivered.

"There's a ridge on my middle..."

She pressed along the indent she felt. Ace grabbed her shoulder and grunted.

"Not so hard."

"Sorry."

"It's okay. Rub slowly."

Irene watched his face as she rubbed his testicle and felt the tougher skin along his ball. Ace held his breath and let out a groan. Irene felt the sound from him as it hit her like being struck by a strong wind. It knocked her back. She bit back the growing yearning and tried to stay focused on not hurting Ace. She massaged him slowly until his knees buckled and he went down to the bed. Sweat trickled from his temples as he held onto control. She touched his thigh. Ace grabbed her hand and squeezed it while she caressed his testicle. Irene placed her other hand on his chest. Ace moaned once more. This time the sound shot straight to her sex. She clenched her thighs together. The orgasm hit her so hard she saw stars. Before she could come down, Ace's weight was on top of her. His lips pushed into hers in a hungry kiss. His hands grabbed at her breasts through her shirt. He thrust his tongue between her lips. A bit of pain hit her tongue and made her jump. She realized his suckers had latched onto her tongue before he broke away and worked down her throat. He struggled with the zipper on her jeans.

"I need you, Irene. I can't hold on much longer. I need to be inside you and taste you."

"Then do it."

His fingers delved under the thin material of her panties and found her clit. Irene pressed up against him. She moaned when he fondled her. Ace grunted and worked his lips down her throat, sucking in her skin. Irene moved her neck to the side. Pain hit her for a quick second as he latched on with his sucker. The sting faded as the pleasure took her while he drew blood.

"Ace," Irene groaned his name.

He stopped taking her blood and tugged down her panties until she felt the fabric give way. The look on his face was as if he didn't see her. She tried to touch him, but he snarled, widened her legs with his knee, and shoved himself inside her. He nestled his face between her breasts, over her heart. The sting of the pain came as he drank from her. Irene struggled to keep up with the rhythm he'd started. Each time he delved into her, he hit her clit. The ecstasy of the orgasm consumed her. His fingers gripped her hips as he impaled her. Irene screamed as another wave grabbed her. She held onto his shoulders to keep herself anchored in her body. Ace pushed into a few more times and slowed. He continued to take her blood until her fingers grew numb.

Once he stopped, a warm tingling flushed from her neck and rushed downward. She felt it hit her heart and then spread to her fingers. Irene gasped at the strange sensation. Ace looked up. His eyes had returned to normal.

"Are you okay? I didn't mean to be so rough. I'm sorry if I hurt you." He stroked her cheek and brushed his lips along hers.

Irene sighed as she snuggled against him. The warmth moved into her toes and receded. "I'm okay. Just a bit warm." She touched her neck where the heat came from. The metal disk on her neck remained cool.

Ace moved his hand over hers. "Is it hurting you?"

"No. I felt a heat from it move down my neck and into my body."

"It's the nanos rushing to heal any damage. I must've taken too much blood. I got a little carried away. I've wanted you so badly since I heard you groan in my dressing room. I prayed I wouldn't frighten you. That's why I sent you the flash drive so you would see I wasn't lying about not taking advantage of you."

"I guess your plan worked. Here we are."

He kissed the top of her head. "Here we are and I can't quite believe it. What is the press going to say about my new flame? They're going to want to dig into your life. I hope you're ready."

She looked into his eyes and saw the amusement. Irene walked her fingers over his pecs and noticed their smoothness. "You don't have any nipples."

"Didn't seem to bother you before."

"It doesn't. The press can dig all they want. I work at a used bookstore. I don't have any skeletons in my closet. Although Bev might try and dig up some dirt."

"She's the friend you were with at my concert? Nicole said Bev kept hanging all over her trying to get an invitation back to my house. She never once asked if you were okay. Why are you friends with her?"

Irene shook her head. "I'm not, actually. Today she came by the store at the same time as the delivery. She showed me the article in the first place. Bev wanted me to spill the beans about our night together. I told her to get lost and she threatened to make my life a living hell."

"Why do you tolerate her?"

"I met her at a sci-fi convention. We struck up a conversation and started to hang out. For a long time, I never minded being her tagalong. Slowly, I saw she used me."

"Good."

"You don't have to worry about her being in my life anymore." Irene kissed his chest and heard him sigh. The double beats of his hearts calmed her. Ace trailed his fingers along her back.

"Next time I'll be more in control. It won't be so unpleasant."

She looked up at him. "I enjoyed myself. Twice, I think."

"Twice! I must've been doing something wrong."

"You're used to your lovers having more than two orgasms?"

"Of course. I can make it so you can go all night or for days if I program the nanos correctly."

Irene felt her throat go dry. She didn't know what to say about having intercourse for days. All that came to mind was how sore she would be after days of sex. The idea didn't sound appealing. "I'm not sure..."

Ace chuckled. "Believe me... you'd enjoy it. We can

always work up to it."

"What about you? Do you have nanos, too?"

"No. They aren't compatible with my species. I can go for a long time without food as long as I have blood. Of course, the nanos would replace what I take from you. Therefore, we could go until you tire of me. We wouldn't be able to do it for a while, though. I have a string of shows I have to do. You sure you can't come with me?"

Irene sighed and lay back thinking about the opportunity. Traveling around with a rock star and having mind-blowing sex. It sounded exciting and she could get some time off. She hardly took vacations except when she went to conventions. *Pages'* owner was on her to get out into the world. She did want to know more about Ace being an alien and all. "Where are you playing?"

"The next leg of my tour brings me to England, Norway, Spain, Italy, then Eastern Europe. I was going to see Dracula's castle. It'd be great to share it with someone I trust."

"What about your assistant and your driver? They know what you are."

"Nicole and I aren't sexually compatible. I tried, but she doesn't do anything for me. Simeon's a dear friend. We have similar tastes, but I don't find him attractive."

"What happens to them when you decide to leave here?"

"You mean when I pack up the ship and head back to Tilleron?"

"Yeah. Ace, you can't be in the spotlight forever."

He leaned down and captured her lips. "No, it doesn't last forever. I have another five or ten years before I step away again."

"Again?"

"I've been here a long time. Ace Hendrix is my most recent persona."

"What's your real name?"

Ace yawned. "How about I tell you another time?"

Irene nodded, wondering who he had been in the past. She snuggled against him and felt his breathing even out. She wasn't far behind.

Chapter Seven

Irene opened her eyes to an empty bed. She half expected Ace to have left her during the night given that was what rock stars were supposed to do. Instead the aroma of freshly brewed coffee lured her out of bed. She tugged on her shirt and headed into the kitchen. As she got closer, she heard Ace talking to someone.

"What... oh shit!" Irene saw Simeon next to Ace showing him something on his phone.

Ace glanced up as she dashed back around the corner. He caught her arm, pulled her into him, and grabbed her ass. His mouth claimed hers in a panty-drenching kiss. Simeon coughed behind them until Ace broke away.

"Can't you see I'm busy?" Ace grumbled.

"Sorry, boss, but we have a tight schedule if you want to make the show on time. I did advise you, but..." Simeon shrugged.

Ace hung his head. "Fine. Give me a minute, will you, Si?"

Irene bit her lip as Ace's driver walked back into the kitchen. Ace backed her up against the wall. His cock pressed against her leg. He leaned into her and brushed her lips with a soft kiss. Irene wrapped her arms around his neck. He nibbled her ear as his hand slid down her side and cupped her breast. He didn't stop and went lower until his fingers brushed across her stomach and she squirmed.

"Ticklish?"

"Yeah."

"I'll have to remember that for later."

She poked his shoulder. "You think there's going to be a next time?"

Ace pulled back with a look of disbelief. "I thought you said... Wasn't it fun?"

She held back a giggle. "You should see your face."

"You'll pay for that." He wrenched her head to the side and bit down.

Irene trembled from the sudden pain. He dragged his tongue over her throat. She could feel the sandy texture of it and then the sting. Ace's lips locked to her neck as his fingers slid under her panties and found her slit. Irene groaned as he fondled her clit. She pressed into him as he drank from her. She raked her hands down his back and grasped his ass. He slowed his torture until she hovered on the brink. Irene cried out again. He took her hand from his ass and slid it over his cock. He bit down on her throat once more. Irene moaned.

"Don't you know what your cries do to me?"

She rubbed his shaft. "I can feel what it does."

"Ace, we really have to go. Nicole is outside," Simeon yelled back at them.

"Tell me you'll come with me."

"I can't. I have to talk to my boss. And, God, Ace..." Irene felt her legs go to jelly.

He held her up and kissed her lips. "I love it when you say my name."

"But you haven't told me your true name. How do you expect me to say your name when I don't know it?" She caressed his cock until he groaned. A tremor passed over her flesh. The orgasm hit her until she shivered and tried to hold on so she wouldn't be pushed over the edge. Ace stroked her clit and then took her lips one more time. Irene didn't care that his team was down the hall. She needed him again. His tongue sought hers and she let the ecstasy of their embrace take hold. He swallowed her groan and grasped one of her breasts until she could stand on her own. Ace rested his head against her forehead.

"It's not fair I have to go. You're leaving me with blue balls."

"I thought they were green."

"Very funny."

"Ace, are you ready?" a woman's voice called from down the hall.

"He's still a bit busy," Simeon replied.

Irene didn't want to let him go, but he couldn't stay.

"I'm coming. I have to go. Call me if you know you can come."

"I will."

"Good." He kissed her throat one more time. He tugged on her ear. "My real name is Avaran."

Ace headed into the living room to meet with the rest of his team. Irene snuck into her room and pulled on some pants so she could be halfway decent. She glanced in the mirror really quickly and tried to tame her brown hair. Looking presentable, she went back into the living room. Nicole held up an outfit to Ace, but he dismissed it. Irene watched, wondering if this was a glimpse into his life behind the scenes.

"Do you want to help?" Ace turned around and asked her.

Nicole grumbled and threw the clothes down. "I don't know why I put up with you."

Irene slipped between them and looked at the outfits Nicole had brought for Ace. Leather pants, vests, Ren Faire shirt rejects, and some ratty T-shirts she could have found at a secondhand store. She sorted through the choices and came out with a decent black shirt and a pair of not-too-tight jeans with a price tag on them.

"How can you spend this ridiculous amount on a pair of jeans?" Irene asked. "Five hundred bucks. Really?"

Ace shrugged. "Nicole does the shopping for me. I don't really keep track."

She poked him. "It must be great to have all the money."

"Are you ready to go now?" Simeon asked. "We do have a plane to catch."

"Yeah. Nicole, did you pack the rest of my travel outfits?" Ace asked.

"Always do. I know how you are." She crossed her arms over her chest and rolled her eyes.

"Good." Ace grabbed Irene and kissed her quickly before pinching her ass.

Nicole gathered up the discarded clothes and tossed them back over her arm. Simeon went ahead of them and Ace followed. He winked at Irene before going out of the door. Even as he left, she felt his absence. The echo of what they shared pinged around in her heart. She nearly went after him. Her heart sank as he got into the car. Irene knew she would follow him. But she had to check about taking her vacation. Her boss had always been getting on her about taking some time off. For the first time in a long time, she wanted to get away from *Pages* and see all the places Ace could show her. Nicole hovered at the front door.

"Is there something you forgot? Do you need help with the clothes?"

Nicole glared at Irene. Her smile faded. She threw the clothes down onto the chair and closed the door. She poked her finger into Irene's chest. "Just 'cause you're his new flame, don't expect to get all cozy with him. I've seen him with others before and it doesn't go anywhere. He's special and don't you forget about it."

She's jealous. Holy shit. "Look, Nicole. I understand you've been with Ace for a long time. Sure, you've seen a lot of women go through his life. However, I understand how special he is."

She laughed. "You don't know anything about him except what he wants you to see."

Irene crossed her arms over her chest. "If you're trying to protect him, then you don't have to. You don't have to be green with jealousy."

Nicole face went as white as her T-shirt. She seemed to

wilt as the realization of what Irene said to her. Her voice lowered. "He told you."

"He did more than that. You're close to him. I don't plan on coming between you two. You're his... well, he didn't exactly tell me your title, but I know he saved you and Simeon. I'm not going to reveal what he is either."

Someone knocked on the door. "Hey, you coming, Nicole? Because we're leaving." Simeon opened the door.

"Yeah, coming. I thought I lost one of his shirts. Irene was helping me look for it." Nicole gathered up the bundle of clothes and headed out the door. She shot a look back toward Irene that told her the conversation wasn't over. Bev and other fan girls wore the same look when it came to Ace. Nicole would protect him even if it killed her. Irene didn't understand the weird fascination people had with celebrities. With the public salivating at the smallest tidbit about their personal lives. If they said or did something wrong, people hyper-focused and it could tear someone up.

Irene watched from the window as they drove off. Believing he was an alien was difficult to sink in. She wasn't sure which way she enjoyed him better, in his human guise or as the dark green alien. Her fingers slid along her neck and touched the nodule along her hairline. It remained cool, but she recalled the warmth as it healed her body. The nanos had fixed her vision, so she could see clearly. They kept her body in a healthy state as Ace said they would. All another part of his mystique.

* * *

After showering and eating some breakfast, Irene headed into the bookshop. As she parked her car, she noticed a crowd gathered around the front door. *What in the world is going on?* Irene got out and pushed her way through the first few.

"It's her. The one Hendrix is dating."

A quick flash blinded Irene. She jumped back but hit

more people as they smothered her. Something went into her face. Irene put up her hands as another click came from a camera or a phone. She couldn't tell. With the keys tight in her hand, she hunkered down and worked her way toward the door.

"Tell us a little about yourself? Where did you meet Ace?"

"Have you slept with him yet?"

The questions bombarded her as she wedged the key into the lock of the shop door. Pulling the door open, Irene didn't bother to apologize to the riffraff. One tried to wedge his foot between the door and the frame to keep it open. He pressed up against the glass and yanked the door. The reporter gave her a wide and devilish grin. His blond hair stuck up from too much hair gel. His brown eyes gleamed with excitement. The expression irritated her. Irene glowered at him and pulled the door closed while he yowled in pain. She locked the door and rested her head against the glass as they continued to take pictures of her. Some cupped their hands and peered into the shop trying to see her.

"Having a good morning I take it?"

Irene jumped at the sound of her boss's voice. "What are you doing here this early? "

"I do own the place."

"Dennis on one of his business trips again, or were you bored living in your oversized house?" Irene set her purse behind the counter.

Traci's lips pursed. Her lack of an answer made Irene think it was the former. Traci might have enjoyed the luxury of a rich husband who funded her little shop, but from what Irene had gathered their marriage wasn't a happy one. Why they stayed together was a mystery to her. She wasn't one to judge.

"What's with the circus?" Traci gestured toward the door with her chin. She relaxed in her chair and turned back to the computer screen. Boxes of books sat around the desk.

"Nothing. You go on another shopping spree?" Irene picked up a few. From the swooning women and half naked men on the covers, she gathered they were romance novels. Irene stopped being surprised over the years when she came to the store to find boxes of books waiting to be added to the inventory. Most of the volumes they didn't have space for, but Traci kept buying books.

"I ran across another shop going out of business. I couldn't pass up the deal. You going to tell me about the spectacle outside? I haven't seen that many photographers and mongers since I was dating the Duke."

Irene leaned against the wall. "I'm going to kill Bev. She said she was going to get back at me. I'm dating Ace Hendrix."

"The rocker? I love him. I didn't realize he lived in town. What's he like?" Traci leaned over the desk waiting for Irene to dish out more information about her relationship with Ace.

"It's -- it's great. He's not what people think he is. I'm not much of a fan of his music, but then we ended up... and... well, this started the other day. He wants me to go on tour with him."

"Then you need to go."

"I can't take off. You need me here."

"Irene, you can tell yourself that all you want, but I can manage the store by myself. Go off and have some fun. All you do is go to your conventions."

"I don't know how long I'll be gone for."

"Do you love him? If you do, then you're going to have to learn to put up with that mess out there a whole lot more."

"I love him. I can deal with it."

More pounded on the door. "If you don't go, then I'm going to have to fire you because I can't have them camped out in front of my store. They'll impede business. I say you sneak out the back and go home to pack."

Excitement bubbled in her stomach as she thought about what she was going to tell Ace. "Thank you, Traci. I don't know when I'll be back."

"Give me a few updates on where you are and how it's going. There's always a place here for you."

She hugged her boss and ducked out the back. She didn't expect Traci to let her go so easily but wasn't going to argue. As Irene slipped out, she dug into her purse and pulled out her phone, ready to text Ace about being able to come with him at least for a while.

"There she is. Ace's new squeeze." The reporter who had stuck his foot in the door lingered by the back door. A flash went off in her face again. She gritted her teeth as he rushed her.

"Is it true you've been his secret lover for years and you have a lovechild?"

Irene stopped in her tracks and glared at him. It took everything in her not to hit the guy. Instead she smiled and endured him taking more pictures. She took out her keys and headed toward her car. "I don't know where you get these absurd ideas. No comment. Please let me get to my car."

The reporter sidestepped her. She got to her car, but he wasn't done with her. "My sources are pretty reliable. Wait until I let it slip Ace's new sidepiece is friends with the notorious Traci Waller."

She stared at him, not sure notorious and Traci should be put in the same sentence. "I have no idea what you're talking about." Before he could fuel anymore rumors, she got into her car and drove back to her place.

Someone had given her up. Traffic gave her time to mull over who that might be. One name kept popping into her head. Her stomach churned and her knuckles were white on the steering wheel. She fumed. At least when she pulled into her driveway, no one waited for her. She got inside and took a few minutes to calm down as she pulled up Bev's number. Bev's voicemail picked up.

"You bitch! You told the reporters where I worked. They know where I live and think Ace and I've been lovers for a long time. One way or another you're going to get what's coming to you." She hung up and settled on what she had to do next.

She had to pack, but first she had to get a hold of Ace. Irene had no idea where he was now, but she had to try. She ran her hand through her hair. Her fingers caught on the nodule at her hair line. She tried to get her fingernail underneath it but couldn't. Ace was right; there was no way she could take it off. She took up her phone again and called Ace but got his voicemail instead. Hearing his voice calmed her anger.

"Hi... umm... I got the okay to come with you. I'm not sure where you are now, but I wanted to let you know. Call me when you can."

Irene waited to hear back from Ace, and she started packing. When she had her bag full, she needed to find her passport. The last time she had put it in one of her storage boxes in her second bedroom. She found it buried underneath a sack of clothes she had set aside for the next convention. By the time she got it out, she discovered a couple of hours had gone by. Irene checked her phone and saw several missed calls and voicemails. One from Bev. The rest were from Ace.

"I asked you to share and you told me to take a hike. You deserve all you get. Have fun!" Bev's voice grated on her nerves and confirmed she leaked where Irene worked to the press.

She held her breath and pressed play on Ace's first

message. "Irene, Ace needs your help. You must come to the house immediately." The voice was the computerized intelligence she had heard on Ace's ship. Panic hit her. "Please, he should've arrived on his plane, but I haven't been able to reach him on his communicator. I fear something's happened to him. Dial me back and come to the house."

Irene's stomach turned as she listened to the panic in the Drean's voice. She had no idea where Ace would have gone. As far as she knew, he was supposed to be getting on a plane and flying out to his next show. Something had to have happened to him between him leaving and him going to the airport. Irene didn't even listen to the third voicemail. Instead, she called the phone back and waited for Ace's voicemail to pick up. After the third ring, a series of clicks and beeps sounded on the other end of the phone.

"Irene, you got my messages. I can't locate him. Have you seen him?"

Irene took a breath as she feared the worst. They had gotten into a car accident or his plane had crashed. Certainly, it would have been all over the news by now? "D-do you know if he's still alive? Aren't you connected to him?"

"He went missing after he left your domicile. All contact with him ceased within a half an hour of him leaving you. He never made it to the airport. I have scanned all your news outlets and haven't detected any broadcasts of his demise. I can't raise Simeon or Nicole. You're the only other I'm connected with which is why I reached out to you. Sometimes there are dead zones he travels through, so I did not worry about it until he gets out of them. However, he hasn't reemerged."

"If he's dead and you know there's a void with him, then shouldn't you be able to tell about Simon and Nicole?"

"I've tried pinging their nanos and have gotten back a minimal response so I know they're alive, but I can't get anything on Ace. Not even on his ring. Will you come to the house? I can bring you up to the ship and you can help me from there." Drean's voice sounded as though it was seriously concerned for Ace.

"I'll be there as soon as I can. Tell me one thing, though. How are you talking to me when you're on the moon, anyway?"

"I'm able to access the Earth's satellite network. Through that I can extend my awareness, and I have the frequency of Ace's cellular phone I can tap into."

"Can't you trace it? Most cell phones have an app where you can locate a phone."

"I already tried. Come to the house so I can bring you up to the ship. It will be easier than having to explain all this when I can show you."

"I'm on my way." Irene hung up, not sure she wanted to even think about going back into the transportation device. It wasn't a great ride. The thought of going a second time churned her stomach, but locating Ace was her main concern. She had to find him. If his spaceship couldn't trace him, how was she going to be of any help? That didn't mean she couldn't try. She would do whatever was in her power to make sure Ace was safe. Irene slipped her phone into her purse and then headed over to Ace's house.

She pulled up and the gate opened automatically. She wondered if the computer was tapped into the house's security system as well. Irene tried the door and found it was locked. She walked around the back of the house and tried the back door in the garden. A small lens above the door winked at her as the camera caught her image. Irene heard a click and then the door popped open. Once she got inside, a blast of cool air hit her.

She caught Ace's scent. It warmed her heart and made

her ache for him. Irene made sure the door was locked and headed downstairs to the music room. Irene ran her hand over the piano keys. The vibration of the keys thrummed through her. It reminded her of how his voice turned her on.

The chord died. Her eyes watered. To think she had thought he was some pop airhead who sang whatever songs he was told to. He might have lived the persona, but there was so much more under the mask. Ace had wowed her with his kindness at the concert when he helped her with her broken glasses. He wielded a power over her body she didn't truly understand even if he explained about sound and vibration. Irene wiped her eyes. Warmth radiated down her neck and into her right arm. The wall toward the corner glowed. She hesitated and then placed her hand over the illuminated portion. The wood melted way to reveal the gray metallic room. The warmth retreated from her hand. Irene slipped inside. The wall reformed. A flash of light tingled her skin and made the hair stand up. She didn't have anything to hold onto this time. She closed her eyes and held her breath as the floor dropped out from underneath her. She reached for the wall, but when her fingers brushed nothing, she nearly lost what was in her stomach.

The rush stopped, and her ears popped.

Irene took in a deep breath, feeling a bit lightheaded.

"Good, you made it," the computer's voice said overhead.

Opening her eyes, a transparent male figure stood before her. It was dressed in a white suit with blue hair and eyes to match. Drean's face had human features, but she couldn't make out a particular expression. "Are you sure I made it in one piece? I don't feel like I'm fully here. Or maybe I am, but..." Irene tried to stop her legs from shaking and stumbled through the hologram.

"Here, let me help you up." A firm hand grabbed her

arm and steadied her. "It can take a minute to orient after the transport. Do you need any water?"

"No, I'm fine. I need you to explain what's going on and why you can't find Ace and the others."

"Of course. Follow me to the Viewing Chamber."

"You're taking me to the sex chamber again? Did Ace set this all up?" Irene felt a little bit irate at the thought Ace had orchestrated all this to get her back onto his ship.

Drean chuckled as he winked out. "No. That's the Stimulation Chamber. Follow the lighted panels." The door opened and a panel along the right wall lit up in orange.

Irene followed along the highway and then turned right. It felt like she rounded over a dozen corners and climbed down and then back up via ramps and doorways until the orange panel stopped in front of a door. It slid open. Inside she found a floating model of the Earth. The globe would have filled her apartment.

"Can you make this smaller so I can interact with it?"

The globe shrank down as Drean reappeared next to the spinning Earth. The sphere ceased its rotation and stopped before her where a big red dot was. "The dot is my last read of Ace's position." The picture widened and went closer to the red mark until she could see the actual street and the car Ace had left her house in. She brushed her fingers over the image and felt the jolt of the current.

"So you know he was in his car and then the vehicle stopped moving? Is this a real time photo since you said you could tap into the satellites?"

"Yes, it's a real time photo. The auto hasn't moved in several hours. I thought something might've happened or Ace went back to your house. When you didn't answer your communication device, I began to worry about him."

"I'm sorry. I don't know where he is. I left him a message I'd be able to go on tour with him. I don't even know where to look for him or any of the others. You have access to the house's security system. Did you see anything in the house? Can you look into Simeon's home as well?"

The hologram shook his head. "I don't have any viewing capability into his domicile. Do you think they could be there? Or maybe at Nicole's?"

Irene shrugged. "I have no idea where he could be. I mean... if the car is still there, then..." She looked closer at the satellite photo. "Can you wind back the footage until you lost them? Maybe we can find when they got out of the car."

The images rewound until they blurred. When they stopped, she could see Simeon, Nicole, and Ace getting out of the car. They walked toward the corner of the street and stood there for a few minutes until another car pulled up. It went down the street, and then in a blip it disappeared from the image.

"Where did it go?" Irene asked.

"I don't know. I can't detect anything because the signal goes blank."

"What do you know about Simeon and Nicole? Would they ever do anything to hurt Ace?"

Drean sighed. "Nicole has been with Ace since the 1950s. He went out to a club and watched her perform. Later that night, he found her in the alley. A few men had had their way with her, and she was in a bad way. He made sure they paid for what they did and saved her life by injecting her with the Suppression Module with the nanos. She's been with him ever since."

"Does he know she's in love with him?" Irene asked.

"I have expressed my concern about her behavior, but he brushes it aside. They tried to be lovers, but they weren't compatible. She's been fine these past few years."

"Would she and Simeon want to hurt Ace?" Irene asked, thinking of where they might be. "What about

Simeon?"

"He's been loyal to Ace ever since Ace rescued him from a bear attack over a hundred years ago. They've been friends for as long as I know. Both have been up here and know what Ace is. I don't think Simeon would ever hurt Ace."

"Are you sure about that?" Irene didn't know the bodyguard well, but he had seemed like he was loyal. Irene stared at the picture and couldn't think of where they had gone. It could have been anywhere since the car disappeared. Her hopes sank knowing she was wasting time being up in the ship. "I'm not doing any good up here looking down on Earth. Do you know where Nicole lives? Ace said Simeon lived on the property."

"I have sent her address to your communication device."

"Thanks. Do you know of any technology able to block Ace's signal?"

Drean shook his head. The lights dimmed and the hologram winked out. "Nothing on Earth."

"Okay. Well, I'm going to check out Simeon's and Nicole's places. I'll let you know my progress."

"Good. We'll get you back to the planet as soon as the transporter's recharged."

Chapter Eight

Irene's stomach still roiled after landing on solid ground. She sat on the stone wall in Ace's garden and let it settle. Once she felt better, she headed to the back of the property, following a map she found on her phone along with Nicole's address. A smaller dwelling no bigger than a shed nestled among the foliage. She peered into the window and didn't see anyone. She tried the door and found it to be open.

The small living room was tidy. She crept down the hallway, peeking into the miniscule bathroom, and then into his bedroom. Clothes were thrown everywhere. The bed was messed. The drawers in the dresser hung open with more clothes thrown over the sides as though someone had gone through them. Irene trod carefully as she went deeper into the bedroom and spied the closet. She ducked inside and found shelves were gone through as well and clothes on the floor. Throwing aside a few shoes, she found a picture frame.

She pulled the frame out and looked at the picture. Inside was a faded black-and-white image of Simeon, Ace, and Nicole. Simeon's face was turned toward Nicole almost as if he were going to kiss her. Ace seemed oblivious. The glass of the picture had smudges on it. The wood grain around the edges were smooth. Someone had gazed at this photograph for a long time and held it. Simeon was in love with Nicole. It was clear in the picture. Nicole didn't return the feelings, at least not that Irene could tell. Even Drean had been aware of it.

She studied the picture. In the upper right corner, she caught a glimpse of a sign. It looked somewhat familiar. Irene pulled the picture out of the frame. The sign's shape was something she recognized. At least what was left of it attached to a building on the outskirts of town. From the appearance of Simeon's closet and living room, something had triggered this. *They wouldn't take Ace away from his tour, would they? He's their meal ticket. If he disappeared, then people would talk. The news would be all over it.*

Irene left his house with the picture and headed to Nicole's as her heart sank. When she pulled up out front, the house didn't fit the neighborhood. It was the only ranch-style dwelling amid newer sprawling, three-story houses. The yard was neatly cut. A bed of roses grew under the front window. She pulled into the driveway and her phone buzzed. A text from Drean.

Have you found anything?

Maybe. I'm at Nicole's. Do you have any news?

Nothing.

She bit her lip and looked at the photograph, then typed. *Try looking in the area of Nicole's old club. I found a picture of them in front of it.* Irene took a photo of the picture for Drean to see. *Let me know if you find anything.*

She shoved her phone into her pocket and got out of the car. Glancing around the neighborhood, she saw an older man walking a dog looking over at her. Irene turned back and heard a ball hitting concrete. She couldn't go inside the way she had at Simeon's. People would see her breaking a window. She didn't need to have the police called. She knocked on the door and tried the handle. Locked. Irene glanced around the garden bed. A rock with a plastic sheen. She grabbed the stone and found a key inside that had seen better days. Once the door opened, she slid inside. Nothing seemed out of place. Silence greeted her. The kitchen remained tidy. She opened the fridge and found a box of baking soda with nothing else. She pulled open the cupboards. Empty. Dread pooled into the pit of her stomach. Irene raced into the bedroom and found nothing out of the ordinary. All of it could be explained away.

She leaned back against the wall and shook her head. This was getting her nowhere. Her pocket vibrated. She checked her phone. Drean had sent her a message back. *I checked the area. I'm not getting anything.*

She groaned and nearly threw her phone. It was all a waste of time. Ace could be anywhere or dead. Her eyes burned. She texted back, *Don't know what else to do. Sorry, Drean.*

No. I'm getting a blank spot that shouldn't be there at all. Go check, Dream replied.

Irene slipped her phone back into her pants and headed over to the club. Drean sent her another map. About halfway to the club, the traffic slowed because of some road construction. Each minute ticking by knotted her stomach. She made it through the construction and could see the burnt-out club in the distance with the sign still clinging to the side. Half of the club remained. Drean said there was a blank spot. The car she'd seen while in the spaceship was parked on a side street a block away. She pulled up behind it. The vehicle was empty, but Ace's ring sat on the seat in plain sight. She tried the door and it was locked.

The air stirred. The scent of something burning caught her attention. She turned toward the aroma and saw a yellow flickering. Someone rushed across the street and into the club. It looked like Nicole. Irene didn't have time to investigate as she caught the aroma of gas. She raced back to her car and got inside. Before she could dial emergency services, the car rocked on its tires. The explosion made her cover her ears. Objects pinged against the metal of her car and cracked the windshield. Smoke engulfed her automobile.

Irene gripped her steering wheel as fear settled into the pit of her stomach. Her hands shook as her ears stopped ringing. The smoke and the grit cleared. Broken pieces of brick lay on her hood. Her phone dropped into her lap as she looked at the building. Nothing remained except rubble. All her hopes of finding Ace had been dashed.

Her phone buzzed. She glanced down through her tears and saw the text message from Drean.

Signal's gone. I detected a detonation. I've been monitoring the local emergency services. Leave. Head back to Ace's.

I don't know if I can. He's gone. I saw... I thought it looked like Nicole running into the building.

Come to the house. You won't want to be there when the press gets there.

Irene wiped her eyes. Drean was right. She couldn't be there. She couldn't watch them search for Ace or pull his remains out of the club. She could hear the sirens approaching. She started the car and headed back to Ace's house, although she didn't know what she would do when she got there. Except be in a place that reminded her of him and knowing he was no longer there for her to hold.

The door clicked open when she arrived, and she went inside. The house felt empty. Irene wandered around, ending up in his bedroom. She pulled out one of Ace's shirts from his closet His smell clung to it. She hugged the fabric to her and thought about Ace. He had changed her life. How could she return to her life after he'd opened her eyes? Her phone buzzed again. Drean had sent her another text.

You should look at the news.

She checked the Internet. The first thing she saw was the story she already knew to be true.

Musician Ace Hendrix is believed to be dead in explosion. Details are not yet available as to what caused the blast. It was widely known he had recently purchased the remnants of the old nightclub with hopes of restoring it.

Irene couldn't focus on more of the article, but it confirmed her worst fears. Her phone rang, but she ignored it since the number came up "unavailable." It kept on until she picked it up. "What do you want?"

"I was hoping you could come up to the ship. We can mourn together and then plan the future." The computerized voice sounded as though it had been crying.

"I'm sorry, Drean. I can't even think right now. I can't be here. M-maybe in a while." Irene hung up and raced back out to her car. When she got in, she didn't realize she still had Ace's shirt in her hand.

* * *

The world whizzed by, and she stayed wrapped up in her grief. People knocked on her door. The press left messages on her phone. Drean sent her text messages which she ignored. She couldn't watch anymore tributes thrown together about Ace or hear any more of his music. Most of what the radio played were his earlier albums. Irene could hear the progression in his music. His amazing vocal talent was wasted on those early pop rock songs. Every time she went online for some kind of distraction, fans had posted their memorials to him. Celebrities cherished him with, "What a great talent! He was lost too early like so many others." The pounding continued on her door as it did in her head. She got up to answer it. The headache hadn't left. Even with the nanos repairing her body, it came back. Guess they couldn't fix everything, like her heart.

"What do you want?" She pulled the door open. Outside was the reporter who had bugged her at *Pages*.

"I know this is a horrible time for you, but I wanted to see if you had a quote for me about your boyfriend's untimely death."

She rolled her eyes and shut the door, but it wouldn't close. His foot was stuck in the doorjamb. "Why won't you leave me alone? I have nothing to say to anyone. I want peace to mourn."

"Come on. One quote and I'll leave you alone."

"No comment. Get your foot out of my door and get off my property before I call the police."

"They might have some questions about why you

were at the scene of the explosion."

Irene stared at the reporter. She tried to keep her face a mask and not let her grief and shock show through. "I- I'm not sure what you mean."

He leaned in a little bit and smiled, showing her the gap between his teeth. "Of course, you do. You parked behind your boyfriend's car. You looked inside and then saw someone run across into the abandoned club."

"H-how do you know that?" she whispered.

"I'll tell you if you let me inside. I'll make it worth your while."

"I don't want any money."

"I wasn't offering any. We should compare notes. Don't you want to know why I was there?"

Her curiosity did make her want to know why he had been at the club. She hadn't seen anyone except Nicole dash into the building. *Where has he been hiding? Will he go to the police after if I let him in?* He could bring trouble for her if she didn't let him in. She opened the door and allowed him. He came in and glanced around her apartment.

"Tell me what you know so you can get out of my house."

The reporter took her hand and pressed it to his lips. Irene nearly pulled it away, when she noticed his ring. "You have an interesting ring. Ace had one just like it. I saw it on the seat of his car. Did you steal it?"

He chuckled. "There was no need to steal it. It's been mine all along. The one in the car was a fake."

"You're a groupie! You went into Ace's house and stole it. Or did it happen to fall off his finger?"

His lopsided smile almost reminded her of Ace's, but it tore her heart. He glanced at the ring and then back at her. "It didn't fall off his finger. It never left." The reporter ran his finger along her jawline. His expression softened.

Irene didn't know what to make of what he was telling her. She shook her head and stepped away from the man in front of her. His touch relaxed her a little bit. Irene caught the scent of peppermint. *No. He was blown to bits.* Tears slipped down her cheeks. "It's not funny. Trying to... twist my emotions when I'm grieving. Your type are all hungry for a story. I don't care why you were at the scene of the ex --"

His mouth connected with hers and cut her off. The lips were familiar, as was how he held her. His hand slid around her waist and pulled her close. She tried to fight him, but he tightened his hold on her. He released her lips and worked his mouth down her neck. Some of her will returned. She pushed against his chest to get him away from her. A sting moved down her throat. His lips locked onto her skin. Irene froze. Only one being could do that. His other hand held hers to his chest. Underneath her palm, she could feel the beating of two hearts.

"Ace. How? I don't...?"

He lifted from her neck and nibbled on her ear. Irene held in a groan as her heart melted. She tried to keep it together.

"Not Ace anymore. Ace is dead to the world. Call me by my true name."

"Avaran." The name spilled from her lips.

When he moaned, the sound hit her. She knew this was him when the warmth of the orgasm built within her. He pulled away before she could come. The form of the reporter fell away revealing the green-skinned alien she loved. Grief overwhelmed her. She pounded his chest as a wail came out. Irene screamed and hit Ace until he grabbed her wrists to stop her.

"It's okay."

"You asshole." She ripped herself from him and threw herself onto the couch. Rage engulfed her. She didn't know if she wanted to kiss him or kill him. "I saw the building explode. Drean brought me up to the ship to find you. He's worried sick... which is tough to believe since he's part of your ship or whatever... and then you pose as that horrid reporter. Have you been playing me this whole time? All this…"

"Was necessary after I realized what I wanted when I found you. After what you said to me. It made me think about a lot of things. If you let me explain, you'll understand." Ace took her hands and sat on the couch next to her. Feeling his touch eased the confusion beating within her soul. The whole scenario almost sounded like he was there to fuck her over the way her last boyfriend had.

"Then explain why you had to put me through this misery."

"Oh, love." Her heart warmed when he called her his love. "I never intended for you to witness the explosion or even have Drean bring you up to the spaceship. We originally planned this to happen after I returned from the European leg of our tour. However, Nicole announced her pregnancy. She and Simeon have been trying for years. She didn't want to go on the road in her condition. I heard what you said about being in the spotlight. How you felt you didn't belong and not feeling comfortable. I want you with me."

Irene shook her head. "Nicole is in love with you."

Ace chuckled. "She was a long time ago. Simeon's been after her since the first time he saw her sing. They finally got together. You don't have to worry about her."

"Good to know, but it doesn't explain you faking your own death and us spending time together." Irene pulled some lint off the couch cushion.

"I thought it'd be obvious. The only way we can truly be together is for me to not be Ace. And to be honest, I want to go home. I'm tired of having to hide who I am. Don't get me wrong. I love singing. I want to take you to

Tilleron and show you my home. It's not Earth, but it's beautiful."

Her anger drained away. "You want me to go into space with you? It almost sounds like you're asking me to marry you."

He scratched his head. "I guess in a way I am. Although you're my mate, so we're already joined. I've waited so long for you, searching the planets in hopes one of my Plasma Units might be the one. It never happened until I came here. What do you say?"

"It's a big decision."

"Believe me, I understand. I know what it's like leaving everything you hold dear behind. I can have Drean upload whatever books or movies you like. I can even have him keep a link open or something in this cave to record movies and beam them back to us. Granted it would take a while, but... You could still shop on Amazon or something..."

"How are you going to beam Amazon packages to your planet?"

He shrugged. "I'm sure I can figure it out. What do you say?"

"It's going to take more to convince me. If you were going to leave, then why even fake your death?"

"I like to have some closure. I know you're furious with me. It happened so quickly I couldn't tell Drean about it."

"He showed me the car and how he lost you."

"Yeah, I had to overload the ring so it created a dampening field. The nanos in Simeon and Nicole -- I stopped them for a little while. We planned this on a whim. You were never supposed to be in on this. Drean isn't talking to me, but I hoped we could make up." He took her hand and slid his lips along her wrist. His tantalizing gaze held hers. She lost herself with the softness of his mouth and then the sudden sting. Irene groaned. Ace stiffened at the sound. His grip on her wrist tightened. He drank from her until she touched his face. He looked up with a wild-eyed expression. The hunger still lingered. She longed for his touch. All her anger melted away because he was safe. She needed him more than she'd needed anything before. Could she give up her life and fly away with him? Even if she had a lifetime's worth of books and movies to watch, could she go to another planet? Could she even survive space? All the movies she'd watched made it look difficult. Ace's species were more highly advanced than humans. Maybe it was easier than it looked.

"Ace, I have to think about it."

"Can you think about it while I make love to you?"

A smile tugged on her lips as his hand inched along her thigh. "I won't be doing much thinking."

"That's the whole idea." He tugged on her jeans.

Irene stood up. She pulled her shirt over her head and tossed it away. His mouth dropped as he stood up and came toward her. She held up her hand. "I don't think so. If you want me, then strip."

"But…"

She crossed her arms over her chest. "No buts about it. You made me suffer. This doesn't even begin to make up for it. Now take off those clothes or you don't get to see any more of me." She slid a bra strap down until the lace of her bra folded over nearly showing her nipple. Ace's eyes grew bigger than platters. Irene undid her bra, dropped it to the floor, and walked toward her bedroom. Irene didn't know how to make him truly pay for how she felt, but she knew one way to get at him. Besides she needed to feel him close to her. Have his lips on her skin. She undressed and waited for him on the bed. A moment later, Ace stood in the doorway wearing nothing but his scales. He appeared to be some kind of strange god coming to worship her. He knelt before her. Ace placed his lips on her feet and kissed her toes. Irene tried not to pull away from the light touch of his mouth as his tongue flicked over her flesh. He moved up slowly to her ankle and switched to her other foot. She curled her toes tightly to keep from moaning. This was not what she had in mind.

"Is this what you wanted?"

"Not exactly. Stand up."

Ace stood up. She traced her fingers over his semi-erect cock. He watched her intently. Irene slid her hand underneath his testicles and found the ridge along the middle one. Ace grunted when she pushed against him, but he kept standing while she rubbed. Ace's eyes fluttered. His dick hardened. Irene knew she'd hit the right spot. She pulled his cock into her mouth and wrapped her tongue around the soft head. She inched her away long his shaft, feeling the difference in the pliable scales covering this part of him. He tasted like cinnamon and she only wanted to take more of him in, but she went slowly, wanting it to last. Wanting him to beg her to make him come.

Ace gripped her shoulder. His head fell back as she gripped all three testicles and squeezed them. She used her middle finger to rub the ridge that aroused him and two other fingers to massage its brothers. His shaft hit the back of her mouth. She grazed her teeth along the surface of his dick until a groan slipped from his throat. The tone raised goose bumps along her skin. Her heart raced. Irene stayed focused, her mouth inching along his cock, alternating with her teeth and with her tongue until his moans turned into hisses. Each time she came to the tip, he thrust his hips for her to go faster, but she ignored his pleas. Irene loved having this power over her alien lover. The act alone made her wet. Ace kneaded her breast, but she batted his hand away. He said something to her in his language expressing his unhappiness, but she didn't care.

Crymsyn Hart   Alien Vampires

This gave him an inkling as to how pissed she was.

He grabbed her hair and yanked her head back. "Please, Irene."

She grazed her teeth along his length once more, then brushed the ridge on his testicle one last time. Her gaze roved over his eight-pack and the defined muscles of his pecs. She trailed her fingers over the ridges and rested her hand between his two hearts. Ace took her hand and brought it to his lips. He nipped the flesh, but she pulled away from him.

"No."

"But I hunger for you."

"Good. Now get on the bed."

Ace sighed and settled back amongst the pillows. He seemed out of place against the white sheets with his cock resting along his stomach. Irene crawled over to him. He reached for her breasts, but she kept out of his reach. His pained expression gave her some satisfaction.

"No touching or I'm out, leaving you with blue balls."

"You wouldn't."

"Try me."

He rolled his eyes. "Fine. I'll play along, but you don't understand how tough it is for me to not take you."

"Oh, I know. Welcome to my life while you've been gone."

He didn't respond and made a point of sitting on his hands. Irene straddled him. She grazed her fingers down his cheeks before kissing him. His lips parted and he touched the tip of his tongue to hers. She wove her hands through his hair and deepened the kiss, tasting the cinnamon of his lips. Irene worked along his jaw and nipped at his Adam's apple. She sucked it in and nibbled on it. Ace jumped, but he moaned. The vibration hit her, and she almost lost her control in an instant. She yearned to be with him and have the closeness, but she could feel he was on the verge. His chest rose quicker. She could feel his hearts thumping.

Irene bit his shoulder and raked her nails along his back while she ground against him. Ace held his arms around hers and brought her in closer. "I told you…" She tried to shimmy off him, but Ace shook his head.

"If you don't let me fuck you right now, I'm going to hurt you. I can't…"

Irene wasn't ready to give up control. She moved a little until he slid his cock inside her. Ace pushed his hips up as Irene arched her back. Having him inside her made it all worthwhile. She started a rhythm between them as he moved his hands over her breasts and kissed between them. His tongue flicked over her flesh.

"No."

"I need to taste you," Ace begged.

"You can't always drink me." Irene rocked faster on top of him. He grabbed her hips and changed how fast she rode him. Each time he hit her clit, Irene lost all sense of self as she dug her nails into his shoulders. They moved together as Ace sought her lips. His hands traveled down her back and gripped her ass. He kissed down her throat where he bit her with regular teeth. Irene screamed, which made Ace pound into her. He nibbled on her ear.

"My beloved."

Irene buried her head into his chest as another moan came out. The longing speared her entire being. She lost her control as he kept moving inside her. Ace groaned, which only redoubled her pleasure. She held onto him as the orgasm rode her body and she tried to catch her breath. Their movements slowed until Ace pulled Irene down to him. He rested his head against her chest. Irene held him to her. She couldn't let him go. No matter where it would lead her.

Chapter Nine

Irene glanced around her house and thought about everything she had packed. Ace had told her to bring whatever she wanted. Clothes, memories of her life going to conventions, books, a few movies, were all stacked in the center of the room. Seeing it all piled together made her wonder what kind of a footprint she had left on the world. She told her boss she had to resign, but Traci didn't seem surprised.

Her phone vibrated. *Ready to go?*

I don't know about ready. Irene tapped out her response. *As ready as I'm gonna b. U gonna fly by and pick me up?*

LOL. The car's outside. Figured you want to take one more ride over to the house. I have a surprise for you, Ace replied.

She peered out of the window and his car sat waiting for her. A knock sounded on the door. She opened it to find Simeon. "Hello, ma'am. Ace is waiting for you."

"You don't have to call me ma'am. I think we're a little bit beyond that. I thought you and Nicole had kidnapped Ace and killed him."

He ran his fingers through his hair and his face turned red. "It was a last-minute plan. I'm sure he's told you that by now."

"He has. What are you and Nicole going to do? I mean... Sorry. It's none of my business really."

"It's okay. Ace is taking us back with him to Tilleron. We've been with him for a long time. He's my family since all of mine has died. We're going to settle in with him and you, if you don't mind. We can't exactly stay here with the implants. He could turn them off so we could age, but people could find out about us. We want to be safe. Honestly, Ace is as cool as hell. Why wouldn't we want to travel the universe with him and see sights no human has ever seen? Aren't you excited?"

"I want to be with him. When I thought he was dead,

it felt like I'd been cut in half. It means giving up everything I know, but I'm up for an adventure."

"Come on. Ace is at the house."

"I thought…"

"He asked me to come and get you. I think he wanted to put out some last minute recordings. He does it on occasion, letting some undiscovered music or songs into the world if he needs some money or to watch how the industry reacts." Simeon closed the door for her as she climbed into the car and got into the front seat.

"What do you mean over the years?"

"He hasn't always been Ace Hendrix. He's been a few other celebrity rockers."

"Anyone I might know?"

"You'd have to ask him."

"Another enigma."

"You've seen him play the piano. You should see him play the guitar. The extra fingers come in handy."

"Sounds like you admire him."

"I owe him my life, and we've become friends over the years. You're the one thing he's been searching for all these years. His mate. I don't fully understand how it works with his species even with what he's told me. Something about sound. You know that already."

She sat back against the seat and thought about what she had learned about Ace. What other musicians had he been? It deepened his mystery. They drove the rest of the way in silence. When they got to the house, Simeon let her out. The door opened for her so she went inside. The walls were bare as she walked toward the sound of the piano. Sheets covered furniture. She found Ace at the piano, playing. Her eyes teared as she listened. He set his fingers on the keys and smiled at her.

"My love song to you will be the last thing my fans will hear."

Her cheeks burned. "I'm not sure I know what to say."

"Do you want me to play it for you from the beginning?" Ace patted the bench next to him.

Irene sat down and touched his knee. "I'd love that."

The sad melody was the same one he had played before, but it sounded different when he sang.

> Into my arms you fly,
> Trapped in the cage we wove together.
> Drifting away toward the stars.
> Fly, fly away to be free together.
> Fly high until it all disappears.
>
> Melt into me, darling.
> Time to spread your wings and soar.
> I'll be by your side until it all fades away.
> Stars above call us home, reaching toward eternity.
> Fly, fly away to be free.
> Fly high until it all disappears...

The piano music continued as Ace hummed. The tune made her chest heavy with emotions she couldn't quite put into words. His eyes remained closed as his fingers flew over the keys. The vibration of the composition hit her as though she could actually feel his love in the song going from him and into her. *"Melt into me and drift away into eternity."*

The chords resounded in the room. Irene sniffled and wiped her eyes. "That was amazing."

"You like it?"

She wrapped her arms around him and captured his lips in a kiss. She hugged him hard. His peppermint-hot chocolate-cinnamon scent reminded her of winter mornings. She could eat him up. "The fans will love it."

He trailed his finger down her cheek. "I didn't do it as a last tribute to the fans. I did it for you."

"I know you did. I'm teasing. Simeon said something about you releasing other albums from the dead rock stars you used to be. Anyone I know?"

It appeared the scales along his face darkened as if he blushed. Ace looked away. "Sometimes I like to see how people respond to finding undiscovered tracks, and it's also good if I ever needed money."

"Did you run around impersonating Elvis?"

"No. You wouldn't believe me if I told you."

"Tell me."

"Buddy Holly and Jim Morrison."

"From the Doors?"

His smile widened. "Told you that you wouldn't believe me."

"Those are some pretty big names. How did you..." Irene shook her head, not sure she actually believed what he was telling her.

"I told you. I scarcely believe it myself after all the craziness. But that's the past and I want to look forward to a future with you." He held her to him. "Maybe even have a family if you want one."

"H-how can that be since we're two different species?"

"We're genetically compatible. I checked."

"Good to know. I hadn't even thought about kids, but we can talk about it."

"Are you ready to go?" Ace asked.

"I guess so. Are you going to do a flyby and pick up my stuff?"

"Something like that."

"What about your house and all your money? It's not like it's good in space."

"I've sold the house with the furnishings I'm not taking. All my money has been converted to precious metals and other materials that can be used for trading. I gave a lot of it to charity."

"I guess I'll be depending on you to support us, then."

"Does the idea bother you?"

"A little. I'm used to being self-sufficient. I want to

know what I'm going to do on a distant planet besides being your arm candy."

He kissed her again. "I like you being my arm candy. I'm sure there'll be things to do. We just have to get there. Trust me, okay?"

Irene stood up. "I do."

"Then I guess we'd better get going."

Simeon and Nicole came and went into the hidden room. A flash of light encompassed them, and they disappeared. Ace took her hand and led her into the room. He held her close as the static electricity encompassed her body and the world disintegrated around her. They appeared again in the transportation room. It was packed full of boxes and crates, along with plants and pieces of furniture. He pulled her out of the way when a flicker of light hit the room. His piano appeared.

"Now we can go. Come with me." Ace led her through the ship until they came to a room with modules around the sides. He pressed his hand against one of them. The floor opened up and a chair rose out of the center. He sat inside and rested his head against the back. "Once Drean fires up the engines, I won't be able to talk to you. I'll form a psychic link with the ship. It's how I fly it. Don't worry. I'll be with you after. Sit if you like and watch."

Another chair came up from the floor. Irene slipped into it as the ship rumbled around her. The screen opened before her showing only darkness. The vibration made her hold her breath. Ace's expression went blank. He gripped the arms of the chair and his body arched off the seat. She nearly went to him, but Drean appeared before her and held up his hands.

"No, he'll be fine. He has to acclimate. He hasn't been connected with me in this manner in a long time." Drean's form grew more solid as Ace's body returned to normal. She could actually make out features on the computer's face. Ace's forehead knotted in concentration.

"What's going on?" Irene asked the computer.

"He's probing the ship to make sure all systems are ready. I told him everything passed inspection, but he's stubborn. Hold on. It's going to be a bit bumpy until we leave atmosphere." Drean disappeared.

Irene could hear a hum. The screen remained black and she could feel they were turning. A loud scrape sounded above her. She cringed. The ship shook. It stopped after a moment and then she could feel them picking up speed. In an instant, the blackness cleared. In the view screen she could see land. They hovered over it for a moment.

"We've picked up your things," Drean told her.

"Thank you." Irene nodded, glad to know her belongings had come aboard. Earth grew smaller and smaller until it all but disappeared.

"We're going to have to stay near the sun and recharge our power cells for a while. Drean will let me know when we're at full capacity." Ace opened his eyes and rubbed his temples.

"Are you okay?"

"Fine. It's been a while since I've flown. Linking to the ship can be taxing. I need to rest a bit while we recharge. Care to join me?" His tongue flicked out and the end bloomed open.

"I take it you're a bit peckish."

"A little. We could both benefit from some downtime."

"You're a demon."

"No. I'm a green alien who wants to make you sing, beloved." He grabbed her and pulled her toward him. Irene wrapped her arms around him.

"You don't want to hear me sing."

He sighed and rolled his eyes. "Fine, then. I'll fuck you until you can't scream my name anymore."

She poked him in the ribs and trailed her hand between his legs where she squeezed his balls. He winced. "I think you'll be the one calling my name."

"Irene, I love it when you talk dirty. Come on, sexy, and light my fire."

She chuckled as he swept her up in a consuming kiss. In his arms she knew everything was going to be okay no matter where they went. They were free to fly through the stars together until they all burned out.

Planted by the Alien Vampire Scientist
Crymsyn Hart

When Abigail Pike goes hiking with her sister, she never expected she'd walk right into a seven-foot-tall green alien.

Jaril came to Earth to study its plants. He didn't intend to rescue a human when she falls and hits her head on a rock after she runs into him. To save her, Jaril must implant his technology in her.

Overcoming her fear, Abigail returns to the cave where she first met the alien. This time he's the one who's injured. The longer she's around Jaril, the more she's drawn to him, but Jaril needs to return to his ship to be healed properly.

Abigail doesn't want to give up her life on Earth, but she might not have a choice if she wants to be with Jaril. Whoever said understanding plants was easier than humans has never met a green alien vampire.

Chapter One

"Do you think this is a good idea?"

"We've had this discussion. I'll be fine. The lunar caves will keep you concealed. The humans won't be able to detect you hidden so deep beneath the surface."

"It's not me I'm worried about." Talix leaned against the ship's gray metallic wall and crossed her arms over her chest. Her solid form dissolved until Jaril could see the console behind her.

Jaril rolled his eyes while he gathered more instruments to take to the planet with him. He could always come back up for more. It offered more risk of exposure, though. The idea of all the various specimens he would encounter made him giddy. He scanned the instruments once more and decided he had enough devices to set up his habitat and lab on the planet. "I'll be deep enough in the cave the humans won't find me. The humans are primitive. I'll be fine."

"They're not as primitive as you think. Didn't you go over the manifests brought back by the other ships? The humans have new technologies. They are aware of us. They're planning on going to Mars. You're excited to delve into the vegetation of this puny world. I told you there are better --"

"Talix. Enough." He threw up his hands and closed the case. Jaril hefted it from the workstation and went into the docking bay where the scout ships were moored. He pressed his hand against the side of one. The metal melted away to reveal a door. He ducked inside and set the case next to the others. Jaril would be cramped with everything he was taking, but he preferred it to scattering his atoms. "Do you have the coordinates programmed into the navigation computer?"

"Yes, they're entered because we both know you're a horrible navigator. I'll be doing most of the flying."

Talix's image flashed inside the small ship. The instrument panel lit up and the pilot's chair glided backward for Jaril to sit.

"Yeah, I know I'm better with plants than living creatures."

"You don't have to tell me twice. This is still an isolated planet. We really don't..."

He glanced at the shaky image of his ship's computer. The artificial intelligence had been his constant companion as he went from one planet to another gathering specimens. He had all the different plant species cataloged on his home planet of Tilleron. Each time others of his race returned from their travels, they brought back data about the worlds they had visited or scanned. The last three ships which had returned from Earth had given him the idea to explore this particular planet for himself. Talix had tried to tell him to stay on Tilleron. He hadn't want to hear it. The idea of Earth was stuck in his mind. At the moment, they hovered near Mars.

"We're almost to their moon. We have the coordinates for the lunar cave where you will stay while I'm on Earth. You've programmed the route to the cavern in the planet where I'm going to park the scout ship. I don't intend to be bothered by humans. If I need to go out among them, I have garments to blend in along with our cloaking tech to keep me invisible if needed."

"Let's hope you do. How are you going to survive down there without any Plasma Units?"

"I'll find one among the humans as the others did. I have enough bottled substance to last me a while. If you're done, we're in range. I'll be fine."

* * *

The thought lingered in his mind as he replayed the conversation he'd had with Talix five months ago, before he arrived on the planet. The scout ship remained nestled deep within the caves of the mountain range. Jaril had parked it in an uncharted cave system. The underground caverns led up and into a lush forest area. Each day he discovered new types of vegetation. Each day Jaril ventured outward in the grid he'd set for himself, until his underground lab was full of different plants.

Jaril couldn't help but feel satisfied that he had amassed quite the assortment of plants growing under the lights in his cave hideaway. Many species he couldn't identify. The ship's database contained limited knowledge about all the different types of vegetation on Earth. He'd had Talix download several Earth books on botany to discover more about the plants he encountered. Others of his kind weren't as interested in properly naming and cataloging all the different species he'd encountered.

Seasons changed. A white blanket of snow melted away and gave way to spring. He discovered more signs of humans in the wild than he thought he'd find. So far, he hadn't had to interact with the primitive species except to observe them from a distance. As his stomach tightened and his veins felt stretched, Jaril glanced at the dwindling supply of plasma. He only had three bottles left. He hadn't anticipated the snow blocking the cave entrance and him being cut off from his home ship.

Jaril took one of the last three and opened the bottle. Once the plasma touched his tongue, his sucker bloomed on the end of it. He ached to latch onto a throat or a wrist of a donor, but he drank the life-giving substance down. It hit his stomach and rushed through his system easing the tightness in his veins. He would have Talix scan the population and find him a suitable donor. He finished the bottle and wiped the back of his hand across his mouth. A smear of crimson came away. Jaril flicked his tongue over it to catch the last drops.

With his hunger sated, he could return to testing the

soil and watching the flora. He had set up his sun lamps to help the plants grow and brought more of the native soil into the cave. The one thing he hadn't anticipated was that he couldn't communicate with Talix from this far underground. Some of the minerals made it difficult to obtain a secure signal. He had to go up to the surface to converse with her.

Jaril donned clothing he had replicated from the ship's database which would allow him to blend in if he came upon a human. Some blue leg coverings made of a thick stiff material and an orange vest. He packed a light, took a small case to gather more samples, and a bag he slung over his shoulder in case he discovered something more interesting to bring back. He maneuvered up through a variety of passageways until he arrived at the small cave opening. A splash of yellow sunlight reached across the cave floor. He had observed red stars, purple ones, and even a green one that matched his skin tone. Life always found a way to grow.

Jaril stood by the mouth of the cave and noticed the clusters of red and black fruit. He plucked a few, sniffed the berries, and slipped the bunches into his bag. *I'll test them later to see if they are edible and what the classification is.*

As Jaril pushed away the branches, he heard voices. He stepped back into the cave as two humans walked by. He heard their lyrical speaking, but he couldn't understand what they said. They stopped outside, a few feet from the entrance.

The breeze stirred. Jaril detected a whiff of something sweet. It smelled like a flower, but had another, deeper scent which roused his hunger. His tongue darted out as he tasted the air to get a better sense of who they were. Jaril tasted their sweat and cringed at the sour tang of a chemical aftertaste.

Fascinated, he studied their strange garments. As they turned more toward him, he deduced they were both females by the curves of their body shapes. One had a red head covering, and the other had a dark brown head covering which stretched over her ears. Jaril inhaled again. His mouth watered. This human aroused his hunger. Her dark brown hair nearly matched her head covering. She had a rucksack on her back with other implements. She wore with a bright purple top and dark blue pants.

As they talked, the other female's tone grew more agitated. She moved toward the entrance to the cave. He backed farther into the shadows. The one with the dark hair turned toward him. Her deep electric blue eyes caught him. They lit up her whole face. He licked his lips and thought what it would be like to drink her.

* * *

Abigail Pike bit her lip to keep from letting loose another string of profanity at her sister, Melony who had planned their camping trip in the middle of August when it was sticky and humid. Abigail carried around their tent and her sleeping bag. Mel didn't have a clue where they were, and Abigail couldn't get any signal on her phone. Camping wasn't her thing, but Mel wanted to spend some more time together before she moved away to California for her job. Abigail's sister was the outdoorsy one who'd played all the sports in high school and was good at it. Abigail was the nerdy bookworm who stayed inside and found her world in between the pages of her books.

"Come on. I'm sure the trail is this way." Mel pulled out a map and twisted it around. They had traipsed off the trail, well into the mountains. Abigail insisted they head back, but her sister was as stubborn as their mother. They continued deeper into the woods until they were hopelessly lost.

With the sun high, Abbie wanted to find a place to camp. Then they could figure out where to go instead of trekking higher and higher into the mountains where they might encounter wild animals. Bears and mountain lions -- along with poisonous snakes -- lingered on the edge of her mind, along with her having to pee.

"Mel, enough. I gotta pee. We've been pushing through dense forest and brush for an hour. I don't have a cell signal, and you forgot the compass. Why don't we set up camp here? We walked over a stream a little while ago. There's a clearing a few feet from here where we can pitch our tents. We can turn back in the morning."

Her sister rolled her eyes. "Ab, we can find the trail. I haven't gotten lost in the wilderness never to be heard from again. Have a little faith."

Abagail shifted the weight of her tent and her bag. The load on her back distracted her for a minute from her bladder. "We're losing the light. It's hot as hell. You know this isn't my thing."

Mel put a hand on her hip and pouted. "I know you're only doing this for me. You'd rather be home buried in a book. Suck it up. Fine, you want me to admit we're lost? Then we're lost. I fucked up. Satisfied? Your little sister fucked up again. As you've said, 'The only reason you're going to California is to get away from the string of bad boyfriends and dead-end jobs.' You --"

"I'm happy for you getting the job. Sure, you've had bad luck with men and jobs lately. You're not a fuck-up. I'm here to spend time with you before you go. We've gotten turned around, and I'm a little freaked-out because civilization is a long way away."

Mel sighed. "Okay, there's a flat patch of grass over there. We'll set up the tents and get a fire going. Then we can roast marshmallows and scare away bigfoot with our ghost stories. Does that work for you?"

"Sounds great." Abigail dropped her pack and found the roll of toilet paper she had brought with her. "I'm going to find some bush to pee behind. I'll be back."

"Keep an eye out for poisonous snakes."

"Thanks for the warning." She rolled her eyes. Abigail looked at the wilderness around her. She wanted to keep her sister within visual range. Ahead of her was a good copse of trees to give her enough coverage. Abigail pushed aside the brambles and discovered a cave opening. *This looks like a good place to go.* Cooler air hit her immediately. She didn't see any signs of an animal inside the cavern. She ducked inside and found a spot. When she was done, Abigail noticed the space opened into a bigger room. The rocky, uneven floor made her pick her away carefully as she went around the corner and walked into something. *Shit.* Abigail thought she had staggered into a rock. When her eyes focused, she found herself staring at a very broad-chested man. *What the hell? Was he in here watching me?*

"I'm sorry. I didn't know anyone was in here." He wore a bright orange vest, a color she would expect to see on a hunter. Something about the neon orange didn't mix well with his green skin. *Wait, it has to be a shirt, but why is his face green, too?* His mouth moved and a strange low warble and a click came out. He spoke again, and his forehead creased.

Abigail stepped away from the stranger as her brain tried to comprehend what she was seeing. His long blue hair was braided at the sides and hung down to his shoulders. He reached out his hand. She stepped back and felt herself pitch backward. She tried to catch her balance but couldn't before she felt a sharp pain at the back of her skull. Abigail tried to focus, but the stranger's face filled her vision before everything went black.

* * *

Abagail winced at the bright light. She covered her eyes with her hand until they could acclimate to the light. She took in a breath and tasted dust and dry air. The last thing she remembered was a strange man coming after her. She sat up and felt the back of her head. The spot felt tender. Her vision swam for a second.

"Whoa! You need to remain careful. The nanos are mending your brain shell back together."

The sound sent shivers down her spine. She turned toward the deep voice. Abigail swept her gaze over to the stranger. His red eyes startled her.

I'm hallucinating. Something in the cave made me think he has green skin, blue hair, and red eyes. He's probably a nice guy who's living in a cave and... shit... What did I get myself into? Did he see me pee? Mel's going to wonder where I am. He could be a murderer.

"You're in no danger. I rescued you from certain death. You're not fantasizing this encounter. I am real enough. Why does my appearance bother you? No, I did not observe you while you were dealing with your bodily functions." He turned her head as though he was inspecting her, like some kind of thing instead of a person.

A moment of panic hit her when she realized he had heard her thoughts. Nothing about that was normal. Her fingers grazed something at the bottom of her hairline. The object warmed her fingertips. She ran her fingers around the dime-sized metal disk and tried to pry it off. He grabbed her wrist gently and pulled it away from her nape.

"You can't take off the suppression nodule. It houses the nanites repairing your body and allows you to understand me. It also gives me access to your thoughts and memories. If I had left you on the cave floor, you would have expired. You have no reason to fear me." He released her wrist and took a seat on a rock across from her.

Her fingers brushed over a rough material underneath her. The cloth felt like canvas. As she lifted it up, the color changed in the light until it matched her skin tone. She set it down again, and it replicated the hue of the rock it lay on. A light in the corner flickered and caught her attention. Along the far wall lush greenery of all different kinds grew under the lights. She heard the running water. A stream had been diverted into the trays he had set up to grow the different plants. A small mound of soil took up another nook. *What is this place? It looks like a lab. Am I going to be this thing's next experiment?*

The male something sighed. "I am not a *thing*. I am not one of your species. You will not be experimented on. I am a..."

Abigail didn't enjoy him reading her thoughts. She couldn't understand the last word he said. "I'm sorry. You lost me. What are you doing here?"

He hissed at her. His lips pulled away from his teeth in a sneer. He got up, muttering, and ran his fingers through his hair. Abagail watched his movements in case he might say or do something else to her. As he paced in the light, the green of his skin changed color to a darker green. She could see swirling patterns over his exposed arms. He ran his fingers over the different types of plants.

After minutes ticked by without him speaking, it seemed he'd lost all interest in her. His focus became the plants. She touched the metal circle on her neck. It remained warm, and her skull above it was tender. *I have to get out of here. I need to get back to Mel.* Her captor stopped and plucked a leaf from a plant, held it up to the light, and shook his head.

Abigail got up and went over to him. "Um... I appreciate you helping me out and healing me, but I must return to my sister. Can you show me the way out?"

He looked up at her and seemed to realize she was still there. "You can't leave. I'm sorry." He returned his attention back to the vegetation.

Abigail pushed his arm to get him to notice her. He was all muscle. He sighed and set his plant down. "Hey, whatever your name is... I'm not a flower. Let me go! My sister is going to raise holy hell if she can't find me."

"I apologize for your... sibling's distress, but your home is here now, among my florae. I understand your human genus can't be planted in soil to survive. Truthfully, I don't understand your species. I'm here to gather different plant varieties. I could spend years on your planet gathering various specimens."

Was he talking to her or more to himself? His attention stayed focused on his experiments. He didn't seem dangerous despite his appearance. *Maybe he's not good at interacting with people.* From his monologue, she gathered he was a scientist. *Oh, God, I can't believe this. He's an alien. No human has green skin, blue hair, and red eyes.* His hands were oddly shaped. He had a thumb and five fingers, six digits total. *Holy shit. I've been kidnapped by some alien botanist. He can hear my thoughts, but he's more concerned about his plants than listening in. I gotta play nice to escape him.* "Maybe I can help you understand my species if you have questions. C-can you tell me your name? Unless you want me to call you Master or Sir."

He plucked a bug off a leaf. She didn't know if he was going to eat it or her. He might be pleasant now, but later he could get all crazy and take a bite out of her. "You wish to know my identifier?"

"Er... yes." She pointed to herself. "I'm Abigail Pike."

"Jaril. Forgive me for not giving you my personal identifier earlier. I wasn't sure how much of your motor functions might be affected by smashing your head bone..."

"My skull? Not head bone," she corrected him.

He flinched. "...Your skull on the rock. The nanites should have repaired the damage from your head wound now. Do you feel as though you might fall over or evacuate your bowels?"

"No, I'm fine. It's nice to meet you, Jaril. Y-you said you're on Earth studying plants. Where are you from? Are there others of your kind here?" Abigail gazed around the cave hoping to find a way out.

"If they are, I'm unable to contact them. Of the three ships which have returned to Tilleron, two of them had been on your planet for many revolutions around your sun. My people integrated themselves into your culture. One was a well-known bard on your world."

"What is your world like? Is it tropical or deserts? Oceans? Are the others green like you?"

"You have many questions for one who thought I'd attack her." He turned and stared at her. Pressure built on her temples as though someone pushed on them. His eyes narrowed. She touched her head as the pain in her temples intensified. Jaril caught her chin. She grabbed his wrist and cried out. The intensity on her mind eased. His thumb swiped across her upper lip. A drop of crimson balanced on the pad of his thumb. Jaril flicked his tongue over his thumb and sucked every little bit of her blood off. His eyes shut as though he enjoyed taking her blood.

"W-why did you do that?" Abigail asked, a little out of breath.

"Your blood tastes like a delectable fruit on my world. I haven't had fresh blood in many long months. Forgive me for indulging. I didn't mean to press into your thoughts so forcefully as to cause you to bleed. You are trying to befriend me so you can escape. You can inquire all you wish, but you will not find your way out of this cave system. You are mine now. I will not treat you as an experiment."

"C-can you answer my questions?" Abigail wiped her eyes and tried to squash her rising panic. *He's going to keep me forever AND he can read my mind. What can I do?*

"Would it make you feel more comfortable to know more about me?"

"Are you going to rape me? Is that why you're really keeping me here?"

Jaril flinched. "What is this rape?"

"Are you going to use me for sexual pleasure against my will?"

He scoffed and said something she couldn't interpret. Abigail drew away in case he came at her. "No. I would never assault a female of any species. Others of my kind do keep Body Units, females whom they use for gratification."

"Great. You have sex slaves."

"No, not slaves. They willingly give their bodies. They are treated well and stay with some of us for many years. They can leave whenever they wish."

"If I'm not a Body Unit for you, do you just want my blood, then? Is that why you're keeping me as your prisoner?" Abigail didn't want to think of the other reasons he might want her, but at least this strange alien wasn't going to assault her. "I promise I won't tell anyone about you. You can read my mind and see I'm not. Please, I want to get back to my sister."

He set his plants down. The weight on her forehead returned but not as heavily this time as he looked inside her mind. "You speak truth. I do not have the resources to keep you underground. I have a proposition for you."

"What is it?"

"I have a desire for more of your blood. It nourishes me. I am down on supplies. Let me take from you."

She felt the blood drain from her face. "You're going to kill me?"

He chuckled. "No. The nanos in your body will replace *your* blood. They do not work with our physiology. My people have tried, but something about our metabolism makes us an unsuitable host for them. In a few hours I can replenish my stores. Then I will release you back into your habitat. Do you agree to this exchange?"

If it got her away from the green alien, she would say yes to anything. "Okay."

His lips curled into a smile. "Good. Good. Come here." He patted his knee.

Abigail sat on his knee as he wanted her to. He reached up to brush the hair from her throat. She flinched away from him, but Jaril tightened his grip. "This is part of our agreement. You'll feel a pinch. Nothing to fear." He opened his mouth. His tongue was more pointed than a human's. The end opened like a flower unfurling its petals. Each little barb had small suckers on it. The sucker was a little bigger than a quarter.

She let out a little cry, but he held her down. Jaril trailed his finger over her throat. Abigail shivered. She took in a breath and smelled something she hadn't before. Maple. She knew there was nothing with maple around, but it came from him. His tongue closed and became a regular tongue once more. "What is that?"

"It is how we draw blood from our Plasma Units. Blood sustains my race. I will attach to your neck. Some species find it pleasurable. Some painful. Are you ready?"

Abigail braced herself as Jaril leaned in and flicked his tongue along her throat. His lips wandered over her flesh until he settled under her ear. He nipped her skin with regular teeth. She trembled with a strange longing. Then he struck. The sudden sting made her cry out. His lips latched onto her neck, and his sucker pulled her blood. Abigail clutched his wrist and felt the pleasure of it overwhelm her. She pressed her legs together as she tried to keep herself focused. A moan crept from her throat. Her green captor cupped her cheek, and he increased his suction on her throat, taking more of her blood.

"Oh, God! What are you doing?" Abigail whimpered as she neared an orgasm which she'd never expected to have from this strange encounter.

Jaril lifted his head. His eyes had a glazed-over look. He grunted something and caught her mouth with his. He held her face in his hands and deepened the kiss. His tongue thrust between her lips. Abigail returned the kiss. She wrapped her arms around his neck and pressed her breasts against his chest. Jaril moved to the other side of her throat and struck. Abigail moaned again. This time an orgasm swept through her. She arched her back as he held her head. Jaril drank only a swallow before his lips slid down to her collarbone, sucking in her flesh. He trailed his nose along her neck and nipped her earlobe. He murmured something she didn't understand.

Abigail tried to make sense of it all. This shouldn't be happening and yet her body reacted to him. It was more than just him sucking on her neck like some vampire. He looked up at her and she saw him breathing hard. *What the hell just happened? He drank my blood, and I had an orgasm.*

"T-the sound you made. Why did you make it? Was it because you found sexual arousal in my bite?"

Abigail felt the place he bit her on her throat. She came away with a star-shaped pattern in dots of blood on her palm. "I... um... wasn't expecting it to feel how it did." The scent of maple grew stronger. "It slipped out. I-I'm sorry if I made you uncomfortable."

"You have given me the flush of your warmth. Rest for a little while, and then I shall take more of your blood as agreed upon."

"I'm not tired."

His fingers slid along the back of her neck and pressed the nodule in a couple of places. "Sleep now."

Abigail felt pressure where he touched, and then her eyes grew heavy. She tried to fight it, but whatever he did to her made her body shut down into sleep.

Chapter Two

The female's body slumped in his arms. Jaril carried her back to his sleeping place. She didn't stir from the restorative state he'd sent her into while the nanos replaced the blood he had drawn from her. Her sweet blood lingered on his tongue. He could have drunk her dry if he hadn't been careful. Her blood was the sweetest he'd had in a long while. Nothing in his bottles compared to what ran through her veins. Then there was the sound she made. It had been soft and muffled, but he'd felt it. The impact of it awoke his sexual desires.

Jaril thought about taking Abigail, savoring her. He'd nearly lost control when he tasted the flush of yearning rushing through her when she reached her carnal gratification. He had held onto his control. Jaril told himself his body reacted like that because it had been so long since he had been in the presence of a female.

He hadn't planned on taking the woman after she ran into him near the cave entrance. She'd fallen backward and hit her skull on the ground. Jaril had caught the scent of her blood. He'd tasted it and wanted more. In order to obtain more, he needed to save her. He'd rushed her back down to his lab and implanted a suppression nodule on her. Their technology released nanos into the bloodstream to mend injuries or old cells. It enabled him to read her thoughts and control her movements. Once the nodule attached to her neck, the nanos calibrated to her species and began repairing her broken skull.

Her incessant questions made his head hurt. He understood most of what she said, but there were some things he didn't understand. When he responded to her, it seemed she could comprehend him, but he didn't know if the translation came out right. Jaril wanted nothing more than to keep her quiet, but she knew he existed. Abigail had his technology running through her veins.

There was no way to remove it. He could deactivate it, but the nodule remained with the subject. The deal they had struck made him feel better about letting her go free. She would stay quiet, and he could get blood.

Something about her intrigued him. The round shape of her face was softer than that of his kind. Her eyes were closer together. Her skin was not scaled, but more like a smooth hide. The color of her eyes were flecked with a deep gold he hadn't seen in others of his kind. Her rounded figure gave her a healthy appearance that appealed to him. Jaril trailed his fingers over the pale skin of her hand. The freckles on the back created a star pattern. He brushed his finger over her full lips and recalled the sound she'd made when he drank from her. The vibration caused him to shiver even as he remembered it. Jaril set her hand down and touched her hair. Abigail sighed and murmured something in her sleep. He got up and grabbed what he needed to get her blood.

While she slept, he placed a small silver instrument on her wrist that resembled a *glorab*, a large, multi-legged insect that lived on his planet. It had six legs, and lived on the undersides of leaves on Tilleron. One end pierced her skin and inserted itself into the vein. The mechanism injected an anticoagulant at the wound site. Jaril filled two bottles before he pulled out the device and let her sleep while the nanos replicated her blood. Her pale color grew rosy again. He repeated this procedure three more times until he had filled eight bottles with her blood. When he pulled out the apparatus, his sucker latched onto the wound.

Jaril lost himself until the flow of blood slowed. He drew away and watched her breathing. He touched her lips and wondered what it would be like to mate with the female.

Abigail smelled nice but tasted even better. He'd never

cared about finding a mate. The only things that mattered to him were his plants. This Earth female would never understand his desire to study plant life. *At least plants don't continually ask questions.* Color returned to her skin. She moaned something while she slept. He needed to keep his part of the bargain. Jaril wrapped her in his blanket and slowly worked his way back to the surface with her. He pushed aside the brambles, but the blanket got caught on the briars. He tugged until it came free. The cool night air helped to clear his head as he went into the clearing.

"Talix," he called, knowing his computer was listening for him.

"Where have you been? You were supposed to surface hours ago."

"I ran into a complication. A human female found the cave entrance and injured herself. I had to reveal myself to her."

"She will go to their soldiers, and they will come. How could you be so careless?"

He knew Talix worried about him, but sometimes the computer went overboard. "We came to an agreement. She'll keep our secret. I used a suppression nodule on her so I could see her thoughts."

"Even better, now she has our technology. Deactivate it now!" Talix ordered through the implant he had behind his ear. It allowed him to communicate with her when needed and when he was within range.

"You don't order me around. I'm not going to disable the nodule."

"If you let her go free, you're risking the technology being studied. You know how this goes."

"Talix, enough! Scan the area and tell me where the nearest gathering of humans is. She spoke of another human female with her. I think she has a sibling searching for her. Can you tell me if there is a concentration of humans around here?"

"Scanning." The computer conveyed her anger with him in her flat tone. "They have congregated not too far from your location. Leave her in a clearing at the bottom of the incline. She'll be found shortly."

Jaril followed the instructions and moved down the slope. He held Abigail closer and moved with her toward the coordinates Talix had given him. As he went down the hill, he spotted several different species of plants he hadn't noticed before. His fingers itched to bring back samples, but he could collect them on the way back. Jaril set the human female down in the clearing, lifted her head, and touched the nodule at her nape. With one push and a twist he could neutralize the device. Instead, he pressed it twice, allowing her to regain consciousness after a normal sleep cycle. He leaned down and took in another whiff of her scent and enjoyed the sweetness of her. Abigail groaned. The small sound hit him like a kick in the gut. Jaril shook it off. *I've been alone for too long. It's only my body reacting to her softness.* He pushed a stray hair from her cheek and brushed his lips along hers, tasting her once more.

Jaril pulled away. *She intrigues me, but I made a deal.* He wrapped her up in the blanket to make sure she would stay warm until her people found her. He touched her face one more time. "Goodbye, human. Maybe we will cross paths again."

Jaril retreated into the brush and watched while he hoped her people would find her. After watching the moon cross the sky and no one coming, he knew the woman was not going to be rescued.

"Talix, signal the humans to where they can find the woman."

"*Now* you're speaking to me. I object to this."

"I don't care. Do it. Tap into the frequency of one of their communication devices. It should be easy for you to do. Relay it to my implant. I'll need you to translate as well."

"As you wish. Give me a moment."

Jaril heard a faint click and an echo.

Talix came back on. "Go ahead."

"Give me the coordinates once more, please."

Talix gave him the coordinates again. The signal chirped.

"...searched in an outlying pattern based on the sister's information. Have you found anything in grid five?" Jaril heard a male speaking through his implant. Talix had broken into the humans' transmissions so he could interact with them.

He heard static and then a click. Another, gruffer male, came over their airwaves. "Nothing yet. We should call it a night."

Jaril didn't like the sound of the message. It seemed the searchers were giving up for the night. He had to do something to get their attention. In Tilleron, Jaril said, "I found the woman," and gave the coordinates to find her. Simultaneously, Talix translated Jaril's words into English.

"Who is this?" the impatient male asked.

A moment of panic struck him as how to answer. "Talix?" Jaril whispered, urging Talix to talk.

"Jerry, this is Virgil in grid eight. I found the woman. I'm going to need help to move her," Talix replied, impersonating another male from the humans' search party.

A loud whine hit Jaril's implant, and he winced.

"They will be at your location shortly," Talix said to Jaril.

"Thank you," Jaril whispered and moved farther into the brush. He made sure no one could see him, but he watched until he saw lights.

"Oh, my God! It's her. Abigail." The female's sibling

knelt by Abigail's prone form and shook her.

Jaril smiled as the human came around. He slipped back into the forest and along the way stopped to gather more samples. "She is among her own kind now."

"Yes. I've disconnected from the humans' communications. Your location has been compromised. You need to relocate your lab. The female found the entrance to the cave. There's no telling how many more will come."

He held in his anger. "I don't need to move the lab. Her discovery of me and the cave entry was an accident."

"You trust her not to reveal your whereabouts?"

Jaril crept back into the cave. "I told you. I saw her thoughts. She will not betray me."

* * *

Abigail stared at her reflection in the computer monitor and ran her fingers through her hair. Her fingertips brushed the metal disk on the back of her head. A year later and she hadn't gotten used to it being there. It only reminded her of the strange encounter she'd had with the green-skinned creature who had sucked her blood. After she had been found by the searchers and being checked out by the paramedics, her life had gotten back to normal. Or almost normal. Ever since she'd been found, Melony kept grilling her on what happened. Abbie had been gone for forty-eight hours, and Mel hadn't been able to find her. Abagail told her sister she'd hit her head and had been unconscious. That she didn't remember anything except going into the cave and tripping.

Abigail wanted to share what she had learned. She wanted to find out more about the strange alien who had saved her. Ever since she'd gotten home, she'd been searching the Internet for any kind of clue about what she had seen. Abigail had come across groups talking about gray aliens and others who might be reptilian, but they didn't sound like the one who had helped her. Sure, the alien had originally said he would keep her hostage, but then he had let her go. Jaril had seemed more interested in his plants than he had in her except for obtaining her blood.

After the paramedics looked her over, they couldn't find a scratch on her. Mel had almost not gone off to California to her new job. Abigail tried to get the nodule off many times, but it wasn't budging. He had told her nanos, little robots, were running through her bloodstream and healing her. This past year, she had never felt better and had even lost a few pounds. When she typed in "alien implants," all manner of strange things came up and nothing resembled what was attached to her neck.

She sighed and sat back in her chair. The only way she would find answers was to go back to the cave and see if the alien was still there. Her stomach churned when she thought about him.

If I do find him, what will I say? Hello, I want you to drink my blood again because it felt good. I need you to suck on my neck so I can orgasm.

Abigail got up and paced. Her dreams had delved into the what-if question of them being together. Every time she woke up, it left her wanting more.

I can't keep making excuses on why not to go. Fuck it. I need answers.

She gathered her things and threw them into the car. She had a ride ahead of her. It was already early afternoon when she got to the trailhead. She parked and headed into the wilderness of the mountains. The longer she walked the more unfamiliar the area seemed. Abigail didn't remember exactly where she had gotten lost. She came to a spot where she needed to take a breath. Taking a sip of water, she rubbed the back of her neck. Could the metal nodule lead her to Jaril?

Abigail recalled they had been off the beaten path. This time she had a compass and a map. She marked her coordinates. The environment looked more overgrown than before. She kept heading north. The sun had slipped lower. She took another break in a small glade. Abigail wiped the sweat from her forehead and caught something glinting in the setting sun. She went to investigate.

She reached through the thorns and pulled out a piece of reflective fabric. The elements ravaged it, but she recognized it as part of the blanket the alien had left with her. *He must not have noticed when it tore off.* She held her bag and pushed through the briars. The thorns caught her exposed arms and made her hiss as she came into the cave.

Warmth flushed down her arm. Abigail watched as the skin knitted itself back together. She dug a flashlight out of her bag and used it to look around the cave. Shoe prints showed in the damp earth. She followed them around the corner and saw they led down into a cavern where she could hear rushing water. The cool air made it nicer in the cave than outside. The footprints stopped at the edge of the rushing stream. It was too far across for her to jump. She didn't see any safe way to cross without getting soaked.

"Hello," Abigail called.

She waited but didn't expect to get an answer. She glanced at her watch. It was past eight. She couldn't make it back down the mountain in the dark. The best thing she could do would be to set up her tent and spend the night in the cave. Abigail hoped no animal came looking to bed down. But she hadn't seen any animal tracks.

Abigail backed away from the water and pitched her tent. She crawled inside and zipped up for the night. *I'll give it one night. After that, I'm done.* Abigail settled into her sleeping bag and munched on some protein bars and jerky she'd packed with her. She left her lantern on low in case she needed to see when she woke up. After a while of listening to the water, her eyes drooped, and she drifted off to sleep.

"What are you doing here?" A rough shake followed by an angry growl woke her up.

Abigail opened her eyes to see Jaril's red eyes staring at her. He grabbed her arm and dragged her out of her tent. Abigail struggled to get away, but his hand wrapped around the back of her neck and held her. His fingers pressed upon the nodule while she struggled and suddenly, she froze. Abigail tried to tell her limbs to move, but nothing happened. In the small light of her lamp, his expression did not look happy. Fear moved through her, but she tried to keep her wits about her, recalling he could read her thoughts. The pressure on her mind pushed along her forehead. She whimpered from the sudden pain.

"I-I came to find you," she whispered.

"Who else did you tell? Are there other humans coming?" He looked a little wilder than she remembered, and she could tell he didn't trust her.

"No one. I swear."

Jaril grabbed her chin and stared into her eyes. His grip hurt, but she had to wait him out because she didn't want to anger him further. His lips pulled back in a snarl. He seemed more alien and untamed than she remembered. Abigail tried to calm her fear when he released his hold on her chin and stepped away. "Why did you come back here? We had a deal. I release you, and you go about your life."

"I-I wanted to talk to you again. To find out more about you. You never answered my questions before. C-could you make it so I can move again, please?"

His eyes narrowed. "For you to attack me? Radio your comrades and inform them I remain? I think not."

She sighed. "I won't. I-I brought you some seeds I thought you might like since you were obsessed with plants. They're in my bag. You can even take my blood if you want."

"I don't need your permission to drink you. No one is going to miss you. Your thoughts show no human knows of your whereabouts." Jaril's fingers moved her hair from her throat. His light touch made her shiver. He trailed his nose along the curve of her neck.

Abigail took in a quick breath. His hands slid down her sides. She recalled the last time she was with him and her dreams. "I'd hope you wouldn't kill me, Jaril. I don't mean you any harm," she told him in the calmest voice she could muster.

Saying his name seemed to get his attention. He pushed the nodule at her nape until she regained control of her body. Abigail stumbled backward, and he caught her. She looked into his eyes and saw a questioning look.

He looked paler than before. Healed cuts crisscrossed his cheeks. She reached up to caress his jaw, but he grabbed her hand. Before she could protest, his sucker latched onto her wrist. She gasped at the sudden pinch. His grip tightened as he drew in her blood as though he was parched. She touched his chest only to find it warm. His eyes never left hers as he drank her in. Abigail felt light-headed. Warmth in her neck rushed down her spine as the nanos tried to replace the blood he took in. As he drank from her, she caught the scent of maple. She licked her lips at the aroma and thought about smothered pancakes.

"Stop, please." She pressed against his chest when she felt herself almost ready to faint.

He grunted but lifted his head from her wrist. His color had returned a little bit. "You said you had seeds for me."

Abigail nodded, but her head spun again. The nodule burned for a few more minutes and she wasn't spinning anymore. She went into her tent and came back out with her bag. She had gone to the store and bought different kinds of herbs, vegetable, and flower seed packets in case she ran into him again. She had over three dozen different varieties for him. She had not even wondered why she had bought them at the time because she wasn't into gardening. For some reason, she wanted to see his reaction. Abigail handed them over to the alien and waited. He looked through them, but his expression darkened.

"These are dead things. Humans..." Jaril drifted off into his own language she couldn't understand. He threw down the bag and scattered the different seed packets all over the cave floor.

Seeing them strewn on the ground hit her harder than it should. She knelt and stuffed them back into the plastic bag she'd had them in. The confusion on Jaril's face made her stop.

"You're right. I shouldn't have come back up here. I-I'm sorry to have bothered you. I'll leave in the morning. I won't reveal you're here. I wanted to learn more about you, Jaril."

"Why aren't you afraid of me? Your kind butchers those it doesn't understand."

She shrugged. "I-I was frightened of you for a long time. I thought you might come after me, but you never did. Then I got curious, and I dreamed about you. You're obsessed with plants so I thought you might not have these in your menagerie. They're not dead. You have to plant them."

"I know what you to do with them, human."

"It's Abigail. Remember? Sorry." Abigail noticed the recently healed gash along his side. "What happened?" She reached to touch it, but he moved away from her.

"One of your kind caught me off guard while I was gathering specimens. I barely made it back into the caves. I've exhausted my supply to heal. Forgive me for pouncing on you, Abigail. I needed nourishment." He gave her a tight smile. She didn't know if the expression was his way of showing he was happy or sorry.

"W-well, I could help you. You took my blood last time, and it didn't hurt. Maybe this time in exchange for my blood you can answer my questions."

"Why would you do this for me?"

Abigail touched his cheek. Jaril didn't move away from her, but he seemed as intrigued about her as she was about him. "Because we all need friends. You must be lonely if you're the only one of your kind here."

"F-f-frie-nnds?"

She nodded overwhelmed by the sweet smell coming off him. "Companions. Allies."

"Yes, I understand this. I've been alone before, but your planet is more isolating than I am used to. I think it's time for me to return to Tilleron. I will respond to your questions. Refilling my blood stores might take a while. You need to replenish your body for it to heal. Would you agree to this compromise?"

"Will it hurt?"

"No. It is a painless procedure. I can put you to sleep again as I did before."

"I'd rather be awake."

"Then you can be awake."

"Okay. Take me to your lair."

He looked at her with a blank expression.

Abigail chuckled. "Never mind. Let me pack up my tent first."

Chapter Three

Jaril couldn't believe it when he came up to the surface and saw the tent by the water. Then he smelled her. The scent of her blood drove him so wild he could barely contain himself. He could have drained her dry, but he wanted to savor it. He didn't know what the human female wanted. In her thoughts she had come alone, but he didn't trust what he saw, not after his last encounter with a human. The wound on his side pained him even after taking the female's blood. He hadn't had human blood since he'd drunk up his supply. Animal blood had sustained him, but it did little to nourish his body.

Abigail packed her things and followed him through the passageways. When she got stuck, he helped her. After touching her soft flesh, the taste of her lingered in his mind. They worked their way down into the cavern where he had his lab set up. Most of the plants and specimens he had were overgrown. He had been worried about taking care of himself, and he hadn't tended to the seedlings.

The wound pained him even with all the blood he had taken from her. They got to his workroom, and she set her bag down. Jaril still wasn't sure he could trust the female, even if he could see into her mind. Abigail didn't seem as though she was hiding anything. He grunted as he twisted. His muscles hurt where he had been stabbed. The blood he'd taken assisted in the healing process, but there was still damage.

The sound of her heartbeat made his mouth water. He needed to drink her again. She ran her fingers over the plants. Jaril regretted throwing the seeds she had brought him. The human female had thought about him.

He didn't want to admit he'd dreamed of her. Those fantasies involved him tasting her and also exploring her body. Jaril took her hand again and brought it to his lips.

Her heart stayed steady as he kissed her wrist and didn't gallop away into fear. His tongue flicked over her flesh and his sucker opened.

"May I?" She stretched her hand out.

Jaril nodded. Her fingertip touched the center of his sucker. He resisted the urge to have the sucker close around it. She carefully traced the sides. Jaril shivered as she touched him. He had wondered what it might be like to have her caress him. As if reading his mind, the human drew her finger along his jaw. Jaril took her wrist and pulled in the blood through his tongue.

The human female groaned. He closed his eyes and let the vibration wash over him. It struck a chord. She swayed on her feet while he drank. Her other hand gripped his shoulder. He listened to her pulse and heard its loud song. He pulled away when it faltered. She rested her head against his shoulder.

Jaril wrapped his arm around Abigail and held her to him. Feeling her warmth throughout his body stirred a yearning he hadn't felt in a long time. He lifted her chin and brushed his mouth along hers. He expected her to pull away, but instead she returned the kiss with a hunger to rival his own. Jaril ran his fingers down her back as instinct took over. His kiss deepened until their tongues met. Jaril nipped her lower lip and nibbled along her jaw. He growled his satisfaction as he pressed against her. Her sweet citrus smell overwhelmed his senses.

Jaril needed her. He tugged her hair and wrenched her neck back. She gasped and struggled in his arms.

"Stop." Abigail tried to push out of his grasp.

"You yearn for me. I desire you. I haven't had a female in a long time. We can satisfy one another."

"I didn't come here to have sex with you."

Her heart fluttered. "You lie. I can hear your heart. I can taste it in your blood. We are compatible. Unclothe yourself."

"I'm not lying to you. I..." She sank down onto his sleeping space.

Jaril didn't understand this human female. He didn't understand females of any species. Plants didn't talk back. Jaril sat next to her but kept his distance. He thought about the sound she'd made and how it resonated within him. He needed to hear it again. He wanted to hear his name on her lips. "You fear me?"

"No. I'm not afraid of you. Hell, I dreamed about us together, but I don't know if I can have sex with you."

"I can make you." He chuckled, but from her horrified expression she didn't find the humor in his statement.

"If you did, I'd find a way to cut your dick off."

Jaril placed a hand on her leg and trailed his fingers over her leg garment. She flinched but didn't shy away from him. "I would not force you. I was making a humorous statement."

"A joke."

"A jake?"

The woman giggled. "Joke."

"Joke." He formed his mouth around the strange word.

She nodded. "What does having sex with you entail? Do you have a normal penis? Is it barbed? Maybe you have two."

He smiled at her comment about him having two *findicks*. He understood what she meant. "My *findick* isn't barbed. I don't have two male members. Would you like to see it?" He reached for his pants to unbutton them but stopped when she stroked his hand. Her touch was soft.

Jaril glanced at her and saw her cheeks were reddened. He sensed her trepidation.

"Ahhh... Maybe later. What is a finn-i-dick?" She tried to sound out the word.

"My male member. Copulation can be pleasurable. With the suppression nodule, I can make your enjoyment last hours if you wish. I'm not built like your human males. I would have to show you."

"What about your tongue sucker thingy? Do you drink blood while you're screwing?"

He trailed his hand over her leg. Jaril brushed the hair away from her throat and licked her flesh until he came to her ear. He nipped the end of it. She shivered and squeezed his leg. His other hand rested on the middle of her back.

"I can drink from you if you like or not. I could lose myself to the pleasure. Sometimes it can be quick and more heated. You did say you came here to find out more about me." Jaril hoped she would say yes. Her flesh was supple, and she smelled good. He hadn't realized how much he ached to be with a female. He dragged his lips over her cheek and met her lips. She kissed him slowly. He wanted more of her.

"Do you plan on impregnating me?"

The question made him feel as though he had been struck in the gut. "I only wanted to share pleasure with you. I did not plan on creating life. I would have to test your blood, but would you want a child with me?"

"No. I mean... If we're going to do this, then I want to be sure I'm not going to get pregnant."

"The dilemma can be solved easily." Jaril pressed the suppression nodule with the intent of what he wanted done. He had already formed a telepathic link with the nodule. The device made it easy to control the human. He thought about his purpose and relayed it to the nanos.

"Now you won't have to burden yourself with bearing any young."

"Forever? Can you reverse it?" The panic in her voice made him reconsider his proposal. "It can be reversed. I have programmed the nanos so they will stop the joining of our DNA. Does this bother you?"

"No, I want to have kids someday. If I leave here --"

"When we are done with our exchange, I will reprogram the nanites, then you will be able to reproduce. Would you like to mate?" Jaril asked, hoping she would accept his offer.

Her face darkened to an even redder color. He heard the blood rush to color her skin. Jaril concentrated on her thoughts and felt confusion and longing. He did not want to probe deeper in case he scared the human female away. However, he could sense her curiosity getting the better of her. He might not have understood all of what she felt and thought, but he got the general idea. Humans didn't present their whole array of emotions and actions. This female surprised him by seeking him out after they had struck a bargain. He was glad she'd returned. Not only because he needed the blood she provided, but Jaril found he enjoyed her company as well.

"Okay. I'll mate with you, but I want to be on top."

Jaril smiled, pleased they had come to another accord, but he wasn't sure what her statement meant.

* * *

Abigail chewed her lip at the idea of having sex with a green alien who drank her blood. It was obvious his people -- or alien -- skills were lacking in some areas because he didn't know what to say to her.

I wonder if he's ever been with another of his kind. Maybe he's awkward with everyone. I don't know. He's attractive in his own way for being a green alien. His touch and his kisses were nice.

For whatever reason, his bite turned her on. She wondered how having him inside her would feel. All her dreams leaned toward it being fucking amazing, but those were only fantasies. *Let's see how it feels for real.*

She got up and pulled off her shirt. His crimson eyes widened as she unhooked her bra. He placed his hand on her stomach while trailing his fingers up until he cupped one of her breasts. His thumb brushed across her nipple. She trembled as he flicked his tongue over the other breast. His sucker bloomed and latched onto her pert bud.

She grabbed onto his shoulder at the sudden pain. Then she could feel the suction as he drank her blood. It aroused her. "Fuck!" she whispered. The warmth enveloped her. Her heart galloped against her chest, and her head spun from the quick orgasm.

He released her breast. "You are not pleased?"

Abigail tried to catch her breath. "I wasn't expecting it to feel like that."

"It made you feel good?" Jaril brushed her other breast with his fingers.

"Yes. It felt wonderful." Abigail took his hand and looked at his palm. The darker pigment of his skin made the lines easy to see. She traced them and wondered what they meant. She brought his palm to her lips and kissed the inside of it. He took in a breath, but she wasn't sure if he enjoyed it or not. "I think I might need an instruction manual. I don't know what arouses you."

Jaril stepped away from her and stepped out of his pants. She took in all of him, including his semi-erect cock. He took her hand and brought it down to his balls. She cupped three instead of two like a human man's. "I know human males are built differently from my species. Does my *findick* scare you?"

Abigail rubbed his testicles, feeling their warmth, and moved her hand along the large vein of his cock. She watched his face looking for a reaction. Jaril didn't seem to be stimulated by her touch. She took off the rest of her clothes. His eyes widened.

"You don't scare me. What do you know about human women or human anatomy?" Abigail asked.

He shrugged. "Nothing, but your form is similar to other female species I've copulated with before. Even our women have your mummeries."

"Breasts. We call them breasts." Abigail tried to hide

her smile at his misuse of the language.

"They are lovely. I know if I touch you like this, then it spurs on your desire." He fondled her nipple until he pinched it, and she cried out. The sudden jolt of pleasure went straight to her core. She pressed her thighs together to stay grounded.

"You have an unfair advantage of being able to read my mind and monitor how my body changes when you touch me."

Jaril tweaked her other nipple. "I like how your body reacts. I want to enter you when I am fully stimulated."

Abigail caressed his thigh and went to her knees. She touched his muscular thighs marveling at the smoothness of his skin. She ran her tongue along his cock and took him into her mouth. Abigail didn't know how he would respond, but he jumped. *Do you want me to stop?*" she thought as her tongue ran over the head of his prick.

"No," he groaned.

At least she knew he was reading her thoughts. *This could make things a whole lot more interesting.* Abigail caressed his testicles and rubbed them while she felt him stiffening in her mouth. She tried to take as much of his length as she could, but his shaft grew until she couldn't fit all of him in her mouth. She slowed and dragged her teeth along his soft flesh. Jaril sighed. The light pressure of his hand pushed down on her head, encouraging her to continue. She kept working her tongue around his firmed dick. She moved her mouth faster until he let out a loud moan.

The sound moved through her. Her body tingled as the vibration hit her nerves. "What happened?"

He opened his eyes. His chest rose and fell faster than before. "Why did you stop?"

"You moaned. I felt something…" Abigail wasn't sure how to describe it. The tremor hit her chest. It made her feel as though she hovered on the edge of orgasm. She touched his chest and felt something she wasn't expecting. A thump and then another one. "You have two hearts?"

"Yes. Please do the motion with your lips and tongue again."

"In a minute. What about the sound?"

"I hear nothing."

"No, you made a sound." Abigail needed to hear it again. The sugary aroma of maple caught her nose. She stood and pressed her lips against his in a hungry kiss. Her nipples firmed as she wanted more of him. She stroked his cock, but he didn't make the sound again. "What am I doing wrong?"

"Your mouth on my findick. I was nearly ready. Why did you cease?"

Abigail shook her head. It all sounded like a little bit of nonsense -- or a whole *lot* of nonsense if she thought about it. How could she ever explain this to anyone? She was having sex with an alien. Her head spun from the maple fragrance she smelled around him. "Why do you smell like maple?"

"What is maple?"

"It's a sweet syrup or candy we eat. It's one of my favorite foods."

Jaril moved his palms over her sides and cupped her ass. His hands dragged along the underside of her butt cheeks and then along her crack as he spread her mounds. "Among my people, we give off a pheromone. If someone wishes to mate with us, it makes them crave something they desire. You smell this with me?" He kissed her shoulder and nipped at the flesh.

Abigail let her head sink back as he bit her again. His hands caressed her thighs. "Yes." His fingers slid along her wet slit. She jumped when he found her clit. He pressed his thumb against it. Her back arched at the sudden shock.

"You like this?" He fondled her slowly. Each time it made her squirm. He kissed her throat again.

"God, yes," Abigail groaned.

He glided a finger along her wet slit until he found her opening. Jaril inserted one finger inside her and then another. Abigail squeezed his shoulder. She hadn't expected to feel this way about him exploring her body. "This is your female place."

"You could call it that. My lady parts." Abigail giggled.

Jaril stopped thrusting his fingers inside her and flashed her a darkened look. "Does this not please you?"

She placed a hand on his cheek. "It does. This is a little strange. I'm having an anatomy lesson with an alien. You know a lot about plants. Isn't there a diagram of a human in your computer or something?"

"There is, but I never paid much attention to it. The sexual and mating practices of humans were not detailed in the records. Only that you are sexually compatible. I met a mated pair and they seemed happy. I've never been very good with interacting with others. If you wish to tell me what will make this enjoyable for you, please do. If not, then we can be touching and discovering for many hours. Your body is soft and luscious. I wouldn't mind getting to know it. I'd like your mouth and tongue on my dick, as you put it."

"Later." She took his hand and brought it back to her clit. "This is one spot which arouses me." She then moved it to her breasts. "This is another. You can touch me with your fingers or your mouth."

"I would like to taste your sweetness. Will you lie down?" Jaril asked.

She nodded and lay down on the blanket he had set out for his sleeping place. He knelt before her and ran his hands over the inside of her thighs. Jaril took his time exploring her flesh until Abigail squirmed and giggled.

"You do not like this?"

"It's fine. It tickles."

"This is good?"

"A little, but not a lot. Not if you're doing it on purpose."

His forehead knotted, but he nodded. Jaril dipped his head between her legs. His tongue moved over her slit. Then his tongue found her clit. First, he sucked on it and flicked his tongue over the puckered bud. His tongue felt like fine sandpaper on her. Then his tongue moved faster. His hands settled on her hips. She skimmed her hands along his and held them. He glanced up and wound his fingers through hers. Then his sucker latched onto her clit. Abigail bucked against him at the sudden jab. She squeezed her eyes at the intensity. She couldn't believe him sucking her blood from her clit would feel good. She squashed his fingers and moved her hips, pressing into him. A moan passed over her lips. All she wanted was for him to continue pleasuring her.

"Don't stop!" she groaned.

Jaril seemed to understand what she needed. The wave of ecstasy brought her toward an orgasm. She held onto him to keep her anchored in the world. She let out a scream when she fully came. Jaril didn't stop there. He kept on drinking her blood and massaging her clit with his tongue. Abigail squirmed against him. She didn't have time to prepare for it. It hit her quickly, and she screamed as she came again. Jaril untangled his fingers from hers and kept on drinking from her clit.

"Please, I --" She curled her toes and moaned again.

Jaril stopped and looked. His expression seemed more far away than before. She couldn't understand it, but his lips pulled back in a growl. She tried to touch him, but he pinned her hands above her head.

Abigail felt a moment of fear, but she couldn't act upon it because he plunged his cock inside her. He buried his head between her breasts as he filled her again and again. His dick was longer than she was used to. His tongue flicked over her nipple, and she shuddered. He laid his head against her chest as though he were listening to her heartbeat. Abigail tried to catch her breath as he fucked her. She let out a loud groan.

At the same moment, Jaril trembled, and another moan came from him. Abigail felt the vibration move through her and the sweetness of his smell made her mouth water. The sound settled into her core. It made her come one more time. This time she rode it out with him still inside her. The grip on her wrists lessened as he released her. Jaril let his head remain on her chest as she took in a few breaths. His tongue flicked over her chest.

Abigail slid her fingers through his hair feeling the fine silky strands. "What was that?"

"What was what?"

"You went kind of animal for a second. The way you grabbed my wrists."

"Did I injure you?"

She moved her hands and felt pain. Heat flowed from her nape and touched upon her wrists. She had gotten used to the sensation when her body needed fixing. "The nanos are repairing the damage. I wasn't expecting you to get carried away."

"Forgive me. You made a sound. The way it moved through me, I lost myself. I had to hear you do it again. I needed you more than I've ever required anything else before. I felt like it was... essential to release myself within you." Jaril seemed to be trying to find the words to describe what he wanted to say.

Abigail smiled. "I-I think I know what you mean. When you came, released yourself, the sound you made... It made me want you again. I could fuck you again to hear you. You smell wonderful. Whatever you do with your tongue... I don't know what it is with your sucker, but when you hit me with it…" The recent memory of it flashed in her mind. The light pressure on her forehead told her he was monitoring her thoughts.

Jaril chuckled. "You were pleasured. I am glad. I would like to continue to explore your body, but I would like to take more blood from you first and let you replenish."

The way he spoke made her think about the context of his statement. Abigail got the gist of what he said. "I'm okay with your idea. First, do you have any water? I need something to drink."

He got up and brought her a square silver container. "Water. I use it to let the plants soak up water."

She held the container in her hands and sipped. The cold temperature surprised her, but the clear taste was good as she sipped it. Jaril refilled it, set it down next to her, and then sat back down. He cupped her jaw with his hand and held her. His other palm settled over her heart.

Abigail felt at ease with him. He had saved her life, even if it had meant implanting his technology into her head. She appreciated that now more than anything. Seeing him hurt the way he was, made her heart ache. She couldn't understand her strange, growing feelings for the alien, but Abigail knew she didn't want to leave him right away.

Jaril pressed his lips to hers. Abigail touched his face to feel the smoothness of his flesh and how warm he was. She kissed him slowly and trailed her tongue over his mouth. He returned the kiss and touched her tongue, but his sucker remained closed as they entwined. She wrapped her arms around his neck as his hands came around her back. One hand clasped her nape. The other held her close as he broke the kiss and moved down to her throat. Abigail moaned as he latched onto her neck once more and began to drink.

Chapter Four

Jaril trailed his fingers over the sleeping form of the human woman who shared his bed. He had taken several containers of blood from her while she was awake. She had not complained while he attached the bloodletter to her wrist. He would take more, but he didn't want to overtax her system when it came to the nanos. Her even breathing and steady heartbeat made him relieved she would recover.

Her thoughts were strange as she dreamed, but he only brushed his mind along their telepathic link to see if she feared him. He found she did not. In fact, she wanted more of him. Jaril had to admit he wanted more of her. When he heard Abigail moan, the sound triggered something within him. The vibration had gone to the primal part of his brain. It meant only one thing. He needed to mate with this female. He couldn't fight the animal side of him. Even her scream made him want to be inside her again. The thought of it made him hard again. He pushed aside the idea to wake her because he could take her again later.

To distract himself from her luscious form, he went to check on his plants. His foot hit the bag she had brought with her. The container of different seed specimens spilled out. He picked it up and looked at the different pictures on the front of the packets. Most were some type of floral species, but others were edible. He would have to cross-check the names with the genus listing in the computer. Jaril tore a packet open. Small black seeds spilled into his hand. He sliced a small section off one seed with a laser knife and placed the segment on a flat gray piece of metal. After a moment, an enlarged holographic image hovered above it. The embryotic seedling waited to come out. *Maybe I can crossbreed them and see what happens.*

He took a few of the seeds and placed them in the soil in the accelerated growth chamber. In a few hours, he would have a viable specimen. As he began working, an irritating high-pitched sound came from her bag. Jaril investigated and found a smooth rectangular device with a screen. When he touched the front, a picture appeared of a woman. The resemblance to Abigail made him think they were siblings. He shook the device. It chirped. Obviously, it was important to her. The twittering came again so he brought it to his ear. When he did, he heard a click.

"Jaril, is that you?"

"Talix?" He tapped the device and stared at the blank screen. "How are we communicating? We haven't been able to speak this far underground before."

"I sensed a communication implement with a weak signal. I had to try and open a channel. Keep it close to your implant, and it should boost the connection."

"What is so important? I am due to return to the ship in a few days' time. Have you started the pre-launch sequence?"

"Yes. All systems are reading normal. I've completed a few minor repairs. Nothing for you to be worried about. How is your physical state? Your biometrics show you've been injured. You aren't healing properly. You need to return now and be repaired."

Jaril sighed. Talix was correct that he wasn't recovering as he should. Nanos didn't work on his physiology, but the medical equipment on the ship would heal him. With Abigail's blood, he should be able to make it until he could return to his craft. He checked the wound. It hurt when he moved, but he figured he had a little while longer before he had to return to the vessel.

"I need to gather up my specimens and send the scout ship up with those first before I can return. There is another… complication." He didn't know how to break the news to his ship's intelligence about the human female. Jaril didn't know how to tell Abigail she was his intended mate. They were meant to be together. She reacted to his sounds, and he responded to her moaning. Never before had that happened when he had been with other females to relieve his sexual desires. He found it rather odd that his body reacted to her the way it did, and yet they were two separate species.

"What is this complication?"

Jaril clutched the communication device. "There is a human here with me. I want her to return with me."

"Jaril, do you hear what you're saying? A human female? Has she tricked you?"

"No, she hasn't *tricked* me. I will not have you jealous, Talix. You've always been loyal to me."

"Jaril, my feelings do not include who you sleep with or not. We are bonded on a deeper level. I care that you are alive and well. I do take it *seriously*. Which is another reason why you must come back. I've been monitoring the humans' telecommunications. A human reported running into a green, manlike creature who tried to attack them. The man had blood on him, or so the transmission said."

"How do you know the humans took this report seriously?" He winced at the notion he would have to leave.

"They are gathering a search party. You must come back. The humans can't obtain any more of our technology."

He couldn't abandon his seedlings. Jaril wasn't about to leave Abigail behind. At this point, if the other humans found her with him, they would experiment on her to see if she had been contaminated by him. They would try and take out the suppression nodule. It would kill her in the process. He hissed at the prospect. He glanced at Abigail.

Would she want to come back to Tilleron with me? Maybe I can at least get her back to my ship until the humans have stopped searching for me. They might have experienced searchers who can come underground. It's not safe for her here.

"I have to speak with the human. I can load the scout ship. You bring it up to the hold and send it back down. How long do you estimate we have before the humans are at my position?"

"It is night now. I'd say you have eight hours before they have gathered. I will keep scanning the area and let you know. Try and keep this communicator with you." Talix signed off.

Jaril turned back to his plants. He lovingly touched the leaves of many of the specimens he'd gathered. He didn't want to abandon them to the humans. He glanced at the passage which led down to the ship into which he needed to start loading the plants. Smooth hands came around his waist. He jumped and hissed. He grabbed the hands and pushed them away.

"Ouch. Hey."

He turned around and saw the succulent human woman rubbing her wrist and holding her hip where she landed against the cave wall. "Forgive me. I'm not used to sharing my domain with another." His gaze drifted toward her breasts as they shook when she walked. Her nipples were colored the same shade of her lips. She touched his stomach. Her hands glided lower over his torso. "You don't have a belly button."

"Belly button?"

She took his hand and moved it over the place on her body where she had a hole. "Belly button. When humans are born, they have a cord connecting them to their mother. The doctors cut the cord. It heals, and we are left with a navel. You don't even have nipples. I hadn't noticed before." She touched his chest on his pecs and then moved his hand over her breasts. Her nipples firmed as he passed his fingers over them. Her mouth found his chest, and her tongue flicked over the soft flesh. Jaril shivered. All thoughts of getting his specimens packed in the scout ship tumbled from his mind. All he wanted to do was drink her and claim her again. Her teeth sucked his flesh. His hands slid along the curve of her back and held her ass. The round mounds fit perfectly into his hands.

Her lips drifted along his throat until she bit down again. This time he cried out. She stopped and trembled in his arms. "Are you okay?"

She nodded. Her skin had flushed. He smelled her desire once more. "I don't know what it is, but the sound makes me come."

It calmed him to know he could arouse her with just his sounds. Jaril didn't know if she would accept the explanation of what he needed to tell her. "Do humans have a concept for mates?"

"You mean marriage? When two people want to spend the rest of their lives together?"

"Does this end? This marriage?"

"It can for a whole lot of reasons. Either partner can find another one, or they no longer love each other. Sometimes for other reasons. Is that the case for your kind?"

He shook his head. Jaril moved his hands over her soft flesh and then picked her back up. He liked having the heat of her body next to his. She snuggled against him and rested her head on his chest. She sighed. "I didn't notice you had two different heartbeats."

"It is another difference of my kind compared to humans. When one of my kind finds their mate, it is forever. Sounds are important to us when it comes to mating. When you moan, it makes me need you. I forget about anything else except pleasing you and needing to be inside you. With my species, it means we are meant to be together. The longer we are around one another, the more we resonate. Soon even the slightest sound will make you express your desire. You are my mate."

"How is that possible when I'm human, and you're... Well, I don't know what species you are except green."

Jaril sat down and pulled Abigail close to him. "I'm from Tilleron. My world is ten light-years from your planet. I can show you images of it, but you would have to ascend to my ship."

"Jaril, I don't really know what to say about you being my intended husband. I came back here to find out more about you, not to run off with you to another planet. I have a life here on Earth. I don't want to leave it or my sister."

"I know it is a lot to ask of you, but maybe you can come back to my ship for a little while. If... if other humans were to find you with me, then they would hurt you. I can't have them hurting you." Jaril hoped she would understand what he was trying to say.

"What would they do to you?"

He shrugged. "Your people would cut me up and dismantle my technology. If they found you, they would take the suppression nodule from your head. It would kill you."

She sat up. Jaril used his link to monitor her thoughts. They were racing at all the different possibilities from the information he'd imparted to her. "Can you not do that?"

"What am I doing?"

"You're looking into my head."

"You can feel it?" Jaril had never heard of such a thing before.

"Yes, it's like a pressure on the center of my forehead. Last time you made my nose bleed. It hurt."

He pushed a strand of hair away from her face. "I didn't mean to cause you pain. Forgive me for looking, but I wanted to know what you were thinking."

"It's kinda creepy."

"Creepy?" Jaril tried to say the world, but it felt

strange on his tongue.

"Umm… not pleasant. Strange." Abigail placed her palm against his. "You have six fingers."

"Yes, it's another mutation of my kind." Jaril kissed her throat until she gasped.

"Mutation? Is there something wrong with you?"

"Some of my species would say there is. Among our kind, if we are born with six fingers and six toes, we are sure to develop our suckers. Most fully mature when we hit adolescence. Then they send us away to Tilleron where they prepare us in how to deal with our mutation. When we are old enough, we go out on ships and look the universe over for Plasma Units… blood donors. They stay with us on the vessels as we travel. We are psychically connected to our ships. They have an artificial intelligence, but they are sentient. Mine has kept me company for a long time."

"Is that who you were talking to when you were using my phone?"

"You heard the conversation?"

"Just the end of it. Someone is coming?"

Jaril kissed her throat as his fingers slid between her thighs. He didn't want to discuss any more about his mutations with her soft, warm body perched on his knees. He found the bump within her wet folds. He held her with his other arm as she wiggled in his lap. "Yes, but right now I want to hear you scream my name. Will you come for me again?" Jaril massaged her clit.

"You're not being fair." She grabbed his arm. Her skin flushed pink as her heartbeat raced along to nearly match his double hearts. Abigail leaned her head back. He trailed his nose along her throat. Her blood called to him. He flicked his tongue along her neck and let his sucker attach. Jaril rubbed her slowly and drew the sweet liquid until he heard her cry out. "Jaril."

He lifted his head and shifted her to slide his *findick*

into her pussy. She straddled him and wrapped her arms around his neck. His female brushed her lips across his as she slowly moved her hips with a rhythm. No female had done this with him. Normally, he remained in control. Her movements made that difficult. Jaril slid his hands along her sides and cupped her ass cheeks. He broke the kiss and moved his lips down her throat until he came to the center of her chest. Her breasts bounced against his face. He took one nipple in his mouth, loving of the rough texture of the flesh. His sucker latched on, engulfing the whole thing.

"Yes!" Abigail cried out.

The sound hit him, and he came inside her. Jaril kissed her chest as her heart thundered. They both tried to catch their breath.

"Your naked form is very distracting. You heard the conversation, so you know humans are coming to this location. If they find me and this cave, they will not let me live. I cannot stay here." Jaril lifted Abigail off him and settled her onto his sleeping space.

She curled her knees up to her chest and sighed. "I can't go with you."

He trailed his finger along her jaw. "How about you come with me, and I show you my craft? Spend a few days with me until the humans disperse. You might enjoy it. I am not ready to let you go."

* * *

Abigail let the water wash over her as she thought about Jaril's offer. *It would be interesting to see his spaceship. I don't want him to get hurt.* He'd started packing his seedlings up to transport them back to his ship. If others were coming, she had to leave the cave. *Someone will find my car. They'll come looking for me. What will Mel say? She would think this is a total yarn. Maybe Jaril can bring her, too.* Abigail stepped out of the stream and dried off with the cloth he gave her. It absorbed the water and remained dry. She dressed and walked back into the main part of the cave and stood in the shadows as her green-skinned alien loaded his sprouts into a hovering cart. She watched how his muscles moved and thought back to the way he made her feel. She couldn't explain it, but something connected them. Abigail had come to the cave wanting answers and to confront her fear. She had found something else. Was it enough to give up her life on Earth and travel the stars with a blood-sucking alien?

"Do you need any help?" Abigail asked.

He turned quickly and spilled dirt on his shirt. He said something in his language and brushed off the soil which smeared on his clothing. She bit her lip to keep from laughing. Abigail took the container from him and set the pot into the floating wagon. Hands enclosed her waist as he pulled her into him. She squealed and turned around in his arms.

"This helps me. Having you in my arms. You comfort me."

"You don't even know me. Not really. I don't know anything you, except that you're into plants and you're from a different planet. You drink blood, but do you eat food?"

"I can eat food. It also nourishes, but the blood helps us to heal quicker as our bodies aren't compatible with the nanos. Our scientists have tried. They still try to program them so they can process our need for blood, but no breakthroughs yet. We are long-lived. Some species we interact with think we are gods, and they willingly volunteer themselves as Plasma Units or Body Units if we are attuned with them." Jaril kissed her forehead. "I need to get these down to the shuttle. If you can carry a few of them, I would appreciate it."

"Sure." She grabbed a few of the smaller seedlings and followed him into the blackness of the cave. Once the shadows enveloped them, a light floated before them like a baseball-shaped moon. It lit up the darkness as they ventured deep within the cave. They stopped now and again for Jaril to pull the floating wagon through the smaller gaps. The passageways twisted and turned until they came out into another large cavern. Parked in the middle of the cave was a small saucer-shaped vehicle.

"This is your ship?"

"No, it's a scout ship. Sometimes we send them out from the main ship to collect Plasma Units."

"Against their will?"

"Some do, yes. I don't condone it."

"You were going to take me against my will the first time you met me."

"I didn't want you for a slave. I panicked because you were the first human I had seen, and you had our tech. I couldn't think of anything else to do except take you back to my vessel and keep you there. I didn't think I would ever see you again."

Abigail set the containers down by the floating wagon. "It took me a long time to overcome my fear. Then I had to convince myself it really happened. Once the rescuers found me, they had me looked over by medical people, but they couldn't find anything wrong with me. I told my sister what happened, but she said it was all a hallucination. Although, they couldn't figure out where I got your blanket. When I went home, I tried to rationalize I had imagined it, but the metal piece on the back of my head remained. I couldn't forget you. I was petrified you would abduct me and experiment on me. After a month, when you didn't show up, I finally figured you weren't going to. Then it was wintertime. The snow made it impossible for me to get back. Then I put it off until I got up the courage to come here. It's a miracle I found the cave entrance this time."

"How did you discover it?" Jaril placed his hand on the outside of the ship. The metal appeared to heat under his touch and an opening appeared in the hull.

"A piece of the blanket you gave me snagged on the brambles near the entrance. The sunlight hit it right as I was looking, and I recognized it."

"I'm glad you came back." He unloaded the wagon and placed the greenery into the ship. "I need to load more. Will you help me?"

"Of course, but how are you going to get back to your spaceship if you're sending this back? Where is your craft anyway?"

"She's hiding in a cave on your moon. A few hours of night remain. We need to get this loaded and then send it back to the ship on autopilot. When it's done, we can go to the surface, and Talix can beam us up."

"Beam?"

"Destabilize our atoms and have them reassemble on the ship. It would be the fastest way. Although it is not my favorite way. You could say… I have a fear of it." Jaril shook as though he really didn't like the idea.

Abigail wasn't too keen on it either. "Yeah, I can understand why you wouldn't want to. Can your ship do that this far underground?"

"No, we have to go above. We are too far underground for me to connect with her. Your communication rectangle seems to have boosted the signal when paired with my implant. She warned me with the device, and this was the conversation you heard."

She nodded beginning to understand a little more about him. Jaril left the ship, and they went back to his lab. They gathered more specimens and made two more trips down into the cave. By the third journey, Abigail struggled drawing in air. A strange taste lingered on the back of her tongue. It felt like she was breathing through a wool blanket. Her lungs were starved for oxygen. The back of her neck burned. Jaril didn't seem to have a problem with it. The air weighed on her and she had to slow down a few times. Her head grew a little light as he loaded the rest of the plants and equipment into the ship until there wasn't any more room. What little he had left, he said he would be able to pack into a shoulder bag he had with him. It would take one more trip to gather the rest of his things, and she had left her backpack.

"Are you okay?" Jaril asked.

She clutched her chest. "There's not enough air down here. My neck burns."

His face scrunched up as he touched the nodule. "The nanos are working overtime to make sure your body is able to process the air here. I don't notice it. I didn't realize the composition of it was not suitable. Come, we will only be here another moment." Jaril touched the hull of the scout ship one more time. The back half closed. He pressed another part of the front and a small keyboard appeared as a hologram on the front of the vessel. He pushed a few keys until it disappeared. The craft shook as he backed away. He picked up Abigail and held her close. The ship glowed until the brightness made her close her eyes against it. Jaril moved away, and a blast of air thrust her hair back. Then the glow and the wind dissipated.

Jaril didn't release her but carried her while she struggled to breathe. As they got back up to his sleeping place, she could inhale normally, and the back of her neck had cooled.

"Better?"

She nodded. "Yes."

"Jaril, can you hear me?" the high-pitched voice came from her bag. Abigail turned toward the corner and saw her phone sitting on the top of her things where Jaril had put it back. The screen remained locked but lit up. She grabbed it.

"Hello, who is this?" she asked.

"Give the communication device to Jaril, human

female. I know he is there with you."

She looked at him. "Is this your ship?"

"Yes, she can be a tad overprotective."

"I can hear you conversing with the female. Jaril, you need to evacuate now. The humans are nearing your location."

"I thought you said we had more time. Has the scout ship made it to you yet?" Jaril took the phone.

"The ship has cleared the Earth's atmosphere. I have fired up the engines and am ready to leave the lunar cave to rendezvous with it. Once I'm closer, I intend to bring you up to the ship, but you must abandon your position now." A picture appeared on the phone that showed a heat signature approaching the cave.

"Is there another way out of the cave?" Abigail asked.

"Yes. I mapped it with Talix so we would have a better understanding of the cave system. It has not been discovered by you humans. Come, gather your things, and we will go." Jaril quickly collected a few pieces of equipment he hadn't been able to take with him and placed them in the bag. Abigail stuffed his other blanket into her knapsack.

Jaril grunted as he hefted the bag over his shoulder. She noticed a small disk he had set where they slept. "What is that?"

"It will destroy any cellular matter left behind. It will make the rest of the equipment I can't take back with me inoperable. We must hurry. If we are in the vicinity of the blast, it will also disintegrate you." Jaril took her hand and pulled her into the dark.

Abigail bumped into something and tripped into him. He grunted and caught them before they hit the dirt. The earth rippled below her feet. She pressed her hand to the cave wall to hold herself until the tremor stopped. Once it was over, Jaril shook something, and a small light appeared in front of him. His emerald green color had taken on a greyish tint.

"Are you okay?" Abigail asked.

"I'll be fine." He gave her a reassuring smile, but she didn't believe him.

"What's the matter?"

"We have to keep moving. We go down before we go up again. You're going to get wet."

"Fine, but tell me what is wrong with you."

He touched his side. "The wound I received from the human who attacked me. It hasn't healed properly. An organ was hit. All the blood I've taken has only healed it to a certain point. The damage has to be repaired when I get back to my vessel."

"Well, then, we have to get you there. Can you make it?" Abigail asked, not sure what to make of his situation. The longer she was with Jaril, the more she knew she didn't want to be away from him.

"I should be. All the activity has aggravated the injury. I wasn't expecting to leave this quickly. Come, we need to get to the surface."

Chapter Five

Jaril winced as they walked along the tunnel. They had gotten through the river which had come up to his waist and up to his female's torso. They couldn't stop. The more he walked, the more pain crept up on him. He needed to get above and into the spaceship where he could be repaired. He couldn't tell the woman it was more serious than he realized. The impact of all the activity by loading and unloading his equipment had taken its toll. He could hear her concern and feel it. Jaril concentrated on putting one foot in front of the other. At least he knew the scout ship had reached Talix. She would return the seedlings and his experiments back to Tilleron in case he perished.

They kept on walking until they started to go uphill. Abigail's breathing was labored once again. It was tough for her to convert the thin oxygen into breathable air even with the nanos working to assist her lungs. She didn't complain but kept up as he pushed himself through the growing agony. Finally, they made it up to a small opening. He welcomed the night air. The last time he had come this way all that greeted him were trees and a magnificent view of the mountains. Now, the lights from the humans' camp lit up the darkness nearby. The noise he heard was not a typical encampment.

"Talix, I need an update on the humans. Our second opening has brought us close to a base camp," he whispered.

"The humans have gathered their military. I read weapons and heavily armored vehicles. They have satellite capabilities and have detected my presence. We need to get you out of there."

"She's right. You need to go," Abigail told him. "If they catch you, they'll experiment on you."

"They can't find you either."

"I'll be okay. Get back to your craft so you can be healed. I'll distract them. Is your spaceship ready to pick you up?" Abigail touched his face.

"Yes. I don't want to let you go." He brushed her lips for one more kiss. Jaril ached to hold her. He yearned to bring her with him, but Talix could only atomize one being at a time.

"I'll be waiting."

Jaril could track the nodule in her neck. "I'll make sure to find you."

Abigail made her way down the small hill toward the floodlights. It took a few moments until the alarm sounded and more lights snapped on. He almost started toward them to bring her back. "Talix, bring me up directly into the medical bay."

"I'll be waiting."

Jaril stepped into the clearing. A hot beam engulfed him. He winced as he could feel himself coming apart and transporting through space. It happened in a blink. When he was aware again, he was in his ship. He collapsed to his knees on the floor. The pain from his injury seemed a hundred times worse. He clutched his side and cried out. Hands helped him stand.

"Come, lie down. I have the medical bed ready. It will heal the damage."

Talix guided him over to the bed and helped him lie back. He grunted as he moved and feared the worst. A device descended from the ceiling. A blue light scanned his body starting at his feet and passed over his body to his head and then went back down it again. A projection of his physiology floated above him. The knife wound had penetrated his stomach and some of his intestines.

"We're going to have to open you up and heal you from the inside out. I'm going to put you under."

"There's blood..." He struggled to get the words out.

The AI placed a hand on his shoulder. "I found it and

already have it loaded to give you a transfusion. I know what to do. This is part of my programming."

A sharp jab hit him where she touched his shoulder. Jaril tried to fight it, but he could feel the blackness taking him as the sedative took hold.

* * *

Jaril awoke again and found himself in his sleep chambers. The gray metallic walls were different from the caves he was used to. He tried to sit up, but the pain from his side made him wince, and he lay back down. Next to his bed was a bottle Talix left for him. He opened it. The sweet scent of Abigail's blood made him long for her. He took a long drink -- it took the edge off the pain. He could sit up once he finished it. Jaril needed more.

"Talix."

The artificial intelligence appeared in her solid form. "You're awake. Your color already looks better. We're already en route to Tilleron. I took --"

"No! Turn the ship around."

"Why do you care for the human?"

"She saved my life. Her blood kept me alive, and she's my mate. I won't leave without her."

"The humans are aware of us."

"I don't care, Talix. Do it!"

Her holographic form blinked out. He could feel the engines slow. The ship shook a moment as it turned. The longer he was away from his female, the more anxious he grew. He'd never felt this way about another being, only his plants. *She put herself in danger for me.* He might not understand humans, or even others of his own species, but he loved her. Even among his own species he was considered strange. When he needed blood, he always used a willing donor, but he never took a Plasma Unit on his ship to sustain him.

Jaril slowly left his room feeling better and went to the cargo hold to check on his seedlings. Talix had gotten a few of them set up. He had nothing to do for few hours until they reached Earth again. He rearranged his seedlings and experiments until he came upon the ones he had planted from Abigail's seed packets. The plants were mature enough they appeared to be edible. He plucked one of the thin green leaves and smelled it. The leaf had a sharp aroma. Jaril crushed it between his fingers and tasted it. The plant didn't have an unpleasant taste. Seeing how it had grown made him miss her more. He carefully put the plants in a place where they would grow better. *I'll show Abigail the first thing after I've rescued her.*

"How long until we get there?" he asked Talix.

"Within the hour. I've already gotten a lock on her position. Her vital signs are showing stable. Her heart rate is a little elevated."

"Can you hack into their transmissions?" Jaril asked.

"Their firewalls are primitive. Do you want me to tap into the female's suppression nodule? You can speak with her then."

"Yes. Monitor the communications and let me know what you hear." Jaril held his breath as the silence extended and he waited to hear his mate's voice.

"I've tapped into her suppression nodule. You'll hear what she hears. I've rerouted the nanos. She'll be able to hear you as well."

"Thank you, Talix." Jaril listened, and he could hear his mate breathing.

"Where are we going?" Abigail asked.

"Not too far. Someplace where you'll be a lot more comfortable. Next time, Ms. Pike, it would be much easier if you started with the truth. We examined the contents of your pack and came away with alien DNA. Seems like someone was a naughty girl."

Jaril bristled at the male's words. He clenched his fists. He heard Abigail whimper and then rustling. Then he heard the man again. "Take her to room five. We'll start with a full body scan and, once we get what we need, the dissection. We need to see how she's been altered by the alien."

He could hear the evil in the man's intention. He might not know what that meant, but he knew it wasn't a good thing. If the humans ever caught him or her, then they would experiment on them. Jaril held his breath as he listened, wanting to see what would happen. He picked up other sounds, but he couldn't discern what they were.

"Let me out!" Abigail screamed.

* * *

Abigail paced the tiny space they had put her in. They had taken her bag and left her in a room with a small chair, a table, and a glass of water. She hadn't touched the water, and she could barely sit down more than a few minutes. Her thoughts raced back to Jaril. *Is he all right? Did he make it back to the ship? Did he get the help he needed? Will he really come back for me?*

The longer she was away from him, the more she realized she didn't want to be apart from him. It was the oddest thing. He made her feel complete in some way. *Maybe it's the implant talking.* She sat on the chair and hung her head. Walking into the camp had been a stupid idea, but it had been the only way to make sure Jaril got back to his ship.

"Ms. Pike, isn't it?"

Abigail jumped as a man entered the room. She gave the man holding the clipboard a smile. He wore a white lab coat with no identification. "That's me. Is everything okay? I got a little lost and was telling the guys I didn't mean to wander in, but my phone was dead and…"

The man gave her a small smile, and yet she could see the triumphant look in his eyes. "Ms. Pike, you don't need to spin an entire story. We know you were in contact with an extraterrestrial being."

"You mean like an alien? Spaceship and everything?" She couldn't help but laugh. She prayed they would buy the story. "I'm sorry. I don't believe in little green men. I think you've seen one too many movies."

The scientist wrote something on his clipboard. "I understand it's quite alarming to discover the truth. Like many of the others we've interviewed and studied, it appears your memory has been altered. These beings don't like us to know about them. Fortunately, for you, this one wasn't smart enough to deactivate the tech it implanted in you."

Abigail tried to act surprised. "Implant? Where?" She made a show of pulling up her sleeves and moving her fingers through her hair.

The man moved the hair aside on the back of her neck. "Here, but I think you already knew that." His fingers slid down her shoulder and clutched it as he leaned over her. The pressure of his weight on her shoulder made it so she couldn't stand up. Her heart pounded into her ribcage. "We're going to have a nice conversation about what you know. We haven't figured out how this device works, but we have found out by trying to remove it, unfortunately, the subject expires. You don't want that to happen to you, do you?"

"N-no," she whispered. Each minute she was with this man, her fear ramped up. She had to find a way out of there. What kept her going was knowing Jaril had gotten away.

"Tell me, what you can remember? It'd help us greatly by getting a location as to where the alien might be. Imagine if we can catch a live specimen."

"I don't know where the alien is. Okay. I escaped."

"Or he let you go to throw us off his tracks. I wonder which it is. We have ways of finding out, Ms. Pike. We found your car. Your backpack has a compass and a map in it. Strange for someone who said they got lost. From my understanding, last year you did lose your way in these mountains. Your sister reported you were…" He looked down at his clipboard. "…going on about a large green man who drank your blood and threatened to take you back to his spaceship and make you his love slave."

Abigail winced at hearing the words she had told the police the year before in her statement. "I don't recall much of what I was rambling about. I hit my head pretty hard."

"The EMTs said you didn't have a concussion. Truth would be better here. We already have your sister in custody."

"My sister doesn't have anything to do with this." Abigail clutched her fist and held it back so she wouldn't strike the man. Mel didn't need to be dragged into the situation.

The man in the lab coat released her and flashed her a wicked grin. Two armed men entered followed by two others dressed in lab coats. Abigail got up out of the chair and backed away, but there was nowhere for her to go. She tried to dart away from the guards, but the other two caught her.

"Where are we going?" Abigail asked as he led her out of the room.

The two goons didn't reply but led her from the room. They held on to her upper arms as they moved through the facility, passing several other people in lab coats. Abigail saw another room where they had the contents of her backpack laid out on a table. The door to the area was sealed in a heavy layer of plastic. Her things were being scanned by several scientific instruments.

The two men shoved her into a room and locked it. She banged on the door, but there was no handle. She cupped her hands and peered through the glass at the other end of the room that was meant to be an observation window, but she couldn't see anything. Abigail backed away and looked at the table in the center of the room. Her fear settled in her throat and her stomach turned.

"Let me out!" she screamed as the terror of her situation took hold.

"Hush, love."

"Jaril?"

"Shhh. I need you to hear me."

Abigail wasn't sure how she could hear Jaril, but it sounded like he was right next to her. She nodded and slid down the wall underneath the window. Hope helped calm her down. She held her head in her hands. He was coming back for her.

"I've tapped into your suppression nodule and altered the nanos to hear what you're hearing, and you can hear me. I don't want to think about doing more in case you are damaged. I made it back to the ship. I've been mended. We'll be in your orbit soon enough. We have your location. I'll bring you aboard when we get there. You'll soon be in my arms, my mate."

"Jaril, they're going to examine me. They know…"

"I heard the man. Impede them for as long as you can. I'll let you know when I'm close enough to retrieve you."

His voice gave her more comfort than she had imagined it would. Abigail leaned her head against the wall and breathed a sigh of relief. Jaril was healed, and he was coming to get her. He called her his mate. Something about the moniker rang in her mind like a bell, and she knew it was true. She belonged with him. It was clear now she had no place on Earth.

What am I going to tell Mel? Shit, they have her. I can't leave her with them. I have to convince Jaril to bring Mel along. She's going to hate it.

She pressed her forehead to her knees when she heard the door open. A rustle of footsteps came into the room. Abigail had to keep a calm head to pass the time.

"Come now, Ms. Pike. It's time for you to play nice. Remove your clothing and put this gown on." The same man who talked to her before had returned. He set the garment on the table and waited.

Abigail rose slowly. "Don't you want to know the details of his underground lab? I'm beginning to remember a few things."

The man's eyebrows rose. "Really? What lab is this? You want me to believe this alien had some clandestine base?"

She shrugged. "You have my bag. I'm sure you found some strange gadgets you don't know the purpose of. I can tell you how to use it. What he was doing down there."

The man's mouth twitched at what she said. He was interested. "A lab, you say?" He touched his ear. He wore an earpiece she hadn't noticed before. "What was he doing down in his laboratory? How far down was it?"

"I don't know how far underground it was. I couldn't see most of the time where we were going. He carried me through the maze of tunnels, but we were near an underground stream. Or maybe it was a small river. His lab was full of plants."

"Were they plants you recognized?"

"I have no idea. I wouldn't know a rose from a begonia without looking it up. Even if it had flowers on it. I didn't see any vegetables."

"Ms. Pike, did you see any type of organism that didn't seem to be from Earth?"

"No, he was exclusively interested in our vegetation. He had heat lamps set up and an irrigation system. He found me when he was out gathering more soil. He told me he was a scientist on his planet, and he came here to study our plant life."

"Didn't you find that a tad strange?"

Abigail decided to be honest with the man. The longer

she could keep him talking, the closer Jaril could come. "To be honest, I found it all bizarre. Last year, my sister and I got lost. I needed to pee and found this cave to go in. I wasn't expecting to walk into a seven-foot, green-skinned man. I fell and cracked my head on the cave floor." She touched the metal disk at her neck. "If it weren't for this implant, I'd be dead. He saved my life."

"And he didn't have an agenda?"

"He threatened to keep me as a slave because I knew about him, and I had his technology in my head."

The man leaned against the wall. "How did you get away?"

"He let me go. I think I was talking too much for him. All he wanted to do was go back to his vegetation. He wasn't a very good conversationalist."

"You could understand him? How was that?"

"It's the implant, but you know that since you told me you've interviewed others who had them."

"That information is classified."

Abigail pulled at a loose thread on her shirt. She didn't know how long she could keep talking. "Well, then. I'm not telling you anything you don't already know."

"Please go on. There are some who don't know."

She wound the thread around her finger and then unwound it again. Something to keep her hands busy. Something to keep her mind focused. "The implant allowed me to understand him, but he doesn't have a great grasp of the English language. Maybe it was translated from him to me. I don't know how it works. He told me the nodule had small nanites. They can heal the body. When I'm injured, I feel this warmth move down my neck and into the place where I'm hurt."

"Hmmm… I talked with others, and they said the communication was telepathic. Did you hear his voice in your mind?" He touched his earpiece again. Someone came in wheeling a tray holding surgical instruments in neat rows.

Her fear amped up once more. "What's that for?"

"We want to test your theory. To be sure you're healing as you claim. Don't worry you shouldn't feel much pain if the implant works the way you say it does. Stand up, Ms. Pike, and come over to the exam table."

"You really don't want to do that."

Another man in a lab coat entered carrying some kind of machine. He set it on the bed and set it up.

"What's that?" she asked. Abigail didn't move. She held her breath and waited for Jaril. "How long?" she whispered as low as she could.

"We are almost there. Keep talking," Jaril told her.

She didn't feel like being cut open. Of course, Jaril would have it even worse if he were captured. Two men grabbed her again.

"Let me go!" Abigail kicked, and her foot caught the tray of surgical implements. It sent the instruments flying. They didn't release her.

"Hold her down." The man with the clipboard picked up the surgical knife.

"No!" Abigail screamed. "Get away from me."

They held her down, and the man grabbed her arm. He pressed the blade into her skin. He sliced her arm. She howled in pain. The knife dug deeper as she tried to pull her arm away. The scientist dragged the blade down the inside of her arm. Abigail jerked her arm away causing a jagged slice along her wrist into the heel of her palm. Her captor threw the blade back onto the tray and motioned for the two men to release her. Warmth flashed down to her shoulder as blood seeped from the wound.

"Give me something to bind this," Abigail pleaded.

"No, we need to watch this. Are you taping?" clipboard man asked.

Abigail couldn't see past the pain and the blood rushing down her arm onto the white sheet soaking up the blood. The nanos charged down her arm. The flow of blood slowed. The heat around the wound made her bite her lip. She could feel the nanos working on healing her. The gaping cut began to seal, and the blood stopped flowing. The clipboard man grabbed a cloth and wiped away the blood. Her skin had all but healed, leaving a faint pink scar behind.

"Remarkable. How is this possible? The others had their implants turned off. Did you record it?"

"Did you get what you wanted?" Hot tears streamed down her cheek.

"Oh, yes, Ms. Pike. You will prove to be the best specimen yet. I'm sure there are things in your memory you don't recall yet, but we will get the implant out of you." He came at her again, but Abigail dodged out of the way.

"Jaril, now would be a good time," she muttered.

Mr. Clipboard reached for her, but this time she felt something buzzing along her skin. The hair on the back of her neck stood up. It felt like all the air got sucked from her lungs. Her vision went black. Abigail tried to move and reached out to find out where the room had gone. She couldn't sense anything. Panic overwhelmed her, but before she could even scream, the world came back into view. The light hit her first.

It hurt her eyes. When she blinked, another man stood in front of her. She cringed and pulled away from the arms reaching out to her. Then the hands caressed her face, and the words didn't make sense. She heard whistles and trills. Abigail focused and saw Jaril. She wrapped her arms around his neck. He held her to him. Relief flooded her. Other feelings she didn't know how to express overwhelmed her. Being apart from him was the worst thing she could have felt. He stroked her hair and murmured sentiments into her ear she couldn't understand. She held Jaril closer and squeezed him to make sure he was real and that she was out of the hell she had found herself in.

Jaril pulled away and she felt his absence. He began talking again, but she caught his hand. "I can't understand you."

His forehead creased. His fingers moved along the back of her neck. His touch made her shiver. Jaril pressed the nodule. A sharp jab shot along her spine and hit her brain. She cried out. He moved slightly and the pain dissipated. "Is this better?"

She relaxed as the nanos spread into her body repairing any damage. "Yes." Jaril slipped his hands underneath her and picked her up. Abigail settled her head against his shoulder as he held her. He made her feel safe. "Are we on your craft?"

"Yes. I had to destabilize your atoms and rearrange them back on the ship. It can be quite disorienting. I think that's why your nodule had the reaction with the translation. I had to fine-tune it. Abigail, I can't tell you what you mean to me."

Jaril stopped in a room and set her down on a bed. He kept her cradled in his arms. He kissed the inside of her palm. "They hurt you."

"I'm okay now, but they have my sister. Is there any way you can get her?"

Jaril let out a long sigh. "She does not have a suppression nodule in her. She will be challenging to track."

"I can search for her based on the human female's DNA profile. May I have a sample of your blood?" Talix asked.

Abigail looked at him. "Anything. We can't leave her with them."

"We will find her." Jaril lifted something from the table beside the bed. "I need a drop. May I?" He held out a needle.

Abigail held out her hand. He pricked the center of her finger and drew blood. He set the needle on a lit-up panel on the wall. "Talix is a living ship. She will find the same DNA signature to locate your sister. I will bring her up to this room, but neither of you can return to Earth. I understand what you have sacrificed for this. The people will always be looking for you. They know about us. Talix can hack into their computer system. Your government knows more about my species and others than we imagined. I need to take the information back to Tilleron."

"I have found a familial match for the human female's DNA pattern. Do you want me to bring the other female aboard?" Talix asked.

"Yes, please," Abigail answered.

"I only answer to Jaril."

She rolled her eyes. Jaril smiled. "Talix, please bring her onto the ship."

"Your sister will be disoriented. I'll have to implant her with a suppression nodule as well."

"Can I talk to her first and let her know what happened?" Abigail asked him.

He nodded. Jaril moved out of the way as a form materialized in the room by the side of the bed. Once the figure was completely solid, Mel looked over and screamed. Jaril put up his hands and moved away. Mel lunged at him.

"Whoa, Mel, it's me. Hey, it's okay." Abigail wrapped her arms around her sister. Mel shook in her arms.

"Abby? What the fuck is going on? Where did all the men in lab coats go? They picked me up in the middle of the night and said something happened to you. Then they bring me to this place and won't let me see you. They kept going on and on about doing some testing to make sure I didn't have any radiation poisoning. Who the hell is the big green guy?"

"Remember when you thought I was crazy last year going on about my encounter with large green man taking me underground?"

Mel kept her gaze on Jaril and then sat down on the bed next to Abigail. "Yeah?"

"We're on his spaceship. He beamed you up here to get you away from the lab coats. They were going to experiment on me to find out more about him. They were probably going to do the same thing to you. I couldn't leave you down there. I asked him to bring you up here, but... we can't go back."

"Abby, you're shitting me, right? I mean, come on..."

Abigail knew how her sister felt. She had been there a year before. "It's not a joke. Last year when I hit my head, Jaril saved my life." She lifted her hair and showed her the implant at the back of her neck. "He put this on my head. The technology saved me. It also allows me to understand him."

"Will she let me put the implant on her?" Jaril asked.

Mel backed away from him a little more on the bed. "What did he say?"

"He wants to know if he can put the implant on you. You can stay healthy and understand him. It doesn't hurt. It gets a little warm when it's repairing your body, but nothing bad."

"Are you his slave?"

Abigail giggled. "No, he doesn't control me. I'm not his slave." She glanced at Jaril and thought about how he was learning her body. Maybe she was his slave. She shivered at how he made her feel.

"I know that look. Oh, my God, you've fucked him. Abigail, what if he gave you some disease? Does he expect me to sleep with him, too, so I can stay on his ship?" Mel's gave her a disgusted look.

"What is she saying?" Jaril asked.

"She wants to know if I'm your slave. If she'll have to

sleep with you to stay on the ship or make you happy." Abigail patted the bed for Jaril to sit next to her. "Come here."

Jaril sat on the bed. Mel tried to move, but Abigail held her hand on her sister's knee to keep Mel from leaving. She had to prove Jaril wouldn't hurt them. Jaril wrapped his hand around her waist. She leaned against him.

"Abby, are you sure he won't make you into his zombie or something?" Mel asked.

"I promise. He loves me, Mel. I love him. He's really a good man."

"He's not a man."

"You know what I mean. He has a good heart. If I hadn't gone looking for him, none of this would've happened. I'm sorry, but I had to make sure I wasn't crazy from last year."

"Abby…" Mel sighed. "You are seriously… This is not how I wanted my day to go. I liked Earth, but I am not about to be experimented on. I don't like the idea of having something in my head. What assurances can he give me my brain won't be erased?"

"She wants to know if you're going to make her into a robot slave," Abigail told Jaril.

"Why would I want a servant? I told you I did not keep Plasma Units on board. And I don't have a Body Unit either. I do not see your sister as someone I would bed. Unless you want her to join us?"

"No. That's not…"

"He won't turn you into his slave," Abigail told her sister. "We can work out the details later. Come on, Mel, you're always up for an adventure. Well, here it is."

Her sister rolled her eyes. "I never thought you'd take it literally. Okay. Put the thing in my head so I can talk to him. I'm tired of listening to all the whistling and chirping. He sounds like a woodpecker who learned to whistle."

"She said yes."

"Good. I'll go get one. When she is settled in, I want to make sure you aren't hurt."

"You know I'm not."

Jaril flashed her a large grin. "I want to make sure anyway."

Chapter Six

Jaril moved the hair aside on Abigail's sister's neck. He touched the smooth skin and held the suppression nodule in his hand. He placed the silver disk at the hairline of the human female. Small thin wisps of metal sprouted from the center of the disk no finer than a hair. They lay against her neck and then sank into her skin. From there they would intertwine with her brain stem and her nervous system. The female stiffened. He heard her grunt from the swift pain and discomfort the implantation caused. He tapped the center of it three times to activate the device. He held his thumb against it imprinting the nanos with the frequency of his own implant.

He could feel the rush of the woman's thoughts as they pressed upon his mind and could feel her fear. He glanced at Abigail, who looked worried. "Can you comprehend me?" he asked.

Her sister didn't react.

"He wanted to know if you could understand him?"

"She said not yet," Abigail answered for her sister.

He pushed the center of the nodule again, and then slid his finger around the edge. "How about now?" He glanced at Abigail, who smiled at him.

"Yes." He heard the trill of the sister's voice and knew the nanos were working. Her sister turned to him.

"What is this going to do to me exactly?"

"First, what is your name?"

Her expression fell. He could see some resemblance to his mate in her face, mostly around her eyes and the shape of her nose. Nothing about her made him feel any desire toward her. "Melony. Mel."

"I'm Jaril. You are a guest upon my ship because your sister is my mate. I don't intend to do anything to you. Although, because you have accommodations, I might request your blood to nourish me."

The color drained from her face. "My blood? You didn't say anything about me giving blood. Abigail..."

"Mel, hush. Jaril needs blood to survive. He's taken mine a few times. It doesn't hurt. He can't feed on me all the time."

"It is a small cost to pay for residing on my ship and using the resources. I do understand compensation is required for things in your realm. We also deal with other civilizations that trade." Jaril stared at her. He hadn't discussed taking blood from her with his mate, but he knew Abigail couldn't sustain him forever even with the nanos in her blood. He didn't want to drain her and take advantage.

"Fine. Do you stick me with a needle or what?" Mel asked.

"I can use an instrument and withdraw the blood or use my sucker."

"You might as well show her, love," Abigail said to him.

He stared at her as the word sunk him. He didn't know what to say. She had called him love. Jaril turned Mel's wrist over. He could hear her thoughts as they raced in her mind. She was afraid of him. She was mad at her sister, but she didn't know how to tell Abigail. Once it all settled into Mel's mind, then Abigail would argue with Mel. Her fear consumed her. The heat of her flesh opened his sucker, and he latched onto the vein. The blood hit his mouth. He drained it down, but it had a bitter taste to it. The liquid would feed him, but he craved his mate's. After a couple of swallows, he released her.

Mel looked at her arm and then back at him. She touched it and wiped it on her clothes.

"The feeding will not harm you. Thank you for the blood. I must speak with your sister. Consider this room your quarters. Abigail, will you accompany me?"

He got up and waited for his mate outside of the quarters. Abigail came out a few minutes later. They walked down the corridor. The need for her overtook him. Jaril pushed her against the wall and pressed his body against hers. He held her arms above her head and claimed her lips. He kissed her until he heard her moan, and she molded her body against him. Jaril moved his mouth to her throat. His sucker latched onto her neck. The sweetness of her blood hit him and made him embrace her more.

"Jaril," Abigail groaned.

He broke from feeding. The desire in her eyes mirrored his need for her. "I yearn to be inside you."

She touched his face. "Yes, you drive me crazy. But we need to talk about my sister and us. Besides, I want to be in your bed and not fucking you against a wall."

"Come." Jaril took her hand, led her through the halls of the ship, and down another corridor. He pressed his hand to the door and it opened. He sat on the bed and realized the room was not fit for his mate. He hadn't been in it since he left the ship. He released her hand and looked away.

"What's the matter?"

"This is not a suitable place for you."

"What are you talking about? There's a bed and your things."

"No, you deserve more. You…" He stopped to think about what it was he had heard about others of his kind having mates and what he read in the database about human women.

"Jaril, you saved my sister and me. You don't owe me anything."

He saw she meant it. When he peered into her mind, her love for him radiated from her entire being. "You meant what you said when you called me 'love.' You love me?"

"I love you. I know you're reading my mind. I'm telling you the truth. You don't need to do anything special for me to make your room nicer or whatever. Show me the ship when you're ready. Tell me about your planet. I want to hear about it all. My sister will come around. You're my mate and you saved me."

"We saved each other." He touched her cheek and enjoyed the softness of it. "I'll show you my world and tell you anything you want to know. I love you, too."

Abigail returned his smile. She got up and took off her garments. He struggled to keep from touching her as she stood before him naked. Her luscious flesh and curves were all filled out in all the places he enjoyed. Jaril loved her rounded hips and the flesh of her belly. His gaze traveled along her body wondering what other parts of her he hadn't explored yet. His mouth watered at the idea of drinking her again. He reached for Abigail, but his mate batted his hand away. He frowned.

"You wish to copulate. Why are you forcing me away?" He looked into her mind, but she poked him in the center of the forehead.

"Stop doing that."

"I must know what you desire. For us to --"

"You don't need to know what I *desire* all the time. Every time you go into my head when I don't want you there, I'm going to hit you between the eyes. That way you can know what it feels like for me."

Jaril heard the amusement in her voice and understood she wanted her privacy. "How do I know when I am allowed to monitor your thoughts?"

"I'll inform you when you can."

"But --"

His mate got to her knees and glided her hands over his thighs until she cupped his cock. His *findick* firmed as she touched him. "Take off your pants."

Jaril didn't need for her to tell him again. He removed

his leggings and waited before her. Her finger traced the vein along his shaft. Abigail looked at him with an innocent expression, but he could see the temptress in her gaze. She held his three testicles and weighed them in her hand. He grunted in anticipation. Abigail kissed his thigh and flicked her tongue over his skin.

"What are you planning?"

"You said you wanted me to suck your cock." Her voice came out in a throaty whisper.

He shivered as the vibration of her soft voice hit him. He grabbed onto her shoulder as her lips encompassed his *findick*. She worked her tongue around his length. Jaril had never felt such pleasure as her mouth created a suction around him. She slowly moved along him and then took all of his prick into her mouth as she could. His mate dragged her teeth over him. A little bit of pain came from her attention, but he welcomed it. He wound his fingers through her hair.

"More," he moaned.

Abigail squeezed his thigh and stopped working on him for a moment. He sensed a flash of her pleasure as it washed over him. She continued to work, but Jaril couldn't keep control. He thrust his hips trying to start a faster pace.

"Love, I need to be inside your warm female place again."

She took one more lick on his cock and released him. Abigail giggled. "We're going to have to work on your English translation."

"Did I say it wrong?"

His mate pushed his chest so that he stumbled back onto the bed. She straddled him and impaled herself on his *findick*. Jaril quaked when she rode him. His hands stroked along her sides and cupped her breasts. Her nipples hardened from the pleasure. He kissed her chest and cupped her breasts. His thumbs played over her pert buds. Jaril flicked his tongue over her flesh. His tongue bloomed, but he kept it from attaching. Instead, he sucked in her flesh and bit her. Abigail cried out from his bite. She quickened her pace as she rode him. He didn't know how much longer he could hold off while she took control of their union. Her hands wrapped around his neck.

"Bite me. Drink me. Whatever, just do it," his mate demanded.

Jaril didn't need any more encouragement. He bit her again with regular teeth before his sucker latched onto her throat. Once he tasted the blood, he gripped her ass and thrust into her. Abigail screamed out as he felt her pussy grip his cock. He broke away from drinking her and claimed her lips. He plunged into her one more time and came. Jaril moaned, and he felt his mate orgasm again. She whimpered against him. He moved inside her a few more times before kissing her. Abigail's plump lips were parted as she breathed in. Tempted, he peeked into her mind to see if she was fulfilled until she hit his forehead again.

"Ouch." He pulled away. "I wanted to know if you reached satisfaction."

"You don't need to read my mind to know I did. Twice."

"Only twice? I have treated you poorly, then." Jaril smiled, loving his mate's expression. He slid his hands under her ass. He lifted her up and set her down on the bed, going to his knees before her.

"Jaril, I don't know if I can go again right now."

"Sure, you can. As you have said, I need to fuck you. I want to hear you scream once more." He licked his lips to catch the last taste of her blood. The ship jolted, but it was only the engines kicking in. They were traveling to Tilleron. He had plenty of time to pleasure his mate and make her scream repeatedly.

* * *

Abigail stood on the ship's main deck watching through the view screen as they flew through the clouds and descended toward the planet's surface. Jaril sat in the pilot's seat as he guided the ship down. He didn't even notice her. He was telepathically linked to the vessel. He'd explained that he was connected and could feel all the ship, and he wouldn't be able to communicate with her.

"Are you sure they won't eat us?" Mel asked.

Abigail chuckled. "They won't eat you. Jaril sent along a message to his kind who are mated to other humans. He said they would meet us when we're ready."

"You can talk about how green your men are and what your babies are going to look like. You aren't stranded here," Mel muttered.

Abigail gave her a look. Mel hadn't adjusted well to the idea of leaving Earth. "I don't want to think of it that way. It's an adventure. At least we're not the only ones here. You never know, you might find your own green man."

"Not likely. Nothing about him turns me on." Mel gave Jaril a side glance and shook her head in disgust. "I still don't really understand what you see in him."

"You don't have to understand it, but it's the best sex I've ever had." The clouds parted, revealing a vast jungle greener than she had ever seen. The sky had a purplish hue to it. They flew lower until they could see a lush field. The ship settled down and shuddered to a stop. Jaril opened his eyes and gave her a tired smile. He had been flying for a few hours, and she could see he needed rest.

She touched his face and felt him sigh. He kissed her wrist and his sucker latched on. He took in a few swallows before getting up from the chair. "Just what I needed, love. What do you think of the view?"

"It's amazing. I can see why you're infatuated with

plants."

"I'm not infatuated with them. I have studied their properties all my life. They bring me comfort."

She hit his shoulder, and he gave her a look that made her giggle. She felt a small pressure in the center of her forehead knowing he was reading her thoughts to understand what she was thinking because he didn't quite understand her action. "You are infatuated because I've found you in your lab when you'd forgotten about me."

His eyebrows lifted. "I've never disregarded you. I've only…"

"I'm teasing. I understand." Abigail kissed him one more time.

"You two are disgusting," Mel blurted out.

Jaril frowned at her comment. "Wait until you find a mate amongst my people."

"I don't think I'll end up with a green…"

Abigail shot her sister a look.

"…with a male from your species. I'll stay celibate," Mel finished.

"Don't worry about her. She'll figure it out. Do we stay on the ship, or do you have a house?" Abigail asked him. Jaril hadn't really said what they were going to do when they got to his planet.

"I-I have a house. It's not far from here. There is a cluster of homes. We keep them for when we are on the planet. I normally work from there. I don't normally go on the ship. I'll take you there and you can settle in. Melony, I know it was not your first choice to come with me and settle on my planet. But I promise I will do what I can to make you comfortable. You are *mala*, family. This life will be different for you, but my kind do not shun those who are different. There are others here from your planet and other races. Some come here to be Plasma Units. Some are mates. Our mutation makes us outcasts on our home planet which is why they send us here. Our families disown us. We come here to be with our own, but we can never return home."

"I-I didn't realize," Mel told him.

"It's okay. Come. I want to show you both my home." He held out his hand to Abigail.

"Come on, Mel. Can you at least try?"

"Can I hitch a ride back to Earth with someone else if I hate it?" Mel asked.

Jaril sighed. "I can ask some of the others and see if they can take you back."

She gave them a nod. "Okay, then. I'll give it a chance."

Abigail took Jaril's hand. As he led her out of the ship, she didn't know what to expect in this new world, but she knew it would be fine as long as she had him.

Souped Up by the Alien Vampire Mechanic
Crymsyn Hart

Pulled from her life on Earth, all Melony Pike wants is to return home. Instead, she's on a distant planet with her sister, Abigail, and Abigail's alien mate. She knows they can't return to Earth -- she'd be hunted down and experimented on for the alien technology implanted in her neck. But even with other human women on the planet, she still feels out of place. She sure isn't looking for a green alien mate.

Brax is a fixer, an alien mechanic. He's been alone for a long time and he's not looking for anyone. Then he meets Melony and his world shifts. However, a looming invasion threatens the one thing he wants. He will do anything to cement the relationship between him and Melony and will stop anyone from getting to her.

Chapter One

Melony trailed her fingers through the fine black sand, as smooth as the contents of an hourglass broken open and standing still. The vastness of the beach made her feel as frozen as time did in this place. Turquoise ocean waves lapped at the shoreline, pulling back the sand as the tide went out. With each wave, it felt like more of her previous life washed out into the foreign ocean. The sulfuric tang of the air stuck to her tongue. She let out a long sigh.

While the picturesque landscape reminded her of a Caribbean island, the sky's slightly purple sheen and the three moons hovering above her reminded her daily she was on a planet called Tilleron, ten light years away from Earth. All because her sister, Abigail, had fallen in love with a green alien who sucked blood and was obsessed with plants. Jaril had brought the sisters to his planet to save their lives. The Earth's military had been about to experiment on her sister because they wanted the technology implanted in her neck.

The cool breeze fluffed her auburn hair and her stomach grumbled. The sun glinted off a silver spaceship as it descended from the sky. It sailed over her head and landed somewhere close by. It resembled the ship which Jaril had used to whisk them away, but her green-skinned brother-in-law and her sister were both on the planet enjoying mated bliss. Three months had passed since Melony had last had a decent meal. All the weird fruit and meat from this planet didn't taste bad, but it wasn't an Italian sausage and mushroom pizza. Lord, she missed peanut butter.

"There you are. We haven't seen you all day." Abigail's voice came from behind her.

Melony curled her fingers into the sand and took a deep breath. She had argued with her sister on many occasions about returning home. Melony counted to ten before turning around and forcing a smile. "Just needed some space. You two are worse than teenagers when you get all moon-eyed over each other."

Abigail sat next to her and rubbed her knee. The quick flash of red on Abigail's cheeks reminded Melony how much Abs loved her alien mate. "You don't have to run away every time you see us kissing. I know Jaril's not the easiest person to get along with. He gets on my nerves when he starts on a tangent about his plants -- I have to remind him I'm in the room. But he means well."

"Don't you want to go back to Earth and have a relationship with a human?" The words slipped out, but Melony already knew the answer to this particular argument. They couldn't go back.

Her sister squeezed her thigh. "I've already told you how it works with them. Once he heard me moan, he knew I was his mate. He's my other half. This place is different, but you've always been about unique experiences. It doesn't matter to me he's not human. Why do you hate them? Think about all the sucky boyfriends you've had."

"They were all dead ends, like my jobs. If you recall, the reason I moved to California was to get a fresh start. I don't hate Jaril or the rest of them. I'm just... This wasn't what I had planned." Abigail wasn't wrong. Melony had ended up with some strange guys. The ones with too many tattoos who had a weird fetish and wanted her to pee on them. Mel shivered when she thought of Nicolas. Then there had been Edvard. Everything had been fine for the first couple of months until their date fell on a full moon. He confessed he was a werewolf. She'd had another who yearned to suck on her nose. Melony could rattle off a list of strange men as long as her arm.

The same with her jobs. She'd worked in a bakery and pulled taffy in a sweet shop, and waitressed on roller skates at an old-fashioned diner. Mel had a great resume of life experiences, but it wasn't until she moved to California that she'd had a chance to put her skills together to use with a national chain of sweet shops. It was going great until the military rolled up in a black Hummer and pulled her out of a meeting saying her sister was in trouble. She still had nightmares about them not telling her anything about what was going on with Abigail. Hell, it had been even worse than when her sister had disappeared for several days the year before that. They had been on their last camping trip into the mountains before she departed for California. The panic she'd felt when her sister disappeared replayed in her dreams. Then Abs had reappeared talking about a green man who'd saved her. It sounded like Abigail had gone crazy. Melony didn't take her seriously.

She thought about the men in the white lab coats who'd ushered her into a room and started asking her questions she couldn't answer about Abigail. Who believed in aliens? It wasn't until she got beamed up to Jaril's spaceship and had to listen to the alien's foreign language as Abigail translated for him. Then he implanted their technology into her. Her fingers slid along the nape of her neck until she felt the suppression module -- a small, paper-thin disk the size of a dime -- embedded into her skin. The device contained the nanos which ran through her bloodstream healing any wounds she had. It also worked as a translator. Abigail had the same device on her neck as well. Her sister had fallen and hit her head in a cave, and Jaril had saved her with the module.

A wink of silver caught her eye. She glanced up. Another ship entered Tilleron's atmosphere. A slick of black smoke smeared the sky behind it. The vessel wobbled on its path. A loud boom and an explosion of sparks lit up the sky like fireworks. The ship spun like a football heading in a curve toward the ground. The turbulence blew Melony back onto her butt. Water frothed and pushed back into the ocean against the tide. The craft leveled off some and touched the tree canopy. The leaves burst into flame as the ship went down, leaving a black trail through the trees.

"Come on, we have to go see if the pilot is okay." Abigail tugged on her sister's arm.

Melony got up and followed her sister to the site of the crashed space craft. They stayed along the edge of the damaged area to keep away from the flames and the heat. Black scorch marks on the ship's hull told them something major had happened. The crew of the spaceship must have gotten into some kind of fight with another vessel. Deep scars marred the once-smooth ship's surface. Several other aliens were gathered around the vessel, Jaril included. Abigail rushed over to her mate, and Mel went over to join them. The aliens, all varying shades of green, were trying to force the ship's door open, but none seemed to be having any luck. The aliens had a similar muscular build like swimmers and stood seven feet or more.

"What's going on? Why can't they get into the ship?" Mel asked Jaril.

He shook his head in disbelief. "We should be able to breach the hull. The ship's artificial intelligence must be keeping the door closed, or it's been damaged. The pilot must be incapacitated." His English had gotten better.

"How are you going to get him out if the computer is damaged?"

"Mel, why don't we go off to the side and leave Jaril to help the others?" Abigail tugged on her arm to get her out of the way.

They waited while more aliens came and tried break open the hull of the ship. The groups gathered together once they couldn't get into the vessel. A few more tried, but nothing could crack the seamless metal. Melony stayed on the sidelines, out of the way. It was clear the aliens were trying to figure out what to do.

A few minutes later, the others parted to allow another figure through. The new green alien approached the ship with a large black bag slung over his shoulder. His fingers trailed over the pitted surface. He stopped a quarter of the way down the side of the ship and placed his palm on the marred metal. The ship's surface rippled like a stone being lobbed into the surface of the ship. A doorway formed in the hull. Steam poured from the door as it opened, and a ramp unfurled onto the ground. Lights blinked inside from what she could see. The other aliens crowded around the doorway, shutting out the view.

"Come on, we should head back to the house. The others seem to have it covered. Jaril will return later with news. There's nothing we can do." Abigail tugged on Melony's arm to pull her away from the congregation.

"I'd rather stay to see what's going on."

"I thought you didn't want to be around the aliens." Abigail smirked.

"This is the most excitement I've had in the months since we've been here." Melony didn't need her sister to hover. "I can find my way back to the hut."

"It's not a hut."

"It's made out of woven bamboo."

"Jaril explained they make their homes by weaving trees together and training them into shapes. They are a beautiful blend of technology and natural materials. It's amazing to see how much the integration of the ship's artificial intelligence, Talix, can project herself into the house. And --"

"Abs, go back to the house. I promise to stay out of the way. They won't need me anyway." Melony waved her sister away, interested in seeing what or who would come out of the downed ship.

"Fine." Abigail put her hands up in submission and left the crash site.

Mel turned back to view the commotion at the crashed craft. The male who had gone inside the ship came rushing out with the unconscious pilot in his arms. He laid him on the ground. Purple blood seeped from the deep wounds on the alien's body. Even though the aliens possessed advanced nano technology, the nanos didn't work on Jaril's kind as they did in humans. The onlookers chattered amongst themselves. The alien who had gone into the spaceship came over to her and started talking in their native tongue. All Melony heard were a few low growls and a string of throat whistles.

She shook her head. "I'm sorry. I don't understand you."

The frustrated look on his face said it all. He wanted her for something. He stepped toward her and said something. She shied away as he got closer. The alien frowned, held up his hand, and pointed at her neck. Melony got the idea he wanted to touch her suppression module. *What does he want with me? It must have something to do with the injured pilot. Why don't they give him some blood and help revive him?*

Then it dawned on her. She was the only source of blood around. They needed the substance to survive. Jaril had taken her blood the first time she had come onto the ship. It freaked her out, and she didn't want to repeat the experience. But she didn't want the pilot to die. The alien grunted to get her attention as he gestured toward her neck again, obviously asking permission to touch her module. Mel sighed and turned around. He pushed her hair aside, and his fingertips brushed over the module. He pressed down and said something else. The words translated into a garbled mishmash of sounds. She shook her head. Mel still couldn't understand him. He put a little more pressure on the disk until she grunted. His finger snagged a piece of her hair as he twisted and pulled it out.

"Can you understand me?" The words came out in a deep voice.

"Yes," Melony answered. She turned around and faced him. Brown streaks shot through his white hair. Something in his eyes and the deeper lines in his forehead gave him an older appearance than the others. When he smiled, it almost made her forget he was green and an alien. It made him approachable. She couldn't help but smile back at him. The wind stirred, and Mel caught the hint of citrus and something else she couldn't place. She licked her lips at the thought of eating an orange or a grapefruit -- both things she craved.

"Good. Nes needs your blood. It appears his Plasma Unit was killed in the crash. Will you do this of your free will? I'd rather not have to force you, but he doesn't have long. Since you are Jaril's property, I'm sure he would understand if I took control of you."

"Whoa! I am no one's property."

His expression hardened. She felt a push against her forehead and a pain in her temples as he tried to impose his will upon her. "At this moment, it doesn't matter. Come."

Melony bit her lips and stood her ground. The pressure on her increased, like someone poking her brow, but nothing physically touched her. "Look, I'll help him. Stop trying to boss me around."

"Why didn't you volunteer in the first place?" the alien asked her.

"You didn't give me a chance."

"Come, then, please." He offered her his hand.

Melony contemplated taking it, feeling the caress of his five fingers and his thumb, and wondered how it would feel. She shook her head. *He's green. I'm not into green. What is it about him?* His earnest expression showed he cared for his fellow aliens. *I've been away from Earth for too long, and I'm going native.*

She chuckled at the thought and slid her hand into his. The silkiness of his palm along hers gave her pause. The scent of citrus grew stronger along with what smelled like fir trees. She and the alien walked toward the injured man as the others milled around and waited to see what she would do.

As she walked by, she could understand what they were saying. This alien had fixed her module to be able to comprehend everyone rather than only understanding Jaril. He motioned her to kneel next to the unconscious pilot, whose scales were a dark forest green. Burns and wounds ran all over his body. Purple blood oozed out of his exposed cuts. Short black hair ran along the top of his head in the start of a mohawk. His chest barely rose with his shallow breaths, and she could hear the rattle in his lungs.

"Give me your hand."

She glanced up at the alien who was ordering her around. He had a sharp blade pointed at her. Mel opened her mouth to say something when he grabbed her hand. "Hey."

He sliced a diagonal cut along her wrist. Blood came out quickly. She tried to pull away from him, but he held firm. Blood dribbled onto the pilot's lips. His mouth opened and the tip of his tongue bloomed into a flowerlike sucker with six points, the size of quarter. This was the appendage each alien had to pull blood from their Plasma Units, as they called their donors. The male lifted the injured pilot's head onto his lap and then brought her arm closer so the sucker could latch onto the wound.

Melony gritted her teeth from the sudden pull on her veins. A small moan of pain slid over her lips. Warmth rushed from the back of her neck and down her arm. The nanos moved to repair the damage and seal the wound.

The hurt alien opened his eyes, which were a striking amber. He sucked on the blood until it felt like her veins were collapsing. The warmth in her arm transformed to a burning heat inching along her nerves until it reached her heart. Her pulse raced faster to keep up. The pain turned into something she hadn't felt before.

"Make him stop," she whimpered. Tears from the pain slipped along her cheeks, and another sob came from her lips.

The male's nostrils flared, and his eyes narrowed. It took him a second to pry her out of the wounded alien's grasp. Melony scuttled backward, clutching her injured arm against her chest. Her heart slowed until she could breathe easily. The burning sensation eased after a minute. She glanced down at the knife wound. A faint pink scar remained where the alien had cut her. Small beads of blood scabbed over leaving a star-shaped pattern where the alien had attached its sucker to her. She pressed it to her jeans and wiped it away. When she looked again, her smooth skin had returned. The lingering effects of blood loss left her a little lightheaded. This was the second time an alien had taken her blood, and it was not a pleasant experience. Abigail enjoyed it when Jaril sucked on her. *Maybe you have to find the right one for it not to hurt. Or one who's not dying.*

"Are you still hurt?" the leader asked.

She looked up at him. "No… it's better. Thanks."

He wiped away the last tear dribbling down her cheek. The small gesture made her meet his eyes. His gaze burned into hers. Something ignited within her. Melony could almost feel the ice in her heart melting. She didn't understand it, but part of her wanted him to touch her again. "I wanted to thank you for allowing Nes to take sustenance from you. We normally don't share Plasma

Units among one another unless there's an emergency. I will compensate you and Jaril, of course. Especially since I had to change your suppression module."

"Jaril doesn't use me for a quick snack. I don't belong to him. What did you do to the module anyway? Before, I could only understand Jaril."

His brows lifted. "Jaril didn't have all the settings correctly calibrated. I should actually upgrade your module to make sure the nanos are running properly... if you'd be willing."

"Does it hurt?" Melony asked.

"You shouldn't feel any pain. I'd have to bring you back to my workshop. It's not far from here. It would have to be after I speak with Nes to find out what happened. He's new at piloting his own ship and to this life. I can come by Jaril's and collect you."

"Fine. As long as it gets me away from my sister and her husband for a while. I'll take it."

Another one of the aliens came over to speak to him. "Brax, Nes is asking to speak with you. We've brought more blood for him."

He replied in their language and turned back to Melony. "I will come later. What is your name?" He offered her his hand to help her up.

This time she took his hand without hesitation. A spark passed between them. Melony felt her heart pound against her chest. She took in a quick breath and could taste the balsam from fir trees on her tongue. She glanced around, though she already knew the planet didn't have any such trees. The strangeness made her wonder. She brushed the sand and dirt from her jeans.

"I'm Melony."

"I'm Brax."

Chapter Two

Melony sat outside the house she shared with Abigail and Jaril. The second moon had risen while another shone cobalt blue in the sky with the gold ring of the sun behind it. The outline of one of the three moons was darkened as the three sunk below horizon. Nights and days on the planet were longer and seemed to stretch on forever. Her sister and Jaril were off in the jungle. Jaril had wanted to show Abigail some night-blooming flowers.

When Melony had gotten back after watching the rescue, she'd told them what had happened at the ship. Jaril didn't seem too concerned once she told him Brax had come and that she had given blood to the pilot. She didn't exactly know what to expect when the alien came to upgrade her nanos. Her thoughts drifted back to the alien. She rubbed her palm where he had taken her hand. A light breeze stirred the night air so she could smell the ocean. It had a slight sulfuric taint to it, but she could also smell the sweetness of the flowers in the garden Jaril had in the back.

One of his new experiments was trying to plant some of the seeds he had brought from Earth. Abigail had given him seed packets with flowers, vegetables, and herbs. Jaril had success with the flowers. The vegetables were proving a bit more difficult. The tomatoes didn't grow larger than her thumb, but they were edible. The pumpkins grew with a thick blue skin instead of the orange or white, although they tasted similar to the ones on Earth. Abigail said the garden was a work in progress. She spent her days with Jaril, helping him or learning about the new world she had found. Melony had no interest in tilling the soil or learning about plants.

"It's a lovely night, don't you think?" Brax's voice pulled her from her thoughts of cheeseburgers and rabid vegetable gardens.

She looked up to see the blue moon glinting off the silver in his hair. *It made him look like something from a romance novel coming to sweep his lover off her feet.* She rolled her eyes. *I'm losing it.* "It can be, I suppose."

"You don't like it here." Brax rested his foot on the porch. The boards creaked under his weight.

She shrugged. "Your planet is nice, but I'd rather go home. I miss blue skies and one sun. The stars here are so different. Looking up at them, I guess I feel lonely."

"I'm sorry, but you can't leave right now."

"Because of the nano technology implanted in my neck." Mel reached back and touched the module on her nape. Her frustration flowed at the idea of it. "I'm aware."

"Yes, that's one reason. The other is we can't go off planet right now. Nes... well, he made some enemies, it appears. Other races think we are abominations. They leave us be if we steer clear of their worlds. Nes decided to visit the Itarians. Sowing his wild oats, so to speak. He found a Plasma Unit from their planet and brought her aboard. The Itarians have a strange leadership dynamic. Even with millions on their planet, they only listen to one leader. Almost like a hive-mind structure. The Plasma Unit was the leader's daughter."

"I thought you said the Plasma Unit you found on board had died. Is the Itarian's daughter someone else?" Melony wondered.

"Yes. The deceased Plasma Unit went with Nes when he first left Tilleron. The Itarians sent ships to reclaim the leader's daughter, but so far, we have not been able to find her. Nes isn't revealing where she is. We've searched the ship and have come up with nothing. The Itarians have staged a blockade, threatening to shoot down any of our ships trying to leave our planet or trying to land here."

"Are you going to do something about it?" Mel

questioned.

"Why would I do anything about it?" Brax asked.

"You're the leader here, aren't you?"

He slid his hands through his hair and chuckled. "No. I'm not the leader amongst us. I'm a fixer. Our leader has been informed of the situation. He is negotiating peace. I've already instructed anyone coming back to stay away. Come, there isn't anything to worry about. I promised you I'd fix your nanos. I'm sure they need an upgrade. My workshop isn't far from here. Come on." He offered her his hand once more.

Melony slid her hand into his. The spark raced along her arm and made her shiver. She paused for a moment as his fingers interlocked with hers. The warmth of his flesh comforted her and made her realize how much she missed it. She'd closed herself off, and now her heart was melting. "Let's go."

She and Brax walked along the shoreline. The waves crashed and the warm night air helped to relax her. The scent of the ocean and the light breeze made her feel almost like she was on some kind of date, even if this wasn't anything close to what she expected. They walked until they came to a path cut into the woods leading them inland. They went in the direction opposite the downed spaceship. Melony contemplated the news he had told her about the leader trying to make peace. She didn't want to end up in an intergalactic war. Mel didn't need lasers coming down from the sky and targeting them. She rubbed her arm and shuddered at the thought of being eradicated like an insect.

"You don't talk much, do you?" Brax asked her.

She shrugged. "I don't really have much to say. How come you can speak English better than Jaril does?"

"I've had more experience with the syntax of your language. Didn't Jaril tell you there are other human females on this planet?"

"He doesn't really talk to me much except to go on about his plants and make googly eyes at my sister." Mel didn't need to picture what Abigail and her husband did behind closed doors.

"This term I don't understand. What are google eyes?" Brax stopped at a fork in the footpath. Lights along the path lit up as he put pressure on the stones. They resembled slabs of slate but were perfectly laid without a space between them for any vegetation to grow. The lights came from under the stones, illuminating them so she could see the veins of gold and green running through the gray.

"It's..." She searched for a good way to describe the expression to the alien male. "It's when my sister and Jaril look at one another like they are the only two people in the universe. Nothing could pull their attention from one another."

He nodded and laughed. "I understand this. I felt this once before."

"You had a wife?"

He looked at her for a moment while her words translated. A sad smile appeared on his face and his eyes got a faraway look to them. "Yes, I had a mate once. Most females of our species don't have our particular mutation, but she did. Her name was Marik. She died while giving birth to our daughter, Sura. Even with all our technology, I was unable to fix her."

Her heart broke for Brax. She hadn't thought about anyone here losing someone. It only made her realize how much alike they were. She touched his arm. "I'm sorry. I didn't mean to bring up..."

Brax ran his five fingers along the back of her hand. The light caress sent tremors along her arm, waking up her nerves. It sent another craving deep within her to have him touch her elsewhere. What would it feel like to have him brush his lips across hers?

"It was many years ago. My daughter has gone off planet seeking to strengthen our ties with some of our nearby neighbors, those cultures who share their citizens with us to be Plasma Units or Body Units."

She could still feel the trail of warmth left behind by his touch. She felt a longing for another's touch, besides her sister's. A longing to see if his skin was as soft as it looked. The scent of citrus came up again on the breeze. "How many share their people?" Melony was interested in knowing the people they fed from weren't slaves. Jaril could control her if he asserted his will enough the way Brax had tried to do with her when he wanted to make her give blood to the downed pilot.

"Most of the civilizations we have treaties with are within four or five light years from us. We are lucky to be in a pocket of the universe where there are many diverse species. We have catalogued thousands of worlds. Some of our pilots kidnap Plasma Units or Body Units without their consent. It's frowned upon. We have good relations with a thousand or so different civilizations. Some are more advanced than we are, and others are more primitive. Some think of us as gods and others enjoy the trade we can bring them. And others have no liking for us because they think we are parasites."

"Aren't you?" Melony asked. It was one thing to give blood for the dying pilot, but she didn't see how her sister could let Jaril suck on her all the time. Mel didn't want to be a vampire's snack box.

He sighed as they got to the end of the path. Ahead of them was a house larger than the one Jaril lived in. The land around it had been cleared. A three-story structure rose above the house in the back. "We can't help our mutation. Our priests think it's a punishment from the Origins. Technology has told us it's a genetic anomaly. It's been traced back to our ancestors. A few of my kind without the mutation accept the science, but many others don't want it to rub off onto them. Which is why they send those like me here."

"Then you give the new ones spaceships and send them off into space to look for blood donors? Sounds irresponsible. On my world, teenagers driving cars is worse than adults driving because they make stupid mistakes."

He laughed. The chuckle -- a deep throaty purr -- hit her in the chest. The vibration ran along her arms and made the hairs stand up. *What's wrong with me?* She took in a long breath to clear her head. The aroma of balsam and citrus settled into her nose. Melony curled her fingers into her palm. The pain helped her focus. Something about the sound lingered within her. It settled at her very core and made the sweet spot between her legs throb. She pressed her thighs together. *What is going on? No way there's a fir tree or oranges around here. Though I'm sure Jaril will eventually try to grow them.*

"We don't just give the young ones a ship. They are assigned to one after they pass a few tests. Many of them are here on the planet apprenticing to do many other things. For example, my daughter was under the tutelage of one of the ambassadors to learn diplomacy. Our society is more than the dwellings you see here. We like to be by the water. If you fly inland, we have cities. Some of our pilots who return from other worlds give up their ships. They settle down with their mates. Those mates eventually become their primary Plasma Units and Body Units. They have no need to go off-world unless they want to. Within the past year, we've had two other ships return with human females. The first human female I met was three years ago. Her name is Della. She and her mate, Luris, returned from your planet and settled down the shore from here. They even have a child. We have become friends. I can introduce you to her if you like."

The idea of having other human women around made

her feel a little bit better. People she could relate to. Questions ran through her mind about why those women had left Earth. Had it been the same reason for why she had come -- because of the technology implanted in her body? Had they come because they were deeply in love with the aliens who used them as appetizers? And a child? "Nice to know. I'd like to meet them sometime. Are you going to fiddle with this implant?"

"Yes. Come into my workshop." Brax went ahead of her. He stepped onto the porch and pressed his hand to a wood-paneled wall. It glowed orange and melted away the same way the doors did on their ships. She could see several long tables in this room were littered with all different tools and contraptions. As he entered, lights clicked on above them. Their soft glow didn't blind her. In one corner stood a large fan-like machine taller than him. He wove through a maze of several tables and workspaces until he came to a chair.

He trailed his finger over the top of the chair and patted the cushion. A wave of hesitation rolled over her. He smiled, and it almost reassured her as to what he was going to do. Worry unwound in the pit of her stomach as though he was going to operate on her -- and she was going to be awake for the whole thing. She examined some of his tools. She recognized a magnifying glass-type implement. Wires and small components were strewn over the table's surface.

"What is all this?" Melony touched one of disconnected machine parts. A high-pitched alarm emanated from the machine. She stuck her fingers in her ears. The noise pierced her eardrums. She winced, trying to clear the sound from her head. The siren made her head throb and her teeth hurt. Warmth gathered at the back of her neck until the module burned. The blaze inched up her neck until it encompassed her ears. She removed her fingers and came away with blood. Her head spun and her vision blurred. Her legs wobbled. She tried to grab onto the corner of the table. Brax rushed over to her before her vision completely went black. The high pitch sent a burning needle into her skull. A scream died in her throat. Brax said something to her, but darkness overtook her, and she fainted.

* * *

She opened her eyes and found herself staring up at the star-filled night sky. The silver light of a full moon shone down on her. Stars twinkled in patterns she recognized. When she tried to sit up, her head felt like it was stuffed with cotton. Her ears still rang. A cool hand rested on her forehead. The gentle pressure reassured her.

A soft whisper came into her mind. *Stay down. The nanos are fixing the damage to your ears and brain.*

Brax?

Yes. Forgive me for the intrusion into your mind. The equipment you touched triggered a penetrating alarm. The other sounds damaged your brain, your hearing, and the module housing the nanos. Instead of repairing the damage to your systems, they attacked them. I removed the old one, flushed the previous nanites from your bloodstream, and installed a new suppression module. It's slightly smaller and hidden at your hairline. I apologize for all the trouble. Your system should be equalized in a little while. Try not to speak.

Melony heard his regret and the sincerity. His presence in her mind brushed against her thoughts like a hummingbird's wing beating along her skin. A light pressure pushed along her forehead. Nothing like the force he used earlier. *Why didn't you leave the module out and get rid of the nanos some other way? Jaril told me you can't remove them without killing me.*

He trailed a finger along her forehead. His cool touch sent a surge of desire through her. She inhaled and smelled balsam and citrus again. *Must be something in the air.* His thumb traced the curve of her cheek and down her jaw. Mel took in a quick breath as another wave of nerves lit up and awakened her sleeping passion. Brax's liquid silver eyes studied her. His lips were turned up in a slight smile, but the lines in his forehead showed his confusion. This close to him she could see the small scales on his face. Darker blue scales spiraled from his temples, twisting downward like a compact tornado over his jaw and swooping along his throat until it blended with the scales of his collarbone. His bottom lip was fuller than the top one. She wondered how it would be to kiss him. Would it be as soft as kissing a human man? Would he bite her? *Why am I thinking about kissing him*?

"Jaril and the others don't have the capability to remove the modules. Since I am a fixer, I have the tools to take out the module out and reprogram the nanites." He switched to spoken words, but his presence lingered on the fringes of her mind.

What exactly is a fixer? Melony thought at him. Since he was reading her mind, he didn't seem to pick up on the fleeting thought of wanting to taste his lips.

He leaned back his seat. "I make the ships work if they have an issue. I build equipment or repair systems as you saw in my workshop. I'm one of a few fixers in this sector. There are more inland in our larger cities. I have an understanding of our anatomy as well. I am no healer, but I can patch up our people. It's a shame the nanos don't work with our biology."

Why? Melony asked.

Whenever the nanites are introduced to our blood, they attack our cells and then one another until they shut down. I think it has something to do with the electrical impulses in our bodies. Others are more adept at studying our physiology than I am. Machines and computers are more my expertise.

You sound like a cross between a mechanic and an engineer. Fixing things and building them. Do you like to work with your hands?

"I've always been taking things apart and putting them back together again. My parents thought I'd become a ship builder. Then I developed my mutation, and they wouldn't have me. I've upgraded the nanos in these modules and made them smaller. The one I implanted within you is one of the newer models. I had to imprint it so I could access your thoughts and program it. I have left it open for Jaril to be able to read your thoughts too, since you are --"

I'm not his property. Melony felt the irritation surge within her once more.

"I'm aware. I was going to say his guest."

Oh. Sorry. She glanced up at the sky again as a star shot across the horizon. The familiar image of the Earth's moon calmed her. The vision wavered slowly, showing it to be a holographic projection.

Brax looked up. "Are you enjoying the view of your planet's sky? I programmed my simulation chamber so it would project across the ceiling in here a view of your Earth's night's sky as the planet turns. I saw and felt your longing for your home world. I thought this might soothe you when you woke up, give you a little glimpse of Earth."

"You looked at my memories?" She didn't know if she should be appalled or not. *How much did he see?* The horror of what Brax might have glimpsed ran through her mind.

He frowned. "Only the most recent thoughts. Your mind is set on how much you want to return home. Forgive the intrusion."

Melony sat up slowly. A slight head rush moved through her, but quickly dissipated. Brax offered her some water and she took a sip from the metal container. The cool liquid slipped down her throat, clearing it out. "I don't mean to sound ungrateful. I'm not used to the idea of someone sharing my mind. Thank you for saving me. I guess it's my fault for touching your gadgets. If I had kept my hands to myself, then none of this would've happened." She took another sip of water, and he took the glass from her, letting his fingers slide over the back of her hand. Melony let out a gasp from the slight caress.

Brax gave her a smile, and she noticed how his eyes sparked with interest. "Accidents happen. The high frequencies are not meant for your species. I made sure when I redid your implant none of the frequencies would inhibit the nanos or cause them to attack the host. Attack you."

"Great. I should get back to my sister. I'm sure she's going to be wondering where I am." Melony stood up. Her knees gave way as a rush went from her heart up into her head.

Brax put an arm around her. The warmth of his body comforted her even if she didn't want to admit it. *Why am I reacting to him this way? It has to be some fleeting connection because of the nanos.*

The soft glow of the moon from the projection sank lower on the horizon, displaying the coming sunrise. Yellow and gold broke over the skyline on the opposite end. Melony turned her face toward the light. The warmth reminded her of Earth. She had taken for granted what it felt like and how beautiful a sight it was. Even the artificial sunrise coming over the horizon in the distance, mixing with the twilight blue and crowding out the night, was beautiful. The weight of homesickness hit her. A drop of wetness fell onto her cheek. She sniffled and wiped it away. She watched the projected dawn and found her gaze drifting over to Brax. He might have looked into her thoughts, but he had gone out of his way to give her a taste of home. It showed he cared for her in his own way.

"Are you okay?" Brax asked her, voicing his concern. He swiped his middle finger over another tear.

"Yeah, fine. I didn't realize how much I missed this view. Thank you. How are you doing it anyway?"

"I have a simulation chamber built into the structure of my house. I find it easier, so I can run simulations when it comes to the equipment I'm working on. It also helps that I have Cherin, my AI, built into the house.

"Did you need something, Brax?" a female voice sounded in the room.

"I'm fine, Cherin. I was telling our guest about the simulation chamber and how I can use it to make virtual models of what I'm fixing." Brax seemed to puff up as he talked to the computer intelligence.

"I thought you had the artificial intelligences tied into the ships. How does she exist in your house?" Melony asked, trying to learn more about the alien mechanic. All of it made him intriguing. She'd always enjoyed a man who had grease on his hands. Most of the previous, unfulfilling relationships with losers she had back on Earth were with mechanics or grease monkeys. Sometimes they worked on cars or motorcycles. Sometimes they worked on machinery in bottling plants. Whatever the job, she found herself entwined with them. It always ended badly, but she couldn't get away men who worked with their hands. She'd dated artists and welders who lost themselves in their work. When she moved to California, Melony hoped her new job would set her on a new path to life. She'd had some potential suitors, but none were successful.

"I exist because someone needs to look after Brax. He wouldn't know where he left his tools if it wasn't for me or Sura." A female form flickered in and out like a bad television station, but it wasn't coming into view.

"She doesn't have to look after me. I'm perfectly capable. Cherin, is there something else you needed?" Brax shook his head at the AI.

"Nothing. Don't let him fool you, human. He does need someone to keep him in line."

"Cherin!" Brax ordered.

"I'm going. Nice to meet you, human." The glimmering figure blinked out leaving the two of them alone.

Mel's cheeks burned at Cherin's comments. *She's insinuating there's something between us. Is there? There couldn't be.* Mel thought back to when Brax touched her, even in passing, and how it made her feel. Her heart raced. She anticipated feeling more for him. Her thoughts reeled as she came to understand that maybe the computer was right. She wanted more of him. She wanted him to slip his hands over her body and discover the hidden parts of herself. "Nice to meet you, too, I guess."

"Don't pay her any attention. She can be a little overzealous. Cherin's been with me for a long time. She's been my companion when there wasn't anyone to talk to. My daughter comes and goes. Sura cares, but she has a life of her own. For her, forging ahead, despite being shunned by others in our culture is the greatest thing I can hope for her."

"You sound very proud of her."

"I am. When I see her, I see my mate. She looks more like her than me, which is a good thing." Brax chuckled. "We have a better chance of finding mates outside of our own species. It's another reason why we send others out. We don't tell the young ones because they aren't even thinking about finding mates. They want to explore the universe and find pleasure."

"Sounds like the young men on my world. I'm sorry about your mate." Mel empathized with him.

"Thank you. Come, Jaril and his female will be wondering where you are. I shouldn't have kept you this long." Brax offered her his hand.

Mel took one more look at the sunrise as it broke over the simulated horizon. She took his hand, feeling the firmness of his grip, the warmth of it. It seemed all she could smell were oranges and taste grapefruit. Melony tried to banish the tastes and smells from her senses, but they lingered. "Yeah, I guess you're right."

"You can come back anytime you'd like to watch the stars or something else. I have quite a few moving pictures Luris has introduced me to."

"Moving pictures?" She stopped, wondering what he was talking about.

"Sorry -- mooovies, you humans call them. Luris and his mate, Della, come here often, and we watch them."

"She's the first human you met, right?"

"Yes."

The chance to meet another human eased some of her tension. Having another human female to relate to besides her sister might help her to feel a little more at home. "I'd like that."

Brax grinned. His features lit up when he smiled. "I'll ask them over for tomorrow night. Okay?"

"Great." Melony yearned to touch his face, but she hesitated. All her feelings mixed within her. The growing attraction she had for the alien mechanic made her giddy. However, her mind kept telling her their relationship wasn't possible. How could she want someone outside of her own species? The questions brought on more doubt. While Brax walked her home, she let him take her hand. Even the smallest caress of his fingers along the back of her hand sent her heart aflutter. It made her crave him in a way she'd never craved any of the human men she had been with.

Chapter Three

"You're going on a date!" Abigail giggled. She pulled out an outfit from her closet and held it up to Melony. Jaril had provided them with whatever they wanted in terms of clothes. The house contained a replicator. They could have whatever clothes or food they wanted. Although some of the replicated food didn't taste quite like it did on Earth.

"It's not a date." Melony rolled her eyes. She told her sister what had happened with Brax, and how he'd replaced her suppression module. She kept her growing feelings about him to herself. Abigail was also excited about her meeting Della and her alien husband.

"It sounds like a date, but these guys don't really know what a date is. Tell me something, do you smell anything when you're around Brax?" Abigail asked.

She shrugged. "I'm not leaning in close enough to see if he has alien BO. I wasn't thinking about what he smelled like when my ears were bleeding, or when I woke up to find him leaning over me. I was more about making sure I could hear and hoping he wasn't riffling around my thoughts and pulling out my innermost secrets."

"I told you. They don't keep slaves. Jaril told me Brax is well-respected. From what I gathered, he's some kind of mechanic." Abigail held up another outfit and then tossed it to Melony. "This one. It makes your eyes pop."

"This is not a date. I doubt he cares what I'm wearing." Melony looked at herself in the mirror. The long, blue shirtdress covered her butt. Its long sleeves were split on the tops of her arms and then joined again with cuffs at the wrist. The scooped neck showed off the top of her breasts. The hue of the garment made her recall the blue spirals on Brax's cheek. It was a near match. *Why do I care about matching his scales? Why did Abigail mention smells? Does she know I pick up something when I'm close to him?* "Why did you bring up the thing about aromas?"

"I've told you before. Maybe you weren't listening, which doesn't surprise me. Something about their anatomy. When a mate feels any attraction to them, it makes us smell something we love or crave. For me it was maple." Abigail shivered and her eyes lit up. "It makes me want to lick Jaril all over. My mouth waters and I could eat him all up."

"Jaril is not a stack of pancakes."

"I realize that, but he tastes just as good. Who cares if they're green or have six fingers on each hand and six toes on each foot? Jaril is the best thing that's ever happened to me."

Mel crossed her arms over her chest. "He brought you ten light years from Earth and made it so you can't go back. You have microscopic robots running through your veins. Doesn't it bother you?"

Abigail let out a long sigh and slid down onto the bed. "It did at first, I'm not going to lie. I never thought I'd adjust to a life here. Jaril shows me so many different things with his plants and about his world. I show him ours. He's all I want. At first, maybe it was pheromones, but then we became more than a chemically induced couple. The link we have because of the nanos lets me see into his mind. We're closer than ever. I wish you could understand. Half the time he knows what I want before I do. I love him, Mel. Did I answer your question? You never told me if you pick up any particular odors when you're around Brax."

She let out a long breath. *Can I really be attracted to an alien? Is that the reason why I smell fir trees like Christmas around him?* "I don't know." She couldn't admit it to herself, but Brax intrigued her.

"I know that look. You wouldn't be agreeing to meet with him if you weren't interested."

Melony pulled the shirtdress over her head and

smoothed it out. She slid on some tights and then some dark leather boots. At least she thought they were leather. She couldn't tell what material they were, but they felt like leather. "I'm only interested in meeting this other human woman. Aren't you?"

"Sure, but not right now. I have plans tonight with my green man." The happy look moved over Abigail's eyes as she thought about her man. Doe eyes and happy about being with Jaril.

"Go climb a tree or eat a flower. Jaril will tell you about some kind of new plant he's trying to hybridize." Melony ran a brush through her hair.

"Actually, he's taking me somewhere special. I think he has something planned, but I'll have to see. Have a good night." Abigail pulled her into a quick hug and then left the room.

Mel stayed in her room until the house went quiet. She wandered outside and sat on the porch watching the sun and the other planets set. The moons were rising, casting their cool silvery light down on her. A little bit of panic enveloped her. *Am I doing the right thing? I can tell him I'm sick. Or something came up.* She turned to go inside when Brax walked up to the porch.

"Hello, Melony. Are you ready for tonight?"

"H-hi, Brax." The way he said her name made her heart thump a little faster. She wiped her palms on her thighs. Even if she was attracted to him, she had no idea if he felt the same way. "Yes. Lead the way."

He offered her his arm. They walked together toward his house. She noticed how his black leather pants hugged his muscled thighs and calves. He wore a white shirt of some light material through which she could see his dark green skin. She stumbled over something and tightened her grip on his arm.

"Are you okay?" he asked her.

"Yes, just a little distracted." She coughed to clear her

throat but could still taste the citrus and balsam on her tongue as it also lingered in her nose. The yearning to lean in closer to him and run her nose along his throat nearly got the best of her. *I'm not attracted to him. I'm not.*

"I know the feeling. I'm excited to see the film as well. Maybe it will give you a little bit of home. Luris has picked the movie." Brax patted her arm. The light touch shot desire straight to her core. She bit her tongue to stay focused. Her body was not going to dictate how to act.

Inside Brax's house, he took her back to the simulation chamber. Inside, two long couches were side by side. She'd been lying on one of them last night.

"Larin, get over here." A woman raced after a toddler who giggled and ran right into Mel's legs. The little one had light purple hair. She hugged Melony's legs and looked at her with big brown eyes and chubby cheeks.

"Up!"

"Ahhh..." Melony hadn't expected there to be a child at the house. She bent down and picked up the little girl. The child wrapped her arms around Mel's neck and laid her head on Mel's shoulder. The child's mother came over to her.

"I'm sorry. She's normally shy around strangers. Come here, little one." The mother unlatched her from Mel's neck.

It took her a minute to realize she was speaking English. The woman didn't look to be older than her sister, but she was shorter and a little bit rounder. Her hair had been pulled back into a bun. Her brown eyes were the same as the toddler's. "It's okay. I haven't seen any kids running around here, so it surprised me. You're Della?"

"Yeah, Brax told me all about you. Melony, right? And your sister's Abigail?"

"He did? What did he tell you?" Melony wanted to know what the alien had said about her. Had he told her about how she collapsed? Had he told her if he felt anything for her? *God, I'm losing it.*

Della smiled. "Nothing horrible. There are some other humans, and he thought you would like to chat or get together. Have you met Irene and Ember yet? They don't live too far away either."

"Not yet."

"They are great, and Larin loves them. It's nice Brax has found a mate. He's been alone for a long time."

Her cheeks grew hot, and she cast a glance at the alien mechanic. "Ahh... we... aren't together."

"Oh, I'm sorry. I thought you and he were an item. The way he looks at you... Well, it doesn't matter. Come and meet my mate, Luris." Della motioned with her head. The toddler had her thumb in her mouth, but she also had five other fingers like the rest of the aliens. Her skin was a light green and very pale but one could see the mixture of species. Larin's face was rounder than the aliens. Her eyes were spaced a little farther apart and her nose was thinner. Her fine hair curled around her ears.

"I can't help but ask, your child? You and your mate's?" Melony wanted to know how it worked.

"We're genetically compatible. Luris wasn't sure if he wanted a child, and then it happened even with the nanos being programmed for it not to happen. Sometimes life finds a way."

"You have a module implanted in you, as well?" Melony ran her hand along the one in the back of her neck.

Della pushed away her collar and pointed to the one at the hollow of her throat. "I do."

"How did you get here?" Melony asked.

"I was leaving the grocery store. I used to run my own baking business. I felt a pinch, and then this bright light hit me. I woke up naked with Luris dressed in a kilt, plunging his fingers into the peanut butter I bought, and then licking it. He tells me I'm going to be his Plasma Unit. Here I'm thinking 'What in the hell is a green alien going to do to me while I'm being held prisoner and naked?' You bet I was thinking the worst."

"He didn't..."

"...Rape me? No. Once we got to know one another a bit better, he explained what and who he was. I gave him my blood and saved his life. He promised to bring me back to Earth, but we were attacked by space pirates. I was hurt, and he brought me back here. Brax fixed me up and updated the module. We've gone back to Earth a couple of times to restock on supplies. Luris has a thing for peanut butter. I can't give up chocolate. The replicators work great on clothes and most of the food. Chocolate comes out a little grainy and the peanut butter is a little off. I can compensate when I'm baking and it isn't bad, but the real thing is best."

"You heard about the no-fly zone thing, right?"

"Yeah, it stinks. We had plans to go back to Earth in a couple of weeks and restock."

"When you go, can I get a ride back with you?" Melony asked. The question slipped out before she could think of anything else. Her hopes soared at the idea of returning home. She could figure out how hide herself from the authorities and stay off their radar. Even as the thought raced through her head, her heart rejected the idea. It wanted to be with Brax.

"I'll have to talk to Luris, but it shouldn't be a problem."

"Are you ladies ready for the movie?" Luris stepped out wearing a plaid kilt with nothing else save the leather boots. Seeing his chest and the expanse of his legs she had to say he was quite well-built. She noticed a silver ring on his middle finger and saw an identical one on Della's, showing they were married. She also caught the scent of something familiar.

"You have popcorn?" Melony asked.

Brax sat down with a bowl of the popcorn. "Yes. Luris and Della have helped me load in recipes for many Earth foods. Sit and relax." He patted the spot next to him on the couch.

Melony sank into the couch. She stayed within inches of him and could feel his warmth. Her mouth watered at the buttery morsels sitting in the lap of the alien mechanic. "What are we watching?"

"*Highlander*," Luris stated.

"*Highlander*?" Melony asked.

"It's his favorite movie. You should see him moving with a sword. It's one of the things I saw when we first met. All those muscles." Della rolled her eyes. Larin lifted her head and looked at Melony.

"There can be only one," the toddler said in a singsong voice.

"Yes!" Luris said as he picked her up and hugged her.

"Don't encourage her." Della poked his ribs. He leaned in and kissed her as the opening scene in the movie started.

"Have you seen this film?" Brax asked.

"I don't think so. Fantasy films aren't really my thing. I'm game for watching anything from home, though." Melony stared at the screen. The scent of the popcorn made her almost forget where she was. Brax handed her the bowl. His fingers brushed the back of her hand as he dipped into the bowl and grabbed some of the fluffy white goodness. She caught a hint of balsam. A warmth rushed through her and settled above her heart. She glanced over at Della. Larin snuggled between Della and her husband. Her thumb was in her mouth. Della kissed Luris and rested her head on his shoulder. They cuddled against one another as they watched the movie. Luris mouthed the words to the film. Melony chuckled and then focused back on the screen.

"Melony, can I ask you something?" Brax leaned in close. His breath moved along her skin. She trembled from the warmth caressing her.

"Sure." She glanced at him and noticed the silver in his eyes seemed more pronounced under the dim illumination of the movie. It seemed as if he looked into her soul. A light pressure moved across her mind, but she didn't shy away from it. Abigail said she shared a mental link with Jaril. Maybe the same thing was developing between her and Brax.

"Do you feel any attraction for me?"

Being put on the spot made the warm feeling drain away. Her words caught in her throat. His fingers trailed along her jawline. Her breath quickened as the small caress made her tingle. Her nerves were a light. Mel bit her lip to keep from moaning. She'd wanted him to touch her since yesterday. She'd wanted him to explore more of her body. Now that he'd touched her, she didn't know how to react.

She yanked her hand from the popcorn bowl and raced out of the room. She wove through the house, following panels that lit up as she got near. Almost as though someone knew what she wanted. She suspected the AI had something to do with it. Mel found her way outside and took in gulps of air. Her heart pounded against her chest. She looked up at the moons and the planets and tried to calm down. Tears gathered in her eyes, but she wiped them away. The whole idea of it baffled her, and yet her heart kept telling her what her mind couldn't grasp.

"Are you all right?"

She turned toward Brax. He stayed a few feet away, giving her space, but with the breeze she caught the balsam scent and citrus once more. The aroma kept growing stronger as did the longing to be in his arms. "I'm fine. Sorry. I didn't mean to run out. I hope I didn't ruin the movie."

"You didn't ruin the movie. I shouldn't have been so forward with the question. I have felt things with you. I didn't want to assume anything until I asked you." Brax sighed and ran his fingers through his hair.

"How can you even feel things for me? You don't know me." Mel's gaze traveled down the expanse of his chest. She tried to not feel anything, but her body told her otherwise.

"Yesterday when you were giving blood to Nes, you made a sound. It hit me. I brushed it off at first, but when I replaced your suppression module, your moans, even though they were from the pain, consumed me. I knew you were my mate. I didn't want to frighten you or approach you too quickly. However, I have learned you can't wait with these things. I would have you be honest with me."

"Even if you don't like my answer?"

"I'm a patient man, but I won't ignore this."

"I -- I don't know. When I'm around you, I get this fragrance. My sister says it's some pheromone your species gives off. It makes a potential mate smell something they love or crave."

Brax nodded. "She is correct."

Melony crossed her arms over her chest. *What I've been smelling is real. It means I've been attracted to him. I'm not imagining it.* "Brax, I -- I don't know what to say. When I came here, I never thought I'd want to be with anyone of your species. I -- I..." She stammered as she tried to find the right words to voice her feelings. She wanted him. She wanted to jump him right there and see how he would feel wrapped around her body. Even as she wanted to say more, something else poured from her lips. "Please don't take this the wrong way. I want to go back to Earth when I can. Whatever chemical reaction this might be between us, it's biology. It doesn't mean anything." She hated herself once the words spilled out.

He winced at her words, but he crossed the space between them. The stronger scent of balsam made her take in a long breath. She resisted the urge to bury her head against his chest and inhale the fragrance of Christmas, her favorite holiday. She and Abigail got together, baked, and sang carols off-key until they had plenty of drinks in them and enough cookies to turn into gingerbread women. Hell, she didn't even know if Christmas had come or not. The days were longer. The nights dragged on. She missed Earth's sunsets and sunrises painting the sky gold or varied shades of pink. Here they all had an eerie purplish hue.

"I understand your hesitation. We're of different cultures. Humans, from what I gather, have thought they were alone in the universe. Accepting the idea of aliens must be difficult. This life was thrust upon you. I know I'm not your ideal choice for a companion, but if you let me, I would worship you."

Melony didn't know what to say to him, except he hit the nail on the head. All of what he'd said resonated within her. Her emotions twisted and her eyes started to sting. She couldn't break down in front of him. Instead she shook her head, started to walk past him and head back to the house when he grabbed her arm.

"Can I ask one favor of you before you run off and discard any thought of what this might be? I can feel it in your thoughts you're conflicted."

"Why are you reading my mind?" she whispered, longing to push past her conflicted feelings. Melony could feel the impressions of his fingers through her dress. The warmth of his flesh flared along her arm. She sucked in a breath through her teeth. Her heart doubled its beat. The heat of his body warmed her side. Brax stood a foot taller than she did, so she had to look up into his eyes. His gaze seared into her soul. It felt as if she would lose herself. Never with any other man had she experienced this loss of self.

The lines in his forehead deepened as he sighed. She barely felt the pressure along her mind as he pulled away. "I wasn't doing it on purpose. Your distress showed on your face. The paleness of your skin tone. The frantic beat of your heart. It was instinct when I reached out. I'm sorry."

"Apology accepted. What's the favor?" She forced the words out and tried not to breathe, to prevent his intoxicating scent from enrapturing her further. His words hit her, and she heard his sincerity in his tone.

His other hand cupped her jaw. With the direct contact to her skin, a spark, a jolt of pure desire took over her body. It trampled along her nerves and speared her heart. A low moan slipped out from her lips. Brax went very still. His eyes closed as though he savored a fine wine or a delectable dessert. He took a breath through his nose and let it out slowly. His fingers slid along her throat, settling on her jugular. His fingertips tapped lightly on her skin, keeping time with her heartbeat.

"W-what are you doing?" Mel bit her lip. Everything in her told her to lean against him. Her entire being yearned to be in his arms. It took all her will not to give in.

"Trying to control myself."

"What do you want to do right now?"

His lips curved into a sexy half smile. Her stomach quivered at the sight and her knees went weak. "Besides rip your clothes off and worship you until you come for me? I want to be inside you." He opened his eyes and trapped her with his gaze. "I yearn to taste all of you. Your scent is intoxicating enough. The timbre of your moan... Even the words you speak have me firm. I want to drink from your veins while I make love to you. To hear you call my name would make me fall to your feet."

Shit. What do I say to that?

"You can say whatever you wish," he murmured. His taps increased as her pulse did.

Melony could barely think. She licked her lips and could taste the citrus, a sweet mixture of orange and tangerine with a bite of grapefruit. "You read my mind again." The yearning to be closer to him burned above all else.

His fingers pressed against her throat enough that she tilted her head a little. He stared at her throat as though half drunk. "Forgive me. As I said, it's difficult to control myself when I am this close to you. Hearing the rush of the blood through your veins. The scent of your sex already wet and waiting for me to claim you. Blocking you out was easier before. Will you at least let me kiss you, so I can drown myself in your lips? If you allow me this one last breath, I would die a happy man."

Her heart felt like it stopped at his statement. *One kiss can't hurt. Screw it. Maybe if he kisses me, then I won't feel this way anymore. It'll burn through my system.* She leaned in and pressed her breasts along his chest. Brax trembled, but his fingers didn't move from her throat. Melony touched the side of his jaw expecting to feel the roughness of the scales. Instead, they were soft, almost like velvet. Mel traced the spiral pattern down his cheek. He grabbed her wrist in a light hold and held her palm to his face. She ran the pad of her thumb along his bottom lip. He sucked her thumb into his mouth. The tip of his tongue swiped along her thumb.

Time slowed. Her heartbeat quickened in desire caused by the swipe of his tongue. Her pulse thundered in her ears like a snare drum. With each breath she could taste hints of citrus and balsam. Brax slid his free hand around her waist to hold her to him. Their bodies seemed to fit together as though they were coming together after being apart for a long time. She could feel the pull between them. Melony placed her hand on his chest. Under her palm she felt a double throb. "You have two heartbeats."

Brax released her thumb and chuckled. "Yes. Each one feels as if it will explode if I don't kiss you. May I kiss you, Melony?"

Her name on his lips in that strangled whisper stole her ability to speak. It was the sexiest thing she had ever heard from a man. All she could was nod. Brax slid his fingers under her chin and tilted her head up. His other hand squeezed her waist with a light pressure to hold her against him. He lowered his lips toward hers until they were nearly touching. *I need to hear you say it,* he whispered in her thoughts.

His mental voice was as sexy as his spoken one. The light pressure on her forehead was like a gentle caress. His anticipation beat along her mind like his hearts. The more she focused on it, the more she realized she could sense his other emotions. Fear of her rejection. Fear she would run from him if he told her the truth. She couldn't understand all his feelings but sensing them let her see how vulnerable he was. Behind all of it was a loss so deep it felt like a black well that swallowed anything thrown into it. The loss of his first mate had devastated him. The only spark of joy was his daughter. It was the only thing which gave him the determination to go on. Melony might not have understood how she connected to him to sense his emotions, but she figured it had to be because of the nanos. Her whole body felt hot, but it wasn't from them. It was all because of him.

"Yes," she whispered.

Brax pressed his mouth to hers in the barest of kisses, waiting for her to seal it between them. Melony wrapped her arms around his neck and brought their mouths together and kissed him. She didn't know how his people kissed, but she was going to show him how an Earth girl did. As their lips touched, she tasted him... cinnamon mixed with an earthiness, not the pine or citrus flavor she expected. His mouth was soft against hers. She threaded her fingers through his hair.

His hands slid lower on her back, resting on the top of her ass but still barely holding her as if she would break. Melony could feel the rigidity of his muscles and the firmness of his cock pressing along her upper thigh. She trailed her tongue over his bottom lip and teased his tongue with the tip. He met hers for a swift moment before pushing his lips against hers. Melony broke away from his lips and brushed her mouth along his jaw down to his throat, planting light kisses along the way. As she moved her tongue up his cheek, she could feel the slight hardness of his scales. She nipped his ear. Brax let out a small moan.

Something about the sound -- or maybe it was being so close to him -- spiked her yearning. Her longing gathered in her chest like a tight ball. She worked her way along his throat where she felt the strongest throb of his pulse. Mel circled around it. Feeling the almost electric spark of his life under his flesh. She nibbled at his throat. Once her teeth bit down, Brax squeezed her ass until it hurt. He let out a loud groan. The noise shook her to the core. Melony broke away from his throat and felt the vibration in her chest. She buried her head against his chest. She took in a few deep breaths to stay steady, but it left her panting and wanting. She hovered on the edge of falling into the void of losing herself and fighting the desire to do more with him.

"What's going on?" Melony moaned. She raked her nails along his skull.

"Do you feel it?" Brax forced out.

"I feel... like I'm hovering on the edge of a cliff, and I could fall off. When you moaned, it went straight through me."

"Yes, you understand the longing, then."

She nodded. The attraction between them grew palpable. She wanted his hands on her. To do as he said and have him buried inside her. Melony needed him. She now understood the reason Abigail was obsessed with Jaril, why they were all over one another. "I do."

Chapter Four

He brushed his lips along hers and down to her jaw. "I want to make love to you. I need to be inside you. Melony, I know you are still fighting our bond. You are trying to reconcile your head and your heart. I don't want to push this with you tonight. Your thoughts are written on your face. If you let me, I can ease the attraction for both of us."

Melony squeezed her eyes shut. She had to stop figuring out if she would come or hover in a no-man's-land and end up with the equivalent of blue balls. His words echoed in her mind. If he could read her expression, then he knew how conflicted she was. Melony shook her head and inhaled his scent once more. She moved her hands over his arms feeling the muscles and the form of him. The voice inside her head quieted and she listened to her heart. "Yes."

"Forgive me if this hurts."

A sharp pain struck her throat. Brax wrapped her in his arms and held her close. The beats of his heart flared along her skin. His lips fastened to her flesh. A tug started on her veins. Melony moaned. He held her closer as he drank more of her in. Her breath came in short pants as she felt herself fall over the edge and come.

Again. Please, Brax begged her with his thoughts.

He held her to him and drank her blood. The sudden sucking made her press her thighs together. Heat encompassed her. Mel gripped his arms tighter. She had to stop herself from wrapping her legs around him. Her head spun. The throb at her center grew the longer he drank. She needed him inside her. It was like an itch she couldn't scratch. If he didn't stop, she would rip his pants off and take his cock in her hands. She would wrap her mouth around it and suck on him the way he did with her.

"Stop. Brax, please!" Melony pleaded.

A few seconds passed before he lifted his head. Brax rested his forehead against hers. "You taste... more than I can explain. It's almost as good as being inside you. I smell your pleasure from my bite. Did you enjoy it?"

She couldn't find the right words to explain how he made her feel. Her emotions spun out of control. Her heart said she needed more of him. Her body knew being with him was correct. The bite made her yearn for more. Her body sang, and he'd barely touched her. She had to fight herself into not doing more with him. "More than I ever dreamed I could."

He brushed the hair from her temples. The coolness of his fingers made her tremble and did little to ease her down. Brax ran his thumb down her cheek. His faint touch made her want more. Melony's yearning for him only remained. She wrapped her arms around him and pressed her body along his. She tried to catch her breath, but her heart kept pounding. Her body seemed out of control. She moved her mouth to his and kissed him, sweeping her tongue along his bottom lip. Brax crushed his mouth to hers and growled. The rumble made her insides quiver once more. He tugged on her bottom lip with teeth. He cupped her ass. The sudden bite of pain from his teeth made her cry out. She tasted a little bit of blood, and he kissed her harder, pushing against her. His firm prick pressed into her thigh. Melony raked her fingers down his sides and tore at his pants.

Brax broke away. His eyes had a wild look in them. She shoved her hand under his waistband and felt the warmth of his cock. He growled and grabbed her hand, but he didn't stop her. "Stop before I lose myself to the animal in me. We are mostly civilized, but sometimes the animal comes out."

Melony heard what he said. She felt the pressure along her mind and sensed the hunger within him. This craving infected her through the link they shared. She didn't understand it, but she needed him. She caressed his dick and shook her head. Everything seemed to be in overdrive. She couldn't take a calming breath. Her legs barely kept her upright. She wanted her mouth on his shaft. She glanced around and saw a large rock with a seat-like cleft in its side. "There." Melony gestured with her head. "Fuck me."

"Are you sure?" Brax panted. The excitement in his eyes and in his mind, the fierceness he called the animal, lingered along the surface of the thread between them.

"Yes."

Brax picked her up and brought her over to the large stone. "Turn around. I've gone too far to hold onto control."

Melony splayed her fingers along the stone, feeling its coolness. She glanced behind her. Brax rubbed his firm prick. He lifted her dress in a hurry. His fingers tugged on her tights. She pushed them down, and instead he concentrated on her panties. After growling, he tugged on the thin material. A rip of fabric made her jump. The back of his hand ran over the slit of her ass. She curled her fingers into the stone, scraping her nails along it. His fingers found her wet pussy. Brax's other hand slammed onto the rock next to hers. He wound his fingers through Melony's as his fingers slid inside her.

She gasped from the sudden plunge. He pressed against her. His hot breath blasted against her ear. "You're so tight." He shoved her legs farther apart, pressing her into the rock. His free hand grabbed her ass in a tight grip. Melony hadn't been manhandled like this in a long time. It felt as though she could give into the animal inside her as well.

"Fuck me, please!" she whimpered, needing him inside her to cool the ache.

Brax growled. The sound rumbled along her back. It

sank into her bones. The crest of the orgasm pulsed within her. Brax pushed into her. Mel bucked against him. Their fingers wove tighter as he rode her. He held onto her right hip with his other hand to keep control of their movements. His cock sank in deep.

All she heard was the sound of their coupling and his small groans. Each one brought her to a higher crest. Coupled, with him filling her, she let the orgasm crash over her. Brax roared as he plunged into her pussy one last time and came. The brief union left them both breathless. Melony felt the craving within her retreat along with the animalistic side of Brax along their mental link.

He moved aside the hair from her throat and placed a few kisses along her jugular. She braced herself for the sting of his sucker. Instead, he remained gentle and let out a sigh that resembled a purr. "You are more than I could've hoped for."

"Brax," Melony didn't know what to say to him as her thoughts began to swim.

He kissed her again and pulled away from her. Melony rested her forehead against the stone. Her body hummed, but her mind felt lost. The sex made her question everything, but she wanted him again. She took a moment and then pulled her tights back on and adjusted her shirtdress. She turned back to Brax and saw the triumphant smile on his face. Seeing him in the moonlight made her want him again, but she pushed it aside.

"Can you deny you are my mate after we have shared intimacies?" Brax asked.

"Mate is a heavy word. I can't deny the attraction between us. Obviously. You expect because of this... strange link, we're bound to be together for the rest of our lives. Even if this blows my mind."

"This is a start. I yearn to make love to you properly

on a much softer surface, where I can look at you when you come. I yearn to discover the pleasure of your body. Tonight, is only the beginning of what could be. Tonight you have seen the animal inside me. I wish for you to see the man. I may not be human, but my wish is for you to see how much I love you. You need to discover the connection for yourself and not just react to the longings of our bodies." The pressure of his mind brushed along her thoughts.

Melony understood what he meant. She nodded in agreement. Brax grazed his lips along hers in a soft kiss before releasing her. Something about it made her feel whole in a way she had never thought possible. She leaned in closer, hoping to have him wrap her in his arms again, but Brax stepped back.

"I'm going to ask Della to walk you back to Jaril's. I don't think it's a good idea for me to be alone with you again. I could risk taking you once more." Brax touched her cheek once more and then walked back into his house.

The cool night air caressed her, reminding her where Brax had once been. Their coupling lingered in her mind. She wanted him inside her again, but what he said was right. She needed some space. Melony could think clearly with the space between them. With Brax gone, all she wanted was for him to return. It was the strangest sensation she'd ever had -- like a bad itch she couldn't scratch. She turned back to the house, but Della came out.

"Brax asked me to go home with you. When you didn't come right back in, I thought something might have happened between the two of you. Are you okay?" Della touched her arm and gave her a warm smile.

"Yeah, I'm fine." The sting of tears burned her eyes. She wiped them away.

"What did Brax say to you? You don't have to share if you don't want to, but I might be able to help."

"He said I had to discover for myself about being his mate. Being away from him feels like..."

"Losing a part of yourself?"

Melony nodded.

"Yeah. It feels that way at first when the bond between you two is forming. It won't be so bad after a while."

"How do you do it? I mean they're a different species and you had a child with your man. Don't you want to go back to Earth and stay there? How did you leave it all behind?" Melony asked, trying to rationalize the encounter she and Brax had had and all her feelings.

"I miss home, but I love Luris more. I love our daughter. Neither of us knows if she'll inherit their genetic mutation. Luris thinks she will because she has six fingers on each hand and six toes on each foot, although she was born with a belly button and nipples. Larin responds to nanos which is good because she was born with them. Brax and the others are interested in following her progress as she grows up.

"I can't tell you how you should feel about Brax. Let him into your heart. The connection between you will flare until you act on it. You have to figure out what you want. Brax knows what he wants. All their kind does. He's giving you the choice to figure out if you truly want him or not.

"They didn't ask for their mutation. They can't help it if they live off blood. If you have the implant, then it was probably given to you to save your life. You have some unsettled feelings about being taken away and not being able to say goodbye, or you had notions of what you wanted to do with your life on Earth. Think about it -- this is a strange universe and now you know there is more in it than just Earth people. You have to look beyond the world view you had. There is more to life than you have thought. Brax is trying to do what he can to give you the space. Get to know him. Give him a chance."

Della stopped outside Jaril and Abigail's house and gave her a small pat on the back. "It's not the end of the world."

Melony took in her words. "Thanks for the information. I guess you're right. I've been thinking about it all wrong. I never expected for any of this to happen. I wanted nothing more than to go back to Earth. This puts a wrench in what I thought I wanted."

"I'm here if you want to talk. I'd love to meet your sister. It's nice to know there are other women here who deal with the same issues. I've met some of the other mates from different planets, but they don't understand what we go through." Della smiled at her. "I need to get back."

"Thanks." Melony sat on her sister's porch and stared up at the night sky. The stars appeared to have multiplied from the night before. The pinpoints of light moved across the sky like a faraway plane. Since they didn't have planes on Tilleron, it must have been something else. Ships far above the planet and more coming. Her stomach dropped out and twisted like it was being wrapped in barbed wire. She raced inside the house and knocked on the closed bedroom door.

"Abs, I think you need to get out here," she called.

Abigail came out wrapped in a sheet with red cheeks. Mel, I was in the middle of something. What is so important?"

"Sorry, I didn't realize you were busy. Come outside and look at this." Melony tugged on her sister's arm until they got back outside.

She shrugged as she glanced upward at the night sky. "Stars. Planets. Moons. What about it? Jaril's waiting for me."

"You might want to get him, too." She pointed toward all the moving lights. "He may want to see this. I don't think this is a good thing."

Her sister nodded. "I'll get him."

Jaril came outside a few seconds later wearing nothing. "What is it you needed?"

She turned away from him because she didn't need to see all his anatomy. "You really need to put something on."

"Why are you concerned about my nakedness? It is natural. Your sister and I were engaged in lovemaking. You have seen my physical attributes before. Why do you look away?" Jaril gestured toward his body.

"Jaril, don't I want to see your junk bouncing around. Knowing what you and my sister were doing doesn't make it any better. We've had this conversation before." Melony glanced at Abigail who bit her lip at the exchange. He might have gotten better at understanding humans, but some things he didn't grasp. His love for plants made it tough for him to interact with people at times. She pointed at one of the sheets and gestured for her sister to give it to her alien husband.

Abigail rolled her eyes and unwound a length of material from around her waist and held the other one up to her torso. "Love, as much as I love you, sometimes you can't be walking around showing off. Humans are used to being clothed. Can you wrap this around yourself please?"

"For you, anything." Jaril wrapped the sheet around his waist. "Why did you drag away my love from our alone time?"

Melony pointed up to the sky and all the moving points of light above them. "I'm sure those aren't planes."

Jaril studied the sky and whispered something in his language. He dropped the sheet and rushed back inside. Melony went over to her sister. "This can't be good."

"It's not."

"Do you think this has something to do with what

happened earlier with the downed pilot and the order for everyone to stay on the planet?" Melony asked.

"It makes sense." Abigail tightened the sheet around herself. "I didn't leave Earth to get blown up because some stupid kid decided to kidnap a princess."

"Brax said the younger pilot took the chief's daughter." Melony tried to stay calm but the idea she might lose Brax over this put a strange hole in her heart. She glanced up at the sky. More pinpoints of light, an armada amassing on an endless sea. If they went to war, then what would happen?

Jaril returned dressed in black armor. He carried a holster for a weapon on his side and a sword hilt projected from a sheath on his back. His grim expression told them both what was going on. "I've been called to service. I have to go." He wrapped his arm around Abigail and pressed his forehead to hers. He whispered something to her before they kissed.

He placed a hand on Melony's shoulder. "I know you hate me for taking you from Earth and exposing you to my technology, but you have allowed me to be with my mate. This gesture means much to me. I hold you close to my heart and am glad to call you sister."

Melony's throat closed up at his words. She hadn't been mean to him, but she hadn't been the most hospitable guest either. "T-thank you, Jaril."

She wanted to say more, but he backed up. For an instant, Jaril was there, and then he faded away as someone from one of the ships above pulled him up. Abigail rushed into her arms and sobbed. She held onto her trembling sister. Part of her wanted to wail at the thought she could lose Brax. *Why do I feel like he's my missing piece?*

"Did you hear what I asked you?" Her sister dragged her from her thoughts.

"Sorry, what?" Melony glanced up at the sky. Was

Brax going to be called to fight, too?

"What happened with Brax tonight?" Abigail asked her.

"I'm sure Jaril's going to be okay."

"He can handle himself. Why are you avoiding my question? Something happened, didn't it?" She lost her grip on her sheet.

Melony grabbed it and pushed her sister toward the house. "Let's go back inside, and we can talk. I don't need to see you naked, too."

"Fine. What happened?"

Mel followed Abigail back into her bedroom as her sister slipped on a robe. She took in the room. Plants nestled in most of the space. One of them grew through the window.

Heat lamps lit above them kept them growing. It made the room a little warm, but not uncomfortable. In one corner, a faint green light shone through all the leaves. That was the replicator which made their clothes and a lot of their food. Along another wall was a set of drawers. On top of it were a few knickknacks.

In another corner she noticed a crib. She ran her fingers over the material. It felt like bamboo, but the plants were alive and grew up the walls into an archway and hung over the crib like a mobile.

"Planning something?" she asked her sister.

"Ahh... kinda. Not really. We've been talking about it. Jaril surprised me with the crib. I wasn't exactly sure. I'm still not sure. I mean I know it's possible. We've discussed how the baby might be like him. He's shown me some projections, images of what the child might look like. You never know. But yeah, I think I want to." Her sister's eyes were lit up with the possibility of what might come out of her relationship with an alien. "Stop changing the subject. Brax. What happened there?"

Melony ran her fingers through her hair. She leaned

against the chest of drawers and told Abigail about the whole incident with Brax. Even as she remembered the encounter, the desire for him consumed her again. She bit her lip. The pain distracted her. Even thinking about their encounter gave her pins and needles. She needed to be in his arms once more. She needed to feel him against her. Mel closed her eyes and pushed the need aside as best she could. Her sister needed her more.

"How do you feel about him?"

"I feel like I'm going to come out of my skin. Everything he said makes sense, and yet I can't rationalize this."

"You can't rationalize it. Mel, you used to be good with going with the flow. You got on my case for not being good at it. Brax isn't some long list of bad relationships you've had."

"You're right. He's not. He's a green vampire alien, and I can't get him out of my mind. My body reacts to him, and even thinking about him…" Melony rubbed her arms.

Abigail squeezed her shoulder. "I know how you feel. It's the same way with Jaril. I had to get used to it. I know you're running the questions through your mind. It's the nanos or it's the pheromones."

"Sounds about right."

"It's not, Mel. Call it a combination of biology, fate, and soul mates, but maybe there's a reason you left Earth and came here. He is the one you're supposed to be with. You don't need a human guy. What you need is a green alien vampire mechanic who can give you a tune-up and make your engine purr."

Melony burst out into laughter. He already made her engine purr. She threw a pillow at her sister. "I don't need my engine tuned up."

"Don't make up your mind to fight the possibility of what might happen. If you truly want him, then you need to figure it out for yourself. How about some hot chocolate and you can keep me company while I wait to hear back from Jaril?"

"Sure, thanks," Melony said as her sister's words sunk in.

Chapter Five

Melony paced the length of the porch and looked up at the night sky. Three days and nights had passed, and they had heard nothing. The stars and ships in the sky crowded together. She hadn't seen any of them fall out of the sky like the first ship had. She kept telling herself no news was good news. She had had time to think about her reaction to Brax and the encounter they'd shared. Even with the few days away from him, she wanted to be with him once more. Even the memory of their union stirred her desire for him.

"Hey, you said you met one of the other humans. Why don't we ask her to come over? Something to distract us from what's going on," Abigail suggested.

She shrugged. It couldn't hurt. "Sure. Do you know how to get in touch with her?"

Abigail smiled. "Jaril showed me how to use the communication system. It's actually pretty easy." She went over to the wall with the replicator and pressed another panel above it. This one turned orange. It beeped.

"How can I help you?" A neutral voice sounded in the room.

"We need to speak with…" Abigail looked over at Melony.

"Della, she's Luris's mate," Melony responded to the computer.

"One moment." The silence lasted for a second. An image of Della bouncing the toddler on her knee came into view.

"Melony, is everything okay?" Della asked.

"Yeah, I thought you might want to come over or something?" Melony asked.

She shook her head. "I haven't heard anything. Luris hasn't returned. Nothing has fallen out of the sky, which is a good sign."

"Yeah, I don't want a spaceship crashing on the house," Melony joked, but her worry niggled the back of her mind.

"Hi, Della. I'm Abigail, Melony's sister. I'm sorry to bother you, but I thought it might be a good idea to see if you might have some news. We're all a little bit worried." Abigail waved at the image of Della. "Your daughter is gorgeous."

"Thanks. Nice to meet you, Abigail. Why don't you ask Brax? He'd probably know more than anyone what the latest news is. I tried, but he shut me down."

"I thought he'd be in a ship with the others getting ready to fight. Or guarding. Whatever they're doing," Melony replied.

"He's working on something." Larin began to fuss. "Sorry, I have to get her to bed. She misses her daddy. So do I." The screen blinked out and returned to looking like a piece of gray metal.

Abigail glanced at her. "If you want answers, then you should go see Brax."

"I'm not sure if that's a good idea," Melony whispered. Deep down she wanted to check on him and make sure he was okay.

"You've been jumping out of your skin. How about we go over there?" Abigail tugged on her sleeve. "Come on, Mel. I know how it is. You know I'm right."

She hung her head. "Fuck. I hate it when you're right." Her entire body tingled at the thought of seeing him. She went into her room to find something to wear, all the while her heart skipped a few beats at the idea of what he would say to her when he saw her.

Walking up the path with Abigail toward Brax's house, her palms began to sweat, and her stomach tied itself into knots. She smoothed her dress once more. Abigail poked her arm. "Go ahead."

Melony glared at her as they went up to the door. She

placed her hand on the gray metal panel next to the door. A buzz of electricity passed through her palm. It didn't zap her but warmed further the longer she kept her hand on it. The panel flashed blue, but it didn't open the door. A chime sounded in the distance.

"No one is allowed to enter. Please leave." A hazy image of the AI came into view. Her features were visible, but Mel couldn't make out any specific details like eye or hair color. Her shape was clearly female. Mel recognized Cherin's voice.

"Tell Brax Melony is here. I was hoping to talk to him."

Cherin crossed her arms across her chest. "Brax is not to be disturbed. He's not interested in seeing you."

"How about you ask him instead assuming we're going to go away because you told us to?" Abigail growled.

"He is busy by order of our leader. You can't interrupt him." Her ghostly form faded.

"I'm not going to deal with a computer telling us what we can and can't do!" Melony banged on the door. She was determined to see Brax. After a few minutes of pounding, she heard footsteps on the other side of the door.

"I told you not to allow anyone in. I'm busy." Brax growled at the computer.

"Two human females will not leave the premises. They are insisting on seeing you."

He swore in his language and the door slid open. "What?" he snapped.

Melony took a step backward. Deep scratches marred his chest and his arms. The dark circles under his eyes told the story of him not sleeping. His silver eyes blazed. Grease streaked his hair and painted his arms. It darkened his pants and smudged his face.

"You shouldn't be here." He glanced at her and then

to Abigail.

"We needed some answers. Della said you might be able to give us some information. Can you?" Abigail asked.

He ran his stained fingers through his hair but kept his eyes on Melony. Even in the silence between them, Mel could feel the pull she had to him. "I have strict orders not to mention anything. No one is supposed to come in either. I'm working on a device to help us detect the enemy better. They have a more sophisticated cloaking technology than we do. They could already be on the planet, and we wouldn't know about it. Please leave." He started to go back into the house.

Melony touched his arm. He whipped around so fast she lost balance. Melony landed on her backside. He muttered something and offered her his hand. She hesitated about taking it. If she did, she didn't know how she was going to react. Instead, she got up and dusted herself off. "I need to talk to you."

"Now is not the time. You're a distraction. Please return home with your sister. We can speak when this is all over."

"How can you continue working if you're not resting or eating. You look like hell. Can't I help you?" Melony wanted to say more to him, but it was clear he wasn't in the mindset to listen to her.

His expression softened for an instance. "I have reserves if I need it. Forgive me for being brash, but you *must* return to your home."

"Can't you tell us anything?" Abigail went to him. "I need to know if Jaril's alive. I'm not the only one who is wondering the same thing."

"I haven't heard of any fighting. He is alive. You need to go."

"Thank you for the information, Brax." Abigail pushed Melony toward the mechanic.

"What are you doing?" Mel questioned under her breath.

"You need to be with him. If he's anything like Jaril, then all he cares about is his work and nothing else. You need to remind him you're important. He has to make room for you in his life."

"He made it perfectly clear he doesn't want us here," Melony replied as Brax started to head back inside.

"Come on, Sis. I've watched you these three days. You've barely sat still. I think you've worn a path on the porch. I've never seen you this way when it comes to men. The only time you came close was when you were with Brad Turner. You were sixteen and Mom said you couldn't go anywhere with him, but you found a way to sneak out."

She rolled her eyes. "I was a teenager, and he was a year older than me. I didn't *love* him."

"Yes, you did. And I know you *love* Brax. I can see it on your face. You want to be with him. Believe me. I know you well enough to see you're going to start overthinking this soon enough. Go be with him." Abigail pecked her on the cheek. She pushed her toward the door and rushed away.

The door closed before Mel could get there. Abigail's words sunk in. Her head did get the better of her from time to time. After seeing Brax in this condition, she wanted to make sure he was taking care of himself. Melony placed her hand on the metallic panel once more. The pulse of the mechanism ran up her arm. A faint beep echoed in the house. She figured it opened a channel inside for Brax would hear her. "Brax, you can't get rid of me. I understand you've been given orders not to allow anyone inside, but you don't look good. Please let me in long enough to make sure you're okay. I --" Melony couldn't find the words to express her feelings for him.

The door slid open. He stepped aside to let her into the

dwelling. Brax kept the distance between them with his arms crossed over his chest. It seemed a gulf had opened between them, and she didn't know how to cross it. Melony touched one of the cuts on his arm. He winced.

"Shit. I'm sorry."

"The gash is superficial. It'll heal in time. I don't need rest or any other interruptions. That includes you." Brax kept his gaze fixed on a point beyond her.

"I'm not here to be a distraction. Look, I'll go once I know you're okay. We really did want to know if you knew anything. Abs is going out of her mind not having any communication from Jaril. We look up at the sky every night and see more ships. I didn't know if you were up there fighting. I -- I wanted to be sure you were still alive."

"I'm fine. Fixers don't get conscripted. We stay here to keep an eye on things. If any of the ships crash, then we work on repairing them. There are more of us than you might realize. We are part of a network who share our discoveries with the other scientists. Please, I've said too much. You see I am fine. I need to get back to work. I need…" He stumbled and grabbed onto the nearest wall to keep him upright.

Melony slipped her arm around him and led him over to a long bench. They sat down. This close to him she noticed how the skin stretched over his bones. Exhaustion had caught up to him. His hands shook. Brax kept leaning to the side. "You need food. Or blood. You need something."

"I have blood in the workshop."

She trailed her finger along his jaw, but he jerked away. A strike right to her heart as though he didn't want her. "Right, I can go get it if you like." She went to get up, but he grabbed her arm.

"What I want is for you to be safe. You being here with me like this puts you in danger." Brax rubbed the back of his neck. He slid a little way down the bench.

The distance between them made her feel like she'd been given a sucker punch to the gut. The feelings gathered in her throat, but she focused on keeping her voice steady. "Fine. I understand. I'll leave you alone." Melony got up and headed toward the door, but then she stopped. No one told her what to do. Maybe her sister did, but she was family. Leaving Earth to live on an alien planet hadn't been her own idea. Nothing had been her choice. She'd made the decision to have sex with Brax. She needed him. She took his head in her hands and planted her lips on his. Feeling him tense made her giddy. Brax tried to resist her. She continued to kiss him. Brax slipped his arms around her, and he broke away from her lips.

"Your blood will sustain me. I could hurt you." He gripped her chin and held her gaze.

A flutter flickered across her mind. Melony sensed Brax's trepidation and a spike of hunger which hit her. She stroked his cheek and moved the hair away from her throat. "Just do it. You should know by now I trust you."

The pain came quickly as his sucker locked onto her. Melony let out a low moan. He held her closer. The strength of his arms and being close to him comforted her. She ran her fingers down his back, stroking along his spine. When he broke away from her, Brax's eyes looked brighter. His skin already had taken on a better hue. "Are you okay?"

She nodded. "I'm fine. You look better, but you're still pale."

He kissed the inside of her wrist. Another quick jab nearly made her pull her hand away. Brax started drinking from her again. He twined his fingers through hers. A small spiral of desire caught her up. Melony placed a hand on his chest. The double thuds of his hearts made her feel safe. Brax lifted his head and licked his lips.

"I thank you for your tenacity and the blood. It has restored me, but you really need to go. I have work I have to do."

"You need to sleep and get some food." She rested her head against his chest. The scent of Christmas and oranges assailed her senses. *Why does he smell so different than he tastes?* She wanted to taste the cinnamon of his flesh one more time. Her fingers tapped the beat of his hearts. He slid his hand over hers and she stopped.

"If I eat and sleep, then will you leave?" Brax asked.

She watched him form the words, but her brain didn't comprehend them. She flashed back to the quick bout of passion they'd shared. The need for him nearly overwhelmed her again. The ache she'd experienced being away from him for three days passed. Being with him made all seem right in her world. A rising need built within her. Melony pressed her mouth to his. Brax responded but pulled away. "I will, but not before I tell you... Shit, how do I tell you?"

His mouth curled up into a half smile. His fingers caressed her cheek. "You don't have to tell me. You being here tells me enough, and I can feel it in your thoughts."

"Then let me help you with whatever I can." She snuggled up to him. Mel swept her lips along his throat. Brax moaned and put his hands on her shoulders to push her away. She moved her hands along his chest and stopped at the waist of his pants. "Do you want me to stop?"

He found her lips again in a quick kiss and broke away. "No, but I have things to do."

"I'm one of them."

"You're making it difficult for me to say no to you."

"You didn't say no to me the other night," Mel whispered.

"I couldn't refuse you. Are you sure about this? Once it happens, I won't let you go." Brax kissed her again, this time swiping his tongue over her mouth. His sucker caught her bottom lip. The quick stab made her press against him.

"I'm not going anywhere."

Brax pulled away. His brow furrowed as he studied her face. His mind brushed against hers, but he didn't push into it. "You're serious. You have made up your mind."

Melony's resolve settled. She understood what choice she was making. She stood up and took her shirt off. His eyes widened as she stripped down to her bra and panties. "I'm yours. I was when you made love to me the other day, I just hadn't admitted it to myself yet." Hearing the words come out made her know it was true.

* * *

Brax's lips widened into a smile. He walked around her as if taking her in. His fingers slid along the curve of her back. The small strokes made her shudder. Each one was like a flame licking along her skin, stoking her growing desire. She stood still as he took her in, so she wouldn't combust. He traced her shoulder blades. "You are more beautiful than I ever imagined."

She felt her cheeks sear at his words. "I'm not."

"You are. And the biggest distraction I've ever had. You're also the person I've dreamt about having again but didn't let myself believe it was possible. Having one mate during a lifetime is amazing enough. Finding a second one is miraculous." He trailed his fingers under her chin and gazed at her. She felt the intensity and nearly cringed but felt her cheeks warm from the attention. Not one of her boyfriends had ever looked at her the way he did. As though she became his entire universe.

"I'm nothing special," she whispered.

"You're more than special. You're mine," Brax proclaimed. His hands slid around her waist and settled on her hips. The warmth of his fingers made her melt. Melony never wanted anything more in her life than to be with him. It went against everything she'd ever thought about the green aliens. She never thought she would fall for one of them. Her brain might have been a few steps behind as she tried to rationalize it all, but her heart and her body already knew what it wanted. She wanted him.

"Prove it."

Brax pushed the straps of her bra down, then his fingers slipped along her sides. He cupped her breasts through the material. His thumbs pressed upon her nipples. A low moan slithered from her throat. Brax squeezed her breasts and crushed his lips to hers. He broke away and found her throat. He licked over her flesh, and she looked forward to the pain of him drinking from her. It drove her against him. The sudden heat of pleasure rippled within her as the pain receded. She ran her hands down his back feeling the muscles rippling under his flesh. The smoothness of his leather pants cooled her palms until she clutched his ass. His fingers pressed into her sides. As he drank, she could feel his delight beating across her mind. She closed her eyes and pushed against it. Brax stiffened.

"I felt you along my mind. How did you do accomplish this?" Brax asked. The look of awe in his eyes made her smile.

"Doesn't that go both ways with the link the nanos create?"

"No."

"I feel you here." She touched her forehead.

"Does it hurt?"

"No, it's like a pressure. I don't know how I can feel you. I didn't mean to intrude."

He curled a strand of hair around her ear. "It's not an intrusion, just something different. Something we'll have to explore. Right now, I want to explore you. Yes?"

"Yes."

"Then come with me to my sleeping place."

Brax lifted her off her feet and carried her into his bedroom. He set her down on a long bed, wide enough for three people to lie on comfortably. Melony slid her hands over the dark blue bedspread. The softness of it reminded her of peach fuzz. The walls were bare. The room barely looked lived in. It showed Brax lived more in his workshop than he did in the rest of the house. She undid the fastener on her bra. Her breasts sprang free, and Brax's eyes grew even wider. Mel pressed her lips to his chest in small kisses. His flesh tasted like cinnamon. His muscled pecs had no nipples, marking him apart from a human along with the absence of a navel. Yet, it didn't deter her. Melony swept her lips across his torso. She sucked in the flesh between her teeth. Each time she nibbled on him, Brax stiffened. She trailed her mouth upward and sucked on his Adam's apple. Brax cupped her breasts and pressed his thumbs into her firmed nipples. His touch quickened her desire. Her finger slithered along the waistline of his leather pants. He grabbed her wrist before she could plunge her hand inside and touch his prick.

"I am not like human males. There are anatomical differences."

She stopped and a cold chill passed over her. "You didn't care about that the other night. It didn't feel like you had a stinger or tentacles when you were fucking me before."

Brax chuckled. "It didn't cross my mind the other night. All I cared about was being inside you. If my *findick* had a protrusion to harm you, I'd think it would be very uncomfortable for you. No, my witty mate, let me show you so you can understand more of the differences between us." He stood before her and peeled his pants off.

"Your finn dick?" She tried to repeat the word he'd used for his cock. The shape of his prick resembled a human dick but thicker.

Brax took her hand and slid it over his length. Her eyes widened when she held his green cock. He had three testicles with no hair on them. "Does it repel you?"

"Not at all. I'm not sure I know how to operate three of these."

He frowned. "They are not mechanical items."

She rubbed his cock. It stirred as she rolled his balls in her hand. Brax grabbed her shoulder. His grip tightened. "Does this start your engine?" Melony asked.

"My yearning for you peaks my desire, but you can do more. Do you feel the slight indentation on the middle one?"

Melony rubbed her fingers over the smooth skin until she felt the crease like the lips of a peach. She pushed against it. He grunted. "Too hard?"

He nodded.

"Forgive me." She kissed his stomach where his belly button should be. She enjoyed the smoothness of his flesh while she kissed downward. Mel flicked her tongue over the spongy head of his dick. She drew it into her mouth and trailed her fingers along all three of his testicles. Her lips worked downward until she drew his cock into her mouth. Even his prick tasted like cinnamon. Her mouth moved along his shaft while her fingers rubbed his balls. She wrapped her tongue around his shaft as it firmed.

"What are you...?"

She smiled to herself, hearing his voice break at the end as she circled her tongue around his length. His cock firmed a bit more. She dragged her teeth upward along the silky flesh. Brax moaned. Melony worked her way down, drawing him in as much as she could. Brax gasped and a rumble started in his chest like a cat's purr. Melony swept her tongue along his cock and pressed upon the crease along his middle ball. He grasped her hair and tugged, making her stop working on his prick. Mel looked up. The wild look in his eyes said it all. His thoughts pushed upon her mind. She couldn't quite grasp what he was feeling, but she caught something ferocious.

"Mel... lony, stop."

She released his dick but went lower. Her mouth found his testicles. She sucked one into her mouth. Brax pushed his hips forward. He gripped her shoulders. She listened to his small moans and felt the sudden pain of his nails biting into her flesh. All of this drove her to the edge of pleasure. Mel released his shaft. "Does this not please you?"

Something about his face had taken on a more animalistic appearance. It seemed longer and sharper. He pulled lips back to reveal more teeth as though he snarled at her. The hungry feeling within her mind intensified. "I need to be inside you. The way your mouth is on me, I have not felt this for many years."

Melony unwound his hand from her hair. She kissed his wrist and shimmied back onto the bed. She opened her legs and ran her fingers along her inner thighs. "Take me."

Brax growled and crawled onto the bed like a lion stalking its prey. He buried his head between her breasts and moved to her nipple. His tongue flicked over the tip. She slipped her fingers through the silky strands of his hair. The sucker bloomed on his tongue and covered her nipple. His lips worked on her flesh as the sucker took in her blood. Melony shrieked as he drank from her. The sudden jolt of pleasure shot straight to her clit. She couldn't catch her breath. The rising orgasm threatened to whiteout her mind. Mel wound her fingers through his hair and held him there. His fingers walked over her stomach. Her clit throbbed with sensation at the same time he fed from her. She stroked his cheeks. He didn't stop drinking.

"Brax," she moaned. The need to have him inside her took her.

He broke from her nipple. His eyes burned with passion. He growled something to her. He kissed the center of her chest and circled his tongue around her other nipple but didn't take her blood. His fingers found her thatch of hair. Melony was already wet for him. His thumb pressed against her clit. He worked her slowly, keeping his gaze on her eyes. Her breath came out in short pants, but he only teased her for an instant.

"I need you," Mel begged him. Brax's lips curled up into a sneer. He grabbed her leg and wrapped her leg around his waist. Mel guided him inside her pussy. Brax thrust into her. She dug her nails into his back. The rhythm between them hastened. Melony couldn't keep up with him.

"Not so fast."

This seemed to get his attention as he slowed. "What must I do?"

She put her hands on his hips and concentrated on moving underneath him so he would get the tempo. Feeling him inside her made her hungry for more now they'd found a rhythm. His cock found her clit.

"Yes, Brax!"

He cupped her breasts and kissed her chest above her heart. Mel lost herself to the raw ecstasy riding her nerves. Her moans encouraged him because he urged her a little faster until he started to groan. Once the first echo of his wails hit her, she couldn't hold back. She dug her nails into his back as they pounded into one another. Brax claimed her lips. His tongue pushed into her mouth. The sucker latched on to the tip of her tongue. His mouth opened wider as he fed on her blood. He broke the kiss and moved to her throat. Passion burst in her body. Light overtook her. She lost herself to their lovemaking and fell into the wonderment he brought her. Never had she thought something like this could happen with an alien, but he had shown her they were meant for one another.

Her heart raced. Brax pressed his ear to her chest. His fingers wound through hers. Melony had never felt such peace. Even as she probed their link, she felt the rightness of their union. He kissed her chest and let out a contented sigh.

"Was that worth the distraction?" she asked.

"Yes, very much. It sounded as though you were satisfied, as well."

"Maybe."

The lines deepened around the corners of his eyes. "You were not pleasured?"

Mel rolled her eyes and poked the center of his forehead. "I think you know I was. If I can feel how you are, then you can feel my enjoyment. I'm teasing."

"It will take some getting used to your humor."

"We have to get to know one another. There's a lot I don't know about you, and well, I'm light years ahead of you," she joked, knowing Earth was ten light years from Tilleron.

"You're not traveling and…"

The weight on her mind returned as he tried to read her mood. Melony held in her giggles. "…and…?"

"You're joking with me. I don't think it's because you're human, but you are a woman which, in general, makes you hard to understand."

She trailed her finger down his nose. "Now you're catching on."

Brax took her nipple into his mouth. He sucked on it for a moment until his sucker latched on. Melony jumped and thrust her hips against him. His soft lips kept moving as he slipped his fingers along her belly and settled on her clit once more. His thumb pressed into the pert bud as he enticed her. She shut her eyes and let go. Her mind couldn't process the ecstasy of him manipulating her and drinking from her nipple at the same time. It made her hyperaware of the way his mouth moved on her, the light pressure on her clit, and how he plunged his fingers inside her.

"Brax," she cried out.

He released her nipple and blew over it. The quick breath over the sucker points made her shiver with even more delight from the pain. A gentle throb filled her. "This is the first of my tune-ups. Soon I'll show you what more there is."

Melony barely heard him as her nerves came alive. The heat of his desire took her. She squeezed his hand and moved under him. He kissed her other breast and increased his speed on her clit. "Oh, my!" An orgasm hit her. She crashed down with it leaving her heart racing and her mate with a satisfied grin.

Brax rolled off her. Melony curled up along his side. "Now I can sleep. At least for a little while. Then I must get back to work. Thank you for the distraction."

She chuckled. "You're welcome."

Her mate shifted and pulled her into his arms. He kissed the top of her head as she laid it on his chest. Melony settled into the warmth of his embrace and drifted away to the beats of his heart.

Chapter Six

Melony jumped awake to a blaring alarm. Brax stood at the end of the bed, dressed in the same style armor Jaril had worn when he left. A spear of worry went through her. She pulled the sheets up to her chest and tried to shake off the aftermath of sleep. "What's going on?"

"We've been put on alert. Several ships have gotten past our defenses and landed. As I said before, the Itarians' cloaking technology is better than ours. They slipped in, and we couldn't detect them. It's what I was working on. A way to warn us if the Itarians arrived. Now they are here. They have personal cloaking devices. They might be here amongst us already. You must get dressed. I have to take you to a safe place. Come."

Melony slipped her clothes back on as the severity of the situation took her over. "I need to get back to my sister. Abigail isn't protected."

Brax stood in her way. "I won't let you go. The house is in lockdown. I have a protected place you must go to."

"Brax, I can't --"

He shot her a cold look. Brax wasn't going to change his mind. He touched her cheek. "I know you care for your sibling, but you mean more to me than anything. Now that I found you, I can't let anything happen to you. Will you promise to stay here?"

Her heart softened. She had to trust that Abigail was okay. "I will, but once this is over, I have to check on her."

"Agreed, and I will go with you. Come." He led her through the house and out into his workshop. He went to a corner wall and placed his hand on it. The door melted away, revealing stairs leading down. Lights came on as they descended. The air smelled a little stale. All around, the walls were full of different types of machines.

"What is all this?"

"Spare parts, tools, projects I've been working on but got distracted. You will be safe here. I must go."

"Come back to me," Melony told him.

"I will do my best. Stay here and you should be comfortable. There is a replicator and a living space behind the wall there. Press it here." He put his hand on the wall, and it melted away to reveal another room." He cupped her cheek. "Stay safe and know you are in my heart." Brax kissed her lightly and then left her. The door closed behind him with a slight swoosh. She heard it lock into place. Her heart sank. It felt a part of her would crack and die because he had left her, and she didn't know his fate. She stepped into the living space and sat down on the bed.

"Hello, is there anyone there?" she asked.

The lights dimmed. "Yes."

"Can you tell me what's going on?"

"I can divert a small amount of power to show you what is going on." Cherin answered her.

"Can you show me Brax?"

An image appeared on the screen of him walking around the house one last time and then of him dissolving into nothing. The image focused in on the sky above them. Cherin magnified the image giving Melony a good view of the Itarians' ships. Their vessels were smaller, sleeker, and made of a black metal, but with windows all around to look out. The wall changed and showed a few of the spaceships appearing as they landed. If they were supposed to have highly developed cloaking technology, Melony figured showing their vessels was a deliberate act. Letting the Tillerons know they were on their planet. One of the craft landed near her sister's house. Six orange- and yellow-skinned aliens ventured out of the ship, each carrying a weapon. The Itarians were dressed in thick metallic armor. Helmets covered most of their faces. Red manes hung down their backs from the helmets. They broke off in teams.

"How can I be seeing this?" Melony asked as her panic set her nerves on edge.

"We have surveillance all around our settlements. All the AIs are tapped into the cameras. They monitor for threats. We are network-sharing information."

The pairs went toward her sister's house. They went in to explore, but the house looked empty. Relief flooded her. Abigail had to be somewhere safe. Cherin showed the other Itarians walking through the forest toward the crash site. "What happened to the other team? Where did they --?"

"Shhh... They are here. You must be quiet." Cherin powered down the lights and the wall went blank.

Melony grabbed the pillow and hugged it to her chest. She huddled into the corner and closed her eyes. The dim light flickered. A hollow thud echoed in the room. Someone banging on the wall. The entire room shook. The lights blinked again. She kept her thoughts on Brax and hoped he would be okay. Through the walls, she heard muffled shouts. Melony hunkered down. Time passed. She didn't know how long she stayed in the dark. More yelling came from outside. The room shook again. Dust fell down around her. She hunkered down even more. After a while the voices faded. Fear became her companion. She prayed Brax was okay and that Abigail remained in hiding. She didn't need her sister kidnapped by another alien race. After a while, she lost all sense of time and drifted off.

* * *

Melony opened her eyes. The lights had turned on but remained dim. "Cherin, how long was I asleep?"

"You have slept for fifteen hours," the computer answered.

"Can you give me an update on the invasion?" she asked Cherin, hoping all had resolved itself.

"You don't have to worry. Everything has been taken care of, my love," Brax purred into her ear. She rolled over and saw him sitting on the bed next to her. All her fears fell away. His armor was scorched in several places. He had cuts on his face and along his arms. Other substances covered his armor. She ran her fingers along his jaw and brushed her lips along his. He returned the kiss but kept her at arm's length.

"Are you okay?"

"I am well, though tired and battle-worn. I need to get this armor off and rest. I wanted to see if you were okay."

"I'm fine. What happened?"

He pushed his hair away from his eyes. "A few ships decided they would take a chance to look for the leader's daughter. Others were emboldened to see if they could take some spoils. They boarded our ships, and we had to fight them. Our leader gave strict orders not to kill any of the Itarians. It appears they weren't given the same orders. I lost a few kinsmen. Then, Nes revealed he'd been hiding the Itarian's daughter away. They'd found out they were mates. She contacted her father and proved she was Nes's mate. Fighting ensued, but our leader and theirs called a ceasefire. They are working out a deal for her to stay, as she is their leader's only child. Reparations are being worked out. The combat has ceased, and the Itarians who landed have rejoined their fleet."

"Peace."

"Hopefully."

Relief washed over her. "Thank God."

"Yes, thank the Origins. If you don't mind, I'm going to get this armor off and then soak."

"Soak?"

"Yes, there is a hot spring I frequent just beyond the house. Would you care to go with me?"

Melony nodded. "A soak sounds heavenly."

She followed Brax into his bedroom. He stripped off

his armor and wrapped a towel around his waist. He brought one for her, too. When they walked outside of house, she looked back at the building. Black scorch marks marred the outside. The ground had deep furrows in it. The Itarians had discovered where Melony was hiding and tried to get to her. Maybe they'd thought she was their lost princess. Good thing they hadn't discovered a way into the bunker. Mel rubbed her arms and focused on Brax as they followed another stone path to a clear topaz pool. Tiered stone steps led down into the water. Brax tossed his towel onto the grass and went into the water.

Mel undressed slowly before him. His eyes stayed focused on her body as she set her clothes aside. The warm water, the temperature of a nice bath, helped to relax her. She sat across from him. The small bubbles popped at the surface from an underground spring. He slid his fingers over her naked thigh. She jumped at the caress but took in the view. The inlet opened into a large lake that stretched for as far as she could see. Trees met the sandy shoreline, towering hundreds of feet into the sky.

"How far does it go?" Melony asked.

"Miles. There are other entrances to the tributary. It opens to a vast lake. This whole area sits on top on of an extinct volcano. No need to worry. It's not going to erupt. Our scientists have done scans and continue to monitor it. It's hotter toward the center of the lake. This is one of the perks of living so close to it." Brax squeezed her leg.

The warm water surrounded her body and helped her to relax. She moved off the step and swam around until her feet barely touched the bottom. She headed out a little bit more and the bottom dropped out. Her head went under, and she swallowed a mouthful of water. Brax's arms dragged her back to the surface and over to the steps to sit down.

"I should have warned you to be careful. I don't know what I would do if I lost you." He smoothed the wet hair from her face.

"You won't. I was so afraid you weren't coming back. I went crazy stuck in that room. The darkness got to me. I kept thinking you were dead. If I lost you, then no one would've found me. Or if I was captured and taken from you, what would I do? My heart nearly broke at the idea." She trailed her fingers over the burns on his chest.

He took her head in his hands. "I didn't want to leave you, but I had no choice. I hated to lock you away. Forgive me."

"You had no choice, I understand that. Never leave me again." The words slipped out and Melony felt the warm tears tickling her cheeks.

"Never." He found her lips in a quick kiss.

Melony felt the world righted itself when she was in his arms. Never would she have thought it would be so. Her fingers wound through his hair. She kissed him and slipped her other hand under the water and gripped his cock. She removed her mouth from his lips and began to lick and kiss along his neck. Mel bit his throat and wondered how Brax would react to being the recipient of nibbles this time!

Brax growled and raked his fingers along her sides. "That is dangerous."

She bit down a little harder. "Why? Don't think I can handle you?"

"I didn't say that."

"Then what is it?"

His cock firmed under her touch. Brax pinched her nipples. The quick pain made her cry out. She stroked his cock a few more times. His free hand found her clit and massaged her. His fingers slid inside her, pumping in and out. Brax flicked his tongue over one of her throbbing nipples. The warmth of his mouth on her intensified her desire. Melony bit her lip to fight from coming as his thumb massaged her. She focused on rubbing his prick at the same pace his fingers sank into her.

"I need you," Melony murmured.

"I'm yours," Brax murmured back.

Melony straddled him as she released his cock. She guided his prick inside her and moved slowly. He groaned as his hands found her waist. He held her so firmly... She didn't care if she had bruises. Feeling him inside her made it okay. Knowing he was safe and how much her love for him had grown in the short time they had been acquainted kept her sane. Her body knew what to do as she rode him. Brax crushed her lips and took control of their union. He growled and bit at her throat with his regular teeth. Melony screamed and tried to keep up with him. He got lost in their coupling. His lips locked onto her throat, but he pulled in whatever blood he drew with his teeth.

She clutched her knees to his waist to hold onto him. Brax's fingers gripped her ass, and he slid his other hand into her hair. He wrenched her head to the side revealing more of the curve of her neck when his sucker latched on.

"More," Melony gasped.

He drew more of her blood. Melony felt her mind floating and felt him along their link, a slight pressure and static in her thoughts. Brax had lost himself to their coming together. His pleasure enraptured her. It helped with the building orgasm. He brought her to a crest and eased her back down again, the tug and flow of a tide of pleasure she didn't realize she felt. Each time he pulled on her body, taking her in, she came back into her body. It went on this way until she felt tangled in his mind. Melony didn't understand how it happened, but when he came, the sensation caught her. She cried out but could feel the rush of bliss within him. The experience shoved her back into her body. She heard herself screaming for him.

"Brax!"

He moaned one more time. The vibration shook her very bones. He slid his fingers along her face. The gentle caress brought her back. The warmth of the nanos flushed her body. Her head spun. "Hey, come back to me, love. I feel you in my mind still. Focus on me."

She nodded. "I'm here. I could feel your reactions. I felt your passion."

"Your mind and mine merged. I didn't expect you to bite me, and I lost control. I hurt you."

"No, I enjoyed your bite."

He laid his hand over her heart. "Your heart says otherwise -- it's beating as though it might burst. You are breathing hard. I should reprogram your nanos so you would not be stressed so."

She squeezed his hand. "I don't think so. No tinkering with it. I'll be fine. I'm human, if you recall."

"I'm fully aware of what you are. You're my most precious thing, and I'm never going to let go. I love you, Melony."

"I love you, Brax." The knowing it was true crashed over her. She didn't want to be anywhere he wasn't. They were meant to be together.

* * *

Melony held her breath as she stood by Brax's side. She counted three other human women besides her sister all crowded around the cute little hybrid toddler and the other males who were their mates. Her stomach churned at the idea of meeting the others. Brax ran the back of his hand down her arm. She jumped.

"Are you ready? We can always go back to my dwelling," he suggested.

"If we go back, then you won't let me out of bed again." She poked his side.

His flashed her a triumphant smile. "You weren't

complaining last night."

"Neither were you." She stretched to kiss him. He nipped her bottom lip before he released her.

"Come on." He broke the kiss and led her to the gathering. Brax brushed her arm with his finger and went over to join the other men.

Abigail pulled her into a hug.

"I told you this was a good idea -- to get everyone together," Della reminded her.

"Yeah, it's almost like a cookout back home. Makes me feel a little bit more like being back on Earth. We don't have any beer, though," one of the other women said. She turned and stuck out her hand. "I'm Irene. I belong to Ace. He still thinks he's a rock star." Her brown eyes sparkled as she pointed toward the alien with a dark green skin tone. His hair was black shot through with purple streaks.

"Isn't it more they belong to us?" the other woman said. "I'm Ember. I belong to the two knuckleheads who can't stop talking about hoses. They used to be firemen on Earth, Nash and Ben are their human names." Ember's light brown hair was caught up in a bun. She motioned toward the other two aliens Melony didn't recognize. One was lighter green and slightly thinner than the other. The second alien had short black hair with an emerald hue to his scales.

"I'm Abigail." She gestured to herself and then to Melony. "This is my sister, Mel. We're the newest arrivals. I'm with Jaril, and Melony's with Brax."

"You all know me and the munchkin. Ember was the first to get here. After I got pregnant with Larin, Luris didn't want me traveling, so I haven't been back to Earth since. He's gone back to make supply runs. When I was pregnant regenerated pickles and peanut butter weren't cutting it. Actually, we're heading back to Earth to get more food. All the other girls here have given me a list of things to pick up for them. We can give you a ride." Della flashed her a smile.

The others turned to look at her. If the offer had come a couple of weeks before, she would have jumped at it. Abigail frowned at her. Melony touched the module on the back of her neck and wondered how the others got along with their mates. So many questions stacked up in her mind. Ember seemed nice enough, and Irene reminded her of herself, but she didn't know without talking to them. It was nice to meet them finally in person, though. Larin squealed and ran to her father. Della smiled and let the toddler go. Melony watched as the happy baby was picked up by her father. He spun her in the air and said something to her in their language. The love the alien had in his eyes for his daughter made Mel wonder if it were possible for her to have kids someday.

"I… ahh…"

"Della, don't put her on the spot," Ember chimed in. "Don't mind her, Melony. Do you like it here?"

"It's growing on me," Melony asked.

"Even if you don't hitch a ride, make sure to give me a list of things you want," Della told her.

"How do you pay for all of it?" Ember asked.

"Luris replicates the money. It's worked in the past," Della told them.

"You do know the US military, and I'm sure other countries, are aware of the aliens and their technology," Abigail told them. "It's why we can't go back. The military was going to experiment on me. If you go, you have to be careful."

"We're aware. It's why one of these ladies was going to go with me so we could divide and conquer all the shops. We'll be careful. Luris will be watching and ready to get us out of there if he detects any trouble. We know to stay away from cities and crowded areas," Della told them.

"It'll be an adventure," Ember told Melony.

Larin wailed. Della rolled her eyes. "Excuse me." She rushed over to take care of her daughter.

"My boys want to try. I don't know if I'm ready yet." Ember's cheeks turned scarlet.

"Jaril already made me a crib. He's enthusiastic about it, especially after the invasion. I think it spooked him."

"Either that or all of them have babies on the brain. Ace wants to start a family, too. I've talked him down to letting us be together for a little while longer. I'm not ready to be an incubator. I'm not afraid the baby will come out with tentacles or anything, but it makes me wonder. Larin is cute. I can see species, but yeah, not ready to go there," Irene announced.

"I've kinda wondered the same thing. I'm not ready to have kids. I'm still trying to wrap my head around Brax and me. How it all works and everything," Melony admitted to the group of women.

Ember nodded. "I thought the same thing. You're lucky. You have one mate. I have two. I wouldn't have it any other way, but the whole smell thing and then the sound. It takes some getting used to. Even when you think it shouldn't work out. Your head says one thing and your heart takes over."

Melony nodded. Her heart had already planted its flag in Brax and didn't want to unmold itself. "I know how you feel. I'm still questioning it, but yeah..." She glanced back at Brax and caught him looking at her. The way his eyes roved over her made her feel like she was the best thing in the universe.

"I'm going to get something to eat. You want anything?" Abigail asked Melony.

She shook her head. "I'm good for now. Thanks."

Ember and Irene went over to the spread with her sister. Brax drifted over to her. Her mate wrapped her in his arms and held her against his chest. His double heartbeat vibrated against her back.

"Luris was telling me they were going back to Earth for supplies, and Della offered you a ride."

"She did."

He stiffened and kissed the top of her head. "Are you going back?"

She heard how he forced out the words. Melony knew he wouldn't deny her the opportunity to return to Earth, but she could feel the fear in his mind. He didn't want to lose her. "Maybe on a future run, but no. I'm not going anywhere." She turned in his arms and looked into his eyes. She took his face between her hands. "I love you."

"I love you, too. Hearing you say it warms my hearts." He kissed her deeply and hugged her before releasing her. "You know, the others were talking about their mates and…"

"Don't even tell me you're also on the baby train because I'm not ready for kids anytime soon."

His eyes grew big. "What? No! They asked if we could make this a regular event. They think it's good for their females being around others like themselves. Do you enjoy their company?"

She relaxed. "Yes. Maybe you can see if there are any other humans on this planet. They might like the company too."

"I can ask. But right now, I'd like to get you alone. Do you think we can sneak away?"

She caught the desire in his thoughts. Melony poked him in the stomach. "Not until after we eat, and I say goodbye to the others. You're going to have to wait."

He sighed and pouted. "Women. You are the one thing I can't fix."

Melony laughed. She caught the sarcasm in his tone. If someone had ever thought she'd fall in love with an alien vampire mechanic, she would have laughed in their face. Mel could never love anyone else as much as she loved him. Brax had carved a road into her heart, and she wasn't about to let him go.

"Maybe you aren't supposed to fix anything. Maybe you have to figure out the mechanical issues as you go along."

"Woman, I don't care what issues you have. I'm going to have fun opening you up and making you purr." He came at her to kiss her once more, but Melony darted away and blew him a kiss.

"Later, tiger."

"It's a promise you'd better keep." He growled. She saw a glimpse of the animal inside, knowing he was serious.

"You know I will." She went over to join the others.

"What did I tell you about going green?"

"Shut up, Abs." Melony nibbled on some cheese.

"Mmm-hhhmmm… I told you so."

She rolled her eyes. "Yeah. Best thing I ever did. I don't want to hear it, okay? But you were right."

Abigail bumped her hip against Mel's and giggled. "I'm glad you found someone. Now I don't have to worry about you getting into anymore bad relationships with assholes."

"No, you don't." Melony laughed as she thought back on some of her failed relationships. None of them would ever come close to what she had with Brax. She didn't need her sister to tell her what she knew in her heart. She would be with her green alien for the rest of her life. Since the nanos would keep her at her optimum health for years to come, Melony wasn't sure how long that would be. It didn't matter. She would be with the man she loved. "Hey, I'm going to go. Tell the others I said bye. We need to do this again soon without the men."

Abigail winked at her. "See you later. We need to compare notes."

Melony wrinkled her nose at the idea. "I don't think

so."

"Never know. Could find out something useful." Abigail hugged her. "Love you."

Melony went back over to Brax and threaded her fingers through his. He glanced over at her. "Is everything okay?"

"Yeah, but I really need that tune-up you promised. Can you make my engine purr?"

A wide smile moved across his lips. The pleasure beat against her mind. "Let me get my tools. Of course, I'm going to have to make sure everything is running properly."

"I figured."

Brax picked her up and flung her over his shoulder. Melony screamed as he carried her off. She could see the know-it-all smiles on the other males' faces. She waved as Brax walked back to his dwelling where he would tune her up all night long.

Crymsyn Hart

Crymsyn Hart is a national bestselling author of over eighty paranormal romance and horror novels. Her experiences as a psychic and ghostly encounters have given her a lot of material to use in her books. Vampires, grim reapers, shifters, and other paranormal creatures tend to end up in her books no matter how hard she tries to keep them away.

She currently resides in Charlotte, NC, with her hubby and their three dogs. If she's not writing, she's curled up with the dogs watching a good horror movie or off with friends.

Crymsyn at Changeling: changelingpress.com/crymsyn-hart-a-188

Changeling Press E-Books

More Sci-Fi, Fantasy, Paranormal, and BDSM adventures available in e-book format for immediate download at ChangelingPress.com -- Werewolves, Vampires, Dragons, Shapeshifters and more -- Erotic Tales from the edge of your imagination.

What are E-Books?

E-books, or electronic books, are books designed to be read in digital format -- on your desktop or laptop computer, notebook, tablet, Smart Phone, or any electronic e-book reader.

Where can I get Changeling Press E-Books?

Changeling Press e-books are available at ChangelingPress.com, Amazon, Apple Books, Barnes & Noble, and Kobo/Walmart.

Changeling Press, LLC

ChangelingPress.com